W9-CAE-745

Rachel Swirsky

This special signed edition is limited to 750 numbered copies.

This is copy 530.

How the World Became *Quiet*

Myths of the Past, Present, and Future

RACHEL SWIRSKY

Subterranean Press | 2013

First Edition

ISBN
978-1-59606-550-5

Subterranean Press
PO Box 190106
Burton, MI 48519

www.subterraneanpress.com

Previous publication information

"The Lady Who Plucked Red Flowers beneath the Queen's Window," first published in *Subterranean Magazine*, 2010

"A Memory of Wind," first published *Tor.com*, 2009

"Monstrous Embrace," first published in *Subterranean: Tales of Dark Fantasy*, Subterranean Press, 2009

"The Adventures of Captain Blackheart Wentworth: A Nautical Tail," first published in *Fast Ships, Black Sails*, Night Shade Books, 2008

"Heartstrung," first published in *Interzone*, 2007

"Marrying the Sun," first published in *Fantasy Magazine*, 2008

"The Sea of Trees," first published in *The Future is Japanese*, Haikasoru, 2012

"Fields of Gold," first published in *Eclipse 4*, Night Shade Books, 2011

"A Monkey Will Never Be Rid of Its Black Hands," first published in *Subterranean Magazine*, 2008

"Eros, Philia, Agape," first published in *Tor.com*, 2009

"The Monster's Million Faces," first published in *Tor.com*, 2010

"Again and Again and Again," first published in *Interzone*, 2010

"Diving After the Moon," first published in *Clarkesworld*, 2011

"Scene from a Dystopia," first published in *Subterranean Magazine*, 2006

"The Taste of Promises," first published in *Life on Mars*, Viking Children's, 2011

"Dispersed by the Sun, Melting in the Wind," first published in *Subterranean Magazine*, 2007

"How the World Became Quiet: A Post-Human Creation Myth," first published in *Electric Velocipede*, 2007

To those who were kind enough to share their writing talents:
Chuck Atkinson, Roz Spafford, Micah Perks, Erica Meitner,
Carolyn Martin Shaw, Stuart Spencer, Andy Duncan,
L. Timmel Duchamp, Daniel Alarcon, and many others

Author's note:
Several of these stories include explicit sexual violence, most especially "The Monster's Million Faces" and "With Singleness of Heart."

Table of Contents

The Past

The Lady Who Plucked Red Flowers beneath the Queen's Window

MY STORY should have ended on the day I died. Instead, it began there.

Sun pounded on my back as I rode through the Mountains where the Sun Rests. My horse's hooves beat in syncopation with those of the donkey that trotted in our shadow. The Queen's midget Kyan turned his head toward me, sweat dripping down the red-and-blue protections painted across his malformed brow.

"Shouldn't…we…stop?" he panted.

Sunlight shone red across the craggy limestone cliffs. A bold eastern wind carried the scent of mountain blossoms. I pointed to a place where two large stones leaned across a narrow outcropping.

"There," I said, prodding my horse to go faster before Kyan could answer. He grunted and cursed at his donkey for falling behind.

I hated Kyan, and he hated me. But Queen Rayneh had ordered us to ride reconnaissance together, and we obeyed, out of love for her and for the Land of Flowered Hills.

We dismounted at the place I had indicated. There, between the mountain peaks, we could watch the enemy's forces in the valley below without being observed. The raiders spread out across the meadow below like ants on a rich meal. Their women's camp lay behind the main troops, a small dark blur. Even the smoke rising from their women's fires seemed timid. I scowled.

"Go out between the rocks," I directed Kyan. "Move as close to the edge as you can."

Kyan made a mocking gesture of deference. "As you wish, Great Lady," he sneered, swinging his twisted legs off the donkey. Shamans' bundles of stones and seeds, tied with twine, rattled at his ankles.

I refused to let his pretensions ignite my temper. "Watch the valley," I instructed. "I will take the vision of their camp from your mind and send it to the Queen's scrying pool. Be sure to keep still."

The midget edged toward the rocks, his eyes shifting back and forth as if he expected to encounter raiders up here in the mountains, in the Queen's dominion. I found myself amused and disgusted by how little provocation it took to reveal the midget's true, craven nature. At home in the Queen's castle, he strutted about, pompous and patronizing. He was like many birth-twisted men, arrogant in the limited magic to which his deformities gave him access. Rumors suggested that he imagined himself worthy enough to be in love with the Queen. I wondered what he thought of the men below. Did he daydream about them conquering the Land? Did he think they'd make him powerful, that they'd put weapons in his twisted hands and let him strut among their ranks?

"Is your view clear?" I asked.

"It is."

I closed my eyes and saw, as he saw, the panorama of the valley below. I held his sight in my mind, and turned toward the eastern wind which carries the perfect expression of magic—flight—on its invisible eddies. I envisioned the battlefield unfurling before me like a scroll rolling out across a marble floor. With low, dissonant notes, I showed the image how to transform itself for my purposes. I taught it how to be length and width without depth, and how to be strokes of color and light reflected in water. When it knew these things, I sang the image into the water of the Queen's scrying pool.

Suddenly—too soon—the vision vanished from my inner eye. Something whistled through the air. I turned. Pain struck my chest like thunder.

I cried out. Kyan's bundles of seeds and stones rattled above me. My vision blurred red. Why was the midget near me? He should have been on the outcropping.

"You traitor!" I shouted. "How did the raiders find us?"

I writhed blindly on the ground, struggling to grab Kyan's legs. The midget caught my wrists. Weak with pain, I could not break free.

"Hold still," he said. "You're driving the arrow deeper."

"Let me go, you craven dwarf."

"I'm no traitor. This is woman's magic. Feel the arrow shaft."

Kyan guided my hand upward to touch the arrow buried in my chest. Through the pain, I felt the softness of one of the Queen's roc feathers. It was particularly rare and valuable, the length of my arm.

I let myself fall slack against the rock. "Woman's magic," I echoed, softly. "The Queen is betrayed. The Land is betrayed."

"Someone is betrayed, sure enough," said Kyan, his tone gloating.

"You must return to court and warn the Queen."

Kyan leaned closer to me. His breath blew on my neck, heavy with smoke and spices.

"No, Naeva. You can still help the Queen. She's given me the keystone to a spell—a piece of pure leucite, powerful enough to tug a spirit from its rest. If I blow its power into you, your spirit won't sink into sleep. It will only rest, waiting for her summons."

Blood welled in my mouth. "I won't let you bind me..."

His voice came even closer, his lips on my ear. "The Queen needs you, Naeva. Don't you love her?"

Love: the word caught me like a thread on a bramble. Oh, yes. I loved the Queen. My will weakened, and I tumbled out of my body. Cold crystal drew me in like a great mouth, inhaling.

* * *

I WAS furious. I wanted to wrap my hands around the first neck I saw and squeeze. But my hands were tiny, half the size of the hands I remembered. My short, fragile fingers shook. Heavy musk seared my nostrils. I felt the heat of scented candles at my feet, heard the snap of flame devouring wick. I rushed forward and was abruptly halted. Red and black knots of string marked boundaries beyond which I could not pass.

"O, Great Lady Naeva," a voice intoned. "We seek your wisdom on behalf of Queen Rayneh and the Land of Flowered Hills."

Murmurs rippled through the room. Through my blurred vision, I caught an impression of vaulted ceilings and frescoed walls. I heard people, but I could only make out woman-sized blurs—they could have been beggars, aristocrats, warriors, even males or broods.

I tried to roar. My voice fractured into a strangled sound like trapped wind. An old woman's sound.

"Great Lady Naeva, will you acknowledge me?"

I turned toward the high, mannered voice. A face came into focus, eyes flashing blue beneath a cowl. Dark stripes stretched from lower lip to chin: the tattoos of a death whisperer.

Terror cut into my rage for a single, clear instant. "I'm dead?"

"Let me handle this." Another voice, familiar this time. Calm, authoritative, quiet: the voice of someone who had never needed to shout in order to be heard. I swung my head back and forth trying to glimpse Queen Rayneh.

"Hear me, Lady Who Plucked Red Flowers beneath My Window. It is I, your Queen."

The formality of that voice! She spoke to me with titles instead of names? I blazed with fury.

Her voice dropped a register, tender and cajoling. "Listen to me, Naeva. I asked the death whisperers to chant your spirit up from the dead. You're inhabiting the body of an elder member of their order. Look down. See for yourself."

I looked down and saw embroidered rabbits leaping across the hem of a turquoise robe. Long, bony feet jutted out from beneath the silk. They were swaddled in the coarse wrappings that doctors prescribed for the elderly when it hurt them to stand.

They were not my feet. I had not lived long enough to have feet like that.

"I was shot by an enchanted arrow…" I recalled. "The midget said you might need me again…"

"And he was right, wasn't he? You've only been dead three years. Already, we need you."

The smugness of that voice. Rayneh's impervious assurance that no matter what happened, be it death or disgrace, her people's hearts would always sing with fealty.

"He enslaved me," I said bitterly. "He preyed upon my love for you."

"Ah, Lady Who Plucked Red Flowers beneath My Window, I always knew you loved me."

Oh yes, I had loved her. When she wanted heirs, it was I who placed my hand on her belly and used my magic to draw out her seedlings; I who nurtured the seedlings' spirits with the fertilizer of her chosen man; I who planted the seedlings in the womb of a fecund brood. Three times, the broods I catalyzed brought forth Rayneh's daughters. I'd not yet chosen to beget my own daughters, but there had always been an understanding between us that Rayneh would be the one to stand with my magic-worker as the seedling was drawn from me, mingled with man, and set into brood.

I was amazed to find that I loved her no longer. I remembered the emotion, but passion had died with my body.

"I want to see you," I said.

Alarmed, the death whisperer turned toward Rayneh's voice. Her nose jutted beak-like past the edge of her cowl. "It's possible for her to see you if you stand where I am," she said. "But if the spell goes wrong, I won't be able to—"

"It's all right, Lakitri. Let her see me."

Rustling, footsteps. Rayneh came into view. My blurred vision showed me frustratingly little except for the moon of her face. Her eyes sparkled black against her smooth, sienna skin. Amber and obsidian gems shone from her forehead, magically embedded in the triangular formation that symbolized the Land of Flowered Hills. I wanted to see her graceful belly, the muscular calves I'd loved to stroke—but below her chin, the world faded to grey.

"What do you want?" I asked. "Are the raiders nipping at your heels again?"

"We pushed the raiders back in the battle that you died to make happen. It was a rout. Thanks to you."

A smile lit on Rayneh's face. It was a smile I remembered. *You have served your Land and your Queen*, it seemed to say. *You may be proud.* I'd slept on Rayneh's leaf-patterned silk and eaten at her morning table too often to be deceived by such shallow manipulations.

Rayneh continued, "A usurper—a woman raised on our own grain and honey—has built an army of automatons to attack us. She's given each one a hummingbird's heart for speed, and a crane's feather for beauty, and a crow's brain for wit. They've marched from the Lake Where Women Wept all the way across the fields to the Valley of Tonha's Memory. They move faster than our most agile warriors. They seduce our farmers out of the fields. We must destroy them."

"A usurper?" I said.

"One who betrays us with our own spells."

The Queen directed me a lingering, narrow-lidded look, challenging me with her unspoken implications.

"The kind of woman who would shoot the Queen's sorceress with a roc feather?" I pressed.

Her glance darted sideways. "Perhaps."

Even with the tantalizing aroma of revenge wafting before me, I considered refusing Rayneh's plea. Why should I forgive her for chaining me to her service? She and her benighted death whisperers might have been able to chant my spirit into wakefulness, but let them try to stir my voice against my will.

But no—even without love drawing me into dark corners, I couldn't renounce Rayneh. I would help her as I always had from the time when we were girls riding together through my grandmother's fields. When she fell from her mount, it was always I who halted my mare, soothed her wounds, and eased her back into the saddle. Even as a child, I knew that she would never do the same for me.

"Give me something to kill," I said.

"What?"

"I want to kill. Give me something. Or should I kill your death whisperers?"

Rayneh turned toward the women. "Bring a sow!" she commanded.

Murmurs echoed through the high-ceilinged chamber, followed by rushing footsteps. Anxious hands entered my range of vision, dragging a fat, black-spotted shape. I looked toward the place where my ears told me the crowd of death whisperers stood, huddled and gossiping. I wasn't sure how vicious I could appear as a dowager with bound feet, but I snarled at them anyway. I was rewarded with the susurration of hems sliding backward over tile.

I approached the sow. My feet collided with the invisible boundaries of the summoning circle. "Move it closer," I ordered.

Hands pushed the sow forward. The creature grunted with surprise and fear. I knelt down and felt its bristly fur and smelled dry mud, but I couldn't see its torpid bulk.

I wrapped my bony hands around the creature's neck and twisted. My spirit's strength overcame the body's weakness. The animal's head snapped free in my hands. Blood engulfed the leaping rabbits on my hem.

I thrust the sow's head at Rayneh. It tumbled out of the summoning circle and thudded across the marble. Rayneh doubled over, retching.

The crowd trembled and exclaimed. Over the din, I dictated the means to defeat the constructs. "Blend mustard seed and honey to slow their deceitful tongues. Add brine to ruin their beauty. Mix in crushed poppies to slow their fast-beating hearts. Release the concoction onto a strong wind and let it blow their destruction. Only a grain need touch them. Less than a grain—only a grain need touch a mosquito that lights on a flower they pass on the march. They will fall."

"Regard that! Remember it!" Rayneh shouted to the whisperers. Silk rustled. Rayneh regarded me levelly. "That's all we have to do?"

"Get Lakitri," I replied. "I wish to ask her a question."

A nervous voice spoke outside my field of vision. "I'm here, Great Lady."

"What will happen to this body after my spirit leaves?"

"Jada will die, Great Lady. Your spirit has chased hers away."

I felt the crookedness of Jada's hunched back and the pinch of the strips binding her feet. Such a back, such feet, I would never have. At least someone would die for disturbing my death.

* * *

NEXT I woke, rage simmered where before it had boiled. I stifled a snarl, and relaxed my clenched fists. My vision was clearer: I discerned the outlines of a tent filled with dark shapes that resembled pillows and furs. I discovered my boundaries close by, marked by wooden stakes painted with bands of cinnamon and white.

"Respected Aunt Naeva?"

My vision wavered. A shape: muscular biceps, hard thighs, robes of heir's green. It took me a moment to identify Queen Rayneh's eldest daughter, who I had inspired in her brood. At the time of my death, she'd been a flat-chested flitling, still learning how to ride.

"Tryce?" I asked. A bad thought: "Why are you here? Has the usurper taken the palace? Is the Queen dead?"

Tryce laughed. "You misunderstand, Respected Aunt. I am the usurper."

"You?" I scoffed. "What does a girl want with a woman's throne?"

"I want what is mine." Tryce drew herself up. She had her mother's mouth, stern and imperious. "If you don't believe me, look at the body you're wearing."

I looked down. My hands were the right size, but they were painted in Rayneh's blue and decked with rings of gold and silver. Strips of tanned human flesh adorned my breasts. I raised my fingertips to my collarbone and felt the raised edges of the brand I knew would be there. Scars formed the triangles that represented the Land of Flowered Hills.

"One of your mother's private guard," I murmured. "Which?"

"Okilanu."

I grinned. "I never liked the bitch."

"You know I'm telling the truth. A private guard is too valuable for anyone but a usurper to sacrifice. I'm holding this conference with honor, Respected Aunt. I'm meeting you alone, with only one automaton to guard me. My informants tell me that my mother surrounded herself with sorceresses so that she could coerce you. I hold you in more esteem."

"What do you want?"

"Help winning the throne that should be mine."

"Why should I betray my lover and my Land for a child with pretensions?"

"Because you have no reason to be loyal to my mother. Because I want what's best for this Land, and I know how to achieve it. Because those were my automatons you dismantled, and they were good, beautiful souls despite being creatures of spit and mud. Gudrin is the last of them."

Tryce held out her hand. The hand that accepted drew into my vision: slender with shapely fingers crafted of mud and tangled with sticks and pieces of nest. It was beautiful enough to send feathers of astonishment through my chest.

"Great Lady, you must listen to The Creator of Me and Mine," intoned the creature.

Its voice was a songbird trill. I grimaced in disgust. "You made male automatons?"

"Just one," said Tryce. "It's why he survived your spell."

"Yes," I said, pondering. "It never occurred to me that one would make male creatures."

"Will you listen, Respected Aunt?" asked Tryce.

"You must listen, Great Lady," echoed the automaton. His voice was as melodious as poetry to a depressed heart. The power of crane's feathers and crow's brains is great.

"Very well," I said.

Tryce raised her palms to show she was telling truth. I saw the shadow of her mother's face lurking in her wide-set eyes and broad, round forehead.

"Last autumn, when the wind blew red with fallen leaves, my mother expelled me from the castle. She threw my possessions into the river and had my servants beaten and turned out. She told me that I would have to learn to live like the birds migrating from place to place because she had decreed that no one was to give me a home. She said I was no longer her heir, and she would dress Darnisha or Peni in heir's green. Oh, Respected Aunt! How could either of them take a throne?"

I ignored Tryce's emotional outpouring. It was true that Tryce had always been more responsible than her sisters, but she had been born with an heir's heaviness upon her. I had lived long enough to see fluttering sparrows like Darnisha and Peni become eagles, over time.

"You omit something important," I said. "Why did your mother throw you out, Imprudent Child?"

"Because of this."

The automaton's hand held Tryce steady as she mounted a pile of pillows that raised her torso to my eye level. Her belly loomed large, ripe as a frog's inflated throat.

"You've gotten fat, Tryce."

"No," she said.

I realized: she had not.

"You're pregnant? Hosting a child like some brood? What's wrong with you, girl? I never knew you were a pervert. Worse than a pervert! Even the lowest worm-eater knows to chew mushrooms when she pushes with men."

"I am no pervert! I am a lover of woman. I am natural as breeze! But I say we must not halve our population by splitting our females into women and broods. The raiders nip at our heels. Yes, it's true, they are barbaric and weak—now. But they grow stronger. Their population increases so quickly that already they can match our numbers. When there are three times as many of them as us, or five times, or eight times, they'll flood us like a wave crashing on a naked beach. It's time for women to make children in ourselves as broods do. We need more daughters."

I scoffed. "The raiders keep their women like cows for the same reason we keep cows like cows, to encourage the production of calves. What do you think will happen if our men see great women swelling with young and feeding them from their bodies? They will see us as weak, and they will rebel, and the broods will support them for trinkets and candy."

"Broods will not threaten us," said Tryce. "They do as they are trained. We train them to obey."

Tryce stepped down from the pillows and dismissed the automaton into the shadows. I felt a murmur of sadness as the creature left my sight.

"It is not your place to make policy, Imprudent Child," I said. "You should have kept your belly flat."

"There is no time! Do the raiders wait? Will they chew rinds by the fire while I wait for my mother to die?"

"This is better? To split our land into factions and war against ourselves?"

"I have vowed to save the Land of Flowered Hills," said Tryce, "with my mother or despite her."

Tryce came yet closer to me so that I could see the triple scars where the gems that had once sealed her heirship had been carved out of her cheeks. They left angry, red triangles. Tryce's breath was hot; her eyes like oil, shining.

"Even without my automatons, I have enough resources to overwhelm the palace," Tryce continued, "except for one thing."

I waited.

"I need you to tell me how to unlock the protections you laid on the palace grounds and my mother's chambers."

"We return to the beginning. Why should I help you?"

Tryce closed her eyes and inhaled deeply. There was shyness in her posture now. She would not direct her gaze at mine.

She said, "I was young when you died, still young enough to think that our strength was unassailable. The battles after your death shattered my illusions. We barely won, and we lost many lives. I realized that we needed more power, and I thought that I could give us that power by becoming a sorceress to replace you." She paused. "During my studies, I researched your acts of magic, great and small. Inevitably, I came to the spell you cast before you died, when you sent the raiders' positions into the summoning pool."

It was then that I knew what she would say next. I wish I could say that my heart felt as immobile as a mountain, that I had always known to suspect the love of a Queen. But my heart drummed, and my mouth went dry, and I felt as if I were falling.

"Some of mother's advisers convinced her that you were plotting against her. They had little evidence to support their accusations, but once the idea rooted into mother's mind, she became obsessed. She violated the sanctity of woman's magic by teaching Kyan how to summon a roc feather enchanted to pierce your heart. She ordered him to wait until you had sent her the vision of the battleground, and then to kill you and punish your treachery by binding your soul so that you would always wander and wake."

I wanted to deny it, but what point would there be? Now that Tryce forced me to examine my death with a watcher's eye, I saw the coincidences that proved her truth. How else could I have been shot by an arrow not just shaped by woman's magic, but made from one of the Queen's roc feathers? Why else would a worm like Kyan have happened to have in his possession a piece of leucite more powerful than any I'd seen?

I clenched Okilanu's fists. "I never plotted against Rayneh."

"Of course not. She realized it herself, in time, and executed the women who had whispered against you. But she had your magic, and your restless spirit bound to her, and she believed that was all she needed."

For long moments, my grief battled my anger. When it was done, my resolve was hardened like a spear tempered by fire.

I lifted my palms in the gesture of truth telling. "To remove the protections on the palace grounds, you must lay yourself flat against the soil with your cheek against the dirt, so that it knows you. To it, you must say, 'The Lady Who Plucked Red Flowers beneath the Queen's Window loves the Queen from instant to eternity, from desire to regret.' And then you must kiss the soil as if it is the hem of your lover's robe. Wait until you feel the earth move beneath you and then the protections will be gone."

Tryce inclined her head. "I will do this."

I continued, "When you are done, you must flay off a strip of your skin and grind it into a fine powder. Bury it in an envelope of wind-silk beneath the Queen's window. Bury it quickly. If a single grain escapes, the protections on her chamber will hold."

"I will do this, too," said Tryce. She began to speak more, but I raised one of my ringed, blue fingers to silence her.

"There's another set of protections you don't know about. One cast on your mother. It can only be broken by the fresh life-blood of something you love. Throw the blood onto the Queen while saying, 'The Lady Who Plucked Red Flowers beneath Your Window has betrayed you.'"

"Life-blood? You mean, I need to kill—"

"Perhaps the automaton."

Tryce's expression clouded with distress. "Gudrin is the last one! Maybe the baby. I could conceive again—"

"If you can suggest the baby, you don't love it enough. It must be Gudrin."

Tryce closed her mouth. "Then it will be Gudrin," she agreed, but her eyes would not meet mine.

I folded my arms across Okilanu's flat bosom. "I've given you what you wanted. Now grant me a favor, Imprudent Child Who Would Be Queen. When you kill Rayneh, I want to be there."

Tryce lifted her head like the Queen she wanted to be. "I will summon you when it's time, Respected Aunt." She turned toward Gudrin in the shadows. "Disassemble the binding shapes," she ordered.

For the first time, I beheld Gudrin in his entirety. The creature was tree-tall and stick-slender, and yet he moved with astonishing grace. "Thank you on behalf of the Creator of Me and My Kind," he trilled in his beautiful voice, and I considered how unfortunate it was that the next time I saw him, he would be dead.

* * *

I SMELLED the iron-and-wet tang of blood. My view of the world skewed low, as if I'd been cut off at the knees. Women's bodies slumped across lush carpets. Red ran deep into the silk, bloodying woven leaves and flowers. I'd been in this chamber far too often to mistake it, even dead. It was Rayneh's.

It came to me then: my perspective was not like that of a woman forced to kneel. It was like a child's. Or a dwarf's.

I reached down and felt hairy knees and fringed ankle bracelets. "Ah, Kyan…"

"I thought you might like that." Tryce's voice. These were probably her legs before me, wrapped in loose green silk trousers that were tied above the calf with chains of copper beads. "A touch of irony for your pleasure. He bound your soul to restlessness. Now you'll chase his away."

I reached into his back-slung sheath and drew out the most functional of his ceremonial blades. It would feel good to flay his treacherous flesh.

"I wouldn't do that," said Tryce. "You'll be the one who feels the pain."

I sheathed the blade. "You took the castle?"

"Effortlessly." She paused. "I lie. Not effortlessly." She unknotted her right trouser leg and rolled up the silk. Blood stained the bandages on a carefully wrapped wound. "Your protections were strong."

"Yes. They were."

She re-tied her trouser leg and continued. "The Lady with Lichen Hair tried to block our way into the chamber." She kicked one of the corpses by my feet. "We killed her."

"Did you."

"Don't you care? She was your friend."

"Did she care when I died?"

Tryce shifted her weight, a kind of lower-body shrug. "I brought you another present." She dropped a severed head onto the floor. It rolled toward me, tongue lolling in its bloody face. It took me a moment to identify the high cheekbones and narrow eyes.

"The death whisperer? Why did you kill Lakitri?"

"You liked the blood of Jada and Okilanu, didn't you?"

"The only blood I care about now is your mother's. Where is she?"

"Bring my mother!" ordered Tryce.

One of Tryce's servants—her hands marked with the green dye of loyalty to the heir—dragged Rayneh into the chamber. The Queen's torn, bloody robe concealed the worst of her wounds, but couldn't hide the black and purple bruises blossoming on her arms and legs. Her eyes found mine, and despite her condition, a trace of her regal smile glossed her lips.

Her voice sounded thin. "That's you? Lady Who Plucked Red Flowers beneath My Window?"

"It's me."

She raised one bloody, shaking hand to the locket around her throat and pried it open. Dried petals scattered onto the carpets, the remnants of the red flowers I'd once gathered for her protection. While the spell lasted, they'd remained whole and fresh. Now they were dry and crumbling like what had passed for love between us.

"If you ever find rest, the world-lizard will crack your soul in its jaws for murdering your Queen," she said.

"I didn't kill you."

"You instigated my death."

"I was only repaying your favor."

The hint of her smile again. She smelled of wood smoke, rich and dark. I wanted to see her more clearly, but my poor vision blurred the red of her wounds into the sienna of her skin until the whole of her looked like raw, churned earth.

"I suppose our souls will freeze together." She paused. "That might be pleasant."

Somewhere in front of us, lost in the shadows, I heard Tryce and her women ransacking the Queen's chamber. Footsteps, sharp voices, cracking wood.

"I used to enjoy cold mornings," Rayneh said. "When we were girls. I liked lying in bed with you and opening the curtains to watch the snow fall."

"And sending servants out into the cold to fetch and carry."

"And then! When my brood let slip it was warmer to lie together naked under the sheets? Do you remember that?" She laughed aloud, and then paused. When she spoke again, her voice was quieter. "It's strange to remember lying together in the cold, and then to look up, and see you in that body. Oh, my beautiful Naeva, twisted into a worm. I deserve what you've done to me. How could I have sent a worm to kill my life's best love?"

She turned her face away, as if she could speak no more. Such a show of intimate, unroyal emotion. I could remember times when she'd been able to manipulate me by trusting me with a wince of pain or a supposedly accidental tear. As I grew more cynical, I realized that her royal pretense wasn't vanishing when she gave me a melancholy, regretful glance. Such things were calculated vulnerabilities, intended to bind me closer to her by suggesting intimacy and trust. She used them with many ladies at court, the ones who loved her.

This was far from the first time she'd tried to bind me to her by displaying weakness, but it was the first time she'd ever done so when I had no love to enthrall me.

Rayneh continued, her voice a whisper. "I regret it, Naeva. When Kyan came back, and I saw your body, cold and lifeless—I understood immediately that I'd been mistaken. I wept for days. I'm weeping still, inside my heart. But listen—" her voice hardened "—we can't let this be about you and me. Our Land is at stake. Do you know what Tryce is going to do? She'll destroy us all. You have to help me stop her—"

"Tryce!" I shouted. "I'm ready to see her bleed."

Footsteps thudded across silk carpets. Tryce drew a bone-handled knife and knelt over her mother like a farmer preparing to slaughter a pig. "Gudrin!" she called. "Throw open the doors. Let everyone see us."

Narrow, muddy legs strode past us. The twigs woven through the automaton's skin had lain fallow when I saw him in the winter. Now they blazed in a glory of emerald leaves and scarlet blossoms.

"You dunce!" I shouted at Tryce. "What have you done? You left him alive."

Tryce's gaze held fast on her mother's throat. "I sacrificed the baby."

Voices and footsteps gathered in the room as Tryce's soldiers escorted Rayneh's courtiers inside.

"You sacrificed the baby," I repeated. "What do you think ruling is? Do you think Queens always get what they want? You can't dictate to magic, Imprudent Child."

"Be silent." Tryce's voice thinned with anger. "I'm grateful for your help, Great Lady, but you must not speak this way to your Queen."

I shook my head. Let the foolish child do what she might. I braced myself for the inevitable backlash of the spell.

Tryce raised her knife in the air. "Let everyone gathered here behold that this is Queen Rayneh, the Queen Who Would Dictate to a Daughter. I am her heir, Tryce of the Bold Stride. Hear me. I do this for the Land of Flowered Hills, for our honor and our strength. Yet I also do it with regret. Mother, I hope you will be free in your death. May your spirit wing across sweet breezes with the great bird of the sun."

The knife slashed downward. Crimson poured across Rayneh's body, across the rugs, across Tryce's feet. For a moment, I thought I'd been wrong about Tryce's baby—perhaps she had loved it enough for the counter-spell to work—but as the blood poured over the dried petals Rayneh had scattered on the floor, a bright light flared through the room. Tryce flailed backward as if struck.

Rayneh's wound vanished. She stared up at me with startled, joyful eyes. "You didn't betray me!"

"Oh, I did," I said. "Your daughter is just inept."

I could see only one solution to the problem Tryce had created—the life's blood of something I loved was here, still saturating the carpets and pooling on the stone.

Magic is a little bit alive. Sometimes it prefers poetic truths to literal ones. I dipped my fingers into the Queen's spilled blood and pronounced, "The Lady Who Plucked Red Flowers beneath Your Window has betrayed you."

I cast the blood across the Queen. The dried petals disintegrated. The Queen cried out as my magical protections disappeared.

Tryce was at her mother's side again in an instant. Rayneh looked at me in the moment before Tryce's knife descended. I thought she might show me, just this once, a fraction of uncalculated vulnerability. But this time there was no vulnerability at all, no pain or betrayal or even weariness, only perfect regal equanimity.

Tryce struck for her mother's heart. She let her mother's body fall to the carpet.

"Behold my victory!" Tryce proclaimed. She turned toward her subjects. Her stance was strong: her feet planted firmly, ready for attack or defense. If her lower half was any indication, she'd be an excellent Queen.

I felt a rush of forgiveness and pleasure and regret and satisfaction all mixed together. I moved toward the boundaries of my imprisonment, my face near Rayneh's where she lay, inhaling her last ragged breaths.

"Be brave," I told her. "Soon we'll both be free."

Rayneh's lips moved slowly, her tongue thick around the words. "What makes you think…?"

"You're going to die," I said, "and when I leave this body, Kyan will die, too. Without caster or intent, there won't be anything to sustain the spell."

Rayneh made a sound that I supposed was laughter. "Oh no, my dear Naeva…much more complicated than that…"

Panic constricted my throat. "Tryce! You have to find the piece of leucite—"

"…even stronger than the rock. Nothing but death can lull your spirit to sleep…and you're already dead…"

She laughed again.

"Tryce!" I shouted. "Tryce!"

The girl turned. For a moment, my vision became as clear as it had been when I lived. I saw the Imprudent Child Queen standing with her automaton's arms around her waist, the both of them flushed with joy and triumph. Tryce turned to kiss the knot of wood that served as the automaton's mouth and my vision clouded again.

Rayneh died a moment afterward.

A moment after that, Tryce released me.

* * *

IF MY story could not end when I died, it should have ended there, in Rayneh's chamber, when I took my revenge.

It did not end there.

* * *

TRYCE CONSULTED me often during the early years of her reign. I familiarized myself with the blur of the paintings in her chamber, squinting to pick out placid scenes of songbirds settling on snowy branches, bathing in mountain springs, soaring through sun-struck skies.

"Don't you have counselors for this?" I snapped one day.

Tryce halted her pacing in front of me, blocking my view of a wren painted by The Artist without Pity.

"Do you understand what it's like for me? The court still calls me the Imprudent Child Who Would Be Queen. Because of you!"

Gudrin went to comfort her. She kept the creature close, pampered and petted, like a cat on a leash. She rested her head on his shoulder as he stroked her arms. It all looked too easy, too familiar. I wondered how often Tryce spun herself into these emotional whirlpools.

"It can be difficult for women to accept orders from their juniors," I said.

"I've borne two healthy girls," Tryce said petulantly. "When I talk to the other women about bearing, they still say they can't, that 'women's bodies aren't suited for childbirth.' Well, if women can't have children, then what does that make me?"

I forebore responding.

"They keep me busy with petty disputes over grazing rights and grain allotment. How can I plan for a war when they distract me with pedantry? The raiders are still at our heels, and the daft old biddies won't accept what we must do to beat them back!"

The automaton thrummed with sympathy. Tryce shook him away and resumed pacing.

"At least I have you, Respected Aunt."

"For now. You must be running out of hosts." I raised my hand and inspected young, unfamiliar fingers. Dirt crusted the ragged nails. "Who is this? Anyone I know?"

"The death whisperers refuse to let me use their bodies. What time is this when dying old women won't blow out a few days early for the good of the Land?"

"Who is this?" I repeated.

"I had to summon you into the body of a common thief. You see how bad things are."

"What did you expect? That the wind would send a hundred songbirds to trill praises at your coronation? That sugared oranges would rain from the sky and flowers bloom on winter stalks?"

Tryce glared at me angrily. "Do not speak to me like that. I may be an Imprudent Child, but I am the Queen." She took a moment to regain her composure. "Enough chatter. Give me the spell I asked for."

Tryce called me in at official occasions, to bear witness from the body of a disfavored servant or a used-up brood. I attended each of the four ceremonies where Tryce, clad in regal blue, presented her infant daughters to the sun: four small, green-swathed bundles, each borne from the Queen's own body. It made me sick, but I held my silence.

She also summoned me to the court ceremony where she presented Gudrin with an official title she'd concocted to give him standing in the royal circle. Honored Zephyr or some such nonsense. They held the occasion in autumn when red and yellow leaves adorned Gudrin's shoulders like a cape. Tryce pretended to ignore the women's discontented mutterings, but they were growing louder.

The last time I saw Tryce, she summoned me in a panic. She stood in an unfamiliar room with bare stone walls and sharp wind creaking through slitted windows. Someone else's blood stained Tryce's robes. "My sisters betrayed me!" she said. "They told the women of the grasslands I was trying to make them into broods, and then led them in a revolt against the castle. A thousand women, marching! I had to slay them all. I suspected Darnisha all along. But Peni seemed content to waft. Last fall, she bore a child of her own body. It was a worm, true, but she might have gotten a daughter next. She said she wanted to try!"

"Is that their blood?"

She held out her reddened hands and stared at them ruefully as if they weren't really part of her. "Gudrin was helping them. I had to smash him into sticks. They must have cast a spell on him. I can't imagine..."

Her voice faltered. I gave her a moment to tame her undignified excess.

"You seem to have mastered the situation," I said. "A Queen must deal with such things from time to time. The important thing will be to show no weakness in front of your courtiers."

"You don't understand! It's much worse than that. While we women fought, the raiders attacked the Fields That Bask under Open Skies. They've taken half the Land. We're making a stand in the Castle Where Hope Flutters, but we can't keep them out forever. A few weeks, at most. I told them this would happen! We need more daughters to defend us! But they wouldn't listen to me!"

Rayneh would have known how to present her anger with queenly courage, but Tryce was rash and thoughtless. She wore her emotions like perfume. "Be calm," I admonished. "You must focus."

"The raiders sent a message describing what they'll do to me and my daughters when they take the castle. I captured the messenger and burned out his tongue and gave him to the broods, and when they were done with him, I took what was left of his body and catapulted it into the raiders' camp. I could do the same to every one of them, and it still wouldn't be enough to compensate for having to listen to their vile, cowardly threats."

I interrupted her tirade. "The Castle Where Hope Flutters is on high ground, but if you've already lost the eastern fields, it will be difficult to defend. Take your women to the Spires of Treachery where the herders feed their cattle. You won't be able to mount traditional defenses, but they won't be able to attack easily. You'll be reduced to meeting each other in small parties where woman's magic should give you the advantage."

"My commander suggested that," said Tryce. "There are too many of them. We might as well try to dam a river with silk."

"It's better than remaining here."

"Even if we fight to a stalemate in the Spires of Treachery, the raiders will have our fields to grow food in, and our broods to make children on. If they can't conquer us this year, they'll obliterate us in ten. I need something else."

"There is nothing else."

"Think of something!"

I thought.

I cast my mind back through my years of training. I remembered the locked room in my matriline's household where servants were never allowed to enter, which my cousins and I scrubbed every dawn and dusk to teach us to be constant and rigorous.

I remembered the cedar desk where my aunt Finis taught me to paint birds, first by using the most realistic detail that oils could achieve, and then by reducing my paintings to fewer and fewer brushstrokes until I could evoke the essence of bird without any brush at all.

I remembered the many-drawered red cabinets where we stored Leafspine and Winterbrew, powdered Errow and essence of Howl. I remembered my bossy cousin Alne skidding through the halls in a panic after she broke into a locked drawer and mixed together two herbs that we weren't supposed to touch. Her fearful grimace transformed into a beak that permanently silenced her sharp tongue.

I remembered the year I spent traveling to learn the magic of foreign lands. I was appalled by the rituals I encountered in places where women urinated on their thresholds to ward off spirits, and plucked their scalps bald when their eldest daughters reached majority. I walked with senders and weavers and whisperers and learned magic secrets that my people had misunderstood for centuries. I remembered the terror of the three nights I spent in the ancient ruins of The Desert which Should Not Have Been, begging the souls that haunted that place to surrender the secrets of their accursed city. One by one my companions died, and I spent the desert days digging graves for those the spirits found unworthy. On the third dawn, they blessed me with communion, and sent me away a wiser woman.

I remembered returning to the Land of Flowered Hills and making my own contribution to the lore contained in our matriline's locked rooms. I remembered all of this, and still I could think of nothing to tell Tryce.

Until a robin of memory hopped from an unexpected place—a piece of magic I learned traveling with herders, not spell-casters. It was an old magic, one that farmers cast when they needed to cull an inbred strain.

"You must concoct a plague," I began.

Tryce's eyes locked on me. I saw hope in her face, and I realized that she'd expected me to fail her, too.

"Find a sick baby and stop whatever treatment it is receiving. Feed it mosquito bellies and offal and dirty water to make it sicker. Give it sores and let them fill with pus. When its forehead has grown too hot for a woman to touch without flinching, kill the baby and dedicate its breath to the sun. The next morning, when the sun rises, a plague will spread with the sunlight."

"That will kill the raiders?"

"Many of them. If you create a truly virulent strain, it may kill most of them. And it will cut down their children like a scythe across wheat."

Tryce clapped her blood-stained hands. "Good."

"I should warn you. It will kill your babies as well."

"What?"

"A plague cooked in an infant will kill anyone's children. It is the way of things."

"Unacceptable! I come to you for help, and you send me to murder my daughters?"

"You killed one before, didn't you? To save your automaton?"

"You're as crazy as the crones at court! We need more babies, not fewer."

"You'll have to hope you can persuade your women to bear children so that you can rebuild your population faster than the raiders can rebuild theirs."

Tryce looked as though she wanted to level a thousand curses at me, but she stilled her tongue. Her eyes were dark and narrow. In a quiet, angry voice, she said, "Then it will be done."

They were the same words she'd used when she promised to kill Gudrin. That time I'd been able to save her despite her foolishness. This time, I might not be able to.

* * *

NEXT I was summoned, I could not see at all. I was ushered into the world by lowing, distant shouts, and the stench of animals packed too closely together.

A worried voice cut through the din. "Did it work? Are you there? Laverna, is that still you?"

Disoriented, I reached out to find a hint about my surroundings. My hands impacted a summoning barrier.

"Laverna, that's not you anymore, is it?"

The smell of manure stung my throat. I coughed. "My name is Naeva."

"Holy day, it worked. Please, Sleepless One, we need your help. There are men outside. I don't know how long we can hold them off."

"What happened? Is Queen Tryce dead?"

"Queen Tryce?"

"She didn't cast the plague, did she? Selfish brat. Where are the raiders now? Are you in the Spires of Treachery?"

"Sleepless One, slow down. I don't follow you."

"Where are you? How much land have the raiders taken?"

"There are no raiders here, just King Addric's army. His soldiers used to be happy as long as we paid our taxes and bowed our heads at processions. Now they want us to follow their ways, worship their god, let our men give us orders. Some of us rebelled by marching in front of the governor's theater, and now he's sent sorcerers after us. They burned our city with magical fire. We're making a last stand at the inn outside town. We set aside the stable for the summoning."

"Woman, you're mad. Men can't practice that kind of magic."

"These men can."

A nearby donkey brayed, and a fresh stench plopped into the air. Outside, I heard the noise of burning, and the shouts of men and children.

"It seems we've reached an impasse. You've never heard of the Land of Flowered Hills?"

"Never."

I had spent enough time pacing the ruins in the Desert which Should Not Have Been to understand the ways in which civilizations cracked and decayed. Women and time marched forward, relentless and uncaring as sand.

"I see."

"I'm sorry. I'm not doing this very well. It's my first summoning. My aunt Hetta used to do it but they slit her throat like you'd slaughter a pig and left her body to burn. Bardus says they're roasting the corpses and eating them, but I don't think anyone could do that. Could they? Hetta showed me how to do this a dozen times, but I never got to practice. She would have done this better."

"That would explain why I can't see."

"No, that's the child, Laverna. She's blind. She does all the talking. Her twin Nammi can see, but she's dumb."

"Her twin?"

"Nammi's right here. Reach into the circle and touch your sister's hand, Nammi. That's a good girl."

A small hand clasped mine. It felt clammy with sweat. I squeezed back.

"It doesn't seem fair to take her sister away," I said.

"Why would anyone take Laverna away?"

"She'll die when I leave this body."

"No, she won't. Nammi's soul will call her back. Didn't your people use twins?"

"No. Our hosts died."

"Yours were a harsh people."

Another silence. She spoke the truth, though I'd never thought of it in such terms. We were a lawful people. We were an unflinching people.

"You want my help to defeat the shamans?" I asked.

"Aunt Hetta said that sometimes the Sleepless Ones can blink and douse all the magic within seven leagues. Or wave their hands and sweep a rank of men into a hurricane."

"Well, I can't."

She fell silent. I considered her situation.

"Do you have your people's livestock with you?" I asked.

"Everything that wouldn't fit into the stable is packed inside the inn. It's even less pleasant in there if you can imagine."

"Can you catch one of their soldiers?"

"We took some prisoners when we fled. We had to kill one but the others are tied up in the courtyard."

"Good. Kill them and mix their blood into the grain from your larder, and bake it into loaves of bread. Feed some of the bread to each of your animals. They will fill with a warrior's anger and hunt down your enemies."

The woman hesitated. I could hear her feet shifting on the hay-covered floor.

"If we do that, we won't have any grain or animals. How will we survive?"

"You would have had to desert your larder when the Worm-Pretending-to-Be-Queen sent reinforcements anyway. When you can safely flee, ask the blind child to lead you to the Place where the Sun Is Joyous. Whichever direction she chooses will be your safest choice."

"Thank you," said the woman. Her voice was taut and tired. It seemed clear that she'd hoped for an easier way, but she was wise enough to take what she received. "We'll have a wild path to tame."

"Yes."

The woman stepped forward. Her footsteps released the scent of dried hay. "You didn't know about your Land, did you?"

"I did not."

"I'm sorry for your loss. It must be—"

The dumb child whimpered. Outside, the shouts increased.

"I need to go," said the woman.

"Good luck," I said, and meant it.

I felt the child Laverna rush past me as I sank back into my restless sleep. Her spirit flashed as brightly as a coin left in the sun.

I never saw that woman or any of her people again. I like to think they did not die.

* * *

I DID not like the way the world changed after the Land of Flowered Hills disappeared. For a long time, I was summoned only by men. Most were a sallow, unhealthy color with sharp narrow features and unnaturally light hair. Goateed sorcerers too proud of their paltry talents strove to dazzle me with pyrotechnics. They commanded me to reveal magical secrets that their peoples had forgotten. Sometimes I stayed silent. Sometimes I led them astray. Once, a hunched barbarian with a braided beard ordered me to give him the secret of flight. I told him to turn toward the prevailing wind and beg the Lover of the Sky for a favor. When the roc swooped down to eat him, I felt a wild kind of joy. At least the birds remembered how to punish worms who would steal women's magic.

I suffered for my minor victory. Without the barbarian to dismiss me, I was stuck on a tiny patch of grass, hemmed in by the rabbit heads he'd placed to mark the summoning circle. I shivered through the windy night until I finally thought to kick away one of the heads. It tumbled across the grass and my spirit sank into the ground.

Men treated me differently than women had. I had been accustomed to being summoned by Queens and commanders awaiting my advice on incipient battles. Men eschewed my consult; they sought to steal my powers. One summoned me into a box, hoping to trap me as if I were a minor demon that could be forced to grant his wishes. I chanted a rhyme to burn his fingers. When he pulled his hand away, the lid snapped shut and I was free.

Our magic had centered on birds and wind. These new sorcerers made pets of creatures of blood and snapping jaws, wolves and bears and jaguars. We had depicted the sun's grace along with its splendor, showing the red feathers of flaming light that arc into wings to sweep her across the sky. Their sun was a crude, jagged thing—a golden disk surrounded by spikes that twisted like the gaudy knives I'd seen in foreign cities where I traveled when I was young.

The men called me The Bitch Queen. They claimed I had hated my womb so much that I tried to curse all men to infertility, but the curse rebounded and struck me dead. Apparently, I had hanged myself. Or I'd tried to disembowel every male creature within a day's walk of my borders. Or I'd spelled my entire kingdom into a waking death in order to prevent myself from ever becoming pregnant. Apparently, I did all the same things out of revenge because I became pregnant. I eschewed men and impregnated women with sorcery. I married a thousand husbands and murdered them all. I murdered my husband, the King, and staked his head outside my castle, and then forced all the tearful women of my kingdom to do the same to their menfolk. I went crazy when my husband and son died and ordered all the men in my kingdom to be executed, declaring that no one would have the pleasure I'd been denied. I had been born a boy, but a rival of my father's castrated me, and so I hated all real men.

I ordered that any woman caught breastfeeding should have her breasts cut off. I ordered my lover's genitals cut off and sewn on me. I ordered my vagina sewn shut so I could never give birth. I ordered everyone in my kingdom to call me a man.

They assumed my magic must originate with my genitals: they displayed surprise that I didn't strip naked to mix ingredients in my vagina or cast spells using menstrual blood. They also displayed surprise that I became angry when they asked me about such things.

The worst of them believed he could steal my magic by raping me. He summoned me into a worthless, skinny girl, the kind that we in the Land of Flowered Hills would have deemed too weak to be a woman and too frail to be a brood. In order to carry out his plans, he had to make the summoning circle large enough to accommodate the bed. When he forced himself on top of me, I twisted off his head.

The best of them summoned me soon after that. He was a young man with nervous, trembling fingers who innovated a way to summon my spirit into himself. Books and scrolls tumbled over the surfaces of his tiny, dim room, many of them stained with wax from unheeded candles. Talking to him was strange, the two of us communicating with the same mouth, looking out of the same eyes.

Before long, we realized that we didn't need words. Our knowledge seeped from one spirit to the other like dye poured into water. He watched me as a girl, riding with Rayneh, and felt the sun burning my back as I dug graves in the Desert which Should Not Have Been, and flinched as he witnessed the worm who attempted to rape me. I watched him and his five brothers, all orphaned and living on the street, as they struggled to find scraps. I saw how he had learned to read under the tutelage of a traveling scribe who carried his books with him from town to town. I felt his uncomfortable mixture of love, respect, and fear for the patron who had set him up as a scribe and petty magician in return for sex and servitude. *I didn't know it felt that way*, I said to him. *Neither did I*, he replied. We stared at each other cross-eyed through his big green eyes.

Pasha needed to find a way to stop the nearby volcano before it destroyed the tiny kingdom where he dwelled. Already, tremors rattled the buildings, foreshadowing the coming destruction.

Perhaps I should not have given Pasha the spell, but it was not deep woman's magic. Besides, things seemed different when I inhabited his mind, closer to him than I had been to anyone.

We went about enacting the spell together. As we collected ash from the fireplaces of one family from each of the kingdom's twelve towns, I asked him, *Why haven't you sent me back? Wouldn't it be easier to do this on your own?*

I'll die when your spirit goes, he answered, and I saw the knowledge of it which he had managed to keep from me.

I didn't want him to die. *Then I'll stay*, I said. *I won't interfere with your life. I'll retreat as much as I can.*

I can't keep up the spell much longer, he said. I felt his sadness and his resolve. Beneath, I glimpsed even deeper sadness at the plans he would no longer be able to fulfill. He'd wanted to teach his youngest brother to read and write so that the two of them could move out of this hamlet and set up shop in a city as scribes, perhaps even earn enough money to house and feed all their brothers.

I remembered Laverna and Nammi and tried to convince Pasha that we could convert the twins' magic to work for him and his brother. He said that we only had enough time to stop the volcano. *The kingdom is more important than I am*, he said.

We dug a hole near the volcano's base and poured in the ashes that we'd collected. We stirred them with a phoenix feather until they caught fire, in order to give the volcano the symbolic satisfaction of burning the kingdom's hearths. A dense cloud of smoke rushed up from the looming mountain and then the earth was still.

That's it, said Pasha, exhaustion and relief equally apparent in his mind. *We did it.*

We sat together until nightfall when Pasha's strength began to fail.

I have to let go now, he said.

No, I begged him, *Wait. Let us return to the city. We can find your brother. We'll find a way to save you.*

But the magic in his brain was unwinding. I was reminded of the ancient tapestries hanging in the Castle Where Hope Flutters, left too long to moths and weather. Pasha lost control of his feet, his fingers. His thoughts began to drift. They came slowly and far apart. His breath halted in his lungs. Before his life could end completely, my spirit sank away, leaving him to die alone.

After that, I did not have the courage to answer summons. When men called me, I kicked away the objects they'd used to bind me in place and disappeared again. Eventually, the summons stopped.

I had never before been aware of the time that I spent under the earth, but as the years between summons stretched, I began to feel vague sensations: swatches of grey and white along with muted, indefinable pain.

When a summons finally came, I almost felt relief. When I realized the summoner was a woman, I did feel surprise.

* * *

"I DIDN'T expect that to work," said the woman. She was peach-skinned and round, a double chin gentling her jaw. She wore large spectacles with faceted green lenses like insect eyes. Spines like porcupine quills grew in a thin line from the bridge of her nose to the top of her skull before fanning into a mane. The aroma of smoke—whether the woman's personal scent or some spell remnant—hung acrid in the air.

I found myself simultaneously drawn to the vibrancy of the living world and disinclined to participate in it. I remained still, delighting in the smells and sights and sounds.

"No use pretending you're not there," said the woman. "The straw man doesn't usually blink on its own. Or breathe."

I looked down and saw a rudimentary body made of straw, joints knotted together with what appeared to be twine. I lifted my straw hand and stretched out each finger, amazed as the joints crinkled but did not break. "What is this?" My voice sounded dry and crackling, though I did not know whether that was a function of straw or disuse.

"I'm not surprised this is new to you. The straw men are a pretty new development. It saves a lot of stress and unpleasantness for the twins and the spirit rebounders and everyone else who gets the thankless job of putting up with Insomniacs taking over their bodies. Olin Nimble—that's the man who innovated the straw men—he and I completed our scholastic training the same year. Twenty years later? He's transfigured the whole field. And here's me, puttering around the library. But I suppose someone has to teach the students how to distinguish Pinder's Breath from Summer Twoflower."

The woman reached into my summoning circle and tugged my earlobe. Straw crackled.

"It's a gesture of greeting," she said. "Go on, tug mine."

I reached out hesitantly, expecting my gesture to be thwarted by the invisible summoning barrier. Instead, my fingers slid through unresisting air and grasped the woman's earlobe.

She grinned with an air of satisfaction that reminded me of the way my aunts had looked when showing me new spells. "I am Scholar Misa Meticulous." She lifted the crystal globe she carried and squinted at it. Magical etchings appeared, spelling words in an unfamiliar alphabet. "And you are the Great Lady Naeva who Picked Posies near the Queen's Chamber, of the Kingdom Where Women Rule?"

I frowned, or tried to, unsure whether it showed on my straw face. "The Land of Flowered Hills."

"Oh." She corrected the etching with a long, sharp implement. "Our earliest records have it the other way. This sort of thing is commoner than you'd think. Facts get mixed with rumor. Rumor becomes legend. Soon no one can remember what was history and what they made up to frighten the children. For instance, I'll bet your people didn't really have an underclass of women you kept in herds for bearing children."

"We called them broods."

"You called them—" Misa's eyes went round and horrified. As quickly as her shock had registered, it disappeared again. She snorted with forthright amusement. "We'll have to get one of the historians to talk to you. This is what they *live* for."

"Do they."

It was becoming increasingly clear that this woman viewed me as a relic. Indignation simmered; I was not an urn, half-buried in the desert. Yet, in a way, I was.

"I'm just a teacher who specializes in sniffing," Misa continued. "I find Insomniacs we haven't spoken to before. It can take years, tracking through records, piecing together bits of old spells. I've been following you for three years. You slept dark."

"Not dark enough."

She reached into the summoning circle to give me a sympathetic pat on the shoulder. "Eternity's a lonely place," she said. "Even the academy's lonely, and we only study eternity. Come on. Why don't we take a walk? I'll show you the library."

My straw eyes rustled as they blinked in surprise. "A walk?"

Misa laughed. "Try it out."

She laughed again as I took one precarious step forward and then another. The straw body's joints creaked with each stiff movement. I felt awkward and graceless, but I couldn't deny the pleasure of movement.

"Come on," Misa repeated, beckoning.

She led me down a corridor of gleaming white marble. Arcane symbols figured the walls. Spell-remnants scented the air with cinnamon and burnt herbs, mingling with the cool currents that swept down from the vaulted ceiling. Beneath our feet, the floor was worn from many footsteps and yet Misa and I walked alone. I wondered how it could be that a place built to accommodate hundreds was empty except for a low-ranking scholar and a dead woman summoned into an effigy.

My questions were soon answered when a group of students approached noisily from an intersecting passageway. They halted when they saw us, falling abruptly silent. Misa frowned. "Get on!" she said, waving them away. They looked relieved as they fled back the way they'd come.

The students' shaved heads and shapeless robes made it difficult to discern their forms, but it was clear I had seen something I hadn't been meant to.

"You train men here," I ascertained.

"Men, women, neuters," said Misa. "Anyone who comes. And qualifies, of course."

I felt the hiss of disappointment: another profane, degraded culture. I should have known better than to hope. "I see," I said, unable to conceal my resentment.

Misa did not seem to notice. "Many cultures have created separate systems of magic for the male and female. Your culture was extreme, but not unusual. Men work healing magic, and women sing weather magic, or vice versa. All very rigid, all very unscientific. Did they ever try to teach a man to wail for a midnight rain? Oh, maybe they did, but if he succeeded, then it was just that one man, and wasn't his spirit more womanly than masculine? They get noted as an exception to the rule, not a problem with the rule itself. Think Locas Follow with the crickets, or Petrin of Atscheko, or for an example on the female side, Queen Urté. And of course if the man you set up to sing love songs to hurricanes can't even stir up a breeze, well, there's your proof. Men can't sing the weather. Even if another man could. Rigor, that's the important thing. Until you have proof, anything can be wrong. We know now there's no difference between the magical capabilities of the sexes, but we'd have known it earlier if people had asked the right questions. Did you know there's a place in the northern wastes where they believe only people with both male and female genitals can work spells?"

"They're fools."

Misa shrugged. "Everyone's a fool, sooner or later. I make a game of it with my students. What do we believe that will be proven wrong in the future? I envy your ability to live forever so you can see."

"You should not," I said, surprised by my own bitterness. "People of the future are as likely to destroy your truths as to uncover your falsehoods."

She turned toward me, her face drawn with empathy. "You may be right."

We entered a vast, mahogany-paneled room, large enough to quarter a roc. Curving shelf towers formed an elaborate labyrinth. Misa led me through the narrow aisles with swift precision.

The shelves displayed prisms of various shapes and sizes. Crystal pyramids sat beside metal cylinders and spheres cut from obsidian. There were stranger things, too, shapes for which I possessed no words, woven out of steel threads or hardened lava.

Overhead, a transparent dome revealed a night sky strewn with stars. I recognized no patterns among the sparkling pinpricks; it was as if all the stars I'd known had been gathered in a giant's palm and then scattered carelessly into new designs.

Misa chattered as she walked. "This is the academy library. There are over three hundred thousand spells in this wing alone and we've almost filled the second. My students are taking bets on when they'll start construction on the third. They're also taking bets on whose statue will be by the door. Olin Nimble's the favorite, wouldn't you know."

We passed a number of carrel desks upon which lay maps of strange rivers and red-tinted deserts. Tubes containing more maps resided in cubby holes between the desks, their ends labeled in an unfamiliar alphabet.

"We make the first year students memorize world maps," said Misa. "A scholar has to understand how much there is to know."

I stopped by a carrel near the end of the row. The map's surface was ridged to show changes in elevation. I tried to imagine what the land it depicted would look like from above, on a roc's back. Could the Mountains where the Sun Rests be hidden among those jagged points?

Misa stopped behind me. "We're almost to the place I wanted to show you," she said. When we began walking again, she stayed quiet.

Presently, we approached a place where marble steps led down to a sunken area. We descended, and seemed to enter another room entirely, the arcs of the library shelves on the main level looming upward like a ring of ancient trees.

All around us, invisible from above, there stood statues of men and women. They held out spell spheres in their carved, upturned palms.

"This is the Circle of Insomniacs," said Misa. "Every Insomniac is depicted here. All the ones we've found, that is."

Amid hunched old women and bearded men with wild eyes, I caught sight of stranger things. Long, armored spikes jutted from a woman's spine. A man seemed to be wearing a helmet shaped like a sheep's head until I noticed that his ears twisted behind his head and became the ram's horns. A child opened his mouth to display a ring of needle-sharp teeth like a leech's.

"They aren't human," I said.

"They are," said Misa. "Or they were." She pointed me to the space between a toothless man and a soldier whose face fell in shadow behind a carved helmet. "Your statue will be there. The sculptor will want to speak with you. Or if you don't want to talk to him, you can talk to his assistant, and she'll make notes."

I looked aghast at the crowd of stone faces. "This—this is why you woke me? This sentimental memorial?"

Misa's eyes glittered with excitement. "The statue's only part of it. We want to know more about you and the Kingdom Where Women Rule. Sorry, the Land of Flowered Hills. We want to learn from you and teach you. We want you to stay!"

I could not help but laugh, harsh and mirthless. Would this woman ask a piece of ancient stone wall whether or not it wanted to be displayed in a museum? Not even the worms who tried to steal my spells had presumed so much.

"I'm sorry," said Misa. "I shouldn't have blurted it out like that. I'm good at sniffing. I'm terrible with people. Usually I find the Great Ones and then other people do the summoning and bring them to the library. The council asked me to do it myself this time because I lived in a women's colony before I came to the academy. I'm what they call woman-centered. They thought we'd have something in common."

"Loving women is fundamental. It's natural as breeze. It's not some kind of shared diversion."

"Still. It's more than you'd have in common with Olin Nimble."

She paused, biting her lip. She was still transparently excited even though the conversation had begun to go badly.

"Will you stay a while at least?" she asked. "You've slept dark for millennia. What's a little time in the light?"

I scoffed and began to demand that she banish me back to the dark—but the scholar's excitement cast ripples in a pond that I'd believed had become permanently still.

What I'd learned from the unrecognizable maps and scattered constellations was that the wage of eternity was forgetfulness. I was lonely, achingly lonely. Besides, I had begun to like Misa's fumbling chatter. She had reawakened me to light and touch—and even, it seemed, to wonder.

* * *

IF I was to stay, I told Misa, then she must understand that I'd had enough of worms and their attempts at magic. I did not want them crowding my time in the light.

The corners of Misa's mouth drew downward in disapproval, but she answered, "The academy puts us at the crossroads of myriad beliefs. Sometimes we must set aside our own." She reached out to touch me. "You're giving us a great gift by staying. We'll always respect that."

Misa and I worked closely during my first days at the academy. We argued over everything. Our roles switched rapidly and contentiously from master to apprentice and back again. She would begin by asking me questions, and then as I told her about what I'd learned in my matriline's locked rooms, she would interrupt to tell me I was wrong, her people had experimented with such things, and they never performed consistently. Within moments, we'd be shouting about what magic meant, and what it signified, and what it wanted—because one thing we agreed on was that magic was a little bit alive.

Misa suspended her teaching while she worked with me, so we had the days to ourselves in the vast salon where she taught. Her people's magic was more than superficially dissimilar from mine. They constructed their spells into physical geometries by mapping out elaborate equations that determined whether they would be cylinders or dodecahedrons, formed of garnet or lapis lazuli or cages of copper strands. Even their academy's construction reflected magical intentions, although Misa told me its effects were vague and diffuse.

"Magic is like architecture," she said. "You have to build the right container for magic to grow in. The right house for its heart."

"You fail to consider the poetry of magic," I contended. "It likes to be teased with images, cajoled with irony. It wants to match wits."

"Your spells are random!" Misa answered. "Even you don't understand how they work. You've admitted it yourself. The effects are variable, unpredictable. It lacks rigor!"

"And accomplishes grandeur," I said. "How many of your scholars can match me?"

I soon learned that Misa was not, as she claimed, an unimportant scholar. By agreement, we allowed her female pupils to enter the salon from time to time for consultations. The women, who looked startlingly young in their loose white garments, approached Misa with an awe that verged on fear. Once, a girl who looked barely out of puberty, ended their session by giving a low bow and kissing Misa's hand. She turned vivid red and fled the salon.

Misa shook her head as the echoes of the girl's footsteps faded. "She just wishes she was taking from Olin Nimble."

"Why do you persist in this deception?" I asked. "You have as many spells in the library as he does. It is you, not he, who was asked to join the academy as a scholar."

She slid me a dubious look. "You've been talking to people?"

"I have been listening."

"I've been here a long time," said Misa. "They need people like me to do the little things so greater minds like Olin Nimble's can be kept clear."

But her words were clearly untrue. All of the academy's scholars, from the most renowned to the most inexperienced, sent to Misa for consultations. She greeted their pages with good humor and unjustified humility, and then went to meet her fellow scholars elsewhere, leaving her salon to me so that I could study or contemplate as I wished.

In the Land of Flowered Hills, there had once been a famous scholar named The Woman Who Would Ask the Breeze for Whys and Wherefores. Misa was such a woman, relentlessly impractical, always half-occupied by her studies. We ate together, talked together, slept together in her chamber, and yet I never saw her focus fully on anything except when she was engrossed in transforming her abstract magical theories into complex, beautiful tangibles.

Sometimes, I paused to consider how different Misa was from my first love. Misa's scattered, self-effaced pursuit of knowledge was nothing like Rayneh's dignified exercise of power. Rayneh was like a statue, formed in a beautiful but permanent stasis, never learning or changing. Misa tumbled everywhere like a curious wind, seeking to understand and alter and collaborate, but never to master.

In our first days together, Misa and I shared an abundance of excruciating, contentious, awe-inspiring novelty. We were separated by cultures and centuries, and yet we were attracted to each other even more strongly because of the strangeness we brought into each other's lives.

* * *

THE ACADEMY was controlled by a rotating council of scholars that was chosen annually by lots. They made their decisions by consensus and exercised control over issues great and small, including the selection of new mages who were invited to join the academy as scholars and thus enter the pool of people who might someday control it.

"I'm grateful every year when they don't draw my name," Misa said.

We were sitting in her salon during the late afternoon, relaxing on reclining couches and sipping a hot, sweet drink from celadon cups. One of Misa's students sat with us, a startle-eyed girl who kept her bald head powdered and smooth, whom Misa had confided she found promising. The drink smelled of oranges and cinnamon; I savored it, ever amazed by the abilities of my strange, straw body.

I looked to Misa. "Why?"

Misa shuddered. "Being on the council would be…terrible."

"Why?" I asked again, but she only repeated herself in a louder voice, growing increasingly frustrated with my questions.

Later, when Misa left to discuss a spell with one of the academy's male scholars, her student told me, "Misa doesn't want to be elevated over others. It's a very great taboo for her people."

"It is self-indulgent to avoid power," I said. "Someone must wield it. Better the strong than the weak."

Misa's student fidgeted uncomfortably. "Her people don't see it that way."

I sipped from my cup. "Then they are fools."

Misa's student said nothing in response, but she excused herself from the salon as soon as she finished her drink.

The council requested my presence when I had been at the academy for a year. They wished to formalize the terms of my stay. Sleepless Ones who remained were expected to hold their own classes and contribute to the institution's body of knowledge.

"I will teach," I told Misa, "but only women."

"Why!" demanded Misa. "What is your irrational attachment to this prejudice?"

"I will not desecrate women's magic by teaching it to men."

"How is it desecration?"

"Women's magic is meant for women. Putting it into men's hands is degrading."

"But why!"

Our argument intensified. I began to rage. Men are not worthy of woman's magic. They're small-skulled, and cringing, and animalistic. It would be wrong! *Why, why, why?* Misa demanded, quoting from philosophical dialogues, and describing experiments that supposedly proved there was no difference between men's and women's magic. We circled and struck at one another's arguments as if we were animals competing over territory. We tangled our horns and drew blood from insignificant wounds, but neither of us seemed able to strike a final blow.

"Enough!" I shouted. "You've always told me that the academy respects the sacred beliefs of other cultures. These are mine."

"They're absurd!"

"If you will not agree then I will not teach. Banish me back to the dark! It does not matter to me."

Of course, it did matter to me. I had grown too attached to chaos and clamor. And to Misa. But I refused to admit it.

In the end, Misa agreed to argue my intentions before the council. She looked at turns furious and miserable. "They won't agree," she said. "How can they? But I'll do what I can."

The next day, Misa rubbed dense, floral unguents into her scalp and decorated her fingers with arcane rings. Her quills trembled and fanned upward, displaying her anxiety.

The circular council room glowed with faint, magical light. Cold air mixed with the musky scents favored by high-ranking scholars, along with hints of smoke and herbs. Archways loomed at each of the cardinal directions. Misa led us through the eastern archway, which she explained was for negotiation, and into the center of the mosaic floor.

The council's scholars sat on raised couches arrayed around the circumference of the room. Each sat below a torch that guttered, red and gold, rendering the councilors' bodies vivid against the dim. I caught sight of a man in layered red and yellow robes, his head surmounted by a brass circlet that was studded with lights that rhythmically flared and faded. To his side sat a tall woman with mossy hair and bark-like skin, and beside her, a man with two heads and torsos mounted upon a single pair of legs. A woman raised her hand in greeting to Misa, and water cascaded from her arms like a waterfall, churning into a mist that evaporated before it touched the floor.

Misa had told me that older scholars were often changed by her people's magic, that it shaped their bodies in the way they shaped their spells. I had not understood her before.

A long, narrow man seemed to be the focal point of the other councilors' attention. Fine, sensory hairs covered his skin. They quivered in our direction like a small animal's sniffing. "What do you suggest?" he asked. "Shall we establish a woman-only library? Shall we inspect our students' genitalia to ensure there are no men-women or women-men or twin-sexed among them?"

"Never mind that," countered a voice behind us. I turned to see a pudgy woman garbed in heavy metal sheets. "It's irrelevant to object on the basis of pragmatism. This request is exclusionary."

"Worse," added the waterfall woman. "It's immoral."

The councilors around her nodded their heads in affirmation. Two identical-looking men in leather hoods fluttered their hands to show support.

Misa looked to each assenting scholar in turn. "You are correct. It is exclusionist and immoral. But I ask you to think about deeper issues. If we reject Naeva's conditions, then everything she knows will be lost. Isn't it better that some know than that everyone forgets?"

"Is it worth preserving knowledge if the price is bigotry?" asked the narrow man with the sensory hairs, but the other scholars' eyes fixed on Misa.

They continued to argue for some time, but the conclusion had been foregone as soon as Misa spoke. There is nothing scholars love more than knowledge.

* * *

"IS IT strange for you?" I asked Misa. "To spend so much time with someone trapped in the body of a doll?"

We were alone in the tiny, cluttered room where she slept. It was a roughly hewn underground cavity, its only entrance and exit by ladder. Misa admitted that the academy offered better accommodations, but claimed she preferred rooms like this one.

Misa exclaimed with mock surprise. "You're trapped in the body of a doll? I'd never noticed!"

She grinned in my direction. I rewarded her with laughter.

"I've gotten used to the straw men," she said more seriously. "When we talk, I'm thinking about spells and magic and the things you've seen. Not straw."

Nevertheless, straw remained inescapably cumbersome. Misa suggested games and spells and implements, but I refused objects that would estrange our intimacy. We lay together at night and traded words, her hands busy at giving her pleasure while I watched and whispered. Afterward, we lay close, but I could not give her the warmth of a body I did not possess.

One night, I woke long after our love-making to discover that she was no longer beside me. I found her in the salon, her equations spiraling across a row of crystal globes. A doll hung from the wall beside her, awkwardly suspended by its nape. Its skin was warm and soft and tinted the same sienna that mine had been so many eons ago. I raised its face and saw features matching the sketches that the sculptor's assistant had made during our sessions.

Misa looked up from her calclulations. She smiled with mild embarrassment.

"I should have known a simple adaptation wouldn't work," she said. "Otherwise, Olin Nimble would have discarded straw years ago. But I thought, if I worked it out…"

I moved behind her, and beheld the array of crystal globes, all showing spidery white equations. Below them lay a half-formed spell of polished wood and peridot chips.

Misa's quill mane quivered. "It's late," she said, taking my hand. "We should return to bed."

* * *

MISA OFTEN left her projects half-done and scattered. I like to think the doll would have been different. I like to think she would have finished it.

Instead, she was drawn into the whirl of events happening outside the academy. She began leaving me behind in her chambers while she spent all hours in her salon, almost sleepwalking through the brief periods when she returned to me, and then rising restless in the dark and returning to her work.

By choice, I remained unclear about the shape of the external cataclysm. I did not want to be drawn further into the academy's politics.

My lectures provided little distraction. The students were as preoccupied as Misa. "This is not a time for theory!" one woman complained when I tried to draw my students into a discussion of magic's predilections. She did not return the following morning. Eventually, no one else returned either.

Loneliness drove me where curiosity could not and I began following Misa to her salon. Since I refused to help with her spells, she acknowledged my presence with little more than a glance before returning to her labors. Absent her attention, I studied and paced.

Once, after leaving the salon for several hours, Misa returned with a bustle of scholars—both men and women—all brightly clad and shouting. They halted abruptly when they saw me.

"I forgot you were here," Misa said without much contrition.

I tensed, angry and alienated, but unwilling to show my rage before the worms. "I will return to your chamber," I said through tightened lips.

Before I even left the room, they began shouting again. Their voices weren't like scholars debating. They lashed at each other with their words. They were angry. They were afraid.

That night, I went to Misa and finally asked for explanations. It's a plague, she said. A plague that made its victims bleed from the skin and eyes and then swelled their tongues until they suffocated.

They couldn't cure it. They treated one symptom, only to find the others worsening. The patients died, and then the mages who treated them died, too.

I declared that the disease must be magic. Misa glared at me with unexpected anger and answered that, no! It was not magic! If it was magic, they would have cured it. This was something foul and deadly and *natural*.

She'd grown gaunt by then, the gentle cushions of fat at her chin and stomach disappearing as her ribs grew prominent. After she slept, her headrest was covered with quills that had fallen out during the night, their pointed tips lackluster and dulled.

I no longer had dialogues or magic or sex to occupy my time. I had only remote, distracted Misa. My world began to shape itself around her—my love for her, my concern for her, my dread that she wouldn't find a cure, and my fear of what I'd do if she didn't. She was weak, and she was leading me into weakness. My mind sketched patterns I didn't want to imagine. I heard the spirits in The Desert Which Should Not Have Been whispering about the deaths of civilizations, and about choices between honor and love.

Misa stopped sleeping. Instead, she sat on the bed in the dark, staring into the shadows and worrying her hands.

"There is no cure," she muttered.

I lay behind her, watching her silhouette.

"Of course there's a cure."

"Oh, *of course*," snapped Misa. "We're just too ignorant to find it!"

Such irrational anger. I never learned how to respond to a lover so easily swayed by her emotions.

"I did not say that you were ignorant."

"As long as you didn't *say* it."

Misa pulled to her feet and began pacing, footsteps thumping against the piled rugs.

I realized that in all my worrying, I'd never paused to consider where the plague had been, whether it had ravaged the communities where Misa had lived and loved. My people would have thought it a weakness to let such things affect them.

"Perhaps you are ignorant," I said. "Maybe you can't cure this plague by building little boxes. Have you thought of that?"

I expected Misa to look angry, but instead she turned back with an expression of revelation. "Maybe that's it," she said slowly. "Maybe we need your kind of magic. Maybe we need poetry."

For the first time since the plague began, the lines of tension began to smooth from Misa's face. I loved her. I wanted to see her calm and curious, restored to the woman who marveled at new things and spent her nights beside me.

So I did what I knew I should not. I sat with her for the next hours and listened as she described the affliction. It had begun in a swamp far to the east, she said, in a humid tangle of roots and branches where a thousand sharp and biting things lurked beneath the water. It traveled west with summer's heat, sickening children and old people first, and then striking the young and healthy. The children and elderly sometimes recovered. The young and healthy never survived.

I thought back to diseases I'd known in my youth. A very different illness came to mind, a disease cast by a would-be usurper during my girlhood. It came to the Land of Flowered Hills with the winter wind and froze its victims into statues that would not shatter with blows or melt with heat. For years after Rayneh's mother killed the usurper and halted the disease, the Land of Flowered Hills was haunted by the glacial, ghostly remains of those once-loved. The Queen's sorceresses sought them out one by one and melted them with memories of passion. It was said that the survivors wept and cursed as their loved ones melted away, for they had grown to love the ever-present, icy memorials.

That illness was unlike what afflicted Misa's people in all ways but one—that disease, too, had spared the feeble and taken the strong.

I told Misa, "This is a plague that steals its victims' strength and uses it to kill them."

Misa's breaths came slowly and heavily. "Yes, that's it," she said. "That's what's happening."

"The victims must steal their strength back from the disease. They must cast their own cures."

"They must cast your kind of spells. Poetry spells."

"Yes," I said. "Poetry spells."

Misa's eyes closed as if she wanted to weep with relief. She looked so tired and frail. I wanted to lay her down on the bed and stroke her cheeks until she fell asleep.

Misa's shoulders shook but she didn't cry. Instead, she straightened her spectacles and plucked at her robes.

"With a bit of heat and…how would obsidian translate into poetry?…" she mused aloud. She started toward the ladder and then paused to look back. "Will you come help me, Naeva?"

She must have known what I would say.

"I'll come," I said quietly, "but this is woman's magic. It is not for men."

What followed was inevitable: the shudder that passed through Misa as her optimism turned ashen. "No. Naeva. You wouldn't let people die."

But I would. And she should have known that. If she knew me at all.

* * *

SHE BROUGHT it before the council. She said that was how things were to be decided. By discussion. By consensus.

We entered through the western arch, the arch of conflict. The scholars arrayed on their raised couches looked as haggard as Misa. Some seats were empty, others filled by men and women I'd not seen before.

"Why is this a problem?" asked one of the new scholars, an old woman whose face and breasts were stippled with tiny, fanged mouths. "Teach the spell to women. Have them cast it on the men."

"The victims must cast it themselves," Misa said.

The old woman scoffed. "Since when does a spell care who casts it?"

"It's old magic," Misa said. "Poetry magic."

"Then what is it like?" asked a voice from behind us.

We turned to see the narrow man with the fine, sensory hairs, who had demanded at my prior interrogation whether knowledge gained through bigotry was worth preserving. He lowered his gaze onto my face and his hairs extended toward me, rippling and seeking.

"Some of us have not had the opportunity to learn for ourselves," he added.

I hoped that Misa would intercede with an explanation, but she held her gaze away from mine. Her mouth was tight and narrow.

The man spoke again. "Unless you feel that it would violate your ethics to even *describe* the issue in my presence."

"No. It would not." I paused to prepare my words. "As I understand it, your people's magic imprisons spells in clever constructions. You alter the shape and texture of the spell as you alter the shape and texture of its casing."

Dissenting murmurs rose from the councilors.

"I realize that's an elementary description," I said. "However, it will suffice for contrast. My people attempted to court spells with poetry, using image and symbol and allusion as our tools. Your people give magic a place to dwell. Mine woo it to tryst awhile."

"What does that," interjected the many-mouthed old woman, "have to do with victims casting their own spells?"

Before I could answer, the narrow man spoke. "It must be poetry—the symmetry, if you will. Body and disease are battling for the body's strength. The body itself must win the battle."

"Is that so?" the old woman demanded of me.

I inclined my head in assent.

A woman dressed in robes of scarlet hair looked to Misa. "You're confident this will work?"

Misa's voice was strained and quiet. "I am."

The woman turned to regard me, scarlet tresses parting over her chest to reveal frog-like skin that glistened with damp. "You will not be moved? You won't relinquish the spell?"

I said, "No."

"Even if we promise to give it only to the women, and let the men die?"

I looked toward Misa. I knew what her people believed. The council might bend in matters of knowledge, but it would not bend in matters of life.

"I do not believe you would keep such promises."

The frog-skinned woman laughed. The inside of her mouth glittered like a cavern filled with crystals. "You're right, of course. We wouldn't." She looked to her fellow councilors. "I see no other option. I propose an Obligation."

"No," said Misa.

"I agree with Jian," said a fat scholar in red and yellow. "An Obligation."

"You can't violate her like that," said Misa. "The academy is founded on respect."

The frog-skinned woman raised her brows at Misa. "What is respect worth if we let thousands die?"

Misa took my hands. "Naeva, don't let this happen. Please, Naeva." She moved yet closer to me, her breath hot, her eyes desperate. "You know what men can be. You know they don't have to be ignorant worms or greedy brutes. You know they can be clever and noble! Remember Pasha. You gave him the spell he needed. Why won't you help us?"

Pasha—kin of my thoughts, closer than my own skin. It had seemed different then, inside his mind. But I was on my own feet now, looking out from my own eyes, and I knew what I knew.

When she'd been confronted by the inevitable destruction of our people, Tryce had made herself into a brood. She had chosen to degrade herself and her daughters in the name of survival. What would the Land of Flowered Hills have become if she'd succeeded? What would have happened to we hard and haughty people who commanded the sacred powers of wind and sun?

I would not desecrate our knowledge by putting it in the hands of animals. This was not just one man who would die from what he learned. This would be unlocking the door to my matriline's secret rooms and tearing open the many-drawered cupboards. It would be laying everything sacrosanct bare to corruption.

I broke away from Misa's touch. "I will tell you nothing!"

The council acted immediately and unanimously, accord reached without deliberation. The narrow man wrought a spell-shape using only his hands, which Misa had told me could be done, but rarely and only by great mages. When his fingers held the right configuration, he blew into their cage.

An Obligation.

It was like falling through blackness. I struggled for purchase, desperate to climb back into myself.

My mouth opened. It was not I who spoke.

"Bring them water from the swamp and damp their brows until they feel the humidity of the place where the disease was born. The spirit of the disease will seek its origins, as any born creature will. Let the victims seek with their souls' sight until they find the spirit of the disease standing before them. It will appear differently to each, vaporous and foul, or sly and sharp, but they will know it. Let the victims open the mouths of their souls and devour the disease until its spirit is inside their spirit as its body is inside their body. This time, they will be the conquerors. When they wake, they will be stronger than they had been before."

My words resonated through the chamber. Misa shuddered and began to retch. The frog-skinned woman detached a lock of her scarlet hair and gave it, along with a sphere etched with my declamation, to their fleetest page. My volition rushed back into me as if through a crashing dam. I swelled with my returning power.

Magic is a little bit alive. It loves irony and it loves passion. With all the fierceness of my dead Land, I began to tear apart my straw body with its own straw hands. The effigy's viscera fell, crushed and crackling, to the mosaic floor.

The narrow man, alone among the councilors, read my intentions. He sprang to his feet, forming a rapid protection spell between his fingers. It glimmered into being before I could complete my own magic, but I was ablaze with passion and poetry, and I knew that I would prevail.

The fire of my anger leapt from my eyes and tongue and caught upon the straw in which I'd been imprisoned. Fire. Magic. Fury. The academy became an inferno.

* * *

THEY SUMMONED me into a carved rock that could see and hear and speak but could not move. They carried it through the Southern arch, the arch of retribution.

The narrow man addressed me. His fine, sensory hairs had burned away in the fire, leaving his form bald and pathetic.

"You are dangerous," he said. "The council has agreed you cannot remain."

The council room was in ruins. The reek of smoke hung like a dense fog over the rubble. Misa sat on one of the few remaining couches, her eyes averted, her body etched with thick ugly scars. She held her right hand in her lap, its fingers melted into a single claw.

I wanted to cradle Misa's ruined hand, to kiss and soothe it. It was an unworthy desire. I had no intention of indulging regret.

"You destroyed the academy, you bitch," snarled a woman to my left. I remembered that she had once gestured waterfalls, but now her arms were burned to stumps. "Libraries, students, spells..." her voice cracked.

"The council understands the grave injustice of an Obligation," the narrow man continued, as if she had not interjected. "We don't take the enslavement of a soul lightly, especially when it violates a promised trust. Though we believe we acted rightfully, we also acknowledge we have done you an injustice. For that we owe you our contrition.

"Nevertheless," he continued, "It is the council's agreement that you cannot be permitted to remain in the light. It is our duty to send you back into the dark and to bind you there so that you may never answer summons again."

I laughed. It was a grating sound. "You'll be granting my dearest wish."

He inclined his head. "It is always best when aims align."

He reached out to the women next to him and took their hands. The remaining council members joined them, bending their bodies until they, themselves, formed the shape of a spell. Misa turned to join them, the tough, shiny substance of her scar tissue catching the light. I knew from Misa's lessons that the texture of her skin would alter and shape the spell. I could recognize their brilliance in that, to understand magic so well that they could form it out of their own bodies.

As the last of the scholars moved into place, for a moment I understood the strange, distorted, perfect shape they made. I realized with a slash that I had finally begun to comprehend their magic. And then I sank into final, lasting dark.

* * *

I REMEMBERED.

I remembered Misa. I remembered Pasha. I remembered the time when men had summoned me into unknown lands.

Always and inevitably, my thoughts returned to the Land of Flowered Hills, the place I had been away from longest, but known best.

Misa and Rayneh. I betrayed one. One betrayed me. Two loves ending in tragedy. Perhaps all loves do.

I remembered the locked room in my matriline's household, all those tiny lacquered drawers filled with marvels. My aunt's hand fluttered above them like a pale butterfly as I wondered which drawer she would open. What wonder would she reveal from a world so vast I could never hope to understand it?

"To paint a bird, you must show the brush what it means to fly," my aunt told me, holding my fingers around the brush handle as I strove to echo the perfection of a feather. The brush trembled. Dip into the well, slant, and press. Bristles splay. Ink bleeds across the scroll and—there! One single graceful stroke aspiring toward flight.

What can a woman do when love and time and truth are all at odds with one another, clashing and screeching, wailing and weeping, begging you to enter worlds unlike any you've ever known and save this people, this people, this people from king's soldiers and guttering volcanoes and plagues? What can a woman do when beliefs that seemed as solid as stone have become dry leaves blowing in autumn wind? What can a woman cling to when she must betray her lovers' lives or her own?

A woman is not a bird. A woman needs ground.

All my aunts gathering in a circle around the winter fire to share news and gossip, their voices clat-clat-clatting at each other in comforting, indistinguishable sounds. The wind finds its way in through the cracks and we welcome our friend. It blows through me, carrying scents of pine and snow. I run across the creaking floor to my aunts' knees which are as tall as I am, my arms slipping around one dark soft leg and then another as I work my way around the circle like a wind, finding the promise of comfort in each new embrace.

* * *

LIGHT RETURNED and shaded me with grey.

I stood on a pedestal under a dark dome, the room around me eaten by shadow. My hands touched my robe which felt like silk. They encountered each other and felt flesh. I raised them before my face and saw my own hands, brown and short and nimble, the fingernails jagged where I'd caught them on the rocks while surveying with Kyan in the Mountains where the Sun Rests.

Around me, I saw more pedestals arranged in a circle, and atop them strange forms that I could barely distinguish from shade. As my eyes adjusted, I made out a soldier with his face shadowed beneath a horned helmet, and a woman armored with spines. Next to me stood a child who smelled of stale water and dead fish. His eyes slid in my direction and I saw they were strangely old and weary. He opened his mouth to yawn, and inside, I saw a ring of needle-sharp teeth.

Recognition rushed through me. These were the Insomniacs I'd seen in Misa's library, all of them living and embodied, except there were more of us, countless more, all perched and waiting.

Magic is a little bit alive. That was my first thought as the creature unfolded before us, its body a strange darkness like the unrelieved black between stars. It was adorned with windows and doors that gleamed with silver like starlight. They opened and closed like slow blinking, offering us portals into another darkness that hinted at something beyond.

The creature was nothing like the entities that I'd believed waited at the core of eternity. It was no frozen world lizard, waiting to crack traitors in his icy jaws, nor a burning sun welcoming joyous souls as feathers in her wings. And yet, somehow I knew then that this creature was the deepest essence of the universe—the strange, persistent thing that throbbed like a heart between stars.

Its voice was strange, choral, like many voices talking at once. At the same time, it did not sound like a voice at all. It said, "You are the ones who have reached the end of time. You are witnesses to the end of this universe."

As it spoke, it expanded outward. The fanged child staggered back as the darkness approached. He looked toward me with fear in his eyes, and then darkness swelled around me, too, and I was surrounded by shadow and pouring starlight.

The creature said, "From the death of this universe will come the birth of another. This has happened so many times before that it cannot be numbered, unfathomable universes blinking one into the next, outside of time. The only continuity lies in the essences that persist from one to the next."

Its voice faded. I stretched out my hands into the gentle dark. "You want us to be reborn?" I asked.

I wasn't sure if it could even hear me in its vastness. But it spoke.

"The new universe will be unlike anything in this one. It will be a strangeness. There will be no 'born,' no 'you.' One cannot speak of a new universe. It is anathema to language. One cannot even ponder it."

Above me, a window opened, and it was not a window, but part of this strange being. Soothing, silver brilliance poured from it like water. It rushed over me, tingling like fresh spring mornings and newly drawn breath.

I could feel the creature's expectancy around me. More windows opened and closed as other Sleepless Ones made their choices.

I thought of everything then—everything I had thought of during the millennia when I was bound, and everything I should have thought of then but did not have the courage to think. I saw my life from a dozen fractured perspectives. Rayneh condemning me for helping her daughter steal her throne, and dismissing my every subsequent act as a traitor's cowardice. Tryce sneering at my lack of will as she watched me spurn a hundred opportunities for seizing power during centuries of summons. Misa, her brows drawn down in inestimable disappointment, pleading with me to abandon everything I was and become like her instead.

They were all right. They were all wrong. My heart shattered into a million sins.

I thought of Pasha who I should never have saved. I thought of how he tried to shield me from the pain of his death, spending his last strength to soothe me before he died alone.

For millennia, I had sought oblivion and been denied. Now, as I approached the opportunity to dissipate at last…now I began to understand the desire for something unspeakably, unfathomably new.

I reached toward the window. The creature gathered me in its massive blackness and lifted me up, up, up. I became a woman painted in brushstrokes of starlight, fewer and fewer, until I was only a glimmer of silver that had once been a woman, now poised to take flight. I glittered like the stars over The Desert which Should Not Have Been, eternal witnesses to things long forgotten. The darkness beyond the window pulled me. I leapt toward it, and stretched, and changed.

After Helen and her lover Paris fled to Troy, her husband King Menelaus called his allies to war. Under the leadership of King Agamemnon, the allies met in the harbor at Aulis. They prepared to sail for Troy, but they could not depart, for there was no wind.

Kings Agamemnon, Menelaus, and Odysseus consulted with Calchas, a priest of Artemis, who revealed that the angered goddess was balking their departure. The kings asked Calchas how they might convince Artemis to grant them a wind. He answered that she would only relent after King Agamemnon brought his eldest daughter, Iphigenia, to Aulis and sacrificed her to the goddess.

A Memory of Wind

I BEGAN TURNING into wind the moment that you promised me to Artemis.

Before I woke, I lost the flavor of rancid oil and the shade of green that flushes new leaves. They slipped from me, and became gentle breezes that would later weave themselves into the strength of my gale. Between the first and second beats of my lashes, I also lost the grunt of goats being led to slaughter, and the roughness of wool against calloused fingertips, and the scent of figs simmering in honey wine.

Around me, the other palace girls slept fitfully, tossing and grumbling through the dry summer heat. I stumbled to my feet and fled down the corridor, my footsteps falling smooth against the cool, painted clay. As I walked, the sensation of the floor blew away from me, too. It was as if I stood on nothing.

I forgot the way to my mother's rooms. I decided to visit Orestes instead. I also forgot how to find him. I paced bright corridors, searching. A male servant saw me, and woke a male slave, who woke a female slave, who roused herself and approached me, bleary-eyed, mumbling. "What's wrong, Lady Iphigenia? What do you require?"

I had no answers.

* * *

I HAVE no answers for you either, father.

I imagine what you did on that night when I paced the palace corridors, my perceptions vanishing like stars winking out of the night sky. You presided over the war council in Aulis. I imagine you standing with the staff of office heavy in your hands—heavy with wood, heavy with burdens.

Calchas, priest of Artemis, bowed before you and the other kings. "I have prayed long and hard," he said. "The goddess is angry with you, Agamemnon. She will not allow the wind to take your ships to Troy until you have made amends."

I imagine that the staff of office began to feel even heavier in your hands. You looked between your brother, Menelaus, and the sly Odysseus. Both watched you with cold, expressionless faces. They wanted war. You had become an obstacle to their desires.

"What have I done?" you asked Calchas. "What does the goddess want?"

The priest smiled.

What would a goddess want? What else but virgin blood on her altar? One daughter's life for the wind that would allow you to launch a fleet that could kill thousands. A child for a war.

Odysseus and Menelaus fixed you with hungry gazes. Their appetite for battle hollowed the souls from their eyes as starvation will hollow a man's cheeks. Implicit threats flickered in the torchlight. *Do as the priest says, or we'll take the troops we've gathered to battle Troy and march on Mycenae instead. Sacrifice your daughter or sacrifice your kingdom.*

Menelaus took an amphora of rich red wine and poured a measure for each of you. A drink; a vow. Menelaus drank rapidly, red droplets spilling like blood through the thicket of his beard. Odysseus savored slow, languorous sips, his canny eyes intent on your face.

You held your golden rhyton at arm's length, peering into redness as dark as my condemned blood. I can only imagine what you felt. Maybe you began to waver. Maybe you thought of my eyes looking up at you, and of the wedding I would never have, and the children I would never bear. But whatever thoughts I may imagine in your mind, I only know the truth of your actions. You did not dash the staff of office across your knee and hurl away its broken halves. You did not shout to Menelaus that he had no right to ask you to sacrifice your daughter's life when he would not even sacrifice the pleasure of a faithless harlot who fled his marital bed. You did not laugh at Calchas and tell him to demand something else.

You clutched the staff of office, and you swallowed the wine.

I lost so much. Words. Memories. Perceptions. Only now, in this liminality that might as well be death (if indeed it isn't) have I begun recovering myself.

All by your hand, father. All by your will. You and the goddess have dispersed me, but I will not let you forget.

* * *

NEXT I knew, mother's hands were on me, firm and insistent. She held her face near mine, her brows drawn with concern.

She and her slaves had found me hunched beside a mural that showed children playing in a courtyard, my hands extended toward the smallest figure which, in my insensibility, I'd mistaken for Orestes. The slaves eyed me strangely and made signs to ward off madness.

"It must have been a dream," I offered to excuse the strangeness which lay slickly on my skin.

"We'll consult a priest," said Clytemnestra. She put her hand on my elbow. "Can you stand? I have news."

I took a ginger step. My foot fell smoothly on the floor I could no longer feel.

"Good," said mother. "You'll need your health." She stroked my cheek, and looked at me with odd sentimentality, her gaze lingering over the planes of my face as if she were trying to paint me in her memory.

"What is it?" I asked.

"I'm sorry. I just wanted to look at you." She withdrew her fingers. "Your father has summoned us to Aulis. Achilles wants you as his wife!"

The word wife I knew, but Aulis? Achilles?

"Who?" I asked.

"Achilles!" Clytemnestra repeated. "We'll leave for Aulis this afternoon."

I looked into the familiar depths of mother's eyes. Her pupils were dark as unlit water, but her irises were gone. They weren't colored; they weren't white. They were nothing.

Green, I remembered briefly, *mother's eyes are like new green leaves.* But when I tried to chase the thought, I could no longer remember what *green* might be.

"Where are we going?" I asked.

"You're going to be married, my heart," said mother. "Everything changes all at once, doesn't it? One day your daughter's a girl, and the next she's a woman. One day your family is all together, and the next there's a war, and everyone's leaving. But that's how life is. There's stasis and then there's change, and then before you even know what the next stasis is, it's gone, and all you can do is try to remember it. You'll understand what I mean. You're so young. Then again, you're going to be a wife. So you're not that young, are you?"

"Who is Achilles?" I repeated.

But mother had already released my hands and begun to pace the room. She was divided between high spirits and fretting about the upcoming preparations, with no part of her left for me. She gave orders to her attending slaves. *Pack this. Take those. Prepare. Clean. Polish.* The slaves chattered like a flock of birds, preening under her attention.

I was not quite forgotten; a lone young girl had been assigned to prepare me for the journey. She approached, her hands filled with wedding adornments. "You're going to marry a hero," she said. "Isn't that wonderful?"

I felt a gentle tugging at my scalp. She began braiding something into my hair. I reached up to feel what. She paused for a moment, and let me take one of the decorations.

I held the red and white thing in my palm. It was delicately put together, with soft, curved rows arrayed around a dark center. A sweet, crushed scent filled the air.

"This smells," I said.

"It smells *good,*" said the slave, taking the thing gently from my hand. I closed my eyes and searched for the name of the sweet scent as she wound red-and-white into my bridal wreath.

* * *

ONCE, WHEN I was still a child with a shaved scalp and a ponytail, you came at night to the room where I slept. Sallow moonlight poured over your face and hands as you bent over my bed, your features wan like shadows beneath the yellowed tint of your boar's tusk helmet. Torchlight glinted off of the boiled leather of your cuirass and skirt.

As a child, I'd watched from time to time from the upper story balconies as you led your troops, but I'd never before been so close while you wore leather and bronze. Here stood my father the hero, my father the king, the part of you that seemed so distant from the man who sat exhausted at meals eating nothing while mother tried to tempt you with cubes of cheese and mutton, as if you were any hard-worn laborer. Here you stood, transformed into the figure I knew from rumors. It seemed impossible that you could be close enough for me to smell olives on your breath and hear the clank of your sword against your thigh.

"I had a sudden desire to see my daughter," you said, not bothering to whisper.

The other girls woke at the sound of your voice, mumbling sleepily as they shifted to watch us. I felt vain. I wanted them to see you, see me, see us together. It reminded me that I was Iphigenia, daughter of Agamemnon and Clytemnestra, niece of Helen, descendent of gods and heroes.

How easy it is to be a thing but not feel it. Greatness slips into the mundanity of weaving, of pitting olives, of sitting cooped up in the megaron during storms and listening to the patter of rain on stone.

"Get up," you said. "I want to show you something."

I belted my garment and followed you out of my chamber and down the echoing stairs to the bottom story. Flickers of firelight rumbled through the doors that led to the megaron. The servants who attended the fire through the night gossiped, their laughter rushing like the hiss and gutter of the flames.

You led the way outside. I hung back at the threshold. I rarely left the palace walls, and I never left at night. Yet you stepped outside without so much as turning back to be certain I'd follow. Did it ever occur to you that a daughter might hesitate to accede to her father's whims? Did you ever think a girl might, from time to time, have desires that outweighed her sense of duty?

But you were right. I followed you onto the portico where you stood, tall and solemn, in your armor.

We descended stone steps and emerged at last beneath the raw sky. A bright, eerie moon hung over the cliff's rocky landscape, painting it in pale light. Fragile dandelion moons blossomed here and there between the limestone juts, reflecting the larger moon above. The air smelled of damp and night-blooming plants. An eagle cried. From elsewhere came a vixen's answering call.

The smell of your sweat drifted on the night breeze, mixing with horsehair and manure. The combined scents were both foul and tantalizing. When you visited the women's quarters, it was always after events had ended, when the sweat was stale or washed away. Suddenly, things were fresh and new. You had brought me into the middle of things.

We reached the place where the river cuts through the rocks. You began running. Ahead of us, voices drifted from a copse of trees, accompanied by the clang of metal on metal. I raced behind you, stumbling over the stones that studded the grass. We veered toward the trees. A low fog gathered over the ground, illuminated from above by shifting white streams of moonlight. Needled cedar branches poked through the veil.

I fell behind, gasping with increasingly ragged breath. Your footsteps crunched onto leaves as you crossed into the copse. I trailed after, one hand pressed against the urgent pain in my side.

You turned when I was mere paces behind you. "If you were out of breath, why didn't you tell me?" you asked while I struggled the last few steps.

I leaned against a cedar to take the weight off of my trembling legs.

Ahead of us, your men stood in the thick foliage, enveloped by the fog. They wore bronze breastplates and thick felt greaves that showed darkly through the haze like tree trunks. Their swords emerged from the obscuring whiteness as they swung, metal clanging against metal as blades found each other. The soldiers seemed a ghostly rank of dismembered limbs and armor that appeared with the glint of moonbeams and then vanished into nothing.

The blunt of a sword crashed against a man's breastplate with a sound like thunder. I cringed. Tears of fright welled in my eyes. I felt exposed beneath the vastness of a sky nothing like the ceilings I'd lived below for most of my life.

You were watching me, your eyes focused on my face instead of on the wonder before us. "I told my hequetai to lead the men in exercises. The fog came up, and look! I had to show someone."

I tried to give you what you wanted. "It's marvelous." My voice quivered with fear that sounded like delight.

"I have an idea," you said, a wicked smile nestled in your beard.

You scavenged through the leaf fall with rustle and crunch until you prized out a branch the length of my forearm. You tested its weight against your palm and gave it an experimental swing.

"Try this," you said, presenting me with the branch.

Tentatively, I placed my palm against the bark.

"Go on." You pointed impatiently at your men battling through the fog. "Pretend you're a warrior."

I waved the branch back and forth, the way I thought they wielded their swords. It rattled in my hand.

"Stop," you commanded. You plucked a dandelion from the ground and laid it across a fallen log. "Here, swing at this. One smooth, strong motion."

The dandelion was a fragile silver moon. I swung the branch. Its weight dragged me forward. I stumbled across a stone.

You took the branch away. "No. Like this."

How I loved the smooth arc of your arm as it moved through the air: the strength of your shoulders, the creak of boiled leather moving with your body. I strove to memorize how you moved, but when you returned the branch to me, my fingers felt numb and strange around the bark. I flailed at the leaves and your shins until an accidental swing carried me off balance. My foot came down on the tiny moon of the dandelion. It died with a wet noise.

Wounded petals lay crushed against the wood, releasing the scent of moist soil. You took the branch from me and threw it aside.

"It's a good thing you were born a girl," you said, tugging playfully at my ponytail.

It was, you know. I've never been sorry about that. What I regret most is the children I never bore. I imagined them before you promised me to Artemis: strong boys and dark-haired girls with eyes blue enough to make Zeus lustful. One after the other, each thought-born child disappeared into forgetfulness after you bartered me for wind.

* * *

DO YOU remember that? Perhaps you do. My memories are still strange and partial, like a blanket that has been cut into pieces and then sewn up again. Stitches obscure old connections. The sense of continuity is gone. I no longer remember what it is like to have a normal recollection.

But I'm not speaking solely for your benefit. I need this, too. I cannot articulate the joy of reaching for memories and discovering them present to be touched, and brought forth, and described. I need my memories to transcend the ephemera of thought. I need them to be tangible for the brief moment when they exist as gale winds shrieking in your ear.

Even while I was dispersing, for a long time, I remembered that night when you brought me to see your soldiers. It was one of the last things Artemis took from me. I've pondered it, and polished it, and fretted about it, as if it were a faceted jewel I could turn in my hand and study from many different angles.

Why did you fetch me when you wanted to share that marvel? Why not my mother? Why weren't you content to share the moment with your men, with whom you've shared so many of your days and nights?

Did you really fail to understand why I ran until I staggered rather than ask you to slow down? You seemed confused then, but you've never stopped expecting me to stumble after you. You've never hesitated to see if I will obey your commands, no matter how wild and cruel, any more than you hesitated that night to see if I would follow you past the palace threshold to a place I'd never been.

Maybe it wasn't ignorance that made me fear your men in the fog. Maybe it was prescience: things have never ended well for me when you've led me out of the world of women and into the world of men.

* * *

CLYTEMNESTRA COMPLETED preparations to leave the palace by noon. She packed me in the wagon with the clothing and the yarn and the dried fruit. I was one more item of baggage to bring to Aulis: a bride for Achilles.

Mother placed Orestes in my lap to hold while she supervised the loading. If she noticed my stillness and silence, she must have believed they were part of a bride's normal reticence.

The wagon set off under full day's sun. Our wheels churned dust into the stifling air. It swirled through gaps in our canopy. Choking grains worked their way into our eyes and mouths. I braved more dust to peek through the curtains; beyond our car, the air hung heavy and motionless.

Orestes jounced on my lap as the wagon tumbled over dirt and rocks. He twisted to look up at me, enormous eyes blinking against the dust. He grabbed a lock of my hair in his fists and put it in his mouth, chewing contemplatively.

"Stop that," said mother, tugging my hair out of his mouth. She inspected the ragged, chewed ends and sighed.

I was content to allow Orestes to chew my hair. During his two short years of life, we'd always communicated by gestures. I understood what he meant by taking an expendable part of me into himself.

Oh, Orestes, so steady and sincere. He never rushed into anything, least of all trivial matters like speech. He took his first steps long after his age-mates were already toddling around the palace, getting into mischief. When he did begin to walk, it was with slow, arduous caution, as if he were always gauging whether independence was worth the risk of falling.

Do you know these things about him? You must. And yet, you never knew me. Why should you know your son?

Really, how could you know him? Even when you were at home, you only saw him at feast evenings, during the chilly twilight hours before we women scooped up the babies and took them back to our spaces. I knew Orestes like my own skin. I worried about the day when he would begin the imperfect translation of his thoughts into speech. I worried that words would obliterate the easy understanding of our hands and faces. This is one fear that your betrayal has made moot. I'll never know what words might have passed between me and my brother.

Orestes began to fuss. I rocked him and sang a ditty about a fleet-footed nymph and the god who loved her. Halfway through the second verse, my memory of the song decayed. Orestes fell asleep anyway, tiny fists still clutching my hair.

I began another song. Mother put her hand over my mouth. "He's already asleep, Iphigenia. Give our ears a rest."

She released me, and I turned to regard her. Through the fog of my dissipating mind, I knew there were things I needed her to tell me.

I couldn't ask the questions I didn't remember so I asked the questions I did remember.

"What is it like to be married? Will I have to live with Achilles's family while he fights in Troy? Can I go to live with father in the army camp instead? How long will the fighting last? Is Achilles a good man? When Orestes is grown and becomes king of Mycenae, will you come to live with me so that I can take care of you as you've cared for me?"

Clytemnestra let me ask questions until my words ran out. The wind had spoiled her elaborate braids, and the dust emphasized the lines of her face, making her look weary. Her eyes were wet and red.

"Every marriage is its own," she said. "Achilles will decide where you're to live, and you'll wait for him there, as I wait for your father. Achilles is a hero, which is a good judge of a man, although a good man is not always a hero. I'll visit you when I can, but I'll never be as happy as I was yesterday, with all my children in my house."

Mother worried her hands as she spoke. Her knotted knuckles had grown larger in the past few years as her arthritis worsened in proportion to her worry over the crisis whirling around her sister Helen and the scoundrel who abducted her to Troy. Mother wouldn't have sent a pig into battle for her whore of a sister, but the kings had been called to war by their oaths, and all her men would go. She'd always known she'd be left to raise Orestes without you, but until that morning she'd believed that she would have me. Now I was supposed to wed a stranger and disappear as completely as if I'd gone to war.

My mother, stern and sentimental, always happiest in that moment after she set things in their designated places: dyes by hue, spices from mild to pungent, children in their proper rooms—easy to assess and admire.

* * *

THE FIRST thing my mother told me about Helen was, "She is my sister, but not my sister. Zeus fathered her when he was in the shape of a swan. We share the same mother but she was born in an egg. I was born the normal way. Helen distorts the world around her. Never look at her too closely. You'll go blind."

I was young when she told me that, still so young that I stretched up for her hand when I wanted to take an unsteady, toddling step. Nevertheless, I still sensed that she had said something important, even though I didn't understand what it meant.

When Helen came to Mycenae during my ninth summer, I was old enough to walk on my own, but I still didn't understand the things my mother said about my famous aunt. Helen seemed glamorous and mysterious and unfathomable—like you.

I wove through the maze of the servants' feet and legs, trying to catch a glimpse of her. Hushed words of praise drifted down, all uttered in the same awed tones, whether the speaker was a slave, a servant, or a hequetai, a man or a woman. They marveled over Helen's skin like beaten gold; her deep blue eyes the shade of newly fallen night; the smooth swell of her high, brown-tipped breasts.

You were busy with your brother Menelaus, the two of you clapping each other's shoulders as you exchanged information about recent military encounters. You didn't even glance at your beautiful sister-in-law, or at the way your wife paced uncomfortably, barking at the slaves to carry out orders they were already rushing to fulfill.

Your men retreated to the megaron to drink and discuss. We women went out to the courtyard. Slaves erected a canopy to shelter us from the sun, and set up benches for us to sit on. Clytemnestra walked among them, shouting that the canopy was hung too low, the benches were in the wrong places, bring more food, bring thicker blankets, and don't forget to set aside lamps and oil to set out at dusk.

Helen arrayed herself on a bench near the front of the canopy where fresh breezes would reach her first. She arranged her garments fetchingly around her form as she lay down. She brushed her hand through her braids, allowing the breeze to blow through her stray hairs so that she looked tousled and intimate and all the more beautiful. I thought she was very vain to pose like that.

A girl my age nearly collided with me as I stood watching Helen. She glared, and then turned abruptly away as if I wasn't worth her time. "Put my bench there," she directed a slave, pointing to a spot near Helen. I wanted to ask her who she thought she was, but before I got the chance, my mother caught me by the shoulders.

Her grip was harder than normal, her fingernails digging into my skin. "Come sit down," she said, guiding me to the bench where she sat near Helen.

I sat at Clytemnestra's feet while she ruffled my hair, and looked up at my aunt. From below, Helen was just as beautiful, but her features looked sharper. Braids coiled around her face like snakes, bound back by a beribboned brass headband that caught the gold flecks in her eyes.

Mother kept a firm grip on my shoulders as if she could keep my mind from straying by holding my body in place. She began a monologue about housekeeping, a subject that was impersonal, factual, and utterly under her control. "Next month, we'll begin drying the fruit stores," she said. "It was too cold this year for the figs. We lost nearly half our crop. But we've traded for nuts that will keep us through the winter."

"You're an excellent steward, sister mine," said Helen, not bothering to disguise her boredom.

"Mother," interjected the awkward girl who had collided with me earlier. "I found you a perfect one."

She extended her hand, in which nestled a cube of goat cheese, its corners unbroken. A bemused smile crossed Helen's face as she looked down at the morsel.

"Thank you," she said awkwardly, taking the cheese. She rewarded the girl with an uncertain pat on the head.

The girl lay stretched out on the bench, imitating Helen, but to completely different effect. The languorous pose accentuated her skinny, ungainly limbs. Stray tangles poked out of her braids like thistles.

"You're Hermione? You're my *cousin*?" I blurted.

Hermione bristled. Her mother looked down at me with a slow, appraising gaze. "Why, hello," Helen said. "Are you my niece?"

Clytemnestra's hand tightened protectively on my shoulder. "This is Iphigenia."

Helen's eyes were hot like sunlight on my cheeks. I burned with embarrassment.

"She'll be a beauty someday," Helen said to my mother.

Clytemnestra shrugged. "There's time enough for that."

Hermione pushed a tray of honeyed figs out of a slave's hands. It clattered to the ground. "None of those are good enough for my mother!" she shouted.

Helen looked uncertainly at Clytemnestra, and then over at Hermione, and then up at the sky. She gave a sigh. "I don't know how you do it, Clytemnestra. I was never raised to be a mother. I was only taught to be a wife."

"Children are just small people, Helen," mother said. "Albeit, occasionally stupid ones."

Helen tugged a red ribbon off of her headband and held it out to me. "Here, Iphigenia, would you like this?"

Wordlessly, I accepted. The ribbon was soft and silken and magic with her touch.

"I'd like to talk with you, Iphigenia. Somewhere where other people can't listen in. Just you and me. If your mother will agree?"

Helen lifted her gaze to Clytemnestra's face. Mother's fingers dug into my shoulders.

"Of course," said mother. "She's your niece."

I knew my mother didn't want me to be alone with Helen. I also knew that I wanted to be near that beauty, that glamour, that heat. I pulled the ribbon taut between my fingers.

"All right," I said.

* * *

AS I rode to Aulis, I forgot the day when I was eight when my mother plucked my embroidery out of my lap and held it up to the light. I waited for her to tear out my stitches and return it to my lap for me to do over again, as she had done every morning since I could first grip a needle. Instead she stared at my work with a thoughtful expression. "Hmm," she said. "You're getting better."

I lost that day, but I remembered Helen in Mycenae, her searing eyes and her haughty pose and her daughter sitting forlornly nearby, trying to earn a moment's attention by finding a perfect bite of food.

* * *

THE WAGON stopped at Aulis with a jolt. Prickling dust settled onto our clothing and skin. I pulled the canopy aside and spat onto the ground to clear my mouth. Mother reached out to stop me, but as her hand touched my shoulder, she changed her mind. She leaned over beside me and spat onto the ground, too.

A slave helped my mother down onto the soil of Aulis. He was old and bent, his right leg dragging behind his left. I felt a tug of recognition, but I couldn't remember who he was. *Iamas*, my mind suggested, but Artemis had stolen everything else I knew about him.

I accepted his hand to help me down. He looked up at me and startled. His hand jerked away. I stumbled, only barely catching my balance. Orestes began to cry.

"What's the matter?" mother demanded.

The slave whimpered.

"Iamas," mother repeated, more softly. "What's the matter?"

Iamas trembled. "King Agamemnon said you might not come."

"Don't be ridiculous," said mother. "How could there be a wedding if we didn't come? Help my daughter down."

Iamas offered his hand again. This time, his grip remained steady as I descended. His gaze lingered on the smelly decorations in my hair that I had forgotten were there. I reached up to touch them, and felt their softness, their fragility.

A shudder ran through Iamas. He looked away from me, and clutched himself as if he were cold, even though the air was hot and stagnant. I knew that he was sad and uncomfortable and lying about something. I couldn't care much. He was a stranger.

"You could still ride back to Mycenae," he suggested, softly.

"Iamas!" Mother's voice grew sharp. "What's wrong with you?"

I remember now what I didn't then: Iamas, the old slave, who had been with my mother since before I was born. I remember him holding me when I was so small that I understood the world in images. He was younger then, his nose crooked from a healed fracture, his smile gap-toothed and ever-wide. When his work was mobile, he came to sit near me while I played, watching me run around and chatter as toddlers will. When I exhausted myself, he made a place for me to lie beside him, and told me stories through the sleepy afternoon.

He was little more than a shadow to me. I walked past him, toward the harbor where a thousand ships sat motionless on a sea as flat as glass. Wilted sails drooped from their masts, pining for a wind that refused to come. The painted eyes on the ships' prows stared blankly forward, as if trying to make out the shape of Troy in the distance. Ten thousand oars waited.

"Why are all the ships still moored?" I asked.

Iamas spoke from behind me. "They're trapped. There's no wind to send them to Troy."

"They're just sitting there?"

"They have no choice."

I watched the ships bob up and down with the almost imperceptible motion of the water. Seabirds circled silently beneath the brazen sun. Even they seemed to be waiting.

I turned my back to the water and surveyed the camp. It was larger than I'd thought a camp could be, an immense array of men and equipment. Regiments formed restless circles around banked fires, their strength turned to games of chance played with stones and carved figures.

The soldiers who'd grown bored with games stood, rubbing wax into their armor with strokes as forceful as blows. Metal shone, bright as children's eyes and new-minted coins. As I stared at the men and their armor, the sun blazed off of the metal until it became impossible to tell warriors from breastplates, skin from gold. Orestes laughed and stretched out his hand toward the shining ranks. They seemed an array of golden men, waiting to stretch their flaming limbs and dazzle into battle like animate rays of sunlight.

Left in the harbor with no one to fight, they were burning up fast. They couldn't survive without wind to stoke them, to blow them onto dry firewood. They needed new things to burn. They needed fuel.

* * *

YOU CAME to the tent where Iamas settled us to wait for the wedding. All three of us looked up at your approach. Orestes stretched his arms in the direction of your voice. You called only for Clytemnestra.

Mother slipped out of the tent, leaving Orestes and me to peer out from the shadows. Orestes fussed; I held him close. Mother's garment was bright against the dun ground, her sandaled feet pale and delicate. I heard cloth rustling as she embraced you.

"You've arrived." Your voice splintered with ambivalence.

"Come inside," mother said. "Iphigenia is wearing her wedding flowers. She'll want to see you. She looks radiant."

"I can't. I have things to attend to."

"Just come in for a moment. You have to see your Iphigenia one last time while she's still a maiden."

"I can't!" Your shout was sudden, anguished. "I must go. I'll return later."

Dust swirled around your retreating footsteps. I inhaled it, ready to choke.

* * *

THE NIGHT when you led me out to see the soldiers in the fog—do you remember what happened after that? It has only just come back to me, how you took me by the hand and led me, walking this time, back out of the copse of trees and into the palace, up to my chamber where the other girls lay, half-awake, waiting for us to return.

I stared after your retreating form. I felt as if I were waking from a dream into my mundane existence. I wanted to run after you and make the dream last.

So I did.

* * *

DO YOU feel it now? The sky is darkening. My power grows. I feel the ruffle of waves beneath what has become of my spirit. They churn into crests, surmounted with foam. Boats tremble beneath me. Sails billow with my breath. I tousle the hair of men who have set aside their helmets, and they totter, no longer sure of their footing.

I am still weak, my father. Soon, I will do more than wail in your ear.

* * *

MOTHER SAT at the edge of the tent after you departed, staring out (as I stared after you when you left me to mundanity after showing me marvels). Perhaps she had begun to suspect something from your refusal to see me, from Iamas's shudder as he looked up at my wedding adornments.

Outside: a flash of gold.

Mother squeezed my hand. "That's Achilles's shield," she said. "Stay here. I'll ask your questions for you."

It was not like my stern, proper mother to expose herself to strange men.

I swung Orestes into my lap. I could only see a narrow slice of the camp from where I sat. I saw the arm and chest of the man who must be Achilles, his body rippling with muscles as sharply delineated as those on a statue. His helmet and breastplate were wrought of fine, detailed gold. His oiled brown skin shone as brightly as his armor.

Mother extended her hand. "Greetings, Achilles! May you and my daughter have the happiest of marriages."

Achilles eyed her fingers. Beneath his helmet, his eyes were dark and chary. (Fog, a branch, a dandelion mirroring the moon.) "Woman, why do you offer your hand to a stranger? You may be beautiful, but that is no excuse."

"Forgive me. I thought you'd recognize me from my description. I'm Agamemnon's wife."

"Are you? I would have thought such a powerful man would have better control of his women."

I could not see my mother's face, but I knew the taut smile she would wear in response to such an affront, the cat-like stretch of her lips that would not reach her eyes. (Like the taut smile Helen flashed me in the courtyard, late that night when I had nine summers: "Come walk with me, niece.")

"We'll be related in a few days," said mother. "Just pretend we already are."

"Are you insane?" Achilles's dark eyes examined the length of my mother's body. "No one told me Agamemnon had married a madwoman."

Mother's voice became dangerously low. "Young man. I am not mad."

"You must be. I'm the son of Thetis, goddess of the sea. I've slain a thousand men. I wear glory like other men wear scent. Why would I marry your daughter just because you tell me to?"

"My husband sent for us," said Clytemnestra. "He said that you wanted to marry my daughter."

"Why would I tell him that? I've never even seen her."

For a long moment, mother fell silent. (My head, ringing with emptiness, the sound of forgotten memories.)

"You'll forgive me if I sound skeptical," she said at last, "but either you are mistaken, or my husband is lying. What should a loyal wife believe?"

Achilles's eyes hardened like metal.

Before Achilles could speak, the slave Iamas pushed himself between the two of them. He turned toward Clytemnestra, panting, his face red with exertion.

Mother snapped, "What do you want?"

* * *

IAMAS TOLD them your plans. He revealed how the armies had been delayed in the harbor, waiting for a wind. He told of how the goddess had demanded a sacrifice, and how the wedding was a ruse designed to lure us to my death.

All around us, the air was as still and expectant as a held breath. (Me, in my bed, forgetting green and figs and wool.)

"Tomorrow," Iamas said, "They will do it tomorrow at dawn."

* * *

MY IMAGINATION caught on the moment when you forged your plan with Menelaus, Odysseus and Calchas. My mind had become a scatter of half-forgotten fragments. Tatters of old memories hung in the places of things I could not recall. I couldn't remember Menelaus's face, so I saw my mother's instead, wearing the beard you had when I was younger, black through and through. A restless Achilles paced in the role of Odysseus, sandals of gold kicking up dust as he paced the fog-filled copse. Calchas wore a thin linen robe instead of priestly raiment. He turned to you, and it was Helen's mouth sneering around his demands, her indigo eyes filled with visions of my blood.

Will you sacrifice your daughter?

I will.

Was your voice loud and resonant? Did mother-Menelaus clap you on the back? Achilles-Odysseus would have spoken with grudging respect, a flicker of admiration in his chary eyes. "You're a callous son of a bitch," he'd have said, "but you do what must be done."

Did you sink your head and whisper? Did Helen-Calchas crane her shapely neck to hear you, the red ribbons on her headband fluttering over her ear?

* * *

"TOMORROW," IAMAS said. "They will do it tomorrow at dawn."

He knelt before Clytemnestra.

"I wasn't sure whether I should tell you. A slave owes his loyalty to his master, but he owes his loyalty to his mistress, too. I came to Mycenae with your dowry. I was a young man then. I've always been yours."

"Why didn't you tell us before?" mother pleaded. "We could have ridden back to Mycenae. Agamemnon would never have known."

"I tried to," said Iamas. "I am a coward."

* * *

IF IT was necessary that you kill me, did you have to use a wedding as your ruse? Do you see how cruel it was to promise me all the treasures of womanhood that I would never possess?

Perhaps you thought you were marrying me off after all, one way or another. As I if were Persephone, spending my youth on the arm of Hades. But there will be no spring for me.

* * *

ORESTES STRUGGLED and cried in my arms. He could hear his mother. He reached for her voice. The sounds of Clytemnestra's small, pitiful sobs carried on the air.

As for me, I felt airy, as if I were standing on the top of the limestone cliffs that surround Aulis harbor like the broken half of a bowl. Betrayal forced all our hearts to skip a beat, but mother and Orestes could still cry.

Parts of me were already gone. I knew there was no turning back.

* * *

"TOMORROW," IAMAS said. "They will do it tomorrow at dawn."

* * *

MOTHER'S GRIP was painful on my arm. "Come on," she said, dragging me out of the tent. Orestes screamed as we went. It was the sound I would have made if I could have.

Achilles saw my unprotected face. He shielded his eyes (dark and chary, above a beard like adolescent scrub) with his sword arm. "Does the girl have to be here?"

"My husband has made fools of us all," said Clytemnestra. "He tricked me and used your name to do it. People will think you find it amusing to lure young girls to their deaths."

Achilles paced angrily. The slave, Iamas, flinched each time Achilles's sword clanked against his armor. "He had no right to use my name."

Mother said, "You could make them stop this. They will listen to you. You're a hero. If you tell them to stop, they'll have to take heed."

Achilles halted. "You want me to tell Agamemnon to stop the sacrifice?"

"For the sake of your reputation!"

"But how will we get to Troy?"

Mother approached him. At once, the stern and proper woman I had known all my life vanished. (Helen arraying herself on the bench, the folds of her garment decorating her languorous body.) She became a softer, reticent figure, her eyes averted, her hands gentle and hesitant as they lifted her hem to show her round calves. Her fingers fastened on the laces of Achilles's breastplate. Her lips moved near his neck, so close that her breath stirred the fine golden hair on his nape.

"You'll find a way," she murmured in his ear.

Achilles stayed silent. Mother lowered herself to her knees. She stared up at him, coy and alluring, through lowered lashes. Soft brown curls escaped from her braids to soften the angles of her face. Her breasts rose and fell with her breath.

"Do you want me to beg?" she asked. "My daughter and I are helpless. We have no choice but to implore you. Help us."

Achilles stepped back, repelled by her need. Mother held out her hands, her wrists upturned in supplication. ("My sister was born from an egg. I was born the normal way.")

"Do you want my daughter to beg instead? She will! She's always been virtuous, but what good will her honor do when they send her virgin to her grave?"

There was desire in Achilles's eyes. It was not for nothing that my mother was Helen's sister. But Achilles's gaze was hard and disdainful, too. For my mother was Helen's sister, and Helen was the whore who ran from Menelaus.

"Your daughter need not debase herself on my account. I will settle the matter of my honor with Agamemnon—"

Mother clasped her hands in gratitude. Achilles held out his hand to silence her.

"I will settle the matter of my honor with Agamemnon. And then *we will sail to Troy.*"

For the first time, Achilles's gaze came to rest on me. His eyes searched my face. I wondered what he saw there. I knew that I was not ugly. I thought, perhaps, in different circumstances he might have chosen to save a helpless woman with my youthful complexion and night-dark eyes. But to stir him that day, I would have had to be even more beautiful than Helen. Her beauty had gathered a thousand ships in the harbor. It would take something even greater to convince them to sail home without their war.

* * *

MOTHER TOOK me back to the tent. She tucked me beneath a blanket as if I were still a child. She pulled the wedding adornments from my hair, and stroked my tresses until they lay smooth and shining across my shoulders. Orestes lay beside me. He curled toward my warmth like a sleeping cat, and wrapped his fists around my hair.

"Stay here," mother said. "Rest. Keep out of sight. Keep yourself pure. It will be harder for them to justify what they're doing if they know that you are innocent and obedient."

She ran her fingers across my cheek.

"Don't worry. They aren't monsters. They won't do this terrible thing."

* * *

MY MEMORIES were tipping out of me more and more rapidly. My mind went dark with only a few moments illuminated, like torches casting small spots of light along a corridor.

I wandered into a lamp of memory: it was after you had taken me to see your soldiers and then returned me to my room. I snuck out behind you, moving as your shadow down the steps and across the portico. I walked quietly so that you would not hear me. We emerged into the forest. The fog was dissipating from the copse, revealing men among the trees, their shouts and sword-clashes harsh in the cold, dim air. This time, you were far ahead of me, already meeting with your hequetai, exchanging shouts and strategy.

Hands tightened on my shoulders. I looked up into their faces: two young men with patchy, adolescent beards. Their breath smelled of rotting fish. In my diminishing memory, I could only remember part of the scene: one standing in his nightclothes, the other wearing a helmet and a breastplate but nothing else. Beneath the helmet's shadow, his eyes were dark and chary.

They spoke. Their voices were rapid, unintelligible, drowned out by the pounding of blood in my ears. Their eyes were enormous and sinister, large and white like the dandelion before I crushed it underneath my foot.

Smells: blood, musk, new sweat. A short, blunt limb—like the branch that you gave me to use as a sword—emerged from obscuring whiteness. It pushed blindly against my leg. "Stop," one boy commanded the other. "Here, swing at this. One strong, smooth motion." The breastplate clattered against my flesh with a sound like thunder. My belly, rotting like the stench of rotting fish. My eyes, welling with fright. (Helen in the courtyard: "Come walk with me, niece." Her daughter Hermione looking on, jealous and ignored.)

Rotting fish and sweat. The moon dwindling like a crushed dandelion. The branch swinging. The thin high wail that a girl makes when someone swings at her with a sword that is a branch that is neither thing at all.

"You're hopeless," said one boy to the other. "It's too bad you weren't born a girl."

Then another face, a hequetai in a tufted cloak, shouting like the clash of swords. "What's wrong with you two? Are you stupid? Don't you know who this is?"

The reek of shit and piss. The man's hand on my arm, tighter than the boys' had been.

"What are you doing here? Your father would kill you if he knew. He'd kill all of us. Be grateful I'm sending you back without shoving your slatternly face in the muck in front of him. Do you have any modesty at all? Your mother and her people. Brazen, the lot of you. Walking into men's camps like common whores. You may be beautiful, but that is no excuse. Go! Get out of here! Get back where you came from! Go!"

My feet, pounding on the path back home. The copse of trees; the grass; the empty mouth of the megaron where exhausted slaves tended the coals to keep them warm until morning.

The pounding of my heart as I lay down in bed for the third time that night. Memories of moons and fog and branches. Love for my father: flat like a branch, round like a dandelion, silver like the moon, welling up and out of me into a rush like the wind, but without the power to move a thousand ships.

* * *

ANOTHER MEMORY. Another night. Indigo shaded the sky to evening. Helen smiled a taut smile that I'd seen on my mother's face, one that did not reach her eyes.

She reached for my hand. "Come walk with me, niece."

Hermione watched us. Jealousy darkened her features. "Mother!" she exclaimed. "I have something to show you."

Helen did not look over at her daughter. "Later." She bent closer to me. "Iphigenia?"

I twisted the ribbon from Helen's headband around my fingers. I stepped toward her, but I didn't take her hand.

Hermione upturned the bench she'd been sitting on, and began to cry.

Helen led me past the canopy that sheltered the benches and toward the black scratchings of the olive trees that stood, lonely, in the chilly air.

Helen arrayed herself beneath one, her garment spreading around her in delicate, shadowed folds.

I heard footsteps behind us and turned to see Hermione peering from the shadows, hoping to overhear what her mother had to say to another girl. She was clutching something in her hand. I wondered what delicacy she'd brought to bribe her mother with this time. A honeyed fig? A flask of sweet wine?

I looked back to Helen. Her eyes changed hue with the setting sun, taking on a lighter shade like the grey of water beneath a cloudy sky. Firelight from the lamps near the benches cast flickers across her cheekbones, highlighting an undertone in her skin like bronze. She watched my gaze as it trailed over her features, and gave a little sigh of boredom.

"You'll be beautiful one day, too," she said patronizingly.

"Not as beautiful as you," I demurred.

"No one is as beautiful as I." Her voice was flat, but full of pride.

The night smelled of burning oil and women's bodies. A dandelion hung high in the sky, casting its light down on us. Helen's motives were obscured behind blankness, like soldiers' bodies disappearing into fog.

Helen distorts the world around her. Never look at her too closely. You'll go blind.

"I saw you holding your father's hand today," said Helen. "Do you feel safe with your father?"

I made a moue. I couldn't speak to my beautiful aunt without my mother beside me.

"What was that?"

"Yes," I mumbled.

Helen shifted. The folds of her garment rearranged themselves into new shimmers and shadows.

"There's something I think I should tell you, Iphigenia. About your father. Did your mother ever tell you that she was married before?"

I shook my head. Around and around, the ribbon wove through my fingers.

"She had a husband named Tantalus who was the king of Mycenae before your father came. They had a child together. A son."

Helen paused, scrutinizing my reaction. I didn't know what to do. I looked to the right and the left. There was no one nearby.

"I know this is hard to hear, Iphigenia," said Helen, "but your father came to Mycenae and murdered Tantalus and then he—" She raised her sleeve over her mouth, and looked away. "He took the baby from your mother's arms and he dashed it to the stones and smashed it to pieces. My nephew."

With a quick glance over my shoulder, I saw that the servants were clearing out the benches and the canopy. Iamas helped a young girl douse the lamps. Behind me, there was safety, there was familiarity. I stepped back. Helen caught my hand.

"He was a round, happy baby. I only saw him once before—" She broke off. "After your father killed Tantalus, he forced Clytemnestra to marry him, and became king of Mycenae. I see him holding your hand and I worry. My sister doesn't want you to know, but you need to be warned. Your father isn't what he seems. He's the kind of man who would kill a baby."

I broke away and fled toward the bustling servants. My feet pounded past Hermione who glared at me and then turned toward Helen, her expression aching with desire for her mother's attention.

Jealous woman. Vain woman. Boastful woman. I never believed her. I never believed you would kill a child.

* * *

AFTER MOTHER fell asleep, I took Orestes in my arms and crept out of the tent. We made our way to the shore where the night sea looked like obsidian, reflecting the glow of the dandelion overhead.

I broke off a piece of branch the length of Orestes's arm and gave it to him, but I couldn't remember why. He stared at me with puzzled eyes until I took it away again and threw it toward the boats.

"Why don't you speak?" I asked him. "You're old enough."

Orestes stretched out his chubby hands. He snuggled his face against my chin and throat, warm as a cat. He liked to snuggle when I was distressed. It made him feel powerful that he, too, could give comfort.

"I am dissolving into pieces," I told him. "I need you to remember me for me. Will you do that? Please?"

He stared up at me with sincere, sober eyes.

"I am your sister," I said. "My name is Iphigenia. I love our father very much. I am going to be murdered by our father, but you must not be angry with him for that. To be angry with our father is to be angry with everything. It's to be angry with wind and war and gods. Don't be angry with him.

"I was born on an autumn day when the rain fell. I was born with the sound of thunder, but I was terrified of it anyway. When the palace rattled with strike and clash, I would run to hide behind mother's loom. She would glare at me and tell me to find something useful to do, but when I lay down beside her and stuck my thumb in my mouth, she would lean down to stroke my hair.

"I love music, but I can't sing. Our mother forever tells me to hush. I sang to you often anyway. When I sang, you laughed and clapped your hands. I taught you songs, but I don't remember them anymore. I want you to remember the things I taught you, whatever they were.

"Our grandmother was raped by Zeus when he turned into a swan, and our mother's sister was born out of an egg. Gods are our aunts and cousins, but we are only mortal. I am particularly mortal. I am weak and not very brave and I will die quickly, like those things they put in my hair for my wedding that never happened.

"I am afraid to die. I am afraid of losing simple things. Things like..." My memory cast a net through dark waters, coming up empty. I drew from what I saw. "Things like the smell of salt near a dark sea, and how warm your hand is, and how much you make me feel without ever speaking.

"I've lost so much already. I don't want to lose any more.

"Should I be glad that I'll never see the sun again so that Helen can be led like an errant child back to the marriage bed she desecrated? Should I rejoice that my death will enable my father to slaughter Trojans over a vixen that ran into the hills when she went into heat? Should my life dower the frigid air that passes between my uncle and his whore?

"I used to learn things, but now I forget them. I think I liked learning things. I need you to learn things for me now. Learn how to love someone, and how to survive a tragedy. Learn how to swing a sword, and how to convince an opponent when you have no argument but justice. Learn how to polish your armor until you become a glowing golden man, and then learn to be a flame that fuels itself. Learn to be your own wind. Will you? Will you please?"

I felt my tears falling into Orestes's hair. He hugged me tighter. I breathed in his smell.

"When warm air rises, seeking the sun, cool air rushes in to replace it. That's the way of the world. Joy and youth and love flow ever upward. What they leave behind is the cold consolation of the wind."

Orestes pulled away from me. I studied his solemn face. His mouth opened. For a long second, I thought he would speak, but no words came. For once, I found him inscrutable.

* * *

I FEEL the sea beneath me. I inhale and it waits. I exhale and it tumbles. Can you feel the pressure of my anger as it blows fiercely across your skin? I am the sand in your eyes, and the reek of the camp's midden heap blowing toward the sea. I am the force that rocks you back on your heels so that you flail and stagger. My hatred whistles through the cliffs. It screeches across the rough timber of your boats.

I grow stronger with every moment. I will be wild. I will be brutal. I will encircle you and conquer you. I will be more powerful than your boats and your swords and your blood lust. I will be inevitable.

* * *

I BROUGHT Orestes back to the tent, and we laid down beside Clytemnestra. I stared, sleeplessly, into the dark.

Possible paths stretched before me. I could go to Achilles's tent and plead my case as a whore instead of a virgin. I imagined what Helen would have done in my place, how she would have colored her cheeks and set her hair. She would arrange herself to look like a dandelion, easily crushed, and easily conquered. Unlike my mother, she would not have halted her fingers at the laces of Achilles's breastplate. Unlike my mother, she would have let her lips do more than hover hotly by his ear. Unlike my mother, she would have convinced him.

I could plead my case to Menelaus as his niece and an innocent. Or if he did not care for virtue, I could venture a suit to replace his lost Helen. Such methods might work on Odysseus, too. Only I was not a practiced seductress. My clumsy attempts might only succeed in doing as my mother said they would, and make the monsters feel justified when they gave me to Calchas's knife.

I could have sought you out, in the hope that the eye of night would grant you mercy. But I already knew what you would do if you found me wandering alone through a camp of soldiers.

One path seemed best: I would run out into the cold and wake the first soldier I found. "Take me to Calchas," I would tell him, and march resolutely to my fate. It would give me a fast, honorable end. And there might be a chance, just a small one, that I could be killed without seeing your face and knowing how it changed after you betrayed me.

But Orestes whimpered and tossed beneath his little blanket. Sweat dampened his brow. I'd kept him up too late, overwhelmed him with disturbing confidences. I stayed to soothe him until dawn neared and I was too tired to chase my death.

I was not brave. I was only a girl.

* * *

YOU CAME to fetch me. You didn't know that we knew. You pretended to be overjoyed at the prospect of the wedding that would never happen. You took my hand and whirled me in a circle. "Oh, Iphigenia! You look so beautiful!"

I looked up into your eyes and saw that you were crying. Your smile felt as false as mother's. Your tears washed over the place where I'd once kept the day when Orestes was born.

"Stop this," said mother. She pulled me away from you and pushed me toward the other end of the tent. Orestes sat on the cushions beside me, a wooden toy in his hand, watching.

Mother turned to confront you. "I have heard a terrible thing. Tell me if it's true. Are you planning to kill our daughter?"

Your eyes went blank. "How can you accuse me of such a thing?"

"I'll ask again. Answer me plainly this time. Are you planning to kill our daughter?"

You had no answer. You gripped the hilt of your branch, and set your jaw. Tears remained immobile on your cheeks.

"Don't do this." Mother grasped at your shoulder. You wrenched away. "I've been a model wife. I've done everything you've asked of me. I ran your home and raised your children. I've been chaste and loyal and honorable. How can you repay me by killing my daughter?"

She snatched Orestes from the cushions and held him toward you. He began to cry and kick.

"Look at your son. How do you think he'll react when you murder Iphigenia? He'll shy away from you. He'll fear you." She turned the baby toward her. "Orestes, do you hear me? Do you want your father to take your sister away?"

You tried to grab my brother. Mother held him tight. Orestes screamed in pain and fear.

"He'll hate you or he'll imitate you," mother shouted over his wails. "You'll teach your son to be a murderer! Is that what you want?"

You pushed Orestes further into his mother's arms and stormed away from her. You stopped a short distance from me and reached for my elbow. I flinched away.

"Are you happy, Clytemnestra?" you asked. "You've scared the girl. She could have gone thinking that she was going to be married. Now she's going to be terrified."

You leaned close to touch my hair. (Tugging my ponytail: "It's a good thing you were born a girl.") You dropped a kiss on my brow. ("I know this is hard to hear," said Helen, "but your father is the kind of man who would kill a baby.") I wrenched backward.

"What do you want?" I asked. "Do you want me to take your hand, blithe and trusting as any goat that follows its master back to the camp to see men fighting in the fog? I'm not a little girl anymore."

I looked into your angry, sneering face.

"Or do I have it wrong?" I asked. "Do you want me to kick and scream? Do you want me to have a tantrum like Orestes so that later you can think back on my wailing and berate yourself about the terrible things you've done?"

You tossed your head like a disquieted horse. "You're acting mad."

I laughed. "So I'm right, am I? You're already beginning to make me into an idea. A difficult decision rendered by a great man. Well, stop now. This is only difficult because you make it so. All you have to do is break your vow and spare my life."

"Menelaus and Odysseus would take the armies and bring them to march against Mycenae. Don't you see? I have no choice."

"Don't *you* see? It should never have been your choice at all. My life isn't yours to barter. The choice should have been mine."

"You don't understand."

"I understand that you want me to pity you for my death."

Wind whistled through my brain. The edges of the tent rustled. Sand stirred. Strands of mother's hair blew out from her braids.

"You know, I never believed what Helen told me. Did he look like Orestes, father? Did my elder half-brother look like Orestes when you dashed him to the rocks?"

You glowered at my defiance. "This is how you beg me to save your life?"

"Is it sufficient?" I asked, but I already knew the answer. I inhaled deeply. "Don't kill me."

I had forgotten how to beg.

* * *

WITH ALMOST nothing of myself remaining, I found myself reconsidering my conversation with Helen. Without my ego to distract me, I concentrated on different details, imagined different motivations behind her words. Had I thought Helen was arrogant simply because that was what everyone said about her? Was she boastful or simply honest?

As Helen sat beneath the olive tree, watching me admire her face, she'd sighed. I'd always believed it was a sigh of pride. Perhaps it was weariness instead. Perhaps she was exhausted from always having to negotiate jealousy and desire when all she wanted was to do something as simple as hold her niece's hand.

"You'll be beautiful one day, too." Had she been trying to reassure me?

"Not as beautiful as you," I demurred.

"No one is as beautiful as I."

Her voice was flat. Not arrogant, perhaps, but bitter? How must it have felt, always being reduced to that single superlative?

After she told me the terrible things about my father, I fled into the crowd to search for my mother. I found her holding a stern conversation with one of Helen's women. She wouldn't budge when I tried to drag her away. She dabbed my tears and told me to find Iamas so he could calm me down.

It wasn't until I crumpled at her feet, distraught and wailing, that she realized I was suffering from more than a scrape.

She slipped her arms around me and helped me to stand, her embrace warm and comforting. She brought me to her rooms and asked what was wrong.

I repeated Helen's words. "It isn't true!" I cried. "She's mean and vain. Why would she lie about something like that? Tell me she's lying."

"Of course she is," said mother, patting me vaguely on the head. "No one would be monstrous enough to do that." (She was lying, and I should have known it. I knew how she sounded when she lied. But oh, I wanted to believe her.)

She pulled the blanket to my chin and sat beside me and stroked my hair. I fell asleep, head tilted toward her touch.

Later, I woke to the sound of voices in the corridor. They drifted in, too quiet to hear. I tiptoed to the door and listened.

"I'm sorry," said Helen, her voice raw as if she'd been crying. "I didn't mean to scare her."

"Well, you did. She's inconsolable. She thinks her father kills babies."

"But Clytemnestra, he *did*…"

"Stories like that have no place in this house. I don't understand what was going on in your head!"

"He's a killer. How can you stand to see him with that sweet little girl? I think of my nephew every time I look at her. He's a monster. He'd kill her in a moment if it suited him. How can you let him near her?"

"He won't hurt her. He's her father."

"Clytemnestra, she had to know."

"It wasn't your decision."

"It had to be someone's! You can't protect her from a little sadness now and let him lead her into danger later. Someone had to keep your daughter safe."

Mother's voice dipped so low that it was barely more than a wisp. "Or maybe you couldn't stand to see that I can actually make my daughter happy."

Helen made a small, pained noise. I heard the rustling of her garment, her footsteps echoing down the painted clay corridor. I fled back to mother's blanket and tried to sleep, but I kept imagining your hands as you threw a baby down to his death on the stones. I imagined your fingers covered in blood, your palms blue from the cold in your heart. It couldn't be true.

* * *

YOU CALLED two men to escort me to Calchas. One wore his nightclothes, the other a breastplate and nothing else. Patchy adolescent beards covered their chins.

Mother wept.

You stood beside me. "I have to do this."

"Do you?" I asked.

The soldiers approached. In a low voice, you asked them to be gentle.

My emotions lifted from me, one by one, like steam evaporating from a campfire.

Fear disappeared.

"Don't worry, mother," I said. "I will go with them willingly. It is only death."

Sadness departed.

"Don't grieve for me. Don't cut your hair. Don't let the women of the house cut their hair either. Try not to mourn for me at all. Crush dandelions. Run by the river. Wind ribbons around your fingers."

Empathy bled away.

"Father, I want you to think of all the suffering I've felt, and magnify it a thousand times. When you reach the shores of Troy, unleash it all on their women. Let my blood be the harbinger of their pain. Spear them. Savage them. Let their mothers' throats be raw with screaming. Let their elder brothers be dashed like infants on the rocks."

Love vanished. I turned on my mother.

"Why did you bring me here? You saw him kill your son, and still you let me hold his hand! Why didn't you remember what he is?"

I pushed my mother to the ground. Orestes tumbled from her arms. I could not help but imagine the parallel of how my eldest brother had fallen to the rocks—but my mother twisted herself to cushion Orestes' fall, and he did not share the other infant's fate.

I forgot resignation.

"Why did you write that letter? Am I worth less to you than the hunk of wood they used to make your staff of office? Would it have been so bad to be the man who stayed home instead of fighting? Let Menelaus lead. Let him appease Artemis with Hermione's blood. If a girl must die to dower Helen, why shouldn't it be her own daughter?

"Did you raise me only so that you could trade me in for the best offer you could get? A wealthy husband? Influential children? A wind to push you across the sea?

"Mother, why didn't you take me to the hills? Helen went! Helen ran away! Why didn't we follow Helen?"

You uttered a command. The soldiers took my elbow. I forgot how to speak.

* * *

YOUR SOLDIERS escorted me through the camp to the temple. Achilles found me on the way. "You're as beautiful as your aunt," he said.

The wind of my forgetfulness battered against him. Effortlessly, Achilles buffeted against its strength.

"I've changed my mind," he said. "It takes courage to walk calmly to your death. I wouldn't mind marrying you. Talk to me. I only need a little persuasion. Tell me why I should save your life."

Voiceless, I marched onward.

* * *

I FORGOT you.

They washed and perfumed me and decked me with the things that smell sweet. You came before me.

"My sweet Iphigenia," you said. "If there was anything I could do to stop it, I would, but I can't. Don't you see?"

You brushed your fingers along my cheek. I watched them, no longer certain what they were.

"Iphigenia, I have no right, but I've come to ask for your pardon. Can you forgive me for what I've done?"

I stared at you with empty eyes, my brows furrowed, my body cleansed and prepared. *Who are you?* asked my flesh.

* * *

THEY LED me into Artemis's sacred space. Wild things clustered, lush and pungent, around the courtyard. The leaves tossed as I passed them, shuddering in my wind. Sunlight glinted off of the armor of a dozen men who were gathered to see the beginning of their war. Iamas was there, too, weeping as he watched.

Calchas pushed his way toward me as if he were approaching through a gale, his garment billowing around him. I recognized the red ribbons on his headband, his indigo eyes, his taut and joyless smile.

"You would have been beautiful one day, too," she said.

Not as beautiful as you.

"No one is as beautiful as I."

His breath stank with rotting fish, unless that was other men, another time. He held a jeweled twig in his hand – but I knew it would be your hand that killed me. Calchas was only an instrument, like Helen, like the twig.

He lifted the jeweled twig to catch the sun. I didn't move. He drew it across my throat.

* * *

MY BODY forgot to be a body. I disappeared.

* * *

ARTEMIS HELD me like a child holds a dandelion. With a single breath, she blew the wind in my body out of my girl's shape.

I died.

* * *

FEEL ME now. I tumble through your camp, upturning tents as a child knocks over his toys. Beneath me, the sea rumbles. Enormous waves whip across the water, powerful enough to drown you all.

"Too strong!" shouts Menelaus.

Achilles claps him on the back. "It'll be a son of a bitch, but it'll get us there faster!"

Mother lies by the remnants of the tent and refuses to move. Iamas tugs on her garment, trying to stir her. She cries and cries, and I taste her tears. They become salt on my wind.

Orestes wails for mother's attention. He puts his mouth to her breasts, but she cannot give him the comfort of suckling. I ruffle his hair and blow a chill embrace around him. His eyes grow big and frightened. I love him, but I can only hug him harder, for I am a wind.

Achilles stands at the prow of one of the ships, boasting of what he'll do to the citizens of Troy. Menelaus jabs his sword into my breeze and laughs. "I'll ram Paris like he's done to Helen," he brags. Odysseus laughs.

I see you now, my father, standing away from the others, your face turned toward Troy. I blow and scream and whisper.

You smile at first, and turn to Calchas. "It's my daughter!"

The priest looks up from cleaning his bloody dagger. "What did you say?"

I whip cold fury between your ears. Your face goes pale, and you clap your hands to the sides of your head, but my voice is the sound of the wind. It is undeniable.

Do you still want forgiveness, father?

"Set sail!" you shout. "It's time to get out of this harbor!"

I am vast and potent. I will crush you all with my strength and whirl your boats to the bottom of the sea. I'll spin your corpses through the air and dash them against the cliffs.

But no, I am helpless again, always and ever a hostage to someone else's desires. With ease, Artemis imposes her will on my wild fury. I feel the tension of her hands drawing me back like a bowstring. With one strong, smooth motion, she aims me at your fleet. Fiercely, implacably, I blow you to Troy.

Monstrous Embrace

I AM UGLINESS in body and bone, breath and heartbeat. I am muddy rocks and jagged scars snaking across salt-sown fields. I am insect larvae wriggling inside the great dead beasts into which they were born. Too, I am the hanks of dead flesh rotting. I am the ungrateful child's sneer, the plague sore bursting, the swing of shadow beneath the gallows rope. Ugliness is my hands, my feet, my fingernails. Ugliness is my gaze, boring into you like a worm into rotting fruit.

Listen to me, my prince. Tomorrow, when dawn breaks and you stand in the chapel accepting your late father's crown, your fate will be set. Do nothing and you will be dead by sundown. Your kingdom will be laid waste, its remnants preserved only in the bellies of carrion birds.

There is another option. Marry me.

Rise from your bed and take my hand. We will be as one, husband and wife.

O, my prince, do not answer hastily. It is no ludicrous suggestion for you to love ugliness, marry ugliness. Already, you have wed yourself to hate. She lies beside you even now, your linen sheets tangled around her naked curves, the heat of her flesh close and tempting.

Repudiate her. Rise from your bed and take my hand. We will be as one, husband and wife. It is your only chance for survival. It is your kingdom's only chance for survival. Marry me and you will keep your life and your crown—if you have the courage.

* * *

THE DAY you met your princess, I was the thicket, watching as you rode with your hunters through the snow-swept clearing. Your horses' manes were bright with royal colors. Hounds prowled through your ranks, ears pricked for the rustling of foxes.

One of your knights sounded his horn and the animals were off, hooves and paws crunching through the frosty undergrowth. One dog tore his side on my thorny branches. He whimpered, tail tucked between his legs, blood trickling into the snow.

You kicked your heels into your stallion's sides to urge him forward. He bolted a few steps before halting. He tossed his head wildly, mad eyes darting toward a nearby stand of oaks. You kicked your heels again. He didn't budge. You tugged the reins. He tossed his head as he had before, the muscles in his great neck straining.

This time you followed his gaze with your own, catching a glimpse of blue between the bare-branched oaks. Tugging your steed's reins in that direction, you kicked your heels once more. This time, the horse obeyed.

Your princess sat side-saddle on a white mare, half-obscured by trees. An unhooded hawk perched on her shoulder, beaming its cruel-eyed gaze at you. Yellow and white ribbons adorned her wheat-colored hair. Her kirtle was the soft blue of mid-afternoon. A distant preoccupation glazed her eyes, giving her a fey appearance.

"Who are you?" you asked, awed.

Though your approach had not been quiet, she startled at your words. One alabaster hand flew across her mouth. As though called back from a great distance, her gaze settled on your face.

"My name is Lady Alna. I'm from the north." She paused. "I am faint from thirst. Perhaps…"

You drew a flask of wine from your pack and offered it to her, your eyes brightening as her fingers trailed across the back of your gloved hand. She drank in small, fluttering sips. You gazed at her, entranced by her high forehead and round cheeks.

Flirting her eyes downward, Alna returned the flask. "Might I ask my benefactor's name?"

You laughed with the genuine pleasure of not being recognized. "I am called Raius. I am the prince of this realm."

You failed to notice the brief twitch of her lips that would have revealed to a more perceptive man that she had known your identity all along. She ducked her head. "Pardon my ignorance. I've been traveling a long time. I come from a tiny city called Elithi in the frozen north. Its towers once rose in the valley between the two highest mountains in the world, but vainglorious warlords have burned them down. My father sent me away when his spies learned of the approaching armies. He and my brothers remained to stage a last stand. I have wandered alone since then, riding further than I can reckon."

Her hawk screeched, wings stretched wide. She laughed brightly and held out her bare wrist. It jumped down, talons leaving no mark on her skin.

"Not quite alone," she amended. "This is Karn—my sole companion."

I saw love catch light in your gaze like an ember igniting firewood. I wish I could say that it surprised me that you could be so easily inflamed by beauty. Alas, I know you are only human.

I was everywhere around you, but you did not see me. You looked past the thorny briars ringing the copse, the poisonous mushrooms sprouting between the roots of the trees, the steam rising from the fox guts spilled by your hounds. All you saw was the smooth, pale face of Lady Alna. This is the fate of fools in love. They are blind to half the world.

* * *

I'VE SEEN much since the world began. When the sky was made, there were thick brown clouds that blotted the cleansing light of the sky. I was those clouds. When the earth was made, there were rocks and mud that choked out the green of growing things. I was those rocks, and I was that mud. I was bony-eyed fish swimming through ocean depths. I was centipedes wriggling across the forest floor. I was mildew spreading tendrils across damp cave walls, filling caverns with the stench of decay.

Wherever death is, there is ugliness. And so I have been everywhere.

I recall the first time I learned that I was one thing—one despised thing—and that there was another thing outside me, one that was loved.

At that time, I was a swamp surrounding a band of travelers who had entered my depths at nightfall. They carried with them a creature in a cage, a wretched animal with torn ears and tattered fur. They had not fed it for days and it was starving. That night, they let it out on a rope. They petted and praised it and gorged it on raw meats.

They loved me that night. They petted and fed me, too. They wore the cured skins of their conquered foes and pierced their hands with bone needles. They stomped and shouted and distorted their faces into hideous masks.

When the creature was full and resting, watching them through satisfied half-lidded eyes, they slaughtered it. I was its entrails which they smeared across their arms and faces. I was their grunts and groans and howls; the stench of their rancid sweat; the angry slash of fire and shadow cast by their torches across their gaping mouths.

I came to love them. Ours was a strange, new synthesis. Other creatures had made themselves ugly to ward off rivals or predators, but nothing had ever before approached me with open arms and thinking minds, seeking to understand and become me. I felt myself unbound and remade as they wove me into themselves.

In the morning, they buried the dead creature. Their leader stood over its grave and intoned, "Hideous spirits that danced with us and dwelled with us, attend me. We have feasted and flattered you, and now I banish you."

With that, they left the swamp.

In the meadow beyond, they bathed themselves in the sparkling waters of the river that threaded through the grass. They rubbed their newly clean bodies with oil extracted from crushed flowers and painted their faces with delicate shades of white and red. They sang instead of speaking, danced instead of walking. At dusk, they dined on fresh goats' milk, apples, blackberries, and honey.

I followed them as oozing mud, until there was no more mud. I circled above their heads, calling with the grating voices of birds that feast on dead things. They pretended not to hear my lonely cries. They turned away from me, seeking instead that vixen beauty whose trail I am always following but whom I have never met.

What did she give them? Nothing but the ephemeral favor of her smile. In the end, when she left them, they returned to me. It was I, their jilted lover, who was left to tenderly trail the drool across their wizened jaws, and to twist their limbs in rigor mortis. I could have loved them all along, but they wouldn't take me until beauty fled from the rasp of their dying breaths. That day, I learned hurt. I have never forgotten it.

* * *

YOU, TOO, know hurt.

When you were born, I was born with you. Together, we felt the midwife's rough hands pull you from your mother. However, only I had enough experience of the world to recognize the fear and disgust on her face as she beheld your crippled foot.

She was quick to blink away her disdain. She wrapped us in a tight blanket and laid us on the queen's belly. "Keep them warm and comfortable," she instructed one of the ladies in waiting. "There are herbs I must fetch from my house. I will return within the hour." She was careful not to let her voice betray something had gone wrong. She had guessed that your father, the king, would blame her for your deformity.

By dusk the next day, your father's soldiers had discovered her attempting to flee the kingdom with a caravan of pilgrims headed through the mountains. Your father had her strung up on the castle gate. During your first few weeks, I hung with her, inhabiting her gnarled bones as the crows pecked them clean.

At the same time, I lay with you in your cradle as we nursed on both the queen's milk and her strained expression of mingled sadness and distaste. She and her ladies did their best to conceal their revulsion beneath polished smiles, but even as an infant, you were not deceived. You were raised on the same provisions I'd become accustomed to over the millennia: the darting glances cut quickly away; the whispers beneath raised hands; the unabashed stares of children too young to have learned that civil, transparent lies are considered more polite than honest acknowledgement.

Day after day, you tottered after the other children, desperate to join their games. I longed to tell you that you were not alone. I was always with you, my invisible fingers in your hair, my lips pressed against your crippled foot as a mother's lips kiss away her child's injury. Alas, you could not hear my voice or feel my shadow.

I know your most painful secrets. Oh, yes. The ones you've consigned to memory's dusty, forsaken chambers. Their doors unlock for me. I have trespassed within them.

Don't doubt me, my prince. I could recount tales of your older brother that even you have forgotten you remember. Once, he was the center around which your thoughts revolved. Now you've learned to set him aside as a woman does with a spoiled bit of embroidery, only taking up his memory when regret inclines you to open old wounds. Your courtiers think your tense, stoic silences stem from grief, but we know the truth. Don't we?

Fear not. Your secrets are safe with me. I hated Edrian as much as you did. I loathed the beauty he wore with the entitlement of a crown prince, his shining blond hair and long flawless legs. The imperious expression he wore as he goaded the other children into racing laps through the castle's circular corridors. His grin as he watched you lurch after them, trailing behind them all, even the short, fat daughters of the duke.

Sometimes, Edrian would run beside you, breathing easy as you wheezed with the effort of dragging your useless foot. He reached out to steady you, features arrayed in a mimicry of compassion. "We'll run together," he said. He waited for you to rest your weight on his shoulders, and then he pulled away and rushed ahead, leaving you to stumble and fall as his laughter echoed through the halls.

Again and again, he did this. Always, you thought to yourself, *this time, this time, this time he'll help me,* and offered your trust once more.

As painful as those memories are for you, others of your memories are for me. The news of your brother's death arriving with the knights who'd ridden with him on that doomed hunt—I did not mourn his death, but I mourned what I knew it would mean for you. The sudden shower of attention bestowed on a previously unimportant son; the brocades and perfumes; the haberdashers and seamstresses and tailors.

Even I could not have predicted the southern magician, wrapped in so many layers of grey gauze that his body was blurred and indistinct, whose tales of healing miracles won him entrance into your bedchamber. He set candles smoldering in the corners of your room and knelt over them, chanting for hours before he approached your bed. His hands emerged from his shroud, delicate and dark as carved ebony. I saw the magic on him like a shadow and I despaired.

While you screamed with the pain of his needles and bone-breaking vises, the part of my spirit that lived within you stretched and thinned. I felt myself sifted from your flesh like sand through a sieve.

The magician pulled aside the netting that had veiled his face. I stared into his bald, white eyes. He touched his fingers to his forehead in salute and spoke a few grave syllables to banish me. I reeled away, dizzy and spinning.

As a normal-bodied boy, you grew distant. Sometimes I watched you, inhabiting the decaying corpses of mice left on the flagstones by well-fed castle cats, or the pock marks scarring the chef's daughter. I watched as you lost your thoughtful gravity. The ugly hesitate over their actions, knowing that they survive on the sufferance of the beautiful. You were comfortable, and careless, and free.

Already, you had forgotten me.

* * *

THOUGH YOU don't see it, your new love betrays you as completely as your brother did. I know, for I am the foul taste that coats her tongue when she remembers your kisses, her lingering expression of disgust when she turns from your caress. You've blinded yourself to her ugliness, just as the tribe in the swamp turned deaf ears to my aching calls.

At night, as you prepare for your rest, the Lady Alna lingers outside your bedchamber to speak with your bodyguard. Through the door, you hear the murmur of her voice. You are not suspicious; it reminds you of the pleasant, reassuring hum of her sleeping breath. But I am the scar across your bodyguard's bicep where he took a blow meant for you, and I hear what she says.

She lays her hand across your bodyguard's forearm. "I've been here a year. We've hardly spoken. I don't even know your name."

Then, with a laugh: "You're so strong. Flex again. My husband must be afraid to travel without you."

"Yes, I've seen him in such moods! He does not seem to want my company either. Sometimes, he forgets I am there, and I must sit quietly and wait for his dismissal. It's kind of you to withdraw when he needs his privacy."

And leaning in, voice and lashes lowered: "The prince has confided in me that he's found the preparations for the coronation wearying. His father's death is still new and raw. He is grieving. After the ceremony, I will take him aside for a walk through the apple orchard to look at the new blossoms. Perhaps you would be so kind as to leave us alone…?"

As she withdraws her hand, her fingertips brush his wrist. His muscles tense, his heart rushes, his pupils dilate. She tilts her head to the side, exposing her neck. Her wheat-colored curls are crushed against her shoulder. On the other side of the door, you wait, innocent.

Later, an abstracted look on her face, she tells you that she misses the towers of her father's city. "Go to the wizard's tower," you tell her. She smiles with the pleasure of knowing you think it's your idea, so that you will not become suspicious when she spends her afternoons there, day after day.

I am the skulls and bones and bottled screams your wizard keeps in his chamber, the premature age that gnarls his spine. I watch as the Lady Alna drops her pretense in his presence. Her shy stance becomes imperious.

She releases her hawk. He circles the room, spreading his wings with the confidence of a creature used to owning all he surveys.

Alna lays her hand on the wizard's twisted knuckles. It is her way of establishing control over men. The touch has only a dusting of magic in it, not enough to affect a man of magic like a wizard. She does it anyway, for body-to-body has a magic of its own. Above, the hawk screams and extends his talons. He does not like it when she touches other men.

She laughs at the bird. He lands on me—one of the wizard's skulls. His talons are sharp, even against bone.

She pulls a list from her robe. "I have the Winter's Wit and Spikeleaf," she says. "I need Stitch Brew."

I extend into the wizard's crooked, toothless leer. "Stitch Brew is hard to obtain," he says.

Still, he promises to get it.

* * *

I WAS there the day the City of Towers burned.

The fairies of the north drove to Elithi in their icy chariots. I caught only glimpses of them as they passed, for the fairies are so beautiful that I have never seen their faces.

When they reached the city, the fairies gathered at the base of the towers. Their chancellor, who is so beautiful that I cannot see for twenty yards around him, read a statement from the fairies to the people of Elithi.

Elithi was magnificent—its spires built of finest marble, its willowy nobles dressed in whispering silks. Yet I always resided within its walls, for Elithi's beauty was purchased with ugly deeds. Some days, I watched the city from the wailing faces of maidens stolen from their homes to be sacrificed for magic spells. Others, I inhabited the severed hands and tongues cut from Elithians who'd dared speak against the city's rulers.

On the day when the fairies came to Elithi, I dwelled in the corpses of children whose organs had been harvested to make sweetmeats for the western barbarians. In the body of a disemboweled girl-child, her last breaths rattling with blood, I crawled to the tower window. The fairy chancellor's mellifluous voice echoed through the valley.

"Elithi is a blight on the ice," he said. "Its evil is a spreading blackness. For too long, we have stood aside. Our sorceresses came to us and told us of your sins. We turned them away, for the thought of destroying an entire people was too much to bear.

"Those of us who made that decision are shamed. It was only the most compassionate among us who looked not at the pain it would cause us to destroy you, but at the pain we could prevent. For years, they have traveled, filling bottles with the tears and screams and sorrows your magic has caused. Many among them have gone mad from witnessing such grief. This was their sacrifice, made in order to force us to see the agony caused by our inaction.

"To excise you from the world will hurt us. Yet it is the course of least evil. Some of us remember a world where light and dark were unalterably distinct. Now they are mixed. We stand at the estuary where they flow into each other. To stop evil, we commit evil."

As the echoes of the chancellor's voice faded, the fairies turned toward the city. In unison, they lifted their hands to the heavens. From their icy palms radiated a fiery nimbus which hung in great sheets across the air like the northern lights. Where it touched the tower walls, they burst into flame.

The Elithian nobles made a habit of living in the highest rooms, as removed as possible from the pain and despair wrought on their behalf in the city's cellars. That day, their callousness doomed them. They burned and died, their screams thrown down like falling stones.

High in the tallest tower, below only the king himself, the heir to the throne of Elithi dwelled in rooms draped in brocaded silks. His name was Honorable Karn and he lived with his young wife, the witch Alna.

They fled to the windows. Below, they heard the screams of dying peasants.

Alna stepped backward. Her wheat-colored hair was bound in braids atop her head. She pulled a dagger from the stone altar beneath the window and sawed through one of the braids. Her tongue twisted into the strange, spidery syllables of the mystic language. She had always been a wary, suspicious creature, and so she kept an arsenal of spells at her fingertips, all but complete. The beginning of this one had been cast ten years ago on a moonless midnight, over the still-beating heart cut from a priest.

Her feet rose from the ground. Her gold brocade gown trailed below her, billowing in the snap of the wind.

Her bear of a husband grabbed her skirts. She struggled. "What about me?" he growled. (I was his growl. I was his livid eyes.)

She batted him away. "Let me go, you fool."

"I won't let you desert me," said Karn. "I'll keep you here until we both burn."

Alna grimaced. I was twinned. "What do you want?"

"Make me fly."

"I can't. I only cut out one priest's heart."

"Find another way then, or we'll die together!"

Alna pursed her lips. Her pale brows drew together as she considered. "Very well," she said, "but you may not like it." She bound together another spell she'd been saving, one woven from the anguish of a bride watching her groom murdered before their consummation. Alna smiled as she began the final incantation. Karn looked up in surprise and pain as his fingers stretched out into feathers.

* * *

MY PRINCE, you must marry me. If you do not, she will kill you tomorrow. After the coronation, you will retreat with a small entourage to the castle chapel in order to receive private blessing from your priest. Alna will catch the holy man's eye. He will avert his gaze. Still, his hands will shake as he anoints your face with oil—for she has corrupted him with her whispers and wiles. He no longer has the power to call on God's protection.

The oil will dry sweet and cool on your forehead. Your wife will clasp your hand. She will lean against you, her silk gown caressing your skin. The carved gold leaves on her coronet will shine against her elaborate coiffure.

"Come walk with me," she will whisper. "I want to be alone with you."

Perhaps a tatter of memory will rustle in your mind, but you will cast aside this night's revelations as the unpleasant echoes of a nightmare.

You will take her hand. The two of you will leave the chapel. The perfume of apple blossoms will waft toward you. Your steward will release a cloud of doves that flap across your path before disappearing into the bright summer sky.

Alna will step off the path, her slippered feet pale as the blossoms. She will tug your hand and pull you into the trees. Your bodyguard will follow a few steps, a nettlesome suspicion turning in his stomach, until Lady Alna turns to soothe him with her smile.

You will walk together to the orchard's heart. The sun will warm to the gold of afternoon, gilding the trunks. Veiled in the canopy's deep shadows, you will feel calm and tired. You will lie at the foot of a massive tree, resting your head on a thick, gnarled root. Your thoughts will drift back to those days when you were an unwanted extra son, set loose to range the castle grounds alone.

Your first warning will be Karn's shadow, inscribing aerial circles with you at their center. The primordial, frightened part of your mind will recognize what it is to be prey before your reasoned self understands. You will convulse with tension, heart thumping as you struggle to your feet.

It will be too late.

Karn will descend from the sky, golden beak glinting as he dives to peck out your eyes. Behind you, Alna will begin her spell.

When your blood mixes with the packets of herbs Alna carries at her belt, a violent shuddering will overtake you. You will bleed through the skin as your soul is forced from your body. Your limbs will seize. You will choke on your tongue. Your thoughts will rush with her betrayal.

What more could she want? you will wonder. You will have made her queen, the most powerful woman for kingdoms around.

It is not your kingdom she desires. She is not interested in paltry command over meadows and sheep. She craves the power of your death: the agony of a good-hearted king betrayed by his queen on the day of his coronation. In Alna's skilled hands, it will yield more power than any sorceress has possessed since the liminal years.

Karn will circle your corpse, beak bloody and glistening with the remnants of your eyes. He will caw with delight, wings spread to the wind. Alna will smile again, and hold out her wrist. He will alight there, ready to gain the first rewards of her power.

Alna will have become so powerful that she can ignite a spell with a simple gesture. She will fan her fingers, light will flare, and then Karn will be standing before her, admiring his strong hairy hands.

"Welcome back, my love," Alna will say, laughter in her voice. For she will have left him with the beady eyes and cruel beak of a hawk, commanded by a hawk's stupidly focused brain.

"I do what I please," she will tell him. "I've had enough of your jealousy."

She will fix a leather hood over his head, and a silver chain around his ankle, and she will lead him north to the frozen lands. She will kill or enslave every fairy who breathes, and then she will set them to rebuilding the elegant spires of Elithi. This time, she will be the one to sit on the throne in the highest tower. Karn will stand beside her, beak bared, a curved sword of ice grasped in his huge hairy hands as he acts both as Alna's bodyguard and as a warning to those who would oppose her.

Here, in the warm lands, your enemies will be emboldened. Your nation, deprived of leaders, will languish in chaos. Neighboring kingdoms will squabble over your fields. Your nobles will die on the invader's blades, and your serfs will be marched north and sold in Alna's Elithi.

I will dwell in more places than ever before, rolling in hideous waves across the world. Yet the heart of me will wait with you as you die, seeking to soothe your pain. Do not do that to me, my prince. Do not force me to die with you.

* * *

ACCEPT MY hand and none of this shall come to pass.

Instead, the magic will come from your professed love. Its power will allow me to take human form.

"Close your eyes," I'll say, newly incarnated. When you have, I will ease you from your bed and settle you elsewhere while I do what I must.

I will approach your queen as she sleeps in your bed and lay my hand gently on her cheek. She will wake and behold the full, terrible strength of my ugliness. Her heart shall seize and fail. She will die with a curse on her lips.

Down in the rookery, Karn will let out a wailing cry. His talons will rip through his bonds. He will fly free, seeking to avenge his mate. As he wings to your bedroom window, I shall turn to face him. He, too, shall perish and fall.

This is the downfall of evil. They have not the courage to see the full face of ugliness, for they know it to be the appearance of their secret selves.

When they are gone, I will allow you to open your eyes. Despite how well we have known each other, you will wince, but you will not be able to draw your gaze away from me. I am riveting.

Arm in arm, we will march to the chapel. When we throw open the door, your corrupt priest will fall under the weight of his guilt. I will take his place at the altar, for ugliness has witnessed many marriages.

After we have pronounced our vows, I will take you into my arms and we will be one again. Do not mistake me for male or female. Ugliness has no sex. Yet for you, I will be all that is feminine, that which absorbs but is yielding. I will be for you a swamp, rising around you in muddy tides that caress and engulf.

Ugliness does not deserve your rebuff. I am neither evil nor virtuous. I simply am. Since the beginning, I have been with you, yearning.

Enthroned as your queen, I will transform your lands into my flesh so that you may better rule them. Your verdant forests will lose their leaves, skeletal branches scratching against hazy skies. Dirt will choke your rivers. Your village's fair youths will stoop, their lovely maidens be afflicted with warts and lazy eyes.

The armies that lurk even now on your borders will turn back. I shall ride on their fear and transform their lands, too, into my domain. Your rule shall extend, out through all the warring kingdoms into the great empire beyond, and then further, across the vast expanse of the ocean into realms your people have never even imagined.

Without beauty, ugliness will become the way of the world. Flowers and weeds will be tended together. Women whose ill favor has left them as lonely spinsters will be sought with the same fervor as their younger, maidenly sisters. A poorly glazed pot will hold the same value as one hammered from gold. Our reign will flourish forever, untroubled by beauty's petty jealousies.

This is the vision I offer, should you take the brave and noble risk of holding out your hand to me.

Or, refuse my offer if you must, and return to your fitful sleep beside your traitorous wife. Put aside my warnings as ghastly dreams and follow the scent of apple blossoms to your death.

Either way, I will gain your kingdom, riding in on the bloody blades of conquerors, or mounting the gilded dais on your arm. The only choice is whether I will be a slave, forced to do the will of destruction, or a wife, striving to serve my liege.

Well, my prince? Are you brave? Will you stand tall and marry me?

Or will you quiver in your bed, ridden by your cowardice until the breaking of a dim and restless dawn?

The Adventures of Captain Blackheart Wentworth: A Nautical Tail

I. BURIAL AT SEA

WITH A splash, the body of Cracked Mack the Lack went overboard. Captain Blackheart Wentworth, Rat Pirate of the Gully by the Oak, stared after Mack into the turgid brown waters. Wentworth's first mate, Whiskers Sullivan of the beady eyes and greedy paws, slunk deckside, muttering madly about the pitter patter of fleas rushing along his spine so loud he couldn't sleep or shit or make water—and when a rat can't shit or make water, tis a dark day indeed.

Cracked Mack the Lack had been the last of their dastardly crew. Sully'd found him that morning, gone tail over snout in the stern. Arsenic done him in. Mack had a taste for it, reminded him of that crack in the wall called home when papa took the boys out of a morning to learn their way in the world: how to tweak a cat's whiskers and pry cheese from between spring-loaded jaws. Now Mack was gone, wrapped in a spider web shroud to decay in his watery grave.

"We two rat jacks is all that's left," Wentworth said to Sully. "A ship with but two pirates is hardly a pirate ship at all."

Sully swiveled one ear toward his captain's voice. He scratched his head with his back foot.

"Tis time for a new mission," said Wentworth. "This old girl's been plundering these shores since you and I were press-ganged pups. We coarsened our hair on this route. Its bounty allowed our balls to grow low and pendulous.

"But now, I say, enough! Enough of hustling gulls, robbing their garbage as if twas treasure. Enough of gobbling eggs and spooking minnows. Like our venerable ancestors who carried the plague across Europe on their backs, we must spread our scourge throughout the seven seas! You hark?"

Sully scrabbled in circles, claws scratching on leaf-planks. His naked tail whipped; his beady eyes sparkled; his snout raised to sniff the invigorating maritime breeze. Whether he danced for joy or to exorcise the demon fleas what haunted him was anyone's guess.

II. LAUNCH

WENTWORTH OVERSAW the repairs which would see them off to parts unknown. Finest acorns restocked the canon. Deadfall to replank the deck was collected from the base of the Great Oak on the riverbank, the tree with bark too slick for any cat to climb, where ancestral rats had taken refuge through dark winters. Fresh twigs, roots and tubers replaced the rotting hull, bound together with whiskers plucked from captured hounds. The old anchor was replaced with a ripe plum, plucked from a pie still cooling on the windowsill belonging to the tabby Sharp Tooth. Under Wentworth's supervision, Sully secured the fruit to a catgut line and dropped it to the riverbottom.

As for the ragged pelts hanging from the fishspine mast, Wentworth ordered them taken down.

"Tis the banner of death what sees us off," said Wentworth. "Our flag should be the same."

Wentworth ordered that a black squirrel should be caught and skinned, one with fur fine as the down on a mother rat's breast and dark as Wentworth's withered heart. Muttering and grumbling, Sully hunted squirrels through the windswept grass. He cornered his quarry near the briar patch, ignoring the squirrel's prayers and promises. He dispatched the creature merciful quick: with but an exhalation of Sully's fetid breath, the squirrel perished.

They hung the pelt—skull and femurs attached—and prepared to launch.

In the stern, Sully stood watch, grumbling to his fleas. Standing at the snail-shell wheel, Wentworth opened the rusty trunk that had belonged to the captain before him, and the captain before him. He pulled out an ancient map. Looking to the overhanging stars, he guided the ship toward a place marked in the shaking script of a rat close to death: The Open Seas.

The ship plunged through dark waters, ghastly sail billowing in the wind, black-furred tail trailing behind them like the hem of death's own garment. Above hung the moon, green as the finest rotting cheese.

III. BATTLE

DAWN ROSE over the water, shards of reflected orange and rose mingling with foam. The ship bobbed through the estuary leading into the sea. Frogs and toads leapt, squelching, through the mud. Sully drew his scimitar to teach the tadpoles a thing or two about pirates, but Wentworth stayed his hand. "Wait til they have legs. Tis fair play," he advised.

Midmorning waters deepened to cobalt. Sully filled his tin cup and used the water to salt his dried meat ration. The treeline thinned to a distant green fringe.

"At last, the sea," said Wentworth. "I feel its goodness deep in my piratical bones."

Sully appeared to agree, or at least the mad twinkle brightened in his eye.

In the afternoon, they caught sight of a duck followed by a line of puffy yellow ducklings.

"Stand down!" shouted Wentworth, brandishing his sword. "We demand treasure! Give us your eggs and nest lining! Lay algae and water bugs at our feet."

The duck turned a matte eye on him and gave an uncomprehending honk.

"A rebel, eh?" Wentworth turned to Sully. "To the cannons, rat!"

The first shot fired across mama's feathered bow. She flapped her wings, but surrendered no treasure.

"Down the fleet!" ordered Wentworth.

The cannon boomed. One, two, three fluffy chicks disappeared into a puff of yellow feathers. Mama honked her outrage. She flew at the ship, pecking the prow. The ship careened beneath ardent avian assault. The whittled ears of the rat maiden figurehead snapped free. Wentworth ducked as they crashed around his head. Sully slammed against the hull and slumped.

"Retreat!" shouted Wentworth. He scrambled over Sullivan's unconscious form and wrenched the wheel to the left. The ship veered. The duck flapped after them, feet dragging in the waves, then skidded back to her remaining youngsters.

IV. UNCHARTED WATERS

SULLY PLUCKED splinters from his fur. "No lasting damage, eh?" said Wentworth.

They sailed til the water turned the steely grey of their swords. Overhead, web-winged creatures wheeled through the sky. "Wok, wok," they called, "Jabberwock."

Sully tested the depths by dropping anchor. The catgut line unspooled til it broke.

Wentworth went to fill his flask and found the supply of good brisk drink had pitched overboard. Ah, and the water barrels were gone, too.

He found Sully perched on the side of the boat, fishing with the broken catgut line. "We're to die out here," said Wentworth. "There's no booze left and no water neither."

Something tugged at Sully's line. He staggered back to ho-heave-ho.

Up on deck came a-sprawling a strange creature with a fish's bright green tail and the furry, cherubic face of a rat maid not long weaned.

"My whiskers," said Wentworth, "a merrat!"

Where her fur merged into scales, it flushed deep emerald like a branch giving way to leaves. Six pink shells covered the delights of her nipples.

Fancies of seduction raced through Wentworth's brain. Sully had other ideas. Drawing his saber, he slashed her tender throat. Her dying squeak rose high above her thumping death throes.

That evening they dined on roast fish while Sully wove himself a coat from the merrat's fur. Twas too close to cannibalism for Wentworth's gut, but a mad rat like Sullivan would slay his mother for her pelt.

"You're a cruel rat, Sully," said Wentworth.

Sully looked up, whiskers twitching. Wentworth could almost see the fleas rushing through his fur.

"Maybe your fleas'll move from your pelt to hers," suggested Wentworth.

Laughter danced in the inky wells of Sully's eyes. Baring the yellowed squares of his teeth, he ripped off a chunk of the merrat's pelt and threaded the needle he'd carved of her bone.

On the horizon, Wentworth glimpsed a white tentacle glowing in the pale dusk. "A monster! Rat your station! It's like to be guarding a hoard."

V. HERE THERE BE KRAKENS

WENTWORTH ORDERED Sullivan to quiet their running. They cut silently through darkening waters, hushed as a coward's footsteps.

They sailed round the tentacle like a peninsula, for twas almost as massive. Suckers big as pampered housecats pulsed, tasting the briny air.

"We'll sail to its center," Wentworth told Sullivan. "I'd lay ingots the beast's treasure lies near its heart."

The monster's head rose from the ocean like the great white dome of a cathedral. It was garbed in seaweed and encrusted with barnacles. A vast obsidian eye stared with diffuse gaze at the horizon.

Wentworth fetched his best harpoon, point honed to the soul of sharpness, and aimed at the creature. He threw strong but false. His harpoon sank into the waves.

The wind of its passing woke the monster. Its great, murky eye flashed alert. The massive head reared, barnacles snapping off and falling into the sea. A tentacle crashed across the ship, knocking the wheel askew. A second wrapped Wentworth in its sinuous grip.

Undaunted, Wentworth drew his dagger and hacked away. Green blood burned Wentworth's fur and sprayed across the ocean surface like oil. The tentacle pulsed with pain, squeezing tighter. At last, Wentworth hacked the tentacle through and thumped onto the deck.

Behind him, Sully led another tentacle in circles. It wrapped around the fishspine mast like a maypole.

Wentworth dashed to Sully's side. "Faster! Faster!" he called.

They whirled in a merry, desperate dance. The tentacle spiraled tighter and tighter 'til white flesh strained.

"Keep running her round," shouted Wentworth. He ran to the merrat's corpse where Sully's half-sewn coat lay, wet and bedraggled. He heaved the coat toward the mast.

Feeling coarse, soaked rat fur, the monster grasped and pulled. The mast came loose in its formidable grip. It dragged both pelt and mast toward gaping maw, stabbing its own throat with splintered fish spine. Green blood spurted. It began to sink.

Doused in burning blood, Wentworth and Sullivan danced a celebratory jig. Over the noise of massive tentacles sliding into the water, the pirates heard a female's distressed wail.

"Help! Help!"

VI. RESCUE

A PEA-GREEN skipper floated beside the nearest tentacle, in danger of being submerged in its wake. Wentworth directed Sullivan to the wheel. "Swiftly, rat," he ordered, buttoning his waistcoat.

They veered toward the small vessel, its deck obscured by churning waters. Wentworth knotted the catgut line and threw it down.

What vision of loveliness awaited them? Wentworth wondered. A sleek sable tail-swinger with cherry-red eyes? A midnight-furred scrambler with whiskers fine as dandelion fluff?

He felt a hitch in the catgut line as the fair maiden trusted her weight to him. "Thank you, kind sir," said she, coming into view: a green-eyed, ginger-coated, ravishing damsel of a…cat.

VII. DINNER AT THE CAPTAIN'S TABLE

THEY GATHERED round a knotted pine table stolen from a child's dollhouse. Oil lamps fueled by finest seal fat cast orange light across their repast of roast fish and "recycled" water.

"Avoid the drink," Wentworth advised their guest. "Tis less than potable."

The cat pulled a flask from her lacy garter. "I come supplied for all occasions." Feline she might be, but she still seemed a lady, bonnet and petticoat pristine. "Gin. Would you like a snifter?"

Wentworth grunted. Was it his imagination or had Sullivan polished the bones on his necklace? Did his flea-ridden fur seem fluffier from, perhaps, a mid-ocean bath?

"I'm Pussy La Chat," said the ginger jezebel. "My story is terrible sad. A fortnight ago, I set off with my bridegroom hoping to be married by the turkey on the hill. Alas, now my love is gone, and I'm alone." She smiled demurely. Lamplight could not help but glisten on her fangs. "How lucky I am to have found two strong sailors."

She set her paw on the table. Wentworth noted the fetching white sock on her foreleg.

Now Wentworth came to think of it, her tail had a rather shapely curve, and her green eyes—well, was not green the color of leaves and grass and cool spring meadows?

"Lucky and lovely," he agreed.

Sullivan glared jealously at his Captain.

"I wonder," said Pussy, voice honeyed with purr, "if I might join your crew. Weak though I am, perhaps I could be of some small assistance."

"That could be arranged."

"Purrfect."

Wentworth loosened his ascot. "Would you care to join me for a moonlight stroll?"

"Would that I could, Captain, but I find myself accounted for this evening." Pussy perked her ears. "Your first mate has offered to show me the constellations. Perhaps another time?"

Sullivan offered his arm to the feline intruder. She *mrrowwed*, fur ruffling prettily along her back. Oh, Wentworth had seen the signs of love before. How fast women fell. How illogical and intractable their affections.

He drained his goblet. Blast. He shouldn't have let Sully slay the merrat.

VIII. A BETTER BATTLE

PUSSY SPOTTED the galleon. "A nautical masterpiece," said Wentworth, admiring the five masts and graceful lateen sail. Plump, well-dressed hamsters bustled along deck.

"To the cannons!" called Wentworth.

Sully paused, shoulders hunched.

"To the cannons!" Wentworth repeated. "Are you a rat or a mouse?"

Hesitantly, Pussy raised her paw. "Your first mate has regaled me with your adventures," she began. "Your aggressive strategy, while admirable, may not be wise."

"Is that what Sully said?"

Under his Captain's betrayed gaze, Sullivan slunk away.

"Innovation is a sailor's way!" Pussy continued. "Else we'd all sail battered skiffs, like me and my poor bridegroom." She sniffed, dabbing her eye.

Wentworth tugged down his waistcoat. "What's your suggestion?"

"Deception!" Pussy licked her chops. "Good nautical men are always eager to assist their fellow voyagers."

"As we assisted you?"

"Our mast is gone. Our figurehead broken. I must say, we're quite a sight."

Grudgingly, Wentworth assented. He and Sullivan secreted themselves beneath the fallen sail, awaiting Pussy's signal.

"We must not allow Pussy to come between us," whispered Wentworth. "We're pirates. We kill without remorse. We do not romance. You hark?"

Sully pricked his ears.

"Good."

Dimly, they heard the galleon nearing. Pussy called, "Oh, sirs! Alack and alas, my ship has been caught in a storm, and all hands lost save me! Help, help!"

In low squeaks, the hamsters considered their options. "What's she worth in salvage?" "We'll get but a pittance for the leaves." "But a gross for the wheel!" Planks creaked as they boarded.

"Now!" shouted Pussy.

Wentworth and Sullivan dashed out, sabers flashing. The merchant's captain drew a fancy fencing foil. "I'll save you, milady!" he shouted. Pussy devoured him in a gulp.

A pretentious poof of a hamster flung a knife at Pussy's tail. Fast as a hopping mad flea, Sully chopped off the fellow's whiskers, tail, and head.

Wentworth made short work of the other quivering wretches. Those who surrendered were marched off the plank with a satisfying splash.

Wentworth surveyed the tatters of his once-sturdy vessel. He turned to the galleon. "The time's come to jump ship."

IX. TREASURE AT LAST

"PEARLS!" SAID Pussy. "Rubies!"

"Sapphires, gold, tea and tin." Wentworth rushed between overflowing trunks. "We're rich, rich, rich!"

He tossed a handful of gems, dancing in their glittering fall. "Ow."

Pussy turned. "What's wrong?"

Sully returned from exploring the ship's bowels, brandishing a master-crafted, jewel-encrusted sword—yet twas the object in Sully's other paw that caught Wentworth's eye.

Wentworth relieved Sullivan of the vintage wine. "Nothing," he said. "Nothing at all."

They drank into the night. Sully and Pussy curled up on a silk rug. Abandoned, the wine bottle emptied its dregs onto fine silk. Amid so much bounty, no one paid heed.

"This is so nice," said Pussy. A pearl necklace looped thrice around her neck. Her claws shone with diamonds.

Wentworth wore the hamster captain's tri-corner hat and tiny velvet waistcoat, unbuttoned. "We should sell our bounty and find a tropical island. We'll have servants and order everyone about. If anyone defies us, our blades will drink their blood!"

"That sounds lovely." Pussy rolled across the rug, paws in the air. "Captain Wentworth, will you marry Sullivan and me?"

The evening's joy bled away like the wine. Wentworth paced to the hull, gazing down at the roiling black sea. "What happened to your last bridegroom?"

Pussy burped. A white feather flew from her mouth. "Nevermind that." She joined Wentworth at the hull. "Here, I want you to have this."

She drew from her petticoats a metal object. It glinted in starlight.

"Tis my runcible spoon. My bridegroom and I ate our last meal from it. It's very precious to me."

Wentworth admired the runcible spoon. "No one's ever given me a gift before. Not without a threat."

Pussy purred. "Will you marry us?"

Wentworth glanced at Sully. He stood, paws folded at his waist, whiskers clean and tidy. For the first time in years, he wasn't twitching.

"Very well."

Wentworth married them there, beneath the green crescent moon. Seeing the two of them, rapturous and silhouetted by starlight, a tear came to Wentworth's crusty pirate's eye.

X. A BREWING STORM

WENTWORTH WOKE with a headache. He grabbed the wine and took a swig.

Above, the rosy tint of dawn illuminated the dark underbellies of storm clouds. Distant lightning flashed across the horizon. Thunder followed.

"Storm!" cried Wentworth. He rushed to the captain's cabin where Pussy and Sullivan had made their honeymoon suite. He burst through the door. "No time to lose! A dickens of a squall is on the way!"

He fell silent. Pussy stood over the bed, mouth stretched to reveal shining, dagger-sharp teeth. Sully lay helpless on the sheets, still snoring.

"Stop, you wretch!" Drawing his dagger, Wentworth ran at the cat. She mewled and leapt away.

"You've the wrong idea," began Pussy.

"Cat!" shouted Wentworth. "Feline! Kitten! Domesticated animal!"

Sullivan woke. He jumped to his feet, drawing his sword. He looked between his wife and his friend, unsure which to attack.

Wentworth jabbed at Pussy. "This *felis domesticus* was about to make you a snack!"

"Do nothing hasty, my beloved," said Pussy. "We can work this out."

Mad eyes bright, Sully charged his friend. Wentworth was too stunned to move. The blade's tip drew close to his fur.

With a burst of lightning like a thousand firecrackers, the ship tilted. Sully's blade clattered to the floor. Wentworth was thrown to the ground after it. Pussy clamored over him, escaping to the deck.

"After her," said Wentworth.

XI. LIGHTNING STRIKES

HE FOUND the false feline standing by the mast, long white gown wetted to her body.

"I didn't mean to hurt him!" she called into the wind. "Tis just—that flashing tail, that delectable fur, that delicious, rapid heartbeat! Oh, the trials of a cat in love."

"Is that what happened to your former bridegroom?"

"Tis true, I've succumbed to temptation in the past, but not this time! I would have remembered my vows!"

Sully crawled after Wentworth. His eyes were black as the tumbling waves. He twitched beneath a seething mass of fleas.

"My fate is in your paws," Pussy called to him.

Another lightning bolt crashed into the ship. It lit the mast from tip to deck where Pussy stood. Her dress turned ashen. The odor of burned fur filled the air.

Sully rushed to her side. "Don't comfort the harlot," called Wentworth. "There's no time."

Thunder rumbled. The mast creaked. As it fell, Wentworth pushed Sullivan aside. It crashed across the deck. The ship heaved and tilted. Gems and silks slid into the water. The bow tipped into the waves, prow pointing straight up toward the hidden sun.

Wentworth scrabbled for purchase. He pulled the runcible spoon from his sleeve and stuck it into a groove between planks. He gripped it, hind paws dangling over the water.

Pussy fell past him. Her claws slipped, stuck. Sully shivered on her back, twitches so bad they'd become convulsions. Fleas flashed around his body.

Pussy began to slip. "Hold tight," she yelled.

Her claws pulled free. She scrambled, regained her grip. She couldn't support them both.

Sully's eyes blazed past the black of waves and nighttime. They were black as madness now, black as the rotten cheese at the back of the moon.

He let go.

"No!" shouted Pussy and Wentworth, simultaneously.

Sully slid into the water, naked tail cresting the waves before disappearing.

XII. RAT OVERBOARD

THE STORM cleared to bright, azure sky. Pussy knelt, weeping. Wentworth inventoried the ship to see what treasure remained.

"The jewels are gone. And the rugs and gold and tea and tin and wine. But it looks like some silver survived. Enough to buy a new boat, maybe. A small one."

"Tis my fault," sobbed Pussy. "If I hadn't been tempted, if you hadn't found me, the three of us might have sheltered together."

Long ago as a press-ganged pup, Wentworth had made a vow of solidarity with those who found themselves prematurely estranged from their loved ones. He would not kill orphans or widows. But oh, he was tempted.

"No, we wouldn't," he said. "You'd have eaten him."

Pussy's bitter tears mingled with the drying ocean water on deck. "O, my dark one, my fleet one, my mad dancing one, with eyes black as a moonless night, and fur soft as the master's blanket."

"Should we drink the wine or save it to sell?" asked Wentworth.

"O, that you should die like this, at the hour of my ignominy, sacrificing your noble life for mine!"

"Drink it, I think," said Wentworth.

"Oh, my love! I can't go on without you!"

With a clatter of her claws on the leaf-planks, Pussy mounted the side of the ship. She stood like a figurehead, gown rustling in the wind, tail billowing behind her. Then the leap, and with a splash of spray, she was gone.

Wentworth gazed after her. This journey had been one of death. Cracked Mack had died. Sullivan had died. Even Pussy, poor pirate though she'd been, had taken a watery grave. Wentworth pulled the runcible spoon from his pocket and heaved it overboard. Without the damn thing, he'd be dead too, and maybe it would have been for the best.

XIII. ADRIFT

WEAKENED BY the storm, exhausted timbers broke apart. The captain's quarters capsized, taking the silver with them. The deck cracked into sections. Wentworth clung to the planks beneath him as they split off like a raft.

Long hours passed. A circling gull woke Wentworth's hope he might be approaching land til the bird pitched dead into the sea. Wentworth fished out its corpse and dined upon it.

Wet and miserable, Wentworth lay down and waited to die. He considered his many sins. As a ratling, he'd oft squabbled with his siblings, nipping their whiskers to make off with their breadcrumbs. He'd swindled apples from pups and woven lies as odiferous as rotten cheese. He'd nipped the teats that fed him.

For all that, he didn't think he'd been a bad rat. A bit nasty. A bit merciless. A bit bloodthirsty. No rodent is without flaws.

When he heard the rush of water pushed aside by a well-made prow, he thought perhaps he was gone to heaven. Sharp steel jabbing his ribs set him straight.

"Slavers, eh?" he asked.

"Silence, rat," replied the sword-wielding ferret, cruel nose twitching. He turned tail and two fat guineas marched Wentworth aboard their rickety vessel.

Palm trees swayed on the horizon, black against the sunset. Wentworth stared slack-jawed, aghast that he'd come so close to freedom.

A guinea caught him looking. "That thar's Sweet Summer Isle. They grow sugar thar. You'll spend the rest of yer life workin' the plantations."

He gave a dry and brutal laugh, cuffed Wentworth round the ear for good measure, and led him below decks whence he chained the poor rat to a dank cell wall for the remainder of the journey.

XIV. DESERTED ISLAND

BUT WHAT kind of pirate would Captain Blackheart Wentworth, Oppressor of Vermin and Terror of Things That Go Squeak, be if he couldn't slip free of rusty handcuffs? He knocked out the guinea guard with his own sword and with thundering footsteps marched deckside to conquer his craven captors.

At port, Wentworth sold the slavers for good gold coin and bought a plantation. When no other rat would purchase the cowards, Wentworth reacquired them at a price much reduced and forced them to labor sunup to sundown.

One afternoon, as summer sun shimmered on the sand, Wentworth was surprised to see two familiar figures staggering from the sea. Pussy, fur patched and ears a-tatter, clung to a skinnier flealess Sullivan. Over a feast of tropical fruit, Pussy explained how they'd come to these sunny shores.

Pussy had leapt into the water contrite and ready to die, until accosted by hungry cannibals who dragged her to their camp. Nearby, Sully, having been found inedible, was imprisoned in a cage. When the cannibals dunked Pussy in their wicked cauldron, Sully drew on nameless reserves of strength to wrench apart the cage bars. Quickly, he slew the cannibals and fled with his bride to their captor's ship which they converted to their own piratical ends. Ah, but theft and murder felt wrong without Wentworth to oversee it. The wedded couple spent their gold-strewn hours listless and mournful til they heard rumors of a wealthy white rat with a scurvy temper who ran a tropical sugar plantation. With haste, Pussy and Sully set off, til not two days from the island, their ship was lost to a freak whirlpool. Pussy and Sully swam for shore. Sharks circled and tropical undertows threatened to drag them under, but lo, they arrived at last on this very beach.

Past slights forgiven, Wentworth embraced his long-lost friends. In the sugar cane fields, even the ferret and his crew of guineas, now tanned and sore from their months of punishing labor, wept sentimental tears 'til Wentworth ordered them back to work.

XV. PIRATICAL EPILOGUE

SO IT came to be that the world was not menaced by rat pirates. Port cities flourished unafraid, reaping rich cargos of coffee and tea, sugar and salt, wood and silk and spices and precious stones. Unaccosted gold flowed through marine arteries, sustaining the vast fatherly arms of empires. By turbulent sea, churning river, or trickling tributary, trade reached even the most insignificant peoples stranded in the remotest, uncivilized reaches of the globe.

Sully held Pussy as they sat together on the white sand, admiring the sunset over the water. Wentworth threatened a cowardly guinea with his sword if he did not immediately dash to fetch a goblet of rum and mango juice. The creature scurried off. A smile stirred beneath Wentworth's whitening whiskers. Ah, sun and sand and sea air. Ah, the goodness of reclining on a beach with friends.

The *Present*

Heartstrung

ONE, TWO, three, the needle swoops.

Pamela squirms as the needle cuts into her sensitive heart tissue. "It hurts!"

"Shh," the seamstress says. "It's almost done, honey. Just a few more stitches and you'll be like mommy."

The seamstress bends forward as she presses the needle into her daughter's heart for another stitch, squinting to make sure she sews tight and even. As she pulls the thread taut, she realizes this stitch marks the midpoint—she's now halfway finished sewing Pamela's heart onto her sleeve.

Just yesterday, Pamela's heart lay locked beneath her ribs like a treasure. Then her daddy decided it was time for her to grow up, and now Pamela's heart lies red against the cuff of her pale blue sweater, bright as a cardinal in the summer sky. When the seamstress finishes sewing it on, Pamela will be a woman.

Right now, though, she's just a little girl. The seamstress tries to distract her. "Aren't you excited about the ceremony?"

"Will Beth be there?" Pamela has asked this question several times in the past few days. The seamstress plays along.

"Beth will be there and so will Uncle Jake and Aunt Mattie. Everyone's coming for you! So you have to be good now so you won't disappoint them."

Pamela nods grudgingly. The vinyl chair she's standing on creaks underfoot. The seamstress puts her hand on the back of the chair to keep it from sliding across the linoleum.

"Good girl," she says, slipping her hand underneath the cuff as she sews to make sure that none of the stitches go too deep and prick Pamela's wrist. As the needle goes in, she sees Pamela wince anyway. "Remember how lovely Beth looked after she had it done? Remember when Uncle Jake slapped her across the face at her ceremony and her smile lit up like a light bulb and everyone clapped?"

"Will everyone clap for me?"

"Of course they will, if you'll just stand still."

Mid-stitch, the needle snaps in two. The seamstress glances at the broken pieces in her palm, then tips them into her apron pocket. As she fumbles for a replacement needle, the broken tip catches underneath the heart on her own sleeve. The seamstress pauses for a moment to shake it loose.

Rubbing her wet eye with a closed fist, Pamela shifts her weight to take advantage of the respite. "It hurts," she repeats. Pamela's fingers dig into her palm. Her knuckles have turned white.

Seeing this, the seamstress feels a twinge of anxiety. The flare of emotion flicks past her eyes, which remain dry, and past her lips, which continue to smile. The anxiety travels through her bloodstream into her arm, down the plaid sleeve of her sweater, into the heart that is sewn on her own cuff. The heart absorbs it, as it has absorbed all her strong emotions since she was sewn at thirteen. Only a dull, polite echo of the anxiety remains.

The seamstress grabs a dishtowel from the rack next to the kitchen sink and dabs at her forehead, then begins sewing the curves of her daughter's heart. This part is the trickiest, especially since her needle has a tendency to slip in the loose knit weave.

The seamstress had known the cardigan would be difficult to sew on when she picked it, but she bought the garment anyway. It's timeless and attractive, cut so that the fabric falls close to the skin without revealing too much of the shape underneath, and the knit is a pretty but not intrusive color. The seamstress is pleased with the choice. The only thing that worries her is the plastic flower-shaped button that clasps the sleeve. Will Pamela think it's childish to have a flower button on her sleeve when she's in high school? When she makes love for the first time? When she marries?

The seamstress glances up. Pamela wipes her eye with the back of her hand, trying to hide her tears. Little girls learn to emulate their sewn mothers long before the stitches make it easy, although Pamela hasn't always obeyed the social rules. The seamstress remembers Pamela, at age three, screaming "I won't apologize!" after pinching the arm of a boy she saw in line at the movies. When Pamela's father dragged her by the elbow to the boy's parents, she hurled herself onto the sidewalk. "He's a boy! I won't say I'm sorry!" Her tears didn't roll; they detonated one by one like bullets. Her determination not to cry now looks similar.

Remorse spins through the seamstress' mind before vanishing into the heart on her sleeve. Nine years old is so young to be sewn, but it's done younger and younger these days. The seamstress and her husband had argued about the timing for weeks, late at night after Pamela went to sleep. While they argued, the seamstress restlessly buttoned and unbuttoned the mother-of-pearl clasps on her own sweater. Ultimately, she'd had to yield. Did she want Pamela to be the only girl in her class who hadn't had it done?

The needle swoops. Three stitches left. Two stitches left. One stitch left.

The seamstress tugs on the cuff, examining the heart to make sure none of the stitches are tight enough to pinch or loose enough to come undone.

"Are you done?" asks Pamela.

"I am."

Pamela lifts her sleeve up to her face so she can scrutinize her mother's work more closely. Her covert tears have dried and her fingers have relaxed, leaving faint welts on her palms. Her lips lift into a gentle smile—the same smile the seamstress sees on her neighbor's faces, in the expression of the butcher's wife and the grocer's sister, in the mirror.

"Do you feel better now?" the seamstress asks.

"Yes," Pamela says. Her polished smile is as lovely as the recess beneath the summit of a cresting wave.

Another memory emerges. A few years ago, the seamstress had been late picking Pamela up from school. As she pulled into the school's driveway, she saw Pamela on the playground, perched on the very top of the jungle gym. Pamela waved frantically, leaping down and running across the asphalt until she reached her mother's car, her knees grass-stained and her chin blotted with dirt. Her grin was wide and shameless and luminous.

Pamela will never smile like that again.

The seamstress feels the expected surge of regret—but it doesn't vanish. Surprised, the seamstress pauses to see if it will drain a heartbeat late, but it doesn't. It stings. Her hands freeze on Pamela's shoulders.

"Should I get dressed now?" Pamela asks.

"Why?" The seamstress stares at Pamela uncomprehendingly. She'd forgotten that regret stings. "The ceremony," she reminds herself. Stiffly, she moves her hands back to her sides. "Yes. Go ahead."

Pamela clings to the back of the chair while she slides down to the floor. Her shoes squeak as she leaves the room and disappears up the stairs.

The seamstress pulls a chair out from the kitchen table and sits down. She doesn't know what to do. Should she call her husband? She probes the edges of the heart on her sleeve to see if it's somehow come loose, but the stitches pull tight and strong. She finds a trickle of blood on her cuff and traces it back to a single loose stitch. Feeling underneath, she discovers the tip of the needle she broke earlier. It must have gotten caught there.

She digs it out and stands to get a new needle and a spool of thread. She needs to sew up her heart before she loses too much blood. The trickle down her sleeve becomes a rivulet in her palm, and a drop splashes onto the table. Before long, she'll get dizzy, and her hand will be too unsteady to sew. Best to do it now.

Except, she can't remember the last time she felt regret—at least, felt it long enough for it to settle in her body. The feeling exhausts her, but it also captivates her, salves a craving she hadn't known she possessed. She pulls out the chair and sits again.

Suddenly, the seamstress remembers the last time she felt regret, but the memory is no longer distinct on its own. It's bound up with another memory. The second one took place two years ago, when Pamela was seven. While playing with a tea set she'd received for her birthday, Pamela dropped a cup. All of the cups in the set were painted with roses and embossed with gold around the rim, but this one had been lithographed with Pamela's initials as well, so it was Pamela's favorite.

It was a stormy day. Rain pounded on the windows behind Pamela as she held up the fragments and demanded that they be put back together again.

"I can't. It's broken," said the seamstress.

"I broke it!" wailed Pamela, pushing the two pieces together. She was thinking, no doubt, of the future tea parties that would be ruined by having only three cups for four saucers, but Pamela's distress reminded the seamstress of her own childhood when she'd once left a little shovel and pail on the beach where they were washed away by the tide. She'd felt as though she'd betrayed them; she'd made them lost and lonely, and how would they ever forgive her?

The seamstress lifted her daughter onto her hip and walked over to the trash so that Pamela could drop the pieces of the cup into the bin. She held up Pamela's hands and examined them to make sure there were no cuts, and when she was sure there weren't, she set Pamela down and fetched a broom and dustpan to clean up the rest of the fragments.

"It's okay," the seamstress assured her daughter, "The teacup broke because there was something trapped inside. When the glass was made, a tiny air spirit that flies in the wind crawled into the big oven where they were cooking the sand. 'What's this?' thought the air spirit, and she fell asleep in the oven. When she woke up, she was baked into the teacup. She's been waiting for someone to let her out."

The seamstress didn't know where she'd found that idea; she was only following her fancy. Pamela looked up at her with eyes still half-full of tears. The little girl's expression was skeptical.

"It's true," the seamstress insisted. "Listen. Can you hear that?"

They listened. Outside, the rain swept droves of leaves onto the deck.

"That's the air spirit playing in the wind. She's so happy to be free that she's knocking on all the branches."

Pamela chewed on a strand of her hair thoughtfully before nodding. "Oh," she said, and went back to playing with the tea set.

The next day, all the cabinets in the kitchen were open and the floor was covered in glass. "I wanted to make sure there were no more air spirits!" Pamela said when her father threatened to spank her. "What have you been telling the child?" the seamstress's husband demanded.

So the seamstress had to explain to Pamela how sometimes stories aren't really true outside, they just feel true inside, and the family bought a new set of dinner dishes.

Pamela's footsteps fall heavily on the stairs. The seamstress pulls her chair back, not wanting to be discovered brooding. Pamela has dressed herself all askew: skirt hitched into her tights, hair tumbling out of her self-made bun.

"How do I look?" Pamela asks, spinning on her heel.

"Beautiful," says the seamstress. "Just let me touch you up."

Pamela's eyes light on the blood spilling down her mother's hand. "Mom!"

"It's all right, honey," the seamstress says, watching her daughter's alarm drain out of her eyes and into her sleeve. "I cut myself while I was making dinner. I'll take care of it."

She wraps her arm in a dishtowel and sets about straightening her daughter's clothes and pinning up her curls. Wearily, she considers what will happen at the ceremony. She pictures her husband slapping Pamela across the face, and Pamela still smiling, the same bland, perfect smile that all the women wear, and suddenly she can't imagine going.

She smoothes the shoulders of Pamela's dress. "Go back upstairs and wait for your father to come home, honey. He'll take you to the ceremony. I won't be there."

Pamela frowns. "But Aunt Mattie's coming and you bought a new dress and everything."

"I know, but I...I'm feeling ill. I'll be here when you get home."

The seamstress braces herself for a temper tantrum, but there isn't one. Anger and confusion cross Pamela's face, then her heart pumps and they drain. Her lips curve upward. Without another word, she turns toward the stairs.

"You know you can talk to me," the seamstress says, haltingly, "If there's anything you want to talk about."

"Like what?"

The seamstress tries to foment her regret into words. They fail to come. "Just...things."

"Okay, mom." Without a pause, Pamela waves and leaves. The seamstress chuckles shallowly and feels the heart on her sleeve contract like a clenched fist.

She sinks back into her seat and thuds her elbows onto the table, bowing her head into the bowl of her hands. The heart on her cuff has swollen, red and round as a pomegranate.

Regret heavy in her blood, the seamstress realizes so many things she should have done. She should have told her husband no and spared Pamela for a few more years, even though she knows the little girl would have hated her for not letting her "grow up" like her peers. She should have run away with Pamela into the woods and caught trout bare-handed and built a hut out of sticks. But now it's too late: there's no way to bring Pamela's emotions back without cutting her loose from her heart and starving her body of blood.

A brief fantasy enters the seamstress's mind like a hallucination: she imagines snatching the heart off her sleeve. In her head, the stitches rip free with an immense roar. She imagines slicing open her chest cavity and using the bathroom mirror as a guide while she reattaches her heart to the veins and arteries that have fluttered loose all these years. She knows she would bleed to death long before she could even get to the bathroom.

It's then that the seamstress realizes the end of the air spirit's story. After so long baked in glass, the little thing could never have flown away. When she tried, she would have discovered that her flight muscles were atrophied, her feathers brittle and broken.

The seamstress listens to the traffic outside. Her husband will be home soon. She feels light-headed. She doesn't know how to judge how much blood she's lost. It looks like a lot, but how much more blood does her body contain? If her husband comes home in time, he might try to rush her to the hospital and save her life, but she's tired of being baked into glass.

Her fingers converge at her throat and unclasp the long row of buttons that line the front of her sweater. She parts the cloth around her neck and pulls it open to her rib cage, her belly, her waist. She pushes the sleeves away from her shoulders. Against pale skin that hasn't been bare for over twenty years, the lukewarm air of the kitchen is shocking, like a swab of alcohol applied to a wound.

Carefully, the seamstress pulls her arm out of the right sleeve. Her heart throbs on the left one, just above the neatly folded cuff. Then the seamstress slides her arm out of that sleeve too. Her elbow slips free, her wrist, her knuckles. The cloth is slack between her fingers. She drops it. Her heart sinks to the floor.

As her blood stagnates in her veins, emotions waft into her brain like mosquitoes rising from a still pool. Each faint tinge feels strong in the body long denied. Fear and desire undulate through her brain, unpleasant and fascinating before she passes out and they slide into oblivion.

In a few minutes, Pamela will hear her father pulling into the driveway and scamper down the stairs in her fancy dress, and yes, she will be the one to find the body. When she sees her mother slumped over the table-top like a statue, she'll feel only a twinge of grief. The emotion will flare and drain away. She will take her father's arm and accompany him to the ceremony. And when he slaps her across the face, she will smile and politely receive her applause.

Outside, rain will knock on the branches, and she will ignore it. Like a grown up.

Marrying the Sun

THE WEDDING went well until the bride caught fire.

Bridget's pretty white dress went up in a whoosh, from train-length veil to taffeta skirt to rose-embroidered bodice and Juliet cap with ferronière of pearls. The fabric burned so hot and fast that it went up without igniting Bridget's skin, leaving her naked, singed, embarrassed, and crying.

Of these problems, nudity was easiest to cope with. Bridget pulled the silk drape off the altar and tied it around her chest like a toga.

"That is it," she said. She pried the engagement ring off her finger and threw it at the groom. The grape-sized diamond sparkled as it arced through the air.

Gathering up the drape's hem, Bridget ran back down the aisle. She flung open the double doors, letting in the moonlight, and fled into the night.

The groom sighed. He opened his palm and stared down at the glittering diamond which reflected his fiery nimbus in shades of crimson, ginger, and gold. His best man patted him on the shoulder—cautiously. The bride's father gave a manly nod of sympathy, but kept his distance. Like his daughter, he was mortal.

"Too bad, Helios," said Apollo.

The groom shrugged. "I gave it my best shot. I can't keep my flame on low all the time. What did the woman want? Sometimes a man's just got to let himself shine."

Apollo clapped him on the back. "You said it, brother."

* * *

BRIDGET WENT down to the reception hall. She let the hotel clerk gawk at her knotted drape, and then told him they'd be canceling.

"The hall or the honeymoon suite?"

"Both," said Bridget.

The clerk rapped a few keys on the keyboard. "I'm sorry, but we can't accept cancellations this late. I'll have the staff take down the decorations in the hall, but we'll have to charge you."

Bridget felt too drained to argue. "Fine."

She went down the corridor to the reception hall. She at least wanted to see the chocolate fondue fountain and the ice sculptures, even if they were going to waste. Caterers and hotel staff ran back and forth, clearing away cups of fresh summer fruit and floral arrangements of birds of paradise and yellow tulips.

Bridget approached the six-tiered cake with the tiny bride figurine standing next to a brass sun. She plucked the bride out of the butter cream frosting. "What was I thinking?" she asked the little painted face.

"Don't we all wish we knew the answer to that question?"

Bridget looked up. Her matchmaker, the goddess of childbirth Eileithyia, leaned against the wine bar, tidy in a burgundy pantsuit and three-inch heels.

"I heard what happened," said Eileithyia.

"He couldn't hold it in, even on our wedding day?"

"Isn't that what you wanted? Someone dazzling, someone out of the ordinary, someone who could light a dark room with his smile?"

"But being dazzling isn't just what he is, it's something he does *to* other people. He can't just shine, he has to consume."

Eileithyia sipped her 1998 Chablis. "Good thing you found out before your vows, at least. The pre-nup you signed's a bitch."

* * *

HELIOS AND Apollo settled in at the hotel bar. Floor-length windows overlooked the river where streetlights cast golden ripples on dark water. The scene was twinned in the mirror behind the bar.

Apollo improvised a sonnet about the cocktail waitress and got a free drink. Not to be outdone, Helios earned a shower of applause by lighting a vixen's cigarette from across the room.

Helios still wore his tuxedo, untied ascot draped across his chest like a scarf. He spun on his barstool to face his drink. "I thought she was different," he said.

Apollo had stopped to change into dress shirt and slacks, chic and metrosexual. He waved Helios's point away, marquise cut topaz and agate rings sparkling on his fingers. "They're all the same. I could have told you that."

"How helpful and droll," said Helios.

"It's true. It's the beauty of mortal women. Sure, they're unique, like snowflakes are unique, but who catches a snowflake to marvel over geodesic ice crystals? That's missing the point of snowflakes."

"Which is?"

"All the power and loveliness of the snow birthing this intricate, astonishing thing that's gone in an instant." Apollo winked at the brunette by the piano. "And they melt on your tongue, too."

Helios lifted his index finger, inspiring a tuft of flame on the brunette's bosom. As she beat it out with her cocktail napkin, Helios shaped the smoke above to spell out the phrase *Hot Stuff.* The brunette giggled, averting her eyes coquettishly.

Helios turned back to his friend. "That's not why I go with mortal women."

"Pray tell."

"They have a better understanding of things like joy and grief because their lives are difficult. They appreciate what they get. They make you feel real."

"Be honest, you just like having all the power in the relationship."

"That's not true!"

"If you say so."

Helios went on, "I like being with mortal women because of how different we are. Fire and water is more interesting than fire and fire."

"Interesting if you're fire. Fatal if you're water."

"Fire and earth, then." Helios lit a flame in his palm. He shifted its composition so that it burned rose and then gold and then iris. "The problem is, most mortal women don't get that. They think being with a god is going to make them more than human. They want to be special. They want to be anointed. I thought Bridget was different than that. She was grounded. She knew she was just an ordinary girl. I thought she was happy with who both of us were. But it turns out she wanted me to be just as dishwater dull as she is."

"We should turn them all into laurel trees," said Apollo, draining his drink. He rose from his barstool and ran his fingers through the loose wheat-colored curls of his Caesar cut. "Come on. If we can't find any nymphs, let's at least get us a couple nymphomaniacs."

* * *

BRIDGET REMEMBERED the day she realized the world was populated with gods. Really, it was an old suspicion, stemming from playground hierarchies and high school lunchrooms. Some people just seemed more *there* than others. They gleamed, they glittered. While Bridget and her peers stumbled through adolescence with scrapes and bruises, *they* floated through life without so much as a detention slip.

Wasn't it something everyone sensed? People watched the godly among them raise waves with a pitchfork, inspire love with an arrow, win track meets in winged sandals. Later they were remembered in a jeweled blur, details fuzzy but gist intact: the dare devil surfer, the counselor who saved my marriage, the kid who could run like nothing you ever saw.

But Bridget didn't really figure it out until she was finishing the fifth year of her Ph.D., tabulating data on a thesis few people outside her field could really understand.

Bridget was one of the world's foremost experts on the sun. Parts of the sun, at least. She studied sunspots, the patches of relative cold that blot the sun's surface like tears. She spent her hours in the laboratory, calculating the frequency of coronal loops and checking them against the predicted occurrence of solar flares.

"The sun is a romantic metaphor," she was fond of telling friends over drinks, back when she had friends, and went out for drinks. "These little dark patches are caused by intense magnetic activity. It's all about attraction and repulsion. It can make the sun burn hot, or blow cold, or eject solar flares so vast they leave traces in Greenland."

Bridget had the kind of mind that thrived on solitude and data, or so she convinced herself in the absence of anything but solitude and data to thrive upon. By the fifth year of her Ph.D., the last of her undergraduate friends had gotten jobs and moved away, not that she had much in common with them any longer anyway. Her father lived in a rental house three states away with two bachelor friends, and while he claimed he wanted updates on Bridget's life, Bridget heard the flat grieved tone of his voice when he picked up the telephone. Bridget had her mother's dark, sunken eyes, and hair the hue of corn sheaves. She knew that, to her father, she was one more reminder of her mother's illness and death. It had been hard on him, being a widower. He dealt with grief by making himself a new life. Bridget was part of the old one. She mostly stayed away.

Daily, Bridget woke at dawn. She showered and brushed her teeth and rode her bike onto campus where she grabbed a cup of coffee from a vendor in the student union. She sat in her lab, watching the sun's arc through the office's high window that let in baking heat during mid-afternoon, until the sun sank and the room grew dark, and then she sat there some more. She rode her bicycle home around two in the morning, and went to bed in her clothes.

One afternoon, as Bridget sat in her lab on a day when heavy snow had piled on the campus's hills, sparkling under a bright but distant sun that lacked the power to melt it, Bridget looked down at her keyboard and realized she couldn't feel her fingers. They'd been typing for an hour without her conscious command. They felt more like part of the machine than part of her.

Red and blue lines criss-crossed the screen, mapping her data. Bridget recognized none of it. She pulled her hands away from the keyboard and fanned her fingers in front of her eyes. Slowly, she began to feel the ache of her cold, unheated office settle in her fingertips.

She tried to remember the last time she'd spoken to anyone for more than two sentences. It had been over three weeks. She was twenty-nine years old and she couldn't fathom why she'd ever thought that mapping sunspots was worth the utter lack of human company.

She fled the office early, ignoring the queries of professors and students as she unlocked her bike from the rack outside the building and rode away down the snowy road. When she reached her house, she found an unfamiliar woman standing there, her outfit and coiffure so immaculate that at first Bridget thought she was selling Avon.

"I've been sent by a secret admirer," said the woman, introducing herself as Eilethyia.

Bridget couldn't imagine any student or professor, the only two groups of people she interacted with, hiring this elegant woman to make a suit on their behalf. "Oh, yes?" she asked.

"Indeed," said Eilethyia, unruffled. "My client prefers to woo via a mediator, someone who understands human culture better than he does."

"Human culture?" asked Bridget, wondering what prank was being pulled on her. "Tell this admirer, whoever he is, that I don't go on blind dates."

"It's not a blind date, exactly," said Eileithyia. "You've met before."

"Who is he?" asked Bridget.

A sly smile crossed Eileithyia's lips. She turned and pointed toward the summit of the noontime sky where the sun blazed through the cold air, dazzling. Somehow, Bridget was unsurprised.

"I daresay you're as enamored of him as he is of you," said Eileithyia. "That's probably what he likes about you. Never forget that gods are narcissists. Why do you think we want everyone to worship us?"

Bridget laughed, not at the fact of her admirer's godhood, for that she had already strangely come to accept. She laughed at the frank and unabashed admission of narcissism. At the time, she thought it was a joke.

* * *

MOST GODS dabbled with mortals the way most mortals dabbled with self-love. It was entertaining, it was convenient, it was a way of releasing tension when nothing better presented itself. The chief deity himself liked to season his love life by seducing mortal maidens as a white bull or swan. But it was like an hors d'ouvre to a gourmet meal. Once the champagne framboise and lobster bisque had been sampled, he wasted no time in slipping back into his natural godly form to hightail it home for an entrée of duck Martiniquaise with his lady wife.

Rarely, a god found mortal love affairs becoming not an aperitif, but something altogether too alluring: a fetish.

Apollo denied it was that way with him. He remained aloof and rakish, playing up his persona as the literally eternal bachelor. It worked pretty well for him too, Helios noted, as he watched Apollo cozy up with the tow-headed boy he'd lured over from the piano. The boy wrapped his arms around Apollo's waist, aiming a nip at the god's ear.

Helios set down his pepper vodka. He left a little flame burning on the surface, evaporating the alcohol. Over his shoulder, the cocktail waitress gingerly cleared her throat.

"Would you mind?"

Helios looked down at a pudding en flambé. "But of course," he said, winking, but the reflexive flirtation felt false. His overzealous flare singed the eyebrows of a nearby man in tweed. The waitress rushed over to give him a free drink.

The blond kid slipped his tongue between Apollo's sculpted lips. His giggling drifted on the air with the cigarette smoke. Helios could smell his cologne: sandalwood with a hint of moss. He looked away.

Helios hadn't been with a goddess since his only son, Phaeton, died. At sixteen, the boy had begged to drive Helios's sun chariot across the sky. Helios pleaded with him to choose any other gift, knowing the boy wouldn't be able to control his team. But Phaeton was sixteen. Failure was something that happened to other people.

At dawn, Helios helped his son into the chariot, and watched as it rose into the sky until Phaeton was only a golden blur in the heavens. Helios felt a strange stirring as he beheld it. He'd never before seen the sun rise from below. Was this what he looked like to mortals every day? A flare of brilliance so intense it stung the eyes?

Later, after Phaeton lost control of the team and Zeus brought the boy down with a bolt of lightning so bright it twinned the sun, Helios's daughters wept so fiercely that Zeus changed them into poplar trees. And so Helios lost them, too. Zeus regarded the rivers of their maidenly tears and froze their mourning into amber, which was how that gem first came into the world. The first time Helios slept in Bridget's apartment, he begged her to discard all her amber jewelry. He bought her replacements in jade.

Helios wasn't sure what it was about mortal women that salved his grief. Or maybe they didn't salve it at all. Maybe their appeal was the way their brief earthbound existences—like plants that flowered out of and then decayed back into the ground—rubbed salt and soil into his wounds.

Apollo looked over. He and the boy swung their hands together, like children. "Come on, pick someone," said Apollo. "It'll make you feel better."

"I suppose."

Helios scanned the bar. His gaze settled on a black woman wearing a gold knit sweater that made her skin glow like a bright penny. She sat with a few girlfriends, chatting. Her laugh sounded like a bell on a winter morning. Helios slipped off his barstool.

"Might I interrupt?" he asked.

The woman's friends looked at her to see what she wanted. She gave them a nod. They scooted back their chairs to admit Helios into their circle.

"I wonder if I might beg the honor of your company tonight," he said. Before the woman could reply, he inspired tiny golden flames to dance across her arms. Sparks pirouetted like ballerinas spinning on a stage.

Interest sparkled in her mahogany eyes. She wet her lips. Her breathing became shallow and quick. She was dazzled.

* * *

BRIDGET HAD never lacked for romantic attention, but she'd never found herself enthralled by it either. Men, by and large, bored her. She wanted men who possessed a flame of dedication that ignited something unique and all-consuming within themselves. She'd dated a few. There was a world champion chess player, a computer programmer who built elaborate palaces of code, and a volcanologist who explored volcanoes on the verge of eruption. But one by one, she'd discovered their passions to be other than what they seemed: rote compulsion, unconscious ability no more personally meaningful than breathing, self-hatred becoming high risk behavior.

Bridget and Helios had their first date on the rim of a molten lava lake, its active vents guttering threateningly with the burble of tension barely contained. Sulfur permeated the air.

Eilethyia accompanied them. At first, Bridget chafed at being chauffeured, but when Eilethyia had to talk Helios out of taking Bridget skinny dipping in the lava, Bridget began to understand why the slender goddess had come along.

They sat and talked about nothing in particular, their worlds so different that the small talk had a dreamlike air, but the strange disjointed nature of their conversation did not detract from the connection they both felt warming between them, as if they spoke different languages but intuitively understood the same words. The goddess Eilethyia sat nearby as they talked, reclining laconically against a slab of basalt, her face turned discreetly away but wearing a wry and pleased smile.

An hour before dawn broke, as pale light gathered in the sky preparing for the moment when Helios would burst over the horizon in his chariot, Helios took Bridget by the hands and led her onto an obsidian outcropping, outside the goddess's hearing.

"I can tell you anything you want to know," he said, correctly assuming that Bridget's lust would be inflamed by the promise of knowledge. "What other stars look like, the chemical compositions of distant suns, why magnetic fields pulse and sway the way they do. I could take you to visit strange planets and nebulas and pulsars."

"I don't think I'd survive," said Bridget.

"Then ask me questions, and I'll bring the answers back to you."

Bridget smiled. The god stood before her with his shoulders thrown back, his feet planted in a strong, wide stance. His hands were hot, his eyes fierce upon her. He had a presence of being in himself like no one that Bridget had ever met before. Throughout her life, she had always felt herself fuzzy and indeterminate, collecting knowledge against the specter of her death like a squirrel assembling nuts before hibernation. Here was someone who flared, and burned, and *was*.

Bridget thought back on that first interlude as she stood in the bathroom of Eilethyia's hotel room, exchanging her improvised drape for one of the goddess's dresses. The dress was loose, grey linen, the only thing in Eilethyia's wardrobe that came close to Bridget's size. Bridget had never been overweight, but the goddess was long and narrow as a stroke of calligraphy.

"Do you need help?" called Eilethyia through the door.

Bridget looked up at the blotted tears beneath her eyes that showed in her reflection. She dabbed them quickly away and steeled herself with anger. He burned, but unthinkingly, more like a fire than a man. She had made the right choice.

Bridget slipped out of the bathroom. The goddess stood nearby, watching.

"Thanks for letting me borrow this," said Bridget. "I couldn't face going up to the suite for my luggage."

"Does your family know where you are?" asked Eilethyia.

"I called my father and told him to go home. I don't want to see him now."

"There's no other mortal to comfort you? Sisters? Friends?"

"I'm an only child," said Bridget. "Isolation is an old habit."

Eilethyia nodded, businesslike but not unkind, diamond studs flashing at her ears. "We should get something to eat."

Bridget raised her eyebrows. "At this time of night?"

"I know a good Greek place not far from here."

Bridget followed Eilethyia though the city's winding intersections. Drunk people swarmed in and out of the pubs lining the river. The air smelled of the contrast between crisp wind and stale beer. They entered an alley and Eilethyia led Bridget up a narrow, metal flight of stairs. Bridget winced as the goddess knocked on someone's door.

"It's so late," Bridget began.

Eilethyia raised a silencing hand. Bridget held her tongue.

Soon enough, a heavyset woman in a long white nightdress opened the door. A man with sleepless circles under his eyes stood behind her, dressed in drawstring pants and a sleeveless cotton undershirt. Both looked unsurprised by the intrusion. "Come upstairs," said the woman, her voice flat.

"What did you do to them?" Bridget whispered to the goddess as they were escorted through a narrow, tiled parlor.

"Nothing," said Eilethyia.

She gestured down a shadowed hallway. Bridget saw the small white shapes of pajama-clad children peering around the corner.

"They know me here," said the goddess.

The woman led them up another flight of stairs. They came out in a roof garden where several ironwork tables sat among potted ferns. The man started to hand them menus, but Eilethyia waved him away and ordered for them both. The man bowed his head and retreated.

Eilethyia leaned back in her chair. "So, what do you plan to do now?"

"I don't know," Bridget admitted. "I can't continue with my thesis… spending so much time with him every day would be…maybe I'll go to work in a lab for awhile…"

"I meant in regard to your erstwhile fiancé."

Bridget sighed. "It's not like I can avoid seeing him." She glanced up at the sky where a sliver of moon sliced the dark. "At least we won't have to talk."

"Will you want another god to replace him?"

"Absolutely not!"

Bridget surprised herself with her vehemence. She shifted in her seat, smoothing wrinkles out of the linen dress.

"Looking back, there was always something…strange about our relationship. The way he saw me was…"

"Like an old man looking at a young girl?" offered Eilethyia.

"Sort of…"

"A celebrity admiring his most ardent fan?"

"Something like that."

Eilethyia gave a short sharp nod. "It's always been my theory that gods who fixate on mortals are…what's the word I'm looking for?" She tapped one crimson nail against the table. "Unnatural, perhaps? Not that there's anything wrong with unnatural. Natural childbirth is painful and often fatal. Unnatural can be good."

"Unnatural?" repeated Bridget, skeptically.

"How do I put this? They're like humans who want to make love with beasts."

Bridget flinched sharply.

"Don't take it like that. It's a difference in kind, not scale."

The man arrived with their food, a plate full of meat wrapped in grape leaves for the goddess, and squares of lamb on rice for Bridget.

"You could have told me all this before you matched me with Helios," said Bridget, accusingly. "Why did you let me get engaged to someone you thought was mentally diseased?"

"Ah. Well." Delicately, Eilethyia chewed a leaf from the side of her fork. "I haven't told you what I think is wrong with mortals who want to be with gods."

Bridget pricked with shame. She hated the thought of others seeing wrongness in her. She worked hard to conceal her flaws.

Eilethyia sipped her wine calmly. "Mortals and gods are always seeing in each other what they themselves lack. Divinity, mundanity, exaltation, pain." She set down her glass and fixed Bridget with a frank stare. "If you want my advice, you have two options. Take my card, and when you've had time to recover, I'll pair you with another god. Or, if you want to grow, if you want to become a better, more whole person, then find the spark of divinity within yourself and search for a mortal to share it with."

Goosebumps prickled along Bridget's arms. She felt bruised and earthen and drained. "It's all so easy for you, isn't it? You don't have relations with gods or mortals, do you?"

"No," said Eilethyia.

The goddess glanced over toward a corner of the roof where children's toys lay scattered among the potted plants.

"I'm too familiar with where it all leads," she said, and Bridget saw her smile was sad.

* * *

HELIOS ESCORTED the woman, whose name turned out to be Jody, to a nocturnal street fair sprawling in the city's main square. Her friends tagged along. He entertained them by challenging the fire eater to a contest which ended when Helios devoured a flaming meteor and then sent it rocketing back into space.

Helios selected a mortal man for each of Jody's friends, haloing them with a light touch of flame to make them seem more attractive. One by one, her friends peeled away. Soon Helios and Jody were alone.

"Would you join me in my hotel room?" he asked.

By the time they reached the elevator, Jody's hands were all over him, stroking his hips, unbuttoning his shirt. Her breath on his neck felt damp and hot as a humid afternoon.

When the elevator clanged Helios's floor, they backed out, entwined, stumbling through the corridor. Helios unclasped Jody's bra. She unzipped his fly. He had to clasp her hands to hold them still long enough so that he could work the key card that admitted them into the honeymoon suite.

When they got inside, they found themselves looking at the tow-headed boy from the bar. He sat astride Apollo in the gigantic bathtub. Sprays of bubbles from the jets obscured what was going on beneath the water.

"What is he doing here?" demanded the boy. "Isn't this your room?"

"My friend here just got left at the altar," said Apollo. "I didn't think he'd be needing the room."

Helios turned to Jody. "My apologies."

"I don't mind," said Jody. She traced her finger down Helios's chest. "It's actually kind of a turn-on."

Leaving Apollo and his mortal in the bathroom, Helios and Jody moved to the bed. Jody's skin felt smooth and sweet as flower petals. Her close-cropped natural hair covered her head like delicious brown moss. Helios ran his fingers through it over and over, the sensation delectable and maddening. He pulled the black strap of her bra out from her sleeve, removing the whole lacy garment without taking off her sweater. He slipped his hands beneath the cashmere and took her breasts into his palms. Her hard nipples felt like knots on wood, beautifully textured. Gently, Helios eased her sweater over her head. A gold chain flashed around her neck.

Helios caught the pendant in his palm. "What is this?"

"Alaskan amber," said Jody. "There's part of a bee in it."

Helios examined the gem. It was set in a simple silver oval. Rich, warm colors swirled through its heart: drifts of sienna, umber, burnt orange and carmine suspended like haze in a yellow sky. A bee hung in its center, wings trapped mid-flutter. Helios thought of all the grief that that had been poured into making this chaotic, vibrant thing, all the sorrow his daughters wept out when Phaeton's chariot fell. Their solidified grief was incandescent as the sun. It burned him.

Helios released the necklace. It swung down, a yellow globe between Jody's breasts. She cocked her head and smiled, raising her eyebrows in invitation. Her lips sparkled. Helios moved away from the bed, and began dressing.

"What?" asked Jody. "Do bees gross you out or something?"

Helios's fingers felt numb on his shirt buttons. "I'm sorry. As my friend said, I was left at the altar today."

She hesitated, and then said, "That must be rough."

"As you can imagine, I'm still in a state of shock. I hope you'll forgive me."

"It's okay," she said. She pulled herself into a sitting position, legs tucked beneath her, and began putting on her clothes. "I can meet up with my friends tomorrow."

She tugged on her sweater and pulled a compact out of her purse, checking to make sure her lipstick hadn't smudged from kissing. She gave Helios a sad smile, one side of her mouth pulled up into a dimple.

"Try not to take it too hard, okay?" she said. "A man like you, someone else'll snap you up in no time."

Helios had nothing to say to that. He took Jody's elbow and escorted her to the door. He watched as she walked away down the hall, short black skirt swishing around her thighs.

Apollo called out from the bathroom. "So, do your newfound sexual ethics mean we have to cut out of here too, or can you suffer alone?"

Helios closed the door. All these eons and he could still picture Phaeton's face, every detail crisp as a brushstroke.

"Do whatever you want."

* * *

AFTER DINNER, Eilethyia offered to continue keeping Bridget company. Bridget declined. She wanted time alone. She paced the waterfront, hugging herself against the chill. Pale clouds had drifted over the gibbous moon, and crickets had emerged from the ornamental hedges lining the sidewalk to serenade potential mates. Bridget stared down at the blurred reflections of halogen bulbs in the water, submerged and insignificant suns. *Everything can be overwhelmed*, she thought. *Everything can be drowned.* When her teeth started chattering, she turned back to the hotel, ready to collect her luggage and move on.

In the corridor leading to the honeymoon suite, Bridget collided with a statuesque African American woman. The woman's clothes were rumpled and her makeup smeared. She smelled of Helios: ash and smoke and sparkle.

Bridget's stomach churned as the woman disappeared into the elevator. This soon? This fast? She felt betrayed, and then furious with herself for being surprised at betrayal. She slid the key card into the door without knocking.

As she entered, she heard splashing as a male voice moaned from the bathroom, "Not another one."

Bridget's anger bellowed full-throated. She put her hand over her eyes and pushed blindly past the bathroom. "Don't worry," she snapped. "I'm just here to get my clothes."

Eyes still covered, she turned toward the dresser and began yanking drawers open. Her unpacked suitcase lay on the rug beside her, lid askew. She felt so stupid for having taken the time to put her clothes away in the suite. She'd been all aflutter that morning, expecting to come back a married woman, not wanting to be distracted by luggage. She threw her clothes into the suitcase in massive, hasty piles.

"Do you want help with that?" asked Helios from behind her.

Bridget turned. He sat on the bed, still dressed neatly in dress shirt and tuxedo pants. His jacket lay draped over the arm of an over-stuffed chair by the window.

"Why aren't you in the bathroom with your buddy?" asked Bridget.

"Hi there," called a voice from the bathroom. Bridget spun around, recognizing Apollo's timbre. The debonair god leaned against the doorframe, a hotel towel wrapped around his waist. A slender, young-looking man stood behind him, staring curiously at Bridget from behind his tousled blond hair.

"We were just trying to have some fun in here," Apollo said. "Some of us aren't so hung up on buying the cow."

Apollo's voice seeped with disdain at the word *cow*. Bridget was momentarily taken aback as she realized it wasn't marriage he was mocking, but mortals' animal flesh.

"Get out of here, Apollo," said Helios.

Apollo looked miffed. "You said we could stay."

Helios's voice was level but taut with tension. He spoke slowly. "Just get out."

"Fine." Apollo took the blond's hand. "Let's get out of here."

The blond frowned. "Where are we going? I told my roommate I wasn't coming back tonight."

Apollo shrugged off the blond's protestations. He turned to Helios, his eyes icy. "Mortals come and go. It's your friends you should be careful to keep."

Helios did not soften. "I'll see you tomorrow night."

Apollo led the blond out of the room. The door slammed behind them.

"I see he hasn't changed since this afternoon," said Bridget.

"He hasn't changed in four thousand years. And he won't, either."

Bridget looked out the window. Twelve floors below, cars pushed past on a busy expressway, headlights garish in the darkness.

"I'm sorry about your dress," said Helios. "I didn't mean to burn it. I wanted to look impressive."

"You wanted to show off," said Bridget.

"No, that's not it—"

"You waited until I was walking up the aisle. You couldn't stand someone else having everyone's attention."

"I didn't think about it."

"You never do, do you? You just do what you want and don't worry about the consequences."

Helios neared Bridget, his presence tangibly hot.

"This is silly," he said, voice firm and commanding. "It was an accident. It won't happen again."

He smelled like sparks thrown into cold air, like firefly swarms piercing humid summer evenings. An aura ignited around his solid, golden form, flashing and sparking like the northern lights. Bridget looked up at his smooth burnished skin, his shoulders broad and straight like the line of the horizon. She felt fragile and insignificant under his gaze, overwhelmed by her primal mind's awe of the sun. Her mouth dried and her heart accelerated to match his aura's flicker.

She pulled away. "Don't do that. Don't manipulate me."

Helios's aura winked out. He paced away from her, strides long and angry. "Why do you think you've spent your life alone? No one's ever good enough for you. I should turn you into a laurel tree. I should change your skin to match your heart and make you a woman of ice, and then melt you with my heat."

"Well, I guess that would prove me wrong!" Bridget said. "It's definitely not narcissistic to kill someone because she won't marry you." She barked a laugh. "I don't know why you care anyway. The same night I leave, you have another woman in your room. We're all just mortals anyway. You exchange one for another for another. Can you even tell the difference?"

Helios halted. His face was wet, his hands were shaking. "Is that what you think?" he said.

"Am I wrong?"

A moment of silence hung in the air. Helios exhaled a wracking sigh.

"How long does it take a mortal man to get over the death of his son?"

"I'm not sure," said Bridget, quietly. "I'm not sure they ever do."

She leaned back against the window, the glass smooth and cool. She closed her eyes.

"We've both got problems," she said. "I think we've got to find the solutions on our own."

Helios said nothing. When Bridget opened her eyes, he had become diffuse, the hotel lights shimmering through his increasingly translucent body.

Through the walls, they could hear the noise of party-goers returning to their rooms after the revelry of the wee hours. Traffic thickened on the expressway below. The night was almost over.

"You need to go, don't you?" asked Bridget.

Helios nodded.

"I'll look down on you from time to time," he said.

Bridget almost smiled.

Helios leaned toward her, his lips pressing warm against her own. She was bathed in his heat for a moment, and then he was gone.

Bridget turned toward the window to watch the grey sky slowly brightening with pink and peach. She wondered where she'd be tomorrow, who she'd find to share her long nights in the lab, her ability to find romance in sunspots. Soon, there would be the break of morning, yellow blazing boldly against azure. Now there was the horizon, flat and distant and caught between the worlds of sky and ground.

A Monkey Will Never Be Rid of Its Black Hands

PAPA AND Uncle Fomba told me if I didn't join the army, they'd kill me. They didn't. They cut off my hands.

This was after U.S. forces marched on Syria, but before we invaded Lebanon. On every city block, posters of Uncle Sam entreated every Tom, Duc, and Haroun to get blown up in the name of freedom. Papa and Fomba gave me two weeks to enlist. I ran for Canada instead. They caught me.

Fomba took me to Papa's shed and handcuffed me to a two-by-four. "You can't scare me," I said.

"We're not trying to scare you," said Fomba. "Get the knife, Bayo."

Papa went. Fomba was younger in years, but elder in authority.

"How far are you going to take this?"

Fomba put his hands over my wrists and grinned. "Cocky Momodu. Strutting Momodu. Don't depend on a dead man's shoes when you don't know their size."

That's a proverb from Sierra Leone: don't count your chickens when you may still get a piece of shrapnel eggshell in the gut.

Papa and I emigrated from Sierra Leone as refugees when I was a toddler. Fomba came eight years later. Fomba had been conscripted by the Revolutionary United Front at nine years old. They made him shoot his parents so he wouldn't have a home to run away to. You'd think Papa would have hated him for that, but when Fomba started sending letters to the U.S., Papa was quick to get him here.

Don't get me wrong. Most child soldiers are poor, mistreated little bastards who get blamed for violence they had no choice in. Thing is, in every barrel, you've got mostly apples. There's still always the spoiled one. The kid who would have been figuring out how to shoot people on the sly if no one had given him the okay to shoot them up-and-up.

That was Fomba.

Once, he was telling me memories from before the RUF, and he started describing what a cat does when you cut off its tail. Fomba was the blackest apple in a fleet of barrels.

Papa was the only one who didn't see it. He thought Fomba was polished red as a kiss.

The RUF terrorized Sierra Leone for ten years, murdering hundreds of thousands, including my mother. Other than hating the government, they had no philosophy, so Fomba was used to militarism without ideals. He took to American nationalism faster than American beer. He liked to say, "When you go to a country where people dance on one foot, you should dance on one foot. If you dance on two feet, they'll cut them out from under you."

Every afternoon of my childhood, my father and I sat with Fomba while he drank beer and quoted proverbs like "Cooked beans don't want cold water, only hot water," which meant children needed punishing. We didn't hang out with other refugees. Fomba said it was because other Africans hated anyone from the RUF. Maybe true. Maybe not. But sure enough, they'd have hated Fomba. So Fomba joined a military history society and befriended whites. The Civil War fascinated him, especially the Confederates. Other society members gave him old rifles which he cannibalized to make new guns. They leaned against the wall in Papa's shed, black and slender like shadows.

In summer, the three of us lay on the floor with our shirts off and Fomba doused himself with beer. Wet and sticky, he got nostalgic for the RUF. "During harvest, we went into the villages to find women growing crops. We had to stop them from finishing the harvest or the food would go straight to the government dogs. We chased them through the plantains and cassava until they went to ground, and then we waited." I remember Fomba's grin, viewed sideways as I lay next to him: the corners of his mouth sidling up his cheeks. "They always gave themselves away. They shouted or whimpered or came out after dusk, and we grabbed them. That's when we cut off their hands."

That story—that should have been my first thought when Papa and Fomba handcuffed me in the shed. How could I have ever thought they were joking? For Fomba, this was justice. He looked saner at that moment than he did downing beers over scavenged guns or maps of Gettysburg.

Before he did it, he quoted another proverb from Sierra Leone: "A monkey will never be rid of its black hands." It meant there was nothing I could do to cleanse myself.

As the cut fell, I saw no blood. Instead, I had a vision of my dead hands rising like black ghosts from my wrists. I passed out before the knife hit bone.

* * *

AMPUTATION HAS been a terrorist tactic in Africa since the Belgians required their officers to provide one human hand for every bullet they shot. After Fomba cut me, America added this tradition to its glorious melting pot and did what Americans do so well: made lots of copies.

The first copycat cut off his son's hands on the family dining table three days after Papa and Fomba did me. Some two-bit hick with one tooth and half a brain cell. He shouted the pledge of allegiance as police hauled him off. Isolated crimes scattered across the United States like drops of blood, seeping across the map as the rate of incidents increased. During July, mutilations reached a high of three per day. Student protesters attached red ribbons to their wrists and counter-protestors threatened to help them stop pretending. In Texas and North Carolina, juries commended perpetrators at the same time as they pronounced guilty verdicts. Then, in September, a gang of soldiers on leave chased a twenty-two year old off the road. He pleaded that he was exempt on account of fibromyalgia. They didn't believe him. When his mother appeared on TV with his medical record, the fever broke.

There are almost four hundred of us. They call us the Handless. Demographically, we are small. But at a time when the fighting in the Middle East and Islamic Africa was a mundane fact of political life, we polarized America. Renewed patriotism inspired huge numbers of red-white-and-blue blooded jingoists to volunteer for the front, while newly-converted pacifists bled their hearts at any Handless too slow to escape.

People assume I didn't join the war because I didn't want to kill innocents. They remember I owned a T-shirt that read "Give Peace a Chance." They forget I belonged to no peace organizations, expressed no opinions on the war, watched as many violent movies as anyone else. I wasn't afraid of killing people, but there was no way I was willing to die.

After Fomba cut me, the physicians tried to fit me with prosthetics. But plastic and metal ignited pain in my missing hands, reminding my brain to grieve for severed nerves. Most amputees suffer phantom pain, but mine was exceptional: no test could explain it, no analgesic douse it. The pain amplified until finally I told the doctors to stuff their damn prosthetics where fists went best, and marched out of the hospital. I've bared my naked wounds since. I am what Fomba made me.

Papa and Fomba would have gotten ten years in the normal route of the legal system, but the judge increased the sentence to twenty-five for deliberate cruelty. I haven't seen them since I testified at the trial, but I get the news like everyone else. Papa got caught in another man's brawl and took a knife in the ribs. They buried him in state ground behind the prison. Fomba's still behind bars, but he believes the food is made from dead inmates, so he won't eat. Media photos show him growing skinnier and skinnier, becoming lean and vicious as his scavenged guns.

* * *

I CAN'T do much for myself anymore. I learned how at first, but everything's so much harder when you don't have hands. So when I got Minna, I let her do it.

A lot of girls want to find out what it would be like to screw a hero with no hands. They approach me at the bar and talk about something banal and then start dropping kisses on my neck and shoulders. I'm supposed to act the grateful cripple. They have no idea that there'll be another girl like them along in fifteen minutes. That's one thing I've learned, having no hands: women want to cut men into pieces.

Minna approached me late in the evening after I was drunk on things you don't look stupid sucking through a straw. She was heavy and colorless and her reflection smeared in the mirror behind the bar, giving her a fleshy white halo. The beads on her shirt fractured my shadow into jagged lines like fingers over her breasts.

I was considering whether or not I wanted to fuck her—even dirty water can put out a fire—when she said, "Your stumps are a mess." Her hands were chubby with runt-like fingers, translucent white skin shot through with blue veins like expensive cheese. When I didn't answer, she said, "What's it like, having no hands?" Her tone held no quaver, just blunt curiosity. That's when I decided to take her to my apartment.

She was fatter than I'd had, but a vehicle is never too big for its driver. A man can always have a big woman.

After a few weeks, her things started to appear in my apartment. It was as though a tide had come in and deposited afghans, German novels, balls of yarn and knitting needles. There were also things I didn't let on bothered me: angora gloves, clippers, nail polish.

I fired my expensive nurse and Minna took over. We fit together. She accepted my tongue because I had no fingers to give her, then sat astride me and pulled my penis in since I couldn't adjust myself. She claimed that she felt touched all over when we slept together. "You have a thousand ghost fingers," she said. At night, she tucked the quilt under my chin and opened the window enough so I wouldn't be hot, but not too much, so I wouldn't be cold.

I didn't like her holding me when I pissed or cleaning the toilet if I missed on my own. I didn't mind being fed, but I didn't like her to wipe up my drool and I hated her reaching inside my mouth. After she fed me corn on the cob, I stayed silent about the strings sawing at my gums. She'd try to peek into my closed mouth and ask, "You still have a tongue, right?"

Nights we spent by the fire, cocooned in her afghans. We rolled next to each other in a full tactile press that almost made hands irrelevant.

She asked stupid questions like, "Are you angry, Momodu?"

Of course I'm angry.

"It's all right for you to be angry," she allowed. And then she called me "courageous for refusing to participate in the slaughter" and lauded me for "sacrificing my hands."

I never responded to that, just tried to make out her chubby fingers under the afghan, whether they were tugging at loose threads, or stroking the fabric, or touching her concealed flesh. As I thought about her hands, bright knives of phantom pain daggered to my elbows.

"How do you feel about the copycats?"

It's tragic.

"It must be hard to be the first. The talk shows treat you like an exhibit in a freak show."

You get used to it.

"Do you regret not seeing your father before he died?"

My father was a puppet, not a man. You don't go to a puppet's deathbed.

"What about your uncle? Do you want to see him?"

The sooner Fomba manages to starve himself, the sooner I can spit on his grave.

And then she ducked her head, bangs falling over her eyes. "Have there been other women who wanted to—? Because you're famous?"

Yes, baby, but you're the best.

* * *

I MET Barry working a talk show four months ago. I get most of my money from that and sitting in the background while politicians make speeches.

Talk shows want short-sleeved T-shirts in navy or purple or goldenrod, and they want you to sit with your "hands" folded in your lap so they can pan from your face to your stumps. Democrats want white button-up shirts with the cuffs pulled over the wrist for "subtle" emphasis. There's a Democrat face, too, which involves sucking in my cheeks and widening my eyes until I looked like a hooked fish. Republicans want a dark suit jacket and a somber expression.

A patriotism columnist took the first five minutes of the show. His hands ranged constantly across his lap, lightly freckled with strawberry blond hairs sprouting at the knuckles. He squinted into the spotlights as he spoke. "Without the Handless to act as a catalyst, our nation might have been too demoralized to continue the fight for Freedom. Women wouldn't be able to drive in Saudi Arabia; Iran would still be a theocracy; the new Palestinian territory would never have been carved out of Jordan and Syria. From that perspective, the Handless may be the most patriotic Americans of the decade."

"That's not why they're heroes!" someone in the audience shouted, rushing toward the stage. While security went to calm her down, the show cut straight to commercial, skipping the question/answer session and sparing us all the same tired whining about how Saudi Arabian women are free not only to drive but to die in car bombs too.

My section of the program was the same old questions about Fomba and Sierra Leone—except that the camera stayed focused on me long after the hostess should have gone on to some weeping mother who'd done her son with the family chainsaw.

The phantom pain in my hands flared up. I caught myself scowling at the cameras. Bad for business. I shifted the expression to wounded hound.

Gesturing for the camera to follow her into a close-up, the hostess mounted the stage, clutching her microphone with burnished tan fingers.

She knelt beside me, and it occurred to me that if I'd had a left hand, it would have been on her tit.

"The producers and I have been looking into your life, Momodu," she said. "You don't have many friends or relatives. We're worried about you. Wouldn't it be wonderful to be with others of your kind—people who understand your pain?"

She smiled Mary Sunshine at me and flung her arm toward the wings. Ten men edged onstage. Mostly white, a couple brown, only one black guy like me. But mostly I was looking at their wrists. Cheap plastic prosthetics except for one top-of-the-line pair with realistic joints, the kind I should have had.

The hostess gestured for me to stand. So the circuit had found a new way to extract the sap: they wanted us to hug.

The audience cheered as I pulled myself slowly to my feet. When I came to the first man, I feinted to the side, as if too overcome for a hug.

"Are we going to let Momodu go back to being alone?" the hostess asked the audience. Choruses of "Go on, do it!" and "Just give him a hug!" urged me forward. I pretended to consider their reactions, as if torn. When I finally stumbled into the other guy's arms, relieved applause showered the studio.

The man and I started weeping. I bit my cheek. I don't know what he did to get the faucet started. We reached around each other's backs, but bent our elbows like chicken wings so our stumps wouldn't touch. That would have been too personal.

Oh yeah, the audience bought it. Tissues rose in the crowd like paper ghosts.

What they don't understand is, Handless don't need community. If we're water, it's oil. Or vice versa. Having no hands, you realize how potent the sense of touch is in the rest of your body. You feel socks scraping your feet, dirty hair pricking your scalp. When you want to remember what a flower feels like, you rub one against your cheek and it's soft. It *is* soft. But there's something about the language of touching hands that knocks down the walls of separate flesh. A pop psychiatrist who analyzed me on one of these shows claims the Handless have problems with intimacy because of the sudden shock of brutality in a trusting relationship. But it's more than that. I know. Hands are the pen that inscribes trust on the soul.

I boo-hooed my way through the line until I got to the black guy in the wheelchair at the end. Barry. He had no prostheses either, which made us the only ones. I leaned over to do the chicken wing thing and he threw his arms around me, pushing his stumps against my spine. As he touched me, my pain blazed. Involuntary tears scalded my cheeks.

"You're my hero," he whispered. "You gave me the courage to do what I did."

I was trapped because the cameras were on, so I bit my cheek harder to squeeze out a few more tears, then pressed my forehead into the crook of my elbow. "I need to sit down..." I said, stumbling back. The hostess rushed to help me to my chair.

Next, she wheeled Barry's chair next to mine. Barry was big. Not really fat, just the kind of big tall guys get. He looked young and fresh like a TV high school athlete. He wore a maroon baseball cap and a green plaid blanket over his arms and legs so his stumps didn't show. When it got to be his turn to speak, he peeked over at me.

"I'm not like most Handless," he said. "I volunteered for the army. I was in Iran for a few months, in Hamadan. What got to me were women at windows. You wondered who they were. Was the man you were shooting at her husband? Her brother? How could you kill this woman's brother while she watched?"

His mouth pinched up. "I came back home on leave and tried to talk to my Dad about it. He was an Air Force man. He was furious when I said I wasn't going back. He said he'd cut me. I told him that didn't matter, I still wouldn't go. So he went after me.

"We were in the kitchen. He knocked me back and I hit my head on the stove. He said if I didn't change my mind, he'd cut off my feet too."

Barry dragged his blanket up. Two metal bars jutted out of his pants, disappearing into his sneakers.

"I'd seen Momodu on TV. There was a still shot of him they kept putting on the air, that showed him at the hospital on the first day after. First time I saw it, I couldn't get it out of my head. I thought: he looks like family. Then I realized: not just family, he looks like my Dad when he's doing what he knows is painful but right. That's what Momodu did. What was painful but right." Barry nodded along with his own story. "I had to do what I could to keep things from getting worse over there. I knew I could live through whatever Dad did to me, because Momodu did."

Family? I thought. *Like hell. I'd off myself if I thought I had that sap in my family tree.*

The audience erupted into applause. Barry looked like he wanted to hug me again, but the hostess commandeered the camera. "Our producers have prepared a phone list for the ten of you. We'll hand it out at the end of the show. We hope you'll be able to support each other through these tough times."

Barry turned a goofy grin toward me, and I knew I was fucked.

* * *

THERE'S A proverb from Sierra Leone about guys who won't leave you alone—you can drive me away from your house, but you can't drive me away from your grave. That was Barry.

It started with phone calls. I told Minna not to pick up the phone, but she got sick of it ringing, so I told her if she had to answer to do it in German. The first time she picked up, she spoke English.

"Uh huh, Momodu lives here," she said while I flailed for her to stop. "I know, our phone goes on and off. Why don't I tell you our address?"

I stood by the refrigerator, pretending to bash my head against the door. "Why did you do that?"

She frowned at me. "All these things they said at the talk show, did you ever stop to think maybe they were right? You could use someone to talk to besides me."

"So you give our address to The Witless Wonder?"

"You've got more in common than you think. You're both black."

"I'm *African*. He's African-*American*."

"The things you've been through, you don't talk about them with me. Maybe I'm not the right person. Maybe someone else who's been through it… Maybe a man…"

I didn't like the look she had then. Her eyebrows tilted in concern, her chubby hands laid out to me in supplication, as if she were offering them to me.

"So it's because he's a man," I said, smirking. "So I'm not enough for you? I should have known. It takes more than one man to fill a box."

She hates it when I speak in proverbs. She turned away, her face and hands falling into the shadow of her body. "*Überheblicher Arshloch*," she said quietly.

Every morning after that, Barry came to our apartment. His Swiss nurse, Arline (slender fingers with abnormally large knuckles, like knots on string) pushed him to our door and knocked. Barry suggested coffee or lunch and I said no, no, no, until the day Minna invited Arline in so *they* could share lunch—"It's nothing to do with you, Momodu, I just want to talk to someone else who speaks German. Is that all right?"—and oh, what a coincidence, Barry had to come along too.

After that, I couldn't keep them out of the house. Arline and Minna chattered about German novels while I scowled. Barry stared at me. Constantly. As if I were a statue of a saint.

A few weeks later, over dinner, I told Minna I wanted them to stop coming. "I like Arline," she replied. "Maybe you could go out walking in the mornings while she's here. Our visits don't last long."

I nodded toward the cup of wine and she lifted it so I could sip. I endured the swipe of her napkin.

"I could," I admitted. "But it's my damn house."

She met my eye. "I live here too." She sighed and pushed away her plate. "You know, Arline says Barry takes care of himself, almost totally alone. They've set up a toilet he can use on his own. He can open and close the door to their house. He even feeds himself. Don't you want to be able to do that?"

Pain surged down my forearms. I twisted in my seat. "The phantom pain is getting bad again."

"I know Barry is hard for you to take, but I think if you sat down with him—"

"I'm in pain, damn it! Can't you see that?"

"Sorry. Do you want me to get some ice?"

"No! Just shut up until it goes away."

We sat in silence until the pain subsided. When I could breathe regularly again, I scooted forward in my chair, pushing my chest forward and my elbows back to make my ribs look prominent so I'd favor all those photos of pathetic, starving Africans.

"It's not that I don't like Barry," I said. "It's just—I don't like to be reminded of what I've lost."

Minna harrumphed, but I saw a subtle shift in her expression. I accepted another sip of wine, and reclined into victory.

I realized something was wrong the next night when Minna began cooking Tafelspitz, Rosti, and strawberry pudding. "You invited them to dinner," I accused.

She smiled but didn't answer, just buzzed around the kitchen in her bare feet. Her trailing sleeves fell down to her elbows as she dragged the dishes down. When the food was ready, she took the pot of Tafelspitz off the stove and put it on the table. She dished out food for Barry and me, pre-cutting our portions.

"I don't like the look of my beef," I complained.

Minna pushed my chair closer to the table and tucked a napkin into my collar for a bib. She looked down at me, one corner of her mouth pinched down. "I can't help you on my own anymore."

Her standing there, looking down, made me think of the hostess kneeling next to me at the talk show, looking up. Why is it I'm always sitting down when women want to make decisions about my life?

The bell rang and Minna went to answer the door. She returned, rolling Barry's wheelchair to the table. He smiled at me, raising his elbow in salutation.

"Where's Arline?" I asked.

"Arline and I agreed that you and Barry need some time together," said Minna. "I'm going to stay and feed you, but I'm not going to talk."

"You're kidding."

She wasn't.

"Help me with my strap, please," Barry said. "Arline put it in the front pocket of my backpack. I wear it on my wrist."

Minna reached into the bag on Barry's wheelchair and pulled out a small loop of Velcro with a spork attached. "This helps you eat?"

"I can feed myself with it. Sometimes it's messy. I've been practicing with prosthetics that hook onto my elbows too. The doctors say they could work as well as hands. I'm not good with them yet, so I only wear them at home."

"Wouldn't you like something like that, Momodu?" Minna asked.

"I thought you weren't supposed to be talking tonight." I opened my mouth for Minna to feed me. She rolled her eyes, but she did.

It was early for dinner. Light still poured through the window over the stove, and Minna didn't need to turn on the lamp.

Barry chewed with his mouth open, like a cow. "My skin's too sensitive to wear prosthetics. My wrists break into hives. What about you?"

"Acute phantom pain."

"Really?"

"The doctors can't explain it."

"Maybe it's psychosomatic."

Barry leaned forward. A chunk of brown cud lodged between his teeth. "Minna says you're unhappy, Momodu."

"I'm not unhappy."

"Oh." He leaned back. "Well, I wanted to tell you. You helped me to find the secret to happiness. I mean, I already told you about the one time you saved my life. But you really did it twice."

"More fool me."

If Barry heard me, he ignored it. "The first time you gave me courage to stand up for what I believed in, but the second time you taught me that I couldn't just stop there. I had to keep doing it, and not just for people overseas. For people close to me too.

"When I woke in the hospital after Dad cut me, I was depressed for weeks. Nothing could shake me out of it. Then I saw you on Letterman, and something you said broke my world open."

He paused for a moment, his arms raised, the spork dangling off his wrist like a ridiculous charm.

"What did I say?"

"An empty bag cannot stand."

"Oh, a proverb. I've got a better one. Put the money in her hand and get her back on the ground." I sneered at Minna, but she stayed true to the silent treatment.

"If he wants to stand, a man must be full. He can't cut himself off from his fellow men. That's why I went to visit my Dad when I left the hospital."

"An empty bag refers to *food*. A *hungry* man cannot stand."

"But hungry for what?" Barry bobbed his head up and down, trying to look sage. "When Dad got into prison and looked around at himself and what he'd become, he realized what he'd done was wrong. He says when he gets out that he's going to make signs with my picture on them and march outside Washington every day until the war stops. He says that he knows now making it okay to kill anyone makes people think that it's okay to hurt everyone. Otherwise, how could he have done this to me?"

"I have no idea," I said, contemplating the logistics of cutting out Barry's tongue.

"Exactly."

Barry reached to put his stump on my arm and missed. It rested where my hand should have been.

"What are you doing?"

He looked down. "Sorry," he said, moving his stump to my shoulder. "Have you forgiven your uncle?"

"Excuse me?"

"He's a deeply troubled man."

"The prison doctors pump nutrition into Fomba through an IV when he gets close to starving. That's his deep trouble." I glared at Minna. This whole conversation was her fault. "Don't you have anything to say?"

She looked to Barry. "Did you really let your father cut you so you wouldn't have to go back?"

Barry nodded. I slammed my stumps on the table.

"You want proverbs? How about this one: a dick is a dick even if it has no hands or feet."

Barry's jaw worked as he tried to masticate the idea. "I'm not sure what you mean..."

"Shit doesn't have bones, but if you step on it, you'll tiptoe."

"...forgiving your uncle...is like shit?"

"Something is, that's for sure. Try this one: What's your interest in hog money when your father's not a butcher?"

"I don't understand..."

"It means mind your own business!"

Minna stood. She pulled the napkin out of my shirt and tossed it on the table. "I'll call Arline."

Twenty minutes later, I was still sitting at the kitchen table, but Barry was gone. Minna said goodbye to Arline, and I heard her count very calmly to one hundred.

Then she stormed into the kitchen.

"What the hell were you doing?"

"Even a worm can get angry."

She heaved the pot of beef into the sink, tossing the potholder onto the counter. "You're a worm, all right!"

"Don't try to make this my fault. It was your bright idea to force the two of us together. Don't blame me when the obvious happens."

Turning on the sink, she blasted water into the pot. "If you throw ashes," she recited, "ashes will follow you."

"I'm not making trouble for anyone. I just want to be left alone."

"*Du armes Kind.*" She paused a moment before translating. "Poor baby."

She leaned over the stove to collect the potholder. As her sleeve trailed over the burner, a flame flashed onto her arm. She'd forgotten to switch the burner completely off, and bright daylight had swallowed the flicker of flame. Even after I knew it was there, the fire remained invisible.

Red and yellow raced toward Minna's shoulder. She raised her arm at an awkward angle, like a cut marionette. Her body drew taut around the fire, as if it had become her center of gravity. Slowly, her eyes widened. And then she shrieked, flapping at the flame with her free hand.

I sat rigid. My knuckles throbbed, as if I was clutching my chair.

Minna's shriek metamorphosed into a hideous, sustained wail. Finally, she pitched herself on the floor, writhing on the tile until the fire vanished in a veil of smoke.

She lay still, tears streaking her mascara into jagged raccoon stripes. The smoke alarm blared. I coughed.

Finally, I realized I should talk. "Shit, what was that?" I asked. "Are you okay?"

Minna didn't answer. She reached up to switch off the stove, and grabbed for my stump. "Come on," she growled. Her hand closed on the place Barry had tried to touch me earlier, the space where my hand should have been. I felt her pull me up by nothing.

She dragged me into the hallway and slid down the wall into a crouch. Burns sketched red swirls like henna down her arm.

"Were you going to sit there and watch me burn?"

"What could I do?"

"You could have tackled me, or turned on the water faucet with your elbow, or screamed for help."

"I don't have any hands!"

"You could have gotten out of your goddamn chair."

* * *

TWENTY-FOUR HOURS later, my house was scoured clean of hand lotions and thimbles and nail files.

"I don't know why I ever thought you were a hero," Minna said.

Of course I'm not a hero. That's all my life has been since Fomba cut me. Save my war, be my martyr, raise my flag, inspire my son, take my pity, be what I tell you to be. Why the hell should I? I'm not Barry. He sat down. He anted up. I never asked to get dealt in. Papa shoved me into the chair, fate dealt me suicide kings, and Fomba ensured I couldn't even pick up the hand. I never gave a rat's shit hole whether we blew up a city or snipered civilians or covered the whole Middle East in marzipan, as long as I didn't have to do it. Roll on the floor your own damn self, America, you can put out the fire without Momodu. He looks out for his own damn self.

When Minna finished packing, I followed her to the threshold. She was laden with suitcases, her arms bulging with muscles I hadn't noticed before.

"What am I going to do without you?" I asked.

She shrugged. "I don't know." She walked out without looking back.

I kept thinking about the man she'd end up with. Someone she wouldn't have to feed, someone who could shave his own beard, someone who could lift her chin and guide her into a kiss.

* * *

I SPENT the day after Minna left raging. It shouldn't have happened: No Barry, no dinner. No dinner, no fire. No fire, no suitcases. No questions about heroism. No empty apartment.

And then the most unexpected thing happened.

The war ended.

The landlady came up to tell me. She helped me to her apartment to watch the incoming reports on TV.

After seventy-five thousand American deaths and fighting that sprawled into twelve countries, America finally declared a draw and pulled out. The stated reason was that we had "accomplished our objectives" by "securing freedom for the native populations" and "protecting America from its enemies."

As far as the unstated reason, there was a lot of conjecture. Maybe it was Israel finally withdrawing its troops. Or the outbreaks of hemorrhagic fever in Kenya and Uganda, which were too close to our front lines for comfort. Or maybe Senator Minter, whose eldest son's death in combat six months before had persuaded the patriotic partisan to throw his full weight into departure, finally managed to call in the last of his favors. But whatever the reason, we had suddenly gone to peace.

A few hours into the coverage, a female news anchor with large, masculine hands read a statement Fomba had sent to the TV stations. "Fomba Koromah, the man who cut off his nephew's hands and triggered the national trend that produced nearly four hundred Handless, writes from his cell: 'Politicians can end the war, but they end nothing. The struggle rages in the heart of this country, bringing glory to the brave and damning the cowards.'" The camera angle zoomed in close to her face; she took a moment for a reaction shot, and continued, "Koromah also writes that he will continue his hunger strike even though the war is over. Sources at the prison say that due to long-term lack of nutrition, Koromah's health remains in decline."

So. I'd gotten everything wrong, hadn't I? Minna leaving wasn't Barry's fault. Fomba lay at the root of all my problems.

And if he was ill, this could be my last chance to hurt him.

* * *

AFTER FIVE years of starving himself but not being violent to anyone else, Fomba was in medium-security prison. The security guard, a tall Lebanese, chattered as he searched me for drugs and weapons. His hands were sweaty and red, his fingernails chewed to the cuticle with a precise, even bite. He placed his right hand on my back and rubbed thoughtfully.

"Waited long enough, didn't you? We had a pool on when you'd come see the Thin Man. After a couple years, everyone's time was gone, so we paid off the guy who said you'd never make it. Now the war's over, and here you are. Think I can get my money back?"

He led me through the prison cafeteria. "There'll be guards watching. Regulations. But we cleared it out like you asked. You and the Thin Man will be the only ones in there."

We entered a tiny adjacent room. Plastic chairs ringed round tables. Faded vending machines lined the back wall.

No matter how big a child is, he's never bigger than the man who raised him. Actually, the proverb says he's never bigger than his father. But Papa's dead. Now Fomba's all I have.

Fomba sat at the middle table, presiding over an empty tray. Malnutrition lent his skin a grey cast, and the whites of his eyes had dimmed to the color of ash. His hands steepled over the tray, fingers woven through each other like shark's teeth. Above, his eyes smoldered: alert, violent embers.

I sat in the opposite chair and folded my arms, putting my stumps between us.

Fomba laughed. His teeth seemed gigantic in his sunken face, the ribs of an immense creature emerging from a dark sea. "Trying to get rid of your black hands?"

"I don't have hands anymore."

"They're shadows, but they're still there. They follow you like ghosts."

He inspected my stumps, pursing his lips in distaste.

"People here want to shit, but they don't want to eat. They're spoiled Americans. Even the black ones. What I wouldn't give for one of my guns..."

Black Americans like Barry. Spoiled. I'd been saying it for weeks. In Fomba's mouth, it was filth.

For an instant, I saw him through his eyes: a martyr remaking himself as he'd once pieced together the remnants of dead weapons, transforming flesh to will through starvation.

He was never going to forgive me or whimper regrets. He'd known exactly what he was doing when he cut me. It was nothing he hadn't done before.

I wanted to hurt him. Revelation: I realized I could. Laying my stumps on the table, I moved my head close to his. "Put your hands over my wrists. Lean in."

He looked wary.

"Trust me. I can't hurt you. The guards are watching."

Up close, his eyes were ill and wavery, bright lights in shivering night water. I put my mouth next to his ear and began to shake and breathe rapidly so, from behind, it would look like I was crying. The guards shuffled behind us.

"You want to die, don't you?" I asked. "Why go on fasting? I brought you some pills. Take them tonight and they won't be able to stop you."

Fomba's eyes were hungry, but his tone remained skeptical. His tongue ranged over his teeth, leaving a sheen of saliva. "How did you get them in?"

"They don't suspect me. Why would I help you?"

"Why would you?"

"A peacetime present." I smiled and breathed into his ear. "I want you to die."

Fomba's hands inched up my arm. His breaths became short and shallow with desire.

"Give them to me."

I took the moment to drink in his strained muscles, his trembling want, then let the grin spread outward.

"I don't have any drugs."

A beat.

Vitriolic with victory, I added, "Really, Fomba, what did you think I could carry them in here *with*?"

His expression should have deadened with disappointment. Instead, his features seized into a grimace. He tightened his grip on my arm, fingers digging between layers of muscle as he pulled my stumps off the table. I struggled.

He laughed. "Cocky Momodu. Strutting Momodu. Look now."

My eyes seized on our arms. There were hands in Fomba's grasp, huge and black and ugly. My hands. Textured like smoke, fingers gnarled into branches. As I watched, they twisted into new malformations like nimbus clouds whipped by a furious wind.

The guards pulled Fomba off me and pinned his arms. "That's a ticket back to high security," one of them said.

Fomba turned to respond, but the beginning of a proverb turned into a strangled yelp. He fell, legs clattering against the chair. The Lebanese shouted, "He's having a fit!" and ran back for help.

As his footsteps fell in the hallway, another guard came in, assessed the situation, and came up to me. "I think we should go, sir," he said, placing his hand on my elbow.

Gently, he guided me into chaos. I heard guard's footsteps halt as we passed. Convicts shouted catcalls of praise and condemnation. One rose above the din: "About time someone got the Thin Man!" As we reached the end of a long corridor, an EMT team rushed past us in a squeak of wheels and rubber soles. I didn't see any of it.

I couldn't draw my eyes away from my black hands. The fingers twisted into claws. Jagged digits curled toward me, accusing.

Peace had come. Fomba was dead. I knew my crime.

* * *

AFRICAN SORCERY is not like Western magic. African witches drill tiny holes in their victim's hands and arms. They possess people's bodies the way a puppeteer manipulates a marionette. When you slit open a witch's chest, you find a heart as soft and yellow as a banana.

The prison called to tell me the Thin Man was dead. Even without my mythical drugs, Fomba got what he wanted.

His doctor called it a stroke. I believe it was something else. Perhaps Fomba's witchcraft finally dissolved his withering body.

Fomba cursed me when he cut me. He called the ghosts of my dead hands to haunt me with the sin of cowardice he supposed I'd been guilty of. But instead, he froze me in that moment of apathy when I would have been happy to see the whole world burn, as long as I was fireproof.

My phantom pain is caused by phantoms. The black hands Fomba cursed me with are jealous of trespassers. When I think back, I realize I've been seeing them all these years: in my shadow, in misplaced grasps, in the ghost fingers Minna claims to feel when we make love.

There are a lot more amputees now in Africa than there used to be. Our army left them behind, victims of land mines and jumpy triggers. And here, in this country, there will be many soldiers returning from the front with missing limbs. How will Americans be able to tell us from them? Who will these men be and what will the nation make of them?

If you do not make the effort to do good, you do evil. I should have learned that in my childhood, watching Fomba. But I was too busy listening to his proverbs.

* * *

DO NOT suppose redemption comes all at once. Revelation does, but not redemption.

By the time I returned from the prison, my black hands had vanished from sight again, but I knew they were still there.

The following day, I relearned helplessness. I hadn't realized how much I'd forgotten while I let Minna take care of me. I couldn't cook, remove my clothing, fluff my pillow. Minna found me the second day, lying on the bathroom floor. I'd wet myself.

"I'm not here forever," she said, helping me out of my soiled clothing. "Just until you settle with a nurse."

Her hand rested like a spider on the tile, tensing and relaxing with her pulse.

"Are you still angry?" I asked.

Of course she's angry.

"It's all right for you to be angry," I allowed.

She looked away. Her other hand came to rest in the hollow spot behind my knee.

"Thank you for coming back."

"Today, there's peace. I figured…"

"If they could make peace, we could?"

"If our government could pull out of a war, then anything can change."

The bite in her voice stung. I looked up, startled, and she chuckled. Her fist did not unclench.

* * *

THE NEXT morning, Minna stood in the doorway of our apartment building as she watched me go. She shivered in a heavy sweater, hands tucked into her armpits. "You're sure you want to go alone?" she asked.

I nodded.

As I headed down the sidewalk, I felt the pain in my hands lessen a fraction. I imagined tiny curls of diaphanous vapor drifting away, leaving the ghosts a little thinner.

Traveling without Minna was difficult, but I managed. Strangers helped. An old man in a yellow tie called me a taxi. I gave the driver the address Minna had found in the phone book for me the night before. As we drove through suburban neighborhoods, I saw celebrations of the new peace: olive branches on parked cars, banners emblazoned with doves hung in windows. Only a few houses showed flags with black stripes instead of red to mourn the war. When we reached our destination, I asked the driver to help me count out the change from my wallet. He surprised me by being honest.

I waited until the taxi rounded the corner before turning to climb Barry's front steps. Instead of a knob, his door had long handles. I knocked with my foot.

Barry opened the door. He wore prosthetics on his elbows.

"Momodu?"

"Hi, Barry."

I watched his eye trail down my mismatched clothes and un-tucked shirt.

"I helped dress myself this morning," I explained.

He nodded.

"Can I come in?" I asked.

He gave me that look. That Barry look. Too deep. Too personal. A look that scrubs instead of seeing.

I don't know what he saw there, but I hoped it was more than he'd seen the day before.

He didn't ask for any more explanation. He just wheeled aside to make room for me to enter.

The Sea of Trees

NOT TEN minutes in, I spot yellow electrical tape strung through the trees. Recent, not tattered. I grab, hold on hand-over-hand as I scramble over roots and rocks. Good to have a touch-connection to the way out. If you don't know the way back, the trees might lure you and keep you.

The forest is all shadows. Clinging mist damps the sunlight. Light penetrates at strange angles, casting a glow over lichen-covered roots, shredded bark and rotting logs.

To the left: a rope suspended from a branch that's too weak to support a man's weight. Hung by someone stupid or indecisive or playing a prank. Hope that's not all I'll find today.

To the right: a second tape trail branching into the shadows.

Better stick to the trail I'm on for now. Hope it pays off.

A few meters later: a woman's compact on the ground. Kick it; watch it bounce end over end, mirror flashing. It leaves an indent in the soil. It's lain undisturbed awhile. Good. Makes it more likely I've gotten here before the suicide watch. I slip the compact into my pack.

I'm feeling really good right now. This is a bingo. Can already see yurei shadows hiding behind trunks. Not long dead, this one, not with ghosts still gathering.

The scent of mandarin oranges precedes a yurei flashing next to me. She's all floating with no feet. Her edo-style white burial kimono casts a shadow on the lichen.

Black hair sweeps to her waist, equally covering the back and front of her head. Impossible to locate her face. Tendrils curl toward me, entreatingly.

This yurei's been around as long as I have. Likes jokes. Minor pranks. She's harmless.

"*Your life is a precious gift from your parents,*" she says. "*Please think about your parents, siblings, and children.*"

"*Ha.*"

She's quoting the signs that are posted at the edge of the forest in weak attempts to turn back the suicidal before they add to the body count among the trees. Who gets this far to be stopped by a sign?

Tendril of hair grasps my shoulder. I bug-shudder it off. "*You know that's not why I'm here.*"

"*Don't keep it to yourself,*" she says, still quoting. "*Talk about your troubles.*"

"*Only trouble I've got right now is where to find good scavenge.*"

The yurei rotates slowly in the air. A raven lock gestures down the trail I've been following.

"*Thief-girl.*" She uses her derisive pet name for me. "*That one's got nothing. Couldn't even take a train back to Tokyo.*"

Another tendril points back to the tape-fork.

"*That one came with everything he's got. Red tent under a big tree.*"

Her tone is too helpful. Suspicious. This yurei likes barbs and mischief. She's not sugar unless she's hiding something.

"*Not gone yet, is he?*" I ask.

Ends of her hair curl up in a shrug. "*Neck's broken. Wait ten minutes.*"

All right. I open my hydration pack. Drink.

Yurei keeps floating by. Can't tell where her eyes are behind all that hair, but she's watching me.

"*You want something?*" I ask.

She bobs silently.

Sigh. "Go *ahead.*"

She floats closer. Tendrils of hair reach out like tentacles. I grit my teeth as she feels out my face like a blind person. Hair feels like hair feels, but this hair moves like hair shouldn't. Body knows that. Body does not like being touched by the dead.

The scent of mandarin oranges lingers as her hair withdraws. "*Just wanted to remember,*" she says. "*What it's like. To touch skin that wants to live.*"

I wipe my mouth, reseal the hydration pack. "*It'll be ten by the time I get there. Thanks for the tip.*"

* * *

YOU CAN call this place Aokigahara or you can call it Jukal, the sea of trees. Either way, it's haunted.

The forest grew eight-hundred-and-fifty years ago after an eruption of Mount Fuji. Green things sunk their roots after the lava cooled.

The woods are very quiet. Little lives here except for ghosts and people on their way to joining them. Wind scarcely blows. Mists hang. Overhead, branches and leaves tangle into a roof underneath which the world is timeless and directionless.

Everything is trapped.

Everything is waiting.

A pair of tennis shoes, sitting alone.

Pants, voluminous over leg bones.

A suicide note nailed to a tree: "Nothing good ever happened in my life. Don't look for me."

The yurei, watching.

* * *

THE MAN hanging above the red tent smells like the shit his bowels just released. He has three gold teeth, an expensive watch, brand name trainers, and a pack of money. I'm unclear on the point of taking cash into the forest, but people do what they do.

Good scavenge, that's sure. Most people have nothing when they come here to die. Easier to feel empty when your bank account's the same.

Scissors, nail clippers, a comb. Copy of Wataru Tsurumi's *Complete Manual of Suicide*. Half of everyone who comes here carries that. Stupid book. Stupider people. Can't even reject their lives without instructions.

I'm about to toss it back when I hear a crunch in the undergrowth.

Nearby.

Damn it.

Snap to my feet. Pull on my pack. Now I notice what greed blinded me to: where are the yurei around this fresh death? Other living people must be on their way. Scared the ghosts off.

That yurei must have known. She trying to get me caught?

The suicide watch is not going to be friendly when they realize I'm looting. I scramble, searching for a tree to climb. No way they won't have heard me by now, but some are superstitious, might put noises down to yurei without really looking.

I hear the smack of someone tripping. The swearing that follows is in American English.

"Damn it to bugfucking, motherfucking hell!"

I can see her now. American tourist wearing a downy red sweatshirt over jeans with sandals of all stupid things. Half-empty hydration pack hangs from her backpack. Either she can't ration or she's been hiking awhile.

Young. Maybe fifteen, sixteen. Makeup and clothes are all-American, but can't conceal Japanese eyes. Probably another fucking Nisei looking for her roots.

I push into the shadows, thinking I'll wait her out, but it turns out that despite being clumsy and unprepared, she's not stupid.

"*Sumimasen*," she says, "*Eigo hanashimasuka?*"

She wants to know if I speak English. I have no intention of letting her know I do. "*Gomen nasai. Eigo ga wakarimasen.*"

"Figures," she mutters. "Just another slant-eyed motherfucker with half a brain."

I can't stop my snarl in time. She cracks a grin.

"Ha! Thought you did!"

No point denying it. "What do you want?"

"I'm lost."

I point over her shoulder at the tape-path. "You can get out that way."

She squints. "I recognize you. In town. I stopped to use my phone. You were on the corner."

"Sorry, wasn't me."

"Someone pointed you out. They said there aren't many women who spend time up here. They said an onryo follows you around."

People should set up shop and charge for gossip the way they toss other people's stories around. Everyone figures it's fair game if there's a ghost.

I gesture at the trees. "You see an onryo?"

"They didn't say it followed you all the time."

I cross my arms. "What do you want?"

"I need to find a yurei."

I point to the newly hanged man. "Wait around."

"No. I need to find a particular yurei. I need to find my father."

Here's the thing about me: I came to Aokigahara when I was twenty-two, the year my onryo came for me. I've been here seven years since. Sure, I leave the trees, but I'm always here.

I make my living scavenging. Selling valuables. Or, most of the time, not finding anything valuable and then hunting down buyers with too much death on their minds, people who want to thrill themselves with a hint of the haunted by buying detritus that once belonged to a suicide. Combs. Glasses. Rope from a noose. Remnants of lives abandoned.

I don't need much to live, but I earn less. That's why I listen when the American girl caps her plea with, "I'll pay."

"How much?"

The figure she names is enough to buy a day or two in the forest looking for a ghost.

I won't even have to find her father. Just spend some time searching then turn up any ghost at all. She'll never tell the difference.

Still, I can't help pressing further. See what she's made of.

I sling my backpack off my shoulder. "Sounds like a deal."

She smiles. Gestures to herself. "I'm Melon."

I give her an oddball eye. She laughs.

"Mom thinks nature names sound Japanese."

I exchange mine. "Nao."

"Cool. Where do we start?"

"Nowhere today. It's getting late."

It's early evening; we could go a couple hours. But I want to stop here.

I unpack my sleeping bag. "I'll be fine on the ground."

She nods.

I add, "You take the tent."

I grin as I point. The red tent still smells like the sweat and piss of the man swinging from the tree. The girl looks up. His shadow falls over her, black as bruises. She swallows fast.

Breaking her gaze from the dead man's eyes, she crouches to unzip the flap.

"Look comfy?" I ask.

She glances back. Her too-earnest American face has a closed, hard set.

"Looks fine."

She crawls in. I'm not unimpressed.

* * *

TWO A.M. The ghost hour.

The whistling of wind wakes me. The sound comes alone, unaccompanied by breeze.

Then she's there. My Sayomi. My onryo.

Dead lips on mine. Cold fingers stroking my thighs. Prehensile tendrils of hair circling my waist, teasing my nipples, trailing my spine.

Creep-shudder, gullet to gut. Body does not like being touched by the dead.

But my Sayomi. Body likes being touched by my Sayomi.

Timeless at twenty-one. Smooth-cheeked, willow-bodied, bloodlessly pale. Eyes shining with tears a decade old.

A long skirt flows to her ankles, western-style but cut from white-flowered silk. Low-cut lace shows the apple-tops of her breasts. Lipstick stains her mouth; she opens to moan; blood-color smears her teeth.

She dressed up to die, my Sayomi.

Ashen tongue in my mouth like a cold lump of meat. Hair busy undoing the zip of my jeans, her obi-style waistband. Night air breathes cold on flesh usually hidden.

She pushes me to the ground, roots sharp in my back. Sayomi on top of me. Her hair parting my lips. Her fingers inside me.

I moan.

She always makes me moan.

The creeping horror of her hair. The unchanging beauty of her face.

My body tightens. That moment, near arriving. Her unfinished business with me nearly resolved.

It takes a great deal of will to shove her away before it comes.

She screams. Her hair ties itself in angry knots. I squirm out from underneath. Her fingernails claw the dirt where I'd been.

Someday I won't get away.

Someday I won't want to.

I gain my feet. Her hair stretches for my wrists and ankles. Her eyes are wide and guileless even as she tries to drag me down.

It would be so easy to give in.

Clouds shift. Across her moonlit face, a shadow swings.

I look up. The hanged man. Socks on his dangling feet, robbed of their expensive trainers.

The red tent. The American girl. I'd forgotten where I was.

Desire vanishes.

Sayomi pounds her fists on the air. She screams again. This time, the sound dissolves her. It becomes a windless whistle as she blows away.

Back in the silence of the sea of trees, all I can hear is my ragged breath.

I pull up my jeans. The girl's face peeps through the tent flap. I politely look away, but she won't give me the courtesy of silence.

She asks, "Was that the onryo?"

I shrug. She knows it was.

"Why is she a pile of bones?"

I sigh. "There's an old ghost story. A lonely scholar lives in his house, pining away, until one day a beautiful woman visits at night. He lets her in. They make love. In the morning, she leaves, and the scholar gets sick. Every night after that, she comes to him. They make love, she gives him pleasure, and he gets weaker."

The girl's watching eyes are bright like Sayomi's, but tearless.

"One night, the scholar's worried neighbor looks through the window," I continue. "He sees the scholar in bed with a skeleton. He tells the scholar what he saw, and that night, when the ghost arrives, the scholar knows what she is. But he doesn't see a pile of bones. When he looks at her, he sees a woman."

"What happened to the scholar?"

"He died."

Silence. Then, "What does your onryo look like?"

I shrug again.

"Did you know her? When she was alive?"

That's enough. I don't listen to whatever she asks next.

* * *

A GIRL may love a girl, but eventually both become women.

One goes to university in America. The other studies in Fukuoka. Each misses the other, but one is distracted by learning English and sunbathing by Lake Michigan and eating cafeteria lunches. For the other, Fukuoka is what Fukuoka has always been, but drained of joy. Joy that will never return for girls who've grown into women.

Even across the boundary of life and death, flesh may yearn for flesh. But when the dead pleasure the living, they pull them to their side, as the ghost woman pulled her scholar.

As a ghost, Sayomi doesn't talk, but just before she died, she sent an email. I didn't receive it until after she was gone. Sometimes it feels as if it was written by her ghost.

Come to Aokigahara, she wrote. *We'll finish things there.*

* * *

I WAKE before the girl does.

Three yurei gather around the hanged man. Clawed hands emerge from hair-veils to peck at the corpse. Spectral fingers leave no marks, but the man's body swings back and forth despite the lack of wind. Slowly at first and then faster and faster. The branch creaks as if caught in a hurricane. The yurei make noises I've never heard. Part-shriek and part-scratch, simultaneously the sounds of predators and of terrified things.

I pull the girl out of the tent. Gesturing for silence, I point to the raven-like yurei. The girl's not stupid; she follows my lead, packing without a word. We back away, careful not to make noise with our feet.

When we're a distance removed, she asks, "What was that?"

I feign nonchalance. "Don't know."

Hope she'll think I'm saying *Don't know and it doesn't matter* instead of *Don't know and I thought I knew everything about yurei.*

Not sure she buys my dismissive shrug. She keeps her own counsel for once.

When she does talk again, it's about something else. She pulls a photo from her pack. "This is my father."

I expect a generic, smiling face, but the photo shows a corpse. Dried flesh on bones. A tidy button-down drapes over shoulders that look like a coat-hanger. Hair clumps on remnants of scalp. Part of the nose and cheek remain, but not enough to make a face.

She points to the background. "See those rocks? I thought maybe you'd recognize them."

Tourists.

"It's a big forest," I answer.

"Not that big."

"Big enough."

She should know what I mean without my having to tell her: with all the ghosts here, the sea of trees is as big as it wants to be.

The girl looks like she wants to stomp her feet. "Then how are you going to find him!"

"Wander. Watch the trees." She still looks pissed. I add, "If we keep going deeper, he'll find you."

If he wants to find her.

If someone else doesn't find us first.

She bites her lips. Gazes abstractly at distant trees. "Do you think he'll talk to me?"

"Yurei like to talk."

I shouldn't say more since her optimism is what's paying me, but I can't stop myself.

I add, "No telling what he'll say."

* * *

WE'RE STILL in familiar forest. I can navigate. Would be better to follow tape-trails, but I don't want the strange yurei to find us too easily.

Once we're moving steadily, the girl starts talking.

"My mother met my father while she was backpacking the summer after college. He was older than she was. They didn't stay in touch, but she had his name. Last year when I turned sixteen, she said I was old enough to figure out for myself what to do with it. So I tracked down his family. They told me he'd died, but they wouldn't say anything else."

"He committed suicide," I assume.

"The suicide watch found him here." Melon's voice is thick. She tugs the strap of her backpack so she has an excuse to hesitate. "They sent me photos."

"What makes you think he became a yurei?"

"I read online that the first night after they bring the bodies back, someone from the suicide watch sleeps next to them. In the morgue or wherever they take them. To make sure their souls can rest."

"No one slept next to him?"

"I don't know. I didn't ask. But in the photo of him, of his body…you can see that he's been…that's he's already…"

"Rotted."

She stiffens. Doesn't protest. "No one slept with him then. On the real first night."

Quiet there, in the sea of trees. Just me and her. Me and her and her sadness.

I ask, "Did he know about you?"

"Mom told him. Before I was born." Her tone changes. Last night's hard look returns to her face. "I know what you're asking. No. He never tried to get in touch with me. It doesn't matter. I care even if he didn't. I have to know where I came from."

I don't think much of Melon's reasons, but I like her conviction. I also like the fact that even though I can see she's tired and sore, she hasn't complained.

"Why do you speak English?" she asks.

"I went to college in America."

"Where?"

"Northwestern."

"Oh!" she says. Then, quietly, "I've read a lot about Chicago."

Something mournful there. Something unsaid. Maybe something to do with why she's seventeen and hiking alone half a world from where she grew up, searching for a father she never knew.

I'm so grateful that she's keeping something to herself for once that I leave it alone.

* * *

WE'RE PAST where most suicides go, but we find footprints so I stop. Gives the girl a chance to rest. Gives me a chance to keep my profits up.

Result: a bag half-buried between roots. I shake off loose soil. Dig through canned food and hygiene products.

The girl asks, "Why'd they bring all that in?"

"Some people stay a long time before they do anything."

"Saying goodbye to the world?"

"Or making up their minds."

At the bottom of the bag, a mokume-gane wedding band. Dirty. Sized for a small man or a large woman.

The girl watches the light pick a glint from beneath the grime. "How sad."

I push the ring into my pocket.

Melon continues, "It makes sense to want to say goodbye to the world before you leave it."

Mist drifts through motionless leaves. Trees creep slowly, invisibly, toward the masked sun.

"This place is like a graveyard," she says.

"Whole world is. At least here, it looks like what it is."

* * *

WE GO on. Evening draws closer. Silent and navy instead of silent and white.

I almost lead the girl toward a cave I know when I feel sudden trepidation. I stop abruptly. "Shh!" I hiss to forestall the girl's question.

A yurei, crouched between trees. He hovers midair, hair parting over his nose and sweeping down in two dark curtains. His exposed jaw stretches all the way to the ground: a gaping maw the size of a door. Black, open, waiting to swallow us into hungry dark.

I pull the girl backwards for several meters before I dare turn. We move swiftly through the trees. Takes a while. Navy turns darker. Still doesn't feel safe.

The girl gets sick of following. Demands, "Where are we going?"

I look back through the dark, toward where the mouth gapes. Yurei like ravens. Yurei waiting to swallow us down.

I've lost my nerve.

"We should get out," I say.

"Why?"

"Something's wrong. Something's bringing out the darkest."

In the last light, she looks lost and lonely. Her voice is all breath. "Maybe it's me."

Melon's stupid and young and American. Annoying as she is, I can't imagine what about her would draw darkness from ghosts.

Chill on my nape, though. Says maybe I'm wrong.

Melon asks, "Can you get us out this late?"

It's almost black. Moonlight casts faint silhouettes along nearby trunks.

We're far away from electrical tape and signs entreating us not to end our lives.

I could get us out. I think. But I don't want to be wrong.

"We'll talk in the morning," I say.

Moonlight reveals her guileless grin.

* * *

TWO A.M.

The sound of wind without wind.

Sayomi.

Me on the ground in my sleeping pack. Crisp, night smells. The girl nearby.

Doesn't matter who's watching. Nothing stops Sayomi's devouring kisses. Hair embraces me. Meat-lump tongue laps at my lips. She wants to pull me out through my mouth. Fill her ribcage with my heart. Fill her bones with my marrow.

I want her, too.

Legs scissoring. Pelvises matched. Lips to lips. Pleasure fluttering. Hovering. Rising. I should go with her. I should let her make me come. I should come; I should go; at least then I'd be somewhere.

No. Not now. Not tonight, with the girl watching. There will always be another night to let Sayomi suck me down.

I shove Sayomi away. She screams. Hair lashes my face, leaves stinging marks that will last to morning.

"No." I shove again.

Hair winds around my throat. Pulls tight. An ethereal glow lights the whiteness of her skin. Her teeth are bared, her weeping eyes bloodshot. She strains as her hair cinches tighter.

Throat hot. Lungs searing. I'm suddenly hyper-aware of air on my face, on my thighs—air I can't breathe.

Sayomi's never gone this far before.

Even as her hair strangles me, strands separate to move beneath my waist. The burning cinch. The gentle stroke. Each sensation sharpens other.

My vision sparks. Blue. White. Fading. Can't even struggle.

A rock streaks past Sayomi's cheek, clatters on the ground behind her. She can't be hurt like that anymore, but she recoils with surprise. Her hair withdraws from me, moving reflexively to protect her like a shield. I can just make out Sayomi's eyes behind the veil. Angry. Betrayed.

Air chokes my throat. I grasp my neck. Pain all the worse now that I have oxygen to feel it.

Hands on my back, checking to see if I'm all right. Melon's hands. "Nao!" she exclaims.

Sayomi looks down at us and screams again, that hair-to-heel scream that scatters her into the night.

"I tried not to watch," Melon says.

I clutch my burning throat.

"Her bones are white. I thought you had to be dead a long time for your bones to bleach like that."

Her voice trembles. Her eyes are afraid. Maybe she's realizing the danger now. These aren't American ghosts you can banish with water and chanting. They're yurei. They take what they want.

* * *

I KNEW Sayomi was dead as soon as I read her email. She was long gone by the time I arrived in Aokigahara.

I've spent years reconsidering all the times we'd spent together after I left for school. The phone calls made when one or the other of us should have been sleeping. The emails complaining about classwork. The summer after my second year when I came home and we went hiking but we got too tired to climb and so we laid down near the mountain's base instead, holding each other's hands and watching the sky.

I should have heard the plaintive tone in her voice on the train heading back. "You'll always come back for me, won't you?" She was staring out the window, not even able to look at me. I hadn't understood what that meant.

I didn't give her what she needed then so I give her what I can now. Not much: a few kisses, a nightly embrace.

Until I can muster more.

* * *

THE GIRL and I are both awake by dawn.

She's angry that I still want to go back. "I need to find my father! You deal with ghosts all the time. I thought you were an expert!"

"That's why I know when to leave."

"You can't just stop! I'm paying you!"

I laugh.

Angry surprise lights her face. American girl, used to money buying power. She doesn't expect *dismissal*.

"This is my only chance! I have to fly back to Nebraska on Tuesday. Who knows if I'll ever get back? I have to find my father! Please! You owe me. You wouldn't even be here if I hadn't rescued you last night!"

I wait for her to run out of shouting.

"I'm heading back," I say. "Come with me or go alone."

Her face goes blank, caught between pride and fear.

I throw her a bone.

"Maybe we'll find your father on the way out."

* * *

WHEN WE glimpse sunlight, the trees thicken.

Down past the rocks, the trees thicken.

Along every path, the trees thicken.

Each time, I turn heel and try another way. My heartbeat goes faster. My mouth dries. I tell myself I'm only lost. I'll find the way.

But I already know. There is no way.

The trees have claimed us.

I don't tell Melon. It would only scare her. She'll eventually work it out.

Maybe by then I'll know what to do.

* * *

THE GIRL'S frightened inhalation warns me to halt.

I'm about to step out from underneath the canopy's shadow. In front of us, a lightning-struck tree has fallen across its sisters, creating a small clearing.

Encroaching on its boundaries, dozens of yurei. Flocking. Screeching.

It's daytime, but shadows swarm around the ghosts, creating temporary dark. Some hold torches aloft in locks of their hair. Firelight picks out undertones of blue and green in their white kimonos. They swoop and dart like carrion-eaters, all suddenness with no grace.

Leaders emerge into the clearing. Pass through. There are many, many more behind.

The girl trembles. Goosebumps prick my skin.

Any moment, they could smell us. They may already be watching behind their hair. Clawed hands could part their veils at any instant.

Hundreds stream by until, at last, the grimacing legion is gone, shadows and firelight with them, leaving behind mist and silent trees.

The girl starts forward into the clearing. No! I throw my arm out to stop her. She cringes as she glimpses what I've seen.

One last yurei sitting on the lightning-charred stump.

The air is so cold. My exhalations are ice.

The yurei's scent drifts toward us.

Mandarin oranges.

Relief instantly warms me. "Don't worry," I tell the girl. "I know this one."

* * *

THE YUREI'S head rotates toward our approach. Her body remains motionless. If she had a living neck, it would snap.

"*Thanks for your advice the other day*," I say acidly in Japanese.

"A moment, please!" she replies in English. "Consult the police before you decide to die."

The girl gasps. Her expression shows fear.

"Don't worry," I repeat. "This one always quotes the signs. She thinks it's a joke."

Melon trembles. She braces her hands protectively across her stomach. I think but don't say, *you're the one who wanted to meet a ghost.*

"We can't get out," I tell the yurei.

She switches to Japanese. "*All roads lead to Aokigahara.*"

Melon breathes raggedly. I can't tell how much she understands.

"Hardly anything leads to Aokigahara."

"*All roads lead to death. Aokigahara is death. All roads lead to Aokigahara.*"

"*You are not being helpful!*" I reply angrily in Japanese.

"*The forest wants you.*"

"*I've been here a hundred times! Why does it want me now?*"

I glare at the yurei. I know her pricks and pranks. She's keeping something to herself.

The girl breaks in, using halting Japanese. "*Please! I need to find my father. Can you help me?*"

The yurei turns again, that neck-snapping turn. "Your name is Melon."

Her English is very bad.

"Yes," Melon says. She's afraid, but it doesn't silence her.

The yurei calls back to me, "*You come a hundred times alone and once with this one. What do you think is different?*"

Melon looks between us, confused. The Japanese is too fast for her. "Please," she repeats. "My father's name is Manabu. He died here."

"Why should I help you?" the yurei grumbles. She adds in Japanese, "*She doesn't have anything I want.*"

"*She has the same thing you get from me,*" I say. "*She has skin that wants to live*—"

The words aren't entirely out of my mouth before I realize what the yurei is implying.

I gape at Melon. "What did you really come here to do?"

Melon hasn't understood our words, but she knows how to read my shocked eyes. She tenses. I move forward to catch her, but I'm too late. She flees.

The yurei rises to watch her go. Her hovering form casts a sharp shadow across the lightning-struck log.

For a moment, I'm too confused to pursue. Everything is going wrong. The trees closing in. Sayomi refusing to let go.

"*One girl wants to die,*" the yurei says. "*One girl is marked by a ghost. Both belong to us.*"

"*What do I do? How do I get out?*"

"*The trees have been waiting to claim you. They won't let you out while they're feeding on her.*"

"*Then I'll chop them down! Damn it! What do I do?*"

The yurei says nothing. She won't help. She got what she wanted yesterday and now she's watching her prank play out.

Damn her. I run past, following Melon.

"*Please reconsider!*" the yurei calls after me. "*Think of your family!*"

* * *

MELON'S STILL walking when I find her, but she's turned herself in circles and hasn't made it far.

She jumps when she feels my hand on her pack. She struggles to keep me from pulling it off, but I'm stronger and her straps are loose.

Inside: gear, clothes, hygiene items—and there: I rattle an enormous bottle of analgesics.

"What's wrong with you?" I ask. "Why do you think you need these?"

I push the lid down and twist. Throw the open bottle. Pills rain down in a hyperbola.

I grab another. Melon fights me for it. I twist free of her grip. Scatter another pill rain.

"Do whatever you want!" she shouts. "You think I need pills? Look where we are!"

Bottle of vodka at the bottom of the pack to wash it down. I dump it. Make some mud.

Melon stomps off. Leaving her pack behind. Leaving me behind. I jog after. Catch her in a couple steps.

"Poison's not even a good way to do it. Stick to rope. It's faster."

"Thanks for the advice."

"I'm not giving you advice! How old are you? Sixteen?"

"Seventeen."

"What the hell is wrong with you at seventeen that you think you need to come here?"

She whips around to face me. The ferocious movement makes me stagger back.

"You think I can't have problems because I'm seventeen? My mother ran off. Okay? She ran off to Chicago when I was seven and left me in Omaha with my grandparents. They don't even like kids. Last year, she comes home just long enough to give me my father's name. Only time I've seen her since I was twelve. So I take the money I've been saving for college and I buy a trip here. To meet my father's family. But they don't want me either! Who am I to them? Some kid from another country? I'm here to find my father!"

Spit from her shouting lands on my face. I'm too stunned to answer. Not used to people emptying themselves. Not to me, the woman with the onryo who spends too much time with the dead.

At last, I think of words. "You think you're going to find family here?" I gesture at the trees. "Make a family of ghosts?"

"Why not? You're fucking one."

She can see that hurts. She's happy to have landed a punch.

"Leave me alone," she says.

"The trees won't let me." I hate to say it, but it's true. "I already half-belong to them. They won't let me leave without you."

Doubt flickers across Melon's face. She didn't intend to force me to die with her.

I push at her weakness. "Your father. Will you promise not to kill yourself if I help you find him?"

She hesitates. Nods. I can see from the flicker in her eyes that it's not a real promise. She'll still kill herself to stay with him if she can.

As long as she's with me, I've got time to convince her otherwise.

* * *

WE RETRIEVE her pack and walk in silence.

The girl's shoes squeak as we walk uphill. Our unwashed smell clings to our clothes.

Why do I care if Melon dies and takes me with her? I've been here seven years, flirting with death. Letting death kiss me. Waiting for her to bring me to a height I can't safely leap down from.

I always knew Sayomi would take me eventually, but not now, I never wanted it now. Seven years of soon, later, someday.

Maybe I never wanted to die at all.

We tread on springy feathers of lichen. Creepers wind around tree trunks like yureis' hair, beautiful and confining. Finger-like branches point in a thousand different directions.

Between trees, a shadowed mass blooms where there should be day.

The horde of ghosts.

I grab Melon's elbow. I know where to find her father.

* * *

GHOSTS' SHADOWS black the narrow, winding twists between trees. We run toward them as they stream toward us. Within moments, we're engulfed in dark.

I scream into the mass of ghosts. "We're looking for her father! You know where he is!"

Torchlight illuminates Melon's upturned face. She's all flickers and contrasts.

Something changes in the flow of ghosts. They move around us as if we're an island, leaving an empty space. A yurei floats into the opening.

Melon's father.

He wears the button-down shirt from the picture, faded and grayed. Too-long slacks drape over his feet—if he has feet. Empty cuffs hang two feet above the ground.

He doesn't have tumbling hair like traditional yurei, but what hair he has obscures his eyes. Impossible to tell where he's looking. What he's thinking.

"Manabu?" Melon's voice shakes.

The ghost's words scrape against each other like pumice stones. "*I was alone.*"

"Speak in English?" Melon pleads.

"*They didn't think I could do it. They thought I was a coward.*"

"Please. I know you used to speak English with my mother. She can't even say *domo arigato.*"

"*No one would hire me. I spent all day in the park.*"

A wind that affects nothing else blows around him. His clothing streams away from his body. Sometimes it presses tight against him, revealing the outline of his skeleton. His hair remains motionless, concealing his face.

I shout at Melon, "He's not even listening to you!"

She ignores me. "I'm your daughter! From America! I knew you'd understand me. You know what it's like to be alone."

"*I told my mother I'd talk to her landlord about the plumbing. She said I didn't have anything else to do. She pestered me until I said yes. She called on my cell phone while I was sitting in the park. 'Why haven't you done it yet? You can't even talk to the landlord.' She didn't think I could do it. She thought I was a coward.*"

"Please! I don't understand! Talk to me in English!"

"*I had an interview that day. Maybe I'd have gotten the job. Who knows? I went to the landlord. I told him to fix my mother's plumbing. He said he'd get to it. I slammed him against the wall. 'Get to it now.' He didn't think I was a coward then.*"

"Your...your mother's toilet...?"

"*He said he was going to call the police. I told him, 'Go ahead.' They could find me in the park. I left his house, but I didn't go to the park. I bought a train ticket instead.*"

I grab urgently for Melon's hand. "He's stuck! Listen! It's what they're like. They're fixed...fixed on loneliness, on kissing someone, on playing games..."

"*I was alone. They didn't think I could do it.*"

Her father has reached the end of his story that is also the beginning. He's repeating himself now, but Melon's still listening to him, not me. Yurei stream around us, their hair growing longer and shorter as the torchlight flickers.

I have to do something to get her attention.

I fumble in my pocket. The mokume-gane wedding ring. Polished by my worrying fingers, it glistens. I hurl it toward the yurei.

They descend, magpies after something shiny. Claws emerge from hair. Wordless, screaming voices rise.

"You see?" I shout. "That's all they are! Picking after scraps of lives *they chose* to leave behind!"

One snatches the ring. It disappears under the veil of her hair. Others screech.

Melon's father drones. "*They thought I was a coward. No one would hire me.*"

I rip open my pack and pull out the trash. Scissors, nail clippers, comb, compact.

I throw them toward the trees. Where each item falls, flocks of yurei descend.

"*I spent all day in the park. I told my mother I'd talk to her landlord about the plumbing.*"

"It might make sense to kill yourself if you thought it would stop the pain. But look at them! It doesn't stop! It just keeps going!"

"*She said I didn't have anything else to do.*"

"There's no family here! Look at them!"

Two yurei attack each other in the air. Their claws rake toward each other's throats.

"They'll tear each other apart for a shred of something living!"

"*She pestered me until I said yes. She called on my cell phone while I was sitting in the park. 'Why haven't you done it yet?'*"

It's not enough. Melon's gaze is still on her father. Full of longing. Full of hope.

I grab for a side pocket of her pack. She wrenches away, but I snatch the zipper. Open it, pull out what I saw her tuck there: the photo of her father's corpse.

I throw it at the ghost's feet. At once, he falls silent. As he recognizes himself, he becomes an arrow of greed and obsession. He dives to retrieve it, Melon forgotten.

"Do you see?" I ask. "Do you understand?"

I see the moment when Melon's gaze hardens. She turns away from her father. I grab her hand.

Wordlessly, we run through firelit dark, terrain rough beneath our feet. We stumble over roots and rocks. Barely manage not to fall.

The howling yurei horde pursues. I pull more trash from my pack. Strew it behind us. It slows them down, but they're still too close.

Melon shrugs off her pack. Abandons it.

I follow her lead and throw the expensive stuff. The trainers from the hanged man. A fan of money.

Our temporary lead widens. We glimpse sunlight through the trees. Burst into day so bright it makes us blink.

The shadows speed behind us. We've nothing else to throw.

From ahead, a drifting scent: mandarin oranges.

There she is, floating above the fork of a tree, the twisted thing that tangled me in this. I want to snarl. I want to punish her. But she's our only chance.

"Please!" I shout. "We need to get out!"

She doesn't rotate toward my voice. Was already facing us. Was probably watching all along.

She asks, "*The usual price?*"

"*Yes!*"

She floats toward us. Dread pricks the back of my neck.

"*Why are you helping now?*" I ask.

"*Now there are two of you to pay.*"

In front of us: her hair extending toward our bodies. Behind us: the yurei horde blocking out the light. Her hair reaches us before the horde does. Wraps us in its cocoon.

Tendrils tangle my eyelashes. Intrude into my ears, my nostrils. Horrible bug-shudder of dead-touch all over. Inescapable. We're buried alive in her hair.

Joy sparks her split ends like static electricity. Will she ever let us go?

Eventually, the hair unwinds. I can move my fingers. My limbs. She unveils my sight last. The yurei horde is gone, passed while we were hidden.

"Thanks," I say.

There's acid in my tone. It's hard to thank someone after they risk your life.

Gratitude in my tone, too. Hard not to be grateful after someone saves you.

She floats a meter away from us. Her hair is back to its normal length, sweeping to her knees, no longer voluminous enough to engulf two people.

"*Consider your parents, your siblings, your children,*" she says. "*Tell the police about your troubles.*"

A lock of her hair separates from the rest. Points to a gap between trees. "*End of a tape-road there,*" she says. "*It'll get you out.*"

She rotates to watch us leave.

* * *

"I WONDER who she was," Melon says. "Maybe she's from old Japan. Like her kimono."

"Hard to say."

"Maybe she's the first one who died in the forest."

"Maybe."

Melon and I sit in the parking lot. During the day, it's filled with tourist buses. Now, no one else is here.

We'll go back to town soon. Now we need rest.

"What am I going to do?" Melon asks plaintively.

Hard to answer a question like that. So painfully honest.

"You should call your grandparents."

"They don't care."

"They might."

She shakes her head. Looks away.

"Someone will care."

Her voice is quiet. "Yeah, right."

She inhales raggedly as if she's going to cry, but she doesn't. She doesn't say anything either.

Speaking feelings is hard for me, but I try. "You'll be happy. Someday. Even for a few minutes. It's more than the ghosts get." Remembering what the yurei said in the forest, I add, "All roads lead to Aokigahara. You may as well walk slowly."

The words leave a too-sweet aftertaste. Sentimental. But they make Melon smile.

Maybe a little sweetness will keep her from dying so young.

Isn't that why I've spent seven years in Aokigahara? Wishing to stop a girl from dying young?

We sit quietly for a few more minutes before we walk to town. I sit by while she places an international collect call to her grandparents.

* * *

TWO A.M.

Wind whistles without blowing.

My Sayomi.

She coils hair around my wrists. Draws me closer.

She's different. Almost transparently pale. So cold that her embrace is like spring rain: sudden, drenching, chill.

Hair strips my clothes. Winds between my thighs. A humid smell rises between us. Tears and desire mingle on our skins.

She opens me. Begins her caress. Cold: both shocking and exquisite.

We half-embrace, half-struggle on the floor of my single room. Same as we've been for seven years. Caught between yearning and anger.

Does she blame me? For leaving? For failing to see what I should have seen?

Do I blame her for drawing me back? For tangling me in death while I was still alive?

I push my fingers between her thighs. In her midst, a spot of warmth. She tenses as I find it.

Hair simultaneously pushes me away and draws me closer. Its tips tie themselves in knots. Sayomi's expression is furious, rapturous, relieved.

All things I'm feeling, too.

My tongue, melting her ice.

Her cold, numbing my lips.

We shiver together as she comes.

At the apex, she screams. For once, it's not rage. It's consummation. It's expiation. It's catharsis.

As the sound dissolves her, I know she won't return. Her ghost-form dissipates, leaving behind only bleached, white bones.

My Sayomi.

I curl myself around her skeleton. It's no longer as cold as ice, only as cold as death.

I sleep there, on the floor, with what's left of her, just as the suicide watch sleeps beside the bodies they bring back. For one night at least, someone must stay to console the newly dead. To ease their loneliness as best we can before morning.

When we have to go on.

Fields of Gold

WHEN DENNIS died, he found himself in another place. Dead people came at him with party hats and presents. Noise makers bleated. Confetti fell. It felt like the most natural thing in the world.

His family was there. Celebrities were there. People Dennis had never seen before in his life were there. Dennis danced under a disco ball with Cleopatra and great-grandma Flora and some dark-haired chick and cousin Joe and Alexander the Great. When he went to the buffet table for a tiny cocktail wiener in pink sauce, Dennis saw Napoleon trying to grope his Aunt Phyllis. She smacked him in the tri-corner hat with her clutch bag.

Napoleon and Shakespeare and Cleopatra looked just like Dennis had expected them to. Henry VIII and Socrates and Jesus, too. Cleopatra wore a long linen dress with a jeweled collar, a live asp coiled around her wrist like a bracelet. Socrates sipped from a glass of hemlock. Jesus bobbed his head up and down like a windshield ornament as he ladled out the punch.

Dennis squinted into the distance, but he couldn't make out the boundaries of the place. The room, if it was a room, was large and rectangular and brightly lit from above, like some kind of cosmic gym decorated for prom, complete with drifts of multi-colored balloons and hand-lettered poster board signs. On second glance, the buffet tables turned out to be narrow and collapsible like the ones from Dennis's high school cafeteria. Thankfully, unlike high school, the booze flowed freely and the music was actually good.

As Dennis meandered back toward the dance floor, an imposing figure that he dimly recognized as P. T. Barnum clapped him on the back. "Welcome! Welcome!" the balding man boomed.

An elderly lady stood in Barnum's lee. Her face was familiar from old family portraits. "Glad to see you, dear."

"Thanks," said Dennis as the unlikely couple whirled into the crowd.

* * *

THINGS DENNIS did not accomplish from his under thirty-five goals list (circa age twelve):

Own a jet.

Host a TV show where he played guitar with famous singers.

Win a wrestling match with a lion.

Pay Billy Whitman $200 to eat dirt in front of a TV crew.

Go sky-diving.

Divorce a movie star.

* * *

AS DENNIS listened to the retreating echo of P. T. Barnum's laughter, a pair of cold hands slipped around his waist from behind. He jumped like a rabbit.

"Hey there, Menace," said a melted honey voice.

Dennis turned back into the familiar embrace of his favorite cousin, Melanie. She was the one who'd been born a year and three days before he was, and who'd lived half a mile away when they were kids. She was also the one he'd started dry-humping in the abandoned lot behind Ping's groceries when he was eleven and she was twelve.

"Mel," blurted Dennis.

"Asswipe," Melanie replied.

She stood on her tiptoes to slip a hug around Dennis's neck. She wore cropped jean shorts and a thin white tee that showed her bra straps. She smelled like cheap lotion and cherry perfume. A blonde ponytail swung over her shoulder, deceptively girlish in contrast with her hard eyes and filthy mouth. She was young and ripe and vodka-and-cigarettes skinny in a twenty-one-year-old way, just like she had been the day he was called to view her at the morgue—except that the tracks where her jilted boyfriend had run her over with his jeep were gone, as if they'd never been there at all.

"God," said Dennis. "It's good to see you."

"You're not a punch in the face either."

Dennis reached out to touch the side of her head. At the funeral, the mortician had arranged a makeshift hairpiece made of lilies to cover the dent they hadn't been able to repair in time for the open casket. At first Melanie flinched, but then she eased into his touch, pushing against his hand like a contented cat. Her hair felt like corn silk, the skull beneath it smooth and strong.

She pulled away and led Dennis on a meandering path through the crowd to the drinks table. "How'd you kick it?" she asked conversationally.

"Diabetic coma," said Dennis. "Karen pulled the plug."

"That's not what I heard," said Melanie. "I heard it was murder."

* * *

DENNIS HALTER had married Karen Halter (née Worth) on the twenty-second of November, six months to the day after their college graduation.

Karen was the one who proposed. She bought Dennis a $2,000 guitar instead of an engagement ring. She took him out for heavy carbohydrate Italian (insulin at the ready) and popped the question casually over light beer. "I can still return the guitar if you don't want to," she added.

Karen was an art history major who was being groomed for museum curation. Dennis was an anthropology major (it had the fewest required classes) who was beginning to worry about the fact that he hadn't been discovered yet. Karen was Type A. Dennis's personality begged for the invention of a Type Z.

Melanie was similar to Dennis, personality-wise, except for the mean streak that had gotten her expelled for fist fighting during her senior year of high school. She and Karen had only met once, six months before Karen proposed, at a Halter family Thanksgiving. They didn't need to exchange a word. It was hate at first sight.

"Hillbilly whore," Karen called Melanie, though not to her face.

Lacking such compunction, Melanie had called Karen a "control-freak cunt" over pecan pie. She drunk-dialed Dennis three weeks later to make sure he hadn't forgotten her opinion. "When that bitch realizes you're never going to change, she's going to have your balls on a platter. If you marry her, I swear I'll hand her the knife myself."

Melanie died instead.

* * *

"MURDER?" SAID Dennis. "No, I wanted her to pull the plug. It was in my living will. I never wanted to live my life as a vegetable."

"Unless it was a couch potato, huh?"

Melanie spoke with the too-precise diction of an over-compensating drunk. Her tone was joking, but held a vicious undercurrent.

She flailed one hand at Dennis's spare tire. The gin she was pouring with her other definitely wasn't her first. Probably not her fourth either.

"Worked out for you, didn't it, Menace the Dennis?" she continued. "Spent your life skipping church only to luck out in the end. Turns out we all go to the same place. Saint, sinner, and suicide."

Dennis's jaw clenched. "I didn't commit suicide."

"Didn't say you did. Sinner."

"And you weren't?"

Melanie poured three fingers of rum into a second Solo cup and went to add Coke. Dennis grabbed the two liter bottle out of her hand.

"Can't drink that with alcohol," he said, irritated, remembering that bender when he was fifteen and she'd promised him it wouldn't matter whether his mixers were diet or regular. He'd ended up in ketoacidosis.

Melanie rolled her eyes. "Think your body works the way it used to? You're dead, moron."

"Fine," said Dennis, annoyance clashing with embarrassment. "Give it to me then."

He rescued the Solo cup and poured a long stream of Coke. Melanie watched reproachfully, gulping her gin.

"You were okay before you started dating that stuck-up bitch," she said. "Had time for a beer and a laugh. Maybe you deserved what that cunt did to you."

"I told you. It was in my will."

"That's not what I'm talking about, jerkwad."

"What *are* you talking about?"

For a moment, Melanie looked simultaneously sly and uncomfortable, as though she were going to spill the beans on something important. Then she shook her head, ponytail whipping, and returned to her rant. "If you'd kept doing me, maybe I wouldn't have ended up with Al. Maybe he wouldn't have gone off the deep-end when I broke it off. I could still be alive. I could be the one in that fancy condo."

"Melanie," said Dennis. "Shut up."

Melanie made to throw an honest-to-God punch. Gin splashed over her shirt and onto the floor. "Look at this!" She gestured broadly, spilling even more. "What the hell is wrong with you?"

Before Dennis could answer, she stormed off in a huff, rapidly disappearing into the mass of people.

* * *

WHEN HE was alive, Dennis had told people he'd married Karen because she was his type of girl. He hadn't told them that one skinny blonde with a D-cup was basically as good as another.

When he was alive, Dennis had told people he'd married Karen because she was driven and smart and successful. He hadn't told them she made him feel inferior by comparison, sometimes because she told him he was.

When he was alive, Dennis had told people he married Karen because he was a simple man with simple needs. He hadn't told them he kept those simple needs satisfied by fucking around at least twice a year.

When he was alive, Dennis had told people he'd married Karen because she was the kind of girl who knew what she wanted and went after it. Time was like water in Dennis's hands, always flowing through his fingers, leaving him damp but never sated. Karen drank from the stream of time. She made things happen.

One of the things she made happen was getting married. Well, what else was Dennis going to do? It wasn't as if he had plans. Okay, he did have plans, but diamond albums didn't just fall into your lap.

Karen proposed and it made sense, Dennis had told people when he was alive. That's why they got married.

That part was true.

* * *

THINGS DENNIS did not accomplish from his under thirty-five goals list (circa age nineteen):

Sign with a label.
Hit the charts.
Get into *Rolling Stone.*
Earn $1,000,000.
Have at least one girl/girl threesome.
Screw Libby Lowell, his roommate's girlfriend.
Play in concert with Ted Nugent, Joe Satriani, and Eddie Van Halen.
Get recognized on the street by someone he'd never met.

* * *

DENNIS STARED after Melanie in minor shock. Somehow he'd figured this kind of social terrorism would be one of the things that ended in the stillness of the grave.

But if anyone was going to keep making incoherent, drunken rants fourteen years after going into the ground, it was Melanie. She'd always been a pain in the ass when she was drunk. She'd introduced Dennis to alcohol back when she first learned to pick the lock on her father's liquor cabinet with a bobby pin. They'd experimented together to figure out just how much sugar Dennis could ingest with his booze without over-taxing his liver.

From day one, Melanie had drunk until she couldn't see straight and then used it as an excuse to say exactly what she thought. Not that she wasn't a fun drunk. Some of the best nights of his life were the ones they'd spent together as drunk teenagers. She'd start out hurling insults until he left in disgust, only to show up on his porch at three a.m., laughing and apologizing and determined to convince him to join her in making prank calls and harassing the neighbors' cows.

She was Melanie. She was the kind of girl who goaded a guy into running over her with his Jeep. But it was hard to stay mad. Especially now that both of them were dead.

The smell of old tobacco arrived, along with a cold hand patting Dennis's shoulder. Dennis was startled to find that both belonged to his late Uncle Ed, Melanie's father.

"Always thought we should have spent more time raising her right," Ed said.

The old man looked just as hangdog as he had in the moment twenty years ago when he'd fallen off his roof while cleaning the gutters. There he'd been, his feet starting to slide, but he hadn't looked scared so much as wrung out and regretful, as if someone had just told him the Christmas pie he'd been looking forward to was gone and he'd have to make do with fruit cake instead.

He was wearing his best brown suit with a skinny, maroon tie. Slicked back hair exaggerated his widow's peak. The weak chin and expressive eyebrows were family traits, although Ed had a lean, wiry build unlike most Halter men, on account of a parasitic infection he'd contracted during his military days that left him permanently off his feed.

Uncle Ed. Christ. Back home, everyone Dennis's age cussed blue when they were on their own, but even Mel had kept a civil tongue in front of the 'rents. "How much did you hear?" he asked.

"'Bout all of it."

"I'm sorry."

Ed gave a rueful shrug. "You have no idea what she gets up to. The other day she stripped naked in front of everyone and started sucking off President Garfield."

"Shit," said Dennis without thinking. "Uh, I mean—"

"Sounds right to me. She sure can be a little shit."

Suddenly, a grin split Ed's melancholy face. It was the same grin he'd flashed when fourteen-year-old Dennis let slip that he'd gone through all the senior cheerleaders one by one until Veronica Steader agreed to be his homecoming date.

"Of course, I was into Mary Todd Lincoln at the time." Ed's leer widened to show even more teeth. "Good woman." He slapped Dennis on the back. "You get yourself one of those. You've had enough of the other kind."

* * *

DENNIS HAD never watched his diet very carefully. Not as carefully as he needed to anyway. Other kids got to eat Doritos and Oreos at lunch and they didn't even have to worry about it. When Dennis was eight, that righteously pissed him off.

It didn't piss him off enough that he tried to eat exactly the way they did. He wasn't stupid. But it pissed him off enough that he acted a little reckless, a little foolish. Always just a little, though, so that whatever happened, he could plausibly claim—to everyone including himself—that there was nothing deliberate about it.

Eventually, even he believed he was too irresponsible to take care of himself.

* * *

THE PARTY had moved on to the stage where everyone was too tired to be gregarious but also too drunk to stop partying. Everyone had gathered into small, intense clusters, leaning urgently toward each other to share dramatic whispers, hands cutting the air with emphasis. From time to time, an over-loud exclamation punctured the susurration.

Dennis surveyed the crowd, identifying faces. There was Blackbeard with Grandpa Avery and a buck-toothed redhead. And over there was that

Chinese guy who used to live down the street, chatting with Moses and Aunt Phyllis. Most of the groups consisted entirely of strangers.

These were some of the things Dennis picked up as he wandered through the crowd:

1) Death had its own time frame in which connected events bent around mortal time to touch each other. In dead time, the assassination of Archduke Ferdinand had coincided with the deaths of millions of World War Two soldiers. For reasons widely subject to speculation, so had the sinking of the RMS Titanic and the deaths of several big game huntsmen touring French colonies in Africa.
2) The dead also had their own vocabulary. Recently dead people were called rotters or wormies. People who'd been dead a long time were called dusties. Dusties tended to stay in their own enclaves, secluded from the modern ideas and inventions that scared them. Famous dead people were called celebs and they
3) were considered by popular opinion to be fakes. This allegation caused Blackbeard to roar with anger and threaten to march the speaker off a plank. It was pointed out to him that this was the sort of behavior that had created the theory that celebs were fakes in the first place. Celebrities conformed too closely to their legends. Cleopatra was always seductive and never bored or put-upon. Lincoln declaimed nonstop poetic speeches. And hadn't someone spotted Lady MacBeth earlier that evening when she wasn't even real?
4) Reality, it seemed, was a contentious issue. Mortality shaped the living world by imposing limits. In the limitless afterlife, the shape of things deformed. That was one reason dead people came to parties. Rotters still carried an impression of the living world. It was like going home again for a little while. Besides, there was good food, and who didn't like watching General Sherman march up and down the linoleum, threatening to burn Atlanta?

While Dennis pondered these new pieces of information, he also picked up a number of more personal things. He had an intuitive sense of where these latter were leading, though, and it wasn't somewhere he wanted to go. Consequently, he performed the time-tested mental contortions he'd developed as a third grader who ate too much sugar while pretending he hadn't done anything wrong. Dennis was a master of self-denial; he didn't even let himself realize there was something he wouldn't let himself realize.

For instance:

1) Whenever Dennis passed a group of strangers, they interrupted their conversations to peer as he passed, and then returned to their huddles to whisper even more urgently.
2) Their renewed whispers were punctuated with phrases like "Do you think he deserved it?" and "Poor son of a bitch."
3) At a certain point, they also started saying, "At least the wife got what's coming to her."
4) These last remarks started occurring at approximately the same time as people began disappearing to attend another party.

* * *

AS THE crowd thinned, Dennis finally located someone standing alone, a very drunk flight attendant staring blankly at a tangle of streamers. On being pressed, she identified herself as Wilda. She was unbelievably hot, like a stewardess from a fifties movie, in her mid-to-late twenties with long, straight blonde hair, and a figure that filled out all the tailored curves of her uniform.

The hint of an exotic perfume was all but drowned out by the stench of alcohol. She wasn't currently crying, but tears had streaked her mascara.

Dennis decided to pick her up.

"Melancholy stage?" he asked.

She spoke as if her lips were numb. "What's the point? On this side?"

"Of being melancholy? I didn't know there was ever a point."

"Mortality," she said gravely.

Her expression altered ever so slightly. Dennis tried to echo back an appropriate seriousness.

"I knew a man once," she went on. "Died in the same crash as me. An actor. Very famous. I was so nervous when I poured his in-flight drink I thought I'd spill. He asked for orange juice."

Dennis gestured back toward the buffet tables. "Do *you* want a drink?"

She ignored him. "After we died, he never spoke a word. Not a word. He...his mouth would open and this sound would come out...eeeeeeeeeee... like a dying refrigerator..."

She looked at Dennis urgently. Her eyes focused briefly. They were weird, electric blue, like a sky lit up by lightning.

"He was grieving for himself, I think. Or maybe he just used up all his words in the world? And when he died, he was just so happy to be quiet that he never wanted to talk again?" She blinked, slowly, her wet mascara smudging more black beneath her eyes. "It's like the celebs. You know?"

"Would you like to kiss me?" Dennis asked.

"I bet the real dead celebrities are nothing special. They probably blend in. Like my friend. But the fake ones, I think they're made from a kind of collective pressure. None of us lived our lives the way we wanted to. It gets mixed up, all our needs, our unsatisfied desires, the things we wanted to be back when we were alive. Beautiful. Famous. The best of our potential. We make the celebs to be like that for us. Since we can't."

Wilda gestured vaguely toward the crowd. Dennis turned to see Benjamin Franklin demonstrating his kite, which rapidly became tangled with the multi-colored balloons. Marilyn Monroe struggled with her skirt while standing over an air-conditioning vent tucked next to some bleachers. Gandhi sat in the middle of a group positioned near the buffet tables, pointedly not eating.

"You should stay away from them," said Wilda softly. "They're bright and crazy. They suck you down."

Dennis turned back to look at her beautiful, tear-stained face. "I'd rather be with you anyway."

She blinked at him, too lost in her own drunkenness to hear. Or maybe she just didn't believe him? Dennis glanced over his shoulder at Marilyn, ripe and coy, dark-outlined eyes sparkling. Something dark and furious clenched in his stomach. He was only thirty-five! Marilyn made him so choked up with jealousy he couldn't breathe.

He turned back toward Wilda and leaned in to dab some of the liner from beneath her eyes. She started toward his embrace but got tangled up with her own feet and started to fall. Dennis caught her before she could hit the floor.

She looked up at him, smiling vaguely. "I wanted to be a gymnast. You know? I was good," she said, and then, "Do you think it's cheating?"

"What?" murmured Dennis.

"My husband's still alive."

"So's my wife."

"What if she weren't? Would it be cheating then?"

"I don't know. I wasn't that faithful when we were both alive."

"Neither was I."

Wilda's voice cracked like ice. Tears filled her eyes, colorless like vodka. Dennis looked down at her left hand where she wore a tan line but no ring.

"I don't like being dead," said Wilda.

"I'm sorry," said Dennis.

He held her, silently, until she recovered enough to stand on her own. "I'm sorry, too," she said at last. "I should go to the other party."

Dennis tried to fake a smile. "Don't drink too much while you're there."

Wilda reached out to touch his shoulder. Her fingertips were frozen.

"When you figure it out," she said, "try not to be too sad."

She faded away.

* * *

A FEW of the times Dennis cheated on Karen:

1) The coed who got stuck in the Dallas airport after her flight was canceled who he wooed with four margaritas, his best dozen dirty jokes, and a rendition of Sting's "Desert Rose."
2) The bartender in Phoenix who'd just been dumped by her fiancé and said she needed to know what it was like with a guy who could commit.
3) The drunk divorcée from the Internet ad who got on the hotel bed and dropped her pants without even a word to acknowledge he was there.

A few of the things Dennis pretended not to notice about his marriage:

1) The way Karen's sense of humor about other women had changed. When they were younger, if she saw a pretty blonde who was about her shape walking past them in the mall, she'd say, "I bet she's your type." If she was in a teasing mood, she'd whisper about all the things she and the other girl would do to Dennis if they had him at their mercy. In recent days, her eyes had started getting hard when they even saw blonde girls on TV. She'd angle her face away from him, trying to hide her disgust.
2) How Karen no longer laughed indulgently when he forgot things. She still took care of him: she did his laundry, she

found his keys, she rescheduled his doctor's appointments. But she moved through the actions mechanically, her blank expression never flickering.

3) And then there was the worst thing, the one Dennis had taken the most pains to hide from himself—the flicker he'd seen when Karen came home exhausted from a late night's work and found him still awake at two a.m., sitting on the couch and eating beans out of a can. She picked up the dishes he'd left on the coffee table and carried them to the sink, grumbling to herself so faintly he could hardly hear it, "It's like I'm his mother." He looked up and caught the brief flash on her face. It was the same emotion he'd heard in her voice: contempt.

* * *

THE MORNING of November nineteenth was three days before their thirteenth anniversary and two months and five days before Dennis's thirty-fifth birthday. Karen Halter (née Worth) proposed they stay in that Friday night to celebrate both occasions. She proposed an evening of drinking and making love. Dennis liked having sex when he was drunk, and although it wasn't Karen's preference, she tried to indulge him from time to time. She knew it reminded him of being young.

Fifteen years ago, when they'd started dating, Karen had carefully reviewed the guidelines for mixing type one diabetes and alcohol. The liver was involved in both processing alcohol and regulating blood sugar, and consequently, a type one diabetic who got carelessly drunk could preoccupy his liver with the one so that it couldn't manage the other. Glucose levels required a tricky balance. If they went too high, they could damage a variety of systems. If they went too low, one could become hypoglycemic or even fall into a coma.

It was trivial to give Dennis more insulin than he needed. She let him inject himself, just in case someone checked later. Not that they would. Everyone knew Dennis was too irresponsible to take care of himself.

She worried when he started puking, but he didn't suspect anything. He just thought he was drunk.

The sleeping pills were his idea. He was feeling too sick to get to sleep on his own. He asked if he could borrow one of her Ambien and before she could say yes or no, he'd pulled the bottle out of the medicine cabinet. She watched him drunkenly struggle to unscrew the lid.

She hadn't meant to go this far. She'd wanted to shock him. She'd wanted him to see how bad things could get and grow the fuck up. Yes, she wanted him to suffer a little, too, just so he'd know what it felt like.

If she let him take the pill, it'd be more than that. He wouldn't be awake to monitor his condition. He wouldn't be able to call an ambulance when things started going really wrong. He'd get sicker than she'd intended. He could even die.

Karen had matched Dennis drink for drink. No one would suspect her of wrongdoing. At worst, they'd think she'd also been too drunk to notice his symptoms.

With a shock, it occurred to Karen that maybe she'd been planning this all along. Maybe she'd been slowly taking the steps that could lead to Dennis's death without admitting to herself that was what she was doing. She knew how self-denial worked by now; she'd been married to Dennis for thirteen years, after all.

She eased the bottle from his hand. "Let me do that," she said, unscrewing the cap. She poured out two pills: one for him and one for her.

Now neither of them could call for help.

In the morning, memory clear and heart pounding, Karen called 911 in a genuine panic. She rode with Dennis in the ambulance, weeping real tears. She cried because she'd become a murderess and she didn't want to see herself that way. She also cried because she wasn't sorry she'd done it and that scared her even more.

The doctors proclaimed the coma unusually severe. Brain damage had occurred. Over the next several weeks, using sterile, equivocal comments, they made it clear that there was no hope. They would need a decision.

Karen had set herself on this path. There was no escaping it. Dennis's living will was clear. She told them to pull the plug.

During the weeks when Dennis lay comatose, Karen began having nightmares. She researched bad dreams on the Internet and confirmed that anxiety produced an increase in negative dream imagery. Nothing to be concerned about. Except she kept dreaming about the strangest thing—that trashy cousin Dennis had admitted to fucking when he was a kid. They'd gone to her funeral a few months before Karen proposed. Dennis had bent over the casket and wept for nearly a quarter of an hour. Karen could understand why he was upset; the girl was family. But deep in her gut, whether it was fair or not, she couldn't help being appalled. He was mourning his partner in incest.

Afterward, at the visitation, various family members asked her to stand next to the big, glossy photograph of the deceased they'd hung on the wall. "You look just like her," everyone said, which made Karen even more uncomfortable. She tried to laugh off her reaction as indignance that she'd ever dress like that, but she had a niggling feeling there was something more profound. She *did* look eerily like the girl, the same close-set eyes, the same blunt chin, the same shade of blonde hair. It was as if Dennis was trying to recreate the relationship he'd had when he was eleven, as if it didn't matter to him that Karen had her own thoughts and feelings and personality, as long as she looked like his first, forbidden love.

In Karen's dreams, the blonde cousin had a knife. She chased Karen down winding asphalt streets, upraised metal shining in the shadows. "I don't care what I said," she growled. "I'm not going to let you cut his balls off. I'll cut you first."

The day Karen told them to pull the plug, she woke with her heart pounding so hard that she thought she was going to have to check into the hospital herself. The feeling faded when she went down to give the decision in person, but intensified again as she got in her car to drive home. She'd told them she couldn't handle staying to watch Dennis die, which was true, but not for the reasons they supposed.

Outside, thick, dingy clouds of smog dimmed the sunlight to a sickly brown. Headlights and taillights glared in Karen's windshield, a fraction too bright.

Horns screamed in the wake of near misses. Karen watched carefully, mapping out the traffic in her mind's eye, making sure she didn't veer out of her narrow lanes or crash into the broken-down SUVs on the side of the road. She was the kind of woman who had memorized the safety manual that came with her vehicle, and could recite all the local laws regarding child safety seats even though she'd never had any children in her car.

Despite her meticulousness, as Karen pulled into the intersection after waiting for the green, she failed to see the skinny blonde girl, her white t-shirt thin enough to show her bra-straps, who jogged into the crosswalk. She pounded the breaks and yanked on the steering wheel, but it was already too late. Rubber screeched. Metal crunched against metal. The car next to hers careened sideways with the impact. Karen fell toward the windshield, her airbag failing to deploy, the steering wheel breaking against her head.

It took Karen almost three weeks to die, but in the land of the dead, time twisted around itself to join connected events. So it was only a few hours into Dennis's party that Karen's began, and his gossiping guests faded away to attend the newest scandal.

* * *

THINGS DENNIS did not accomplish from his under thirty-five goals list (circa age thirty-four):

Start another band.
Play some gigs in the area.
Get his sugar under control.
Be nicer to Karen.
Stop cheating.
Go to the gym.

* * *

DENNIS'S SELF-DENIAL had finally reached its breaking point. He ran between the fading guests. "How do I get there? You have to show me! I have to see her!"

They winked out like stars from a graying dawn sky, not one of them letting slip what he needed to know.

The empty gym, if it was a gym, seemed to be disappearing on the edges. Perhaps it was. The dead people had talked about imposing their own shapes on the limitless afterlife. Maybe shapelessness was taking over.

One spot near the buffet tables remained bright, a fraction of the dance floor underneath the disco ball. Uncle Ed stood alone in the middle, fiddling with the coin slot in the juke box.

He turned as Dennis approached. "I wanted 'Young Love,'" he said, "but they've only got 'After You've Gone.' Not worth a quarter." He sighed. "Oh, well. That's the afterlife, I guess."

The juke box lit up as the coin slid into its machinery. It whirred, selecting a record. Dennis recognized the bright, slightly distorted strains as a hit from the forties.

Ed selected a pastel blue balloon and began to whirl it around like a dance partner. Dennis stood tensely, arms crossed.

"Why didn't you tell me?"

Ed dipped the balloon. "About what?"

"About Karen."

"Figured you'd find out sooner or later. No sense ruining a perfectly good party until you did."

"I'd have wanted to know."

"Sorry then."

"How do I get over there? I've got to talk to her."

"You can't."

"I've got to!"

"She doesn't want you. You can't go bothering someone who doesn't want you. That's one of the rules we agree on. Otherwise someone could stalk you forever." Ed gave a mild shrug. "I was used badly by a woman once, you know."

Dennis glared silently.

"My first wife, Lilac," Ed went on. "Not Melanie's mother. Lilac died before you all were born. Your mom never liked her."

"Mom never liked Karen either."

"A perceptive woman, your mother. Well, things were good with me and Lilac for a while. We spent my whole party making out. Afterward, we found some old Scottish castle out with the dusties and rolled around in the grass for longer than you spent alive. It didn't last long, though. Relatively. See, while I was still alive, she'd already met another dead guy. They'd been together for centuries before I kicked it. She was just curious about what it would be like to be with me again. Near broke my heart."

"Ed," Dennis said. "Karen murdered me. I have to know why."

Ed released the balloon. It flew upward and disappeared into grey.

"Have to?" Ed asked. "When you were alive, you had to have food and water. What's 'have to' mean to you anymore?"

"Ed, please!"

"All right, then, I'll take a gander. I've been dead a long time, but I bet I know a few things. Now, you didn't deserve what Karen did to you. No one deserves that. But you had your hand in making it happen. I'm not saying you didn't have good qualities. You could play a tune and tell a joke, and you were usually in a good humor when you weren't sulking. Those are important things. But you never thought about anyone else. Not only wouldn't you stir yourself to make a starving man a sandwich, but you'd have waited for him to bring you one before you stirred yourself to eat. One thing I've learned is people will give you a free lunch from time to time, but only so long as they think you're trying. And if you don't try, if they get to thinking you're treating them with disdain, well then. Sometimes they get mean."

"I didn't treat Karen with disdain," Dennis said.

Ed blinked evenly.

"It's not that I don't think about other people," Dennis said. "I just wanted someone to take care of me. The whole world, everything was so hard. Even eating the wrong thing could kill you. I wanted someone to watch out for me, I guess. I guess I wanted to stay a kid."

"You married a problem solver," said Ed. "Then you became a problem."

When Dennis thought about Ed, he always thought about that moment when he'd watched him fall off the roof. Failing that, he thought of the mostly silent man who sat in the back of family gatherings and was always first to help out with a chore. But now, with his words still stinging, Dennis remembered a different Uncle Ed, the one who'd always been called to finish off the barn cats who got sick, the one everyone relied on to settle family disputes because they knew he wouldn't play favorites no matter who was involved.

Ed didn't look so much like the man who'd fallen off the roof anymore. His wrinkles had tightened, his yellowing complexion brightening to a rosy pink. His hair was still slicked back from his forehead with Brilliantine, but now there were generous, black locks of it.

He straightened his suit jacket and it became a white tee-shirt, snug over faded jeans. He grinned as he stuck his hands in his pockets. His teeth were large and straight and shiny white.

"I always figured we'd have kids," Dennis said. "I can't do that here, can I? And the band, I was always going to get started with that again, as soon as I got things going, as soon as I found the time…"

Dennis trailed off. The juke box spun to a stop, clicking as it returned the record to its place. Its lights guttered for a moment before flicking off.

"I'm dead," said Dennis, plaintively. "What do I do?"

Ed spread his hands toward the gym's grey edges. "Hop from party to party. Find a cave with the dusties. Get together with a girl and play house until the continents collide. Whatever you want. You'll find your way."

A newsboy cap appeared in Ed's hand. He tugged it on and tipped the brim.

"Now if you'll excuse me," he continued. "I need to pay my respects."

"To my murderer?"

"She's still family."

"Don't leave me alone," Dennis pleaded.

Ed was already beginning to fade.

Dennis sprinted forward to grab his collar.

* * *

WHEN DENNIS was four, he found his grandfather's ukulele in the attic, buried under a pile of newspapers. It was a four-string soprano pineapple made of plywood with a spruce soundboard. Tiny figures of brown women in grass skirts gyrated across the front, painted grins eerily broad.

The year Dennis turned six, his parents gave him a bike with training wheels for Christmas instead of the guitar he asked for. After a major tantrum, they wised up and bought him a three-quarter sized acoustic with two-tone lacquer finish in red and black. It was too big, but Dennis eventually got larger. The songbook that came with it included chords and lyrics for "Knockin' on Heaven's Door," "Leaving on a Jet Plane," and "Yellow Submarine."

The summer when Dennis was fifteen, he wheedled his grandparents into letting him do chores around their place for $2.50 an hour until he saved enough to buy a used stratocaster and an amp. He stayed up until midnight every night for the next six months, playing that thing in the corner of the basement his mother had reluctantly cleared out next to the water heater. He failed science and math, and only barely squeaked by with a D in English, but it was worth it.

The guitar Karen bought him when they got engaged was the guitar of his dreams. A custom Gibson Les Paul hollow-body with a maple top, mahogany body, ebony fret board, cherryburst finish, and curves like Jessica Rabbit. He hadn't been able to believe what he was seeing. Just looking at it set off strumming in his head.

As she popped the question, Karen ran her index finger gently across the abalone headstock inlay. The tease of her fingertip sent a shiver down his spine. It was the sexiest thing he'd ever seen.

* * *

EVERYTHING BLURRED.

Dennis and Ed reappeared in the rooftop garden of the museum where Karen had worked. It looked the way it did in summer, leafy shrubs and potted trees rising above purple, red and white perennials. The conjured garden was much larger than the real one; it stretched out as far as Dennis could see in all directions, blurring into verdant haze at the horizon.

Seurat stood at his easel in front of a modernist statue, stabbing at the canvas with his paintbrush. Figures from Karen's family and/or the art world strolled between ironwork benches, sipping martinis. Marie Antoinette, in *robe à la Polonaise* and *pouf*, distributed *petit fours* from a tray while reciting her signature line.

Dennis glimpsed Wilda, seemingly recovered from her melancholia, performing a series of acrobatic dance moves on a dais.

And then he saw Karen.

She sat on a three-legged stool, sipping a Midori sour as she embarked on a passionate argument about South African modern art with an elderly critic Dennis recognized from one of her books. She looked more sophisticated than he remembered. Makeup made her face dramatic, her eyebrows shaped into thin arches, a hint of dark blush sharpening her cheekbones. A beige summer gown draped elegantly around her legs. There was a vulnerability in her eyes he hadn't seen in ages, a tenderness beneath the blue that had vanished years ago.

Dennis felt as if it would take him an eternity to take her in, but even dead time eventually catches up.

Ed, struggling to pry Dennis's fingers off his collar, gave an angry shout. Both Karen and the old man beside her turned to look straight at them.

Ed twisted Dennis's fingers until one of them made a snapping sound. Shocked, Dennis dropped his grip.

"Christ!" said Ed, glaring at Dennis as he rubbed his reddened throat. "What the hell is wrong with you?" He turned away from Dennis as if washing his hands of him, tipped his hat to Karen, and then stalked off into the green.

"How are you here?" Karen sounded more distressed than angry. "They told me you couldn't be."

"I hitched a ride."

"But that shouldn't matter. They said—"

Karen quieted in the wake of the noise from the crowd that had begun to form around them. Ordinary people and celebs, strangers and friends and family and neighbors, all gossiping and shoving as they jockeyed for front row views.

The elderly art critic straightened and excused himself to the safety of the onlookers. Dennis stepped into his position.

"Maybe you let me in," Dennis said. "Maybe you really wanted me here."

Karen gave a strangled laugh. "I want you out and I want you in. I can't make up my mind. That sounds like the shape of it."

"You murdered me," said Dennis.

"I murdered you," said Karen.

Behind them, Dennis heard the noise of a scuffle, some New Jersey guido pitting himself against H. L. Mencken.

"I didn't mean to do it," Karen continued. "I don't think I did, at least."

Dennis swallowed.

"I'm sorry," Karen said. "Sorrier than I can tell you."

"You're only saying that because you're dead."

"No. What would be the point?"

Dennis heard the guido hit the ground as H. L. Mencken declared his victory in verse. A small round of applause ended the incident as the throng refocused on Dennis and Karen. Dennis had thought he'd want to hit her or scream at her. Some part of her must have wanted him to do that, must have known she deserved to be punished. He wondered if anyone would try to stop him if he attacked her. He got the impression no one would.

"I hate you," Dennis told her. It was mostly true.

"Me, too," said Karen.

"I didn't when we were alive. Not all the time, anyway."

"Me, too."

They both fell silent. Straining to overhear, the crowd did, too. In the background, there were bird calls, the scent of daisies, the whoosh of traffic three stories below.

"I don't think," said Dennis, "that I want to be near you anymore."

So, according to the rules of the land of the dead, he wasn't.

* * *

THINGS DENNIS did accomplish from his under thirty-five goals lists (various ages):

Eat raw squid.

Own a gaming console.

Star in an action movie.* (*After a bad day when he was twenty-four, Dennis decided to broaden the definition of "star" to include his role as an extra in *Round Two.*)

Watch Eric Clapton live.

Seduce a girl by writing her a love song.

Screw Pamela Kortman, his roommate's ex-girlfriend.

Clean out the garage to make a practice space.

Play all night, until dawn, without noticing the time.

* * *

HE WAS back in the gym. A single bank of fluorescent lights whined as they switched back on. Only one of the bulbs turned on, casting an eerie glow that limned Dennis's body against the dark.

A figure crept out of the shadows. "Hey."

Dennis turned toward the voice. He saw the outline of a girl. At first he thought it was the stewardess, Wilda. No, he thought, it's—is it Karen? But as the figure came closer, he realized it was Melanie.

"Hey Mel," said Dennis.

"Hey Asswipe," said Mel, but her voice didn't have any edge to it.

"I thought you were at Karen's party."

"That bitch? I wouldn't go to her party if she was the last rotter. I've been waiting here so I could catch you alone."

She crept even closer, until he could smell the sourness of her breath.

"I heard what my dad said. I wanted to say I'm sorry. He was pretty hard on you. You didn't deserve it. I was going to come out and give him a piece of my mind, but I didn't know how you'd feel after all that stuff I said."

She shifted her weight nervously from foot to foot.

"You didn't deserve that either," she said. "I'm sorry."

"It's okay," Dennis said.

"No, really."

"No, really."

Melanie smiled. Her expression looked so young and genuine that Dennis finally felt the fist around his heart begin to relax.

He remembered the late nights when he and Melanie had been kids, when she'd turned up on his porch and begged him to go with her to steal cigarettes or throw aftershave at Billy Whitman's window. The same mischief inflected her pose now: her quirked smile, sparkling eyes, and restless fingers.

"Do you think a man could live his whole life trying to get back to when he was eleven?" Dennis asked.

Melanie shrugged. She was twelve now, young and scrappy, pretty in pink but still the first kid on the block to throw a punch.

"Do you want to go play in the lot behind Ping's?" she asked.

Dennis looked down at himself. He saw the red and purple striped shirt he'd worn every day when he was eleven years old except when his mom took it away for the laundry.

Tall, dry grass whipped the backs of his knees. It rustled in the breeze, a rippling golden wave.

"Yeah," he said.

He reached for her hand. Her fingers curled into his palm.

"We don't ever have to come back if we don't want to," she said. "We can go as far as we want. We can keep going forever."

The sun hung bright overhead, wisps of white drifting past in the shapes of lions and racecars and old men's faces. The air smelled of fresh, growing things, and a bare hint of manure. A cow lowed somewhere and a truck rumbled across the asphalt. Both sounds were equidistant, a world away.

"Come on," said Dennis.

They ran. She led the way, long sandaled feet falling pigeon-toed in the soil. Dennis felt the breath flow sweet and easy through his lungs.

Someday they'd stop. Someday they'd fall exhausted to the ground and sleep curled up together in the dirt. Someday they'd pass into town where Dennis's father would be haggling over the price of wood while Uncle Ed stood in front of the hardware store, sipping lemonade. Someday they might even run straight through the universe, all the way back to the weird land of death where they'd chat with Descartes about the best way to keep mosquitoes off in summer.

For now, their feet beat like drums on the soil. Wind reddened Dennis's ears. Melanie's hair flew back into his face. He tugged her east to chase a crow circling above the horizon. Behind them, the wind swept through fields the size of eternity.

The Future

Eros, Philia, Agape

LUCIAN PACKED his possessions before he left. He packed his antique silver serving spoons with the filigreed handles; the tea roses he'd nurtured in the garden window; his jade and garnet rings. He packed the hunk of gypsum-veined jasper that he'd found while strolling on the beach on the first night he'd come to Adriana, she leading him uncertainly across the wet sand, their bodies illuminated by the soft gold twinkling of the lights along the pier. That night, as they walked back to Adriana's house, Lucian had cradled the speckled stone in his cupped palms, squinting so that the gypsum threads sparkled through his lashes.

Lucian had always loved beauty—beautiful scents, beautiful tastes, beautiful melodies. He especially loved beautiful objects because he could hold them in his hands and transform the abstraction of beauty into something tangible.

The objects belonged to them both, but Adriana waved her hand bitterly when Lucian began packing. "Take whatever you want," she said, snapping her book shut. She waited by the door, watching Lucian with sad and angry eyes.

Their daughter, Rose, followed Lucian around the house. "Are you going to take that, Daddy? Do you want that?" Wordlessly, Lucian held her hand. He guided her up the stairs and across the uneven floorboards where she sometimes tripped. Rose stopped by the picture window in the master bedroom, staring past the palm fronds and swimming pools, out to the vivid cerulean swath of the ocean. Lucian relished the hot, tender feel of Rose's hand. *I love you*, he would have whispered, but he'd surrendered the ability to speak.

He led her downstairs again to the front door. Rose's lace-festooned pink satin dress crinkled as she leapt down the steps. Lucian had ordered her dozens of satin party dresses in pale, floral hues. Rose refused to wear anything else.

Rose looked between Lucian and Adriana. "Are you taking me, too?" she asked Lucian.

Adriana's mouth tightened. She looked at Lucian, daring him to say something, to take responsibility for what he was doing to their daughter. Lucian remained silent.

Adriana's chardonnay glowed the same shade of amber as Lucian's eyes. She clutched the glass's stem until she thought it might break. "No, honey," she said with artificial lightness. "You're staying with me."

Rose reached for Lucian. "Horsey?"

Lucian knelt down and pressed his forehead against Rose's. He hadn't spoken a word in the three days since he'd delivered his letter of farewell to Adriana, announcing his intention to leave as soon as she had enough time to make arrangements for Rose to be cared for in his absence. When Lucian approached with the letter, Adriana had been sitting at the dining table, sipping orange juice from a wine glass and reading a first edition copy of Cheever's *Falconer.* Lucian felt a flash of guilt as she smiled up at him and accepted the missive. He knew that she'd been happier in the past few months than he'd ever seen her, possibly happier than she'd ever been. He knew the letter would shock and wound her. He knew she'd feel betrayed. Still, he delivered the letter anyway, and watched as comprehension ached through her body.

Rose had been told, gently, patiently, that Lucian was leaving. But she was four years old, and understood things only briefly and partially, and often according to her whims. She continued to believe her father's silence was a game.

Rose's hair brushed Lucian's cheek. He kissed her brow. Adriana couldn't hold her tongue any longer.

"What do you think you're going to find out there? There's no Shangri-La for rebel robots. You think you're making a play for independence? Independence to do what, Lu?"

Grief and anger filled Adriana's eyes with hot tears, as if she were a geyser filled with so much pressure that steam could not help but spring up. She examined Lucian's sculpted face: his skin inlaid with tiny lines that an artist had rendered to suggest the experiences of a childhood which had never been lived; his eyes calibrated with a hint of asymmetry to mimic the imperfection of human growth. His expression showed nothing—no doubt, or bitterness, or even relief. He revealed nothing at all.

It was all too much. Adriana moved between Lucian and Rose, as if she could use her own body to protect her daughter from the pain of being abandoned. Her eyes stared achingly over the rim of her wine glass. "Just go," she said.

He left.

* * *

ADRIANA BOUGHT Lucian the summer she turned thirty-five. Her father, long afflicted with an indecisive cancer that vacillated between aggression and remittance, had died suddenly in July. For years, the family had been squirreling away emotional reserves to cope with his prolonged illness. His death released a burst of excess.

While her sisters went through the motions of grief, Adriana thrummed with energy she didn't know what to do with. She considered squandering her vigor on six weeks in Mazatlan, but as she discussed ocean-front rentals with her travel agent, she realized escape wasn't what she craved. She liked the setting where her life took place: her house perched on a cliff overlooking the Pacific Ocean, her bedroom window that opened on a tangle of blackberry bushes where crows roosted every autumn and spring. She liked the two block stroll down to the beach where she could sit with a book and listen to the yapping lapdogs that the elderly women from the waterfront condominiums brought walking in the evenings.

Mazatlan was a twenty-something's cure for restlessness. Adriana wasn't twenty-five anymore, famished for the whole gourmet meal of existence. She needed something else now. Something new. Something more refined.

She explained this to her friends Ben and Lawrence when they invited her to their ranch house in Santa Barbara to relax for the weekend and try to forget about her father. They sat on Ben and Lawrence's patio, on iron-worked deck chairs arrayed around a garden table topped with a mosaic of sea creatures made of semi-precious stones. A warm, breezy dusk lengthened the shadows of the orange trees. Lawrence poured sparkling rosé into three wine glasses and proposed a toast to Adriana's father—not to his memory, but to his death.

"Good riddance to the bastard," said Lawrence. "If he were still alive, I'd punch him in the schnoz."

"I don't even want to think about him," said Adriana. "He's dead. He's gone."

"So if not Mazatlan, what are you going to do?" asked Ben.

"I'm not sure," said Adriana. "Some sort of change, some sort of milestone, that's all I know."

Lawrence sniffed the air. "Excuse me," he said, gathering the empty wine glasses. "The kitchen needs its genius."

When Lawrence was out of earshot, Ben leaned forward to whisper to Adriana. "He's got us on a raw food diet for my cholesterol. Raw carrots. Raw zucchini. Raw almonds. No cooking at all."

"Really," said Adriana, glancing away. She was never sure how to respond to lovers' quarrels. That kind of affection mixed with annoyance, that inescapable intimacy, was something she'd never understood.

Birds twittered in the orange trees. The fading sunlight highlighted copper strands in Ben's hair as he leaned over the mosaic table, rapping his fingers against a carnelian-backed crab. Through the arched windows, Adriana could see Lawrence mincing carrots, celery and almonds into brown paste.

"You should get a redecorator," said Ben. "Tile floors, Tuscan pottery, those red leather chairs that were in vogue last time we were in Milan. That'd make me feel like I'd been scrubbed clean and reborn."

"No, no," said Adriana, "I like where I live."

"A no-holds-barred shopping spree. Drop twenty thousand. That's what I call getting a weight off your shoulders."

Adriana laughed. "How long do you think it would take my personal shopper to assemble a whole new me?"

"Sounds like a midlife crisis," said Lawrence, returning with vegan hors d'oeuvres and three glasses of mineral water. "You're better off forgetting it all with a hot Latin pool boy, if you ask me."

Lawrence served Ben a small bowl filled with yellow mush. Ben shot Adriana an aggrieved glance.

Adriana felt suddenly out of synch. The whole evening felt like the set for a photo-shoot that would go in a decorating magazine, a two-page spread featuring Cozy Gardens, in which she and Ben and Lawrence were posing as an intimate dinner party for three. She felt reduced to two dimensions, air-brushed, and then digitally grafted onto the form of whoever it was who should have been there, someone warm and trusting who knew how to care about minutia like a friend's husband putting him on a raw food diet, not because the issue was important, but because it mattered to him.

Lawrence dipped his finger in the mash and held it up to Ben's lips. "It's for your own good, you ungrateful so-and-so."

Ben licked it away. "I eat it, don't I?"

Lawrence leaned down to kiss his husband, a warm and not at all furtive kiss, not sexual but still passionate. Ben's glance flashed coyly downward.

Adriana couldn't remember the last time she'd loved someone enough to be embarrassed by them. Was this the flavor missing from her life? A lover's fingertip sliding an unwanted morsel into her mouth?

She returned home that night on the bullet train. Her emerald cockatiel, Fuoco, greeted her with indignant squawks. In Adriana's absence, the house puffed her scent into the air and sang to Fuoco with her voice, but the bird was never fooled.

Adriana's father had given her the bird for her thirtieth birthday. He was a designer species spliced with Macaw DNA that colored his feathers rich green. He was expensive and inbred and neurotic, and he loved Adriana with frantic, obsessive jealousy.

"Hush," Adriana admonished, allowing Fuoco to alight on her shoulder. She carried him upstairs to her bedroom and hand-fed him millet. Fuoco strutted across the pillows, obsidian eyes proud and suspicious.

Adriana was surprised to find that her alienation had followed her home. She found herself prone to melancholy reveries, her gaze drifting toward the picture window, her fingers forgetting to stroke Fuoco's back. The bird screeched to regain her attention.

In the morning, Adriana visited her accountant. His fingers danced across the keyboard as he slipped trust fund moneys from one account to another like a magician. What she planned would be expensive, but her wealth would regrow in fertile soil, enriching her on lab diamonds and wind power and genetically modified oranges.

The robotics company gave Adriana a private showing. The salesman ushered her into a room draped in black velvet. Hundreds of body parts hung on the walls, and reclined on display tables: strong hands, narrow jaws, biker's thighs, voice boxes that played sound samples from gruff to dulcet, skin swatches spanning ebony to alabaster, penises of various sizes.

At first, Adriana felt horrified at the prospect of assembling a lover from fragments, but then it amused her. Wasn't everyone assembled from fragments of DNA, grown molecule by molecule inside their mother's womb?

She tapped her fingernails against a slick brochure. "Its brain will be malleable? I can tell it to be more amenable, or funnier, or to grow a spine?"

"That's correct." The salesman sported slick brown hair and shiny teeth and kept grinning in a way that suggested he thought that if he were charismatic enough Adriana would invite him home for a lay and a million dollar tip. "Humans lose brain plasticity as we age, which limits how much we can change. Our models have perpetually plastic brains. They can reroute their personalities at will by reshaping how they think on the neurological level."

Adriana stepped past him, running her fingers along a tapestry woven of a thousand possible hair textures.

The salesman tapped an empty faceplate. "Their original brains are based on deep imaging scans melded from geniuses in multiple fields. Great musicians, renowned lovers, the best physicists and mathematicians."

Adriana wished the salesman would be quiet. The more he talked, the more doubts clamored against her skull. "You've convinced me," she interrupted. "I want one."

The salesman looked taken aback by her abruptness. She could practically see him rifling through his internal script, trying to find the right page now that she had skipped several scenes. "What do you want him to look like?" he asked.

Adriana shrugged. "They're all beautiful, right?"

"We'll need specifications."

"I don't have specifications."

The salesman frowned anxiously. He shifted his weight as if it could help him regain his metaphorical footing. Adriana took pity. She dug through her purse.

"There," she said, placing a snapshot of her father on one of the display tables. "Make it look nothing like him."

Given such loose parameters, the design team indulged the fanciful. Lucian arrived at Adriana's door only a shade taller than she and equally slender, his limbs smooth and lean. Silver undertones glimmered in his blond hair. His skin was excruciatingly pale, white and translucent as alabaster, veined with pink. He smelled like warm soil and crushed herbs.

He offered Adriana a single white rose, its petals embossed with the company's logo. She held it dubiously between her thumb and forefinger.

"They think they know women, do they? They need to put down the bodice rippers."

Lucian said nothing. Adriana took his hesitation for puzzlement, but perhaps she should have seen it as an early indication of his tendency toward silence.

* * *

"THAT'S THAT, then." Adriana drained her chardonnay and crushed the empty glass beneath her heel as if she could finalize a divorce with the same gesture that sanctified a marriage.

Eyes wide, Rose pointed at the glass with one round finger. "Don't break things."

It suddenly struck Adriana how fast her daughter was aging. Here she was, this four year old, this sudden person. When had it happened? In the hospital, when Rose was newborn and wailing for the woman who had birthed her and abandoned her, Adriana had spent hours in the hallway outside the hospital nursery while she waited for the adoption to go through. She'd stared at Rose while she slept, ate, cried, striving to memorize her nascent, changing face. Sometime between then and now, Rose had become this round-cheeked creature who took rules very seriously and often tried to conceal her emotions beneath a calm exterior, as if being raised by a robot had replaced her blood with circuits. Of course Adriana loved Rose, changed her clothes, brushed her teeth, carried her across the house on her hip—but Lucian had been the most central, nurturing figure. Adriana couldn't fathom how she might fill his role. This wasn't a vacation like the time Adriana had taken Rose to Italy for three days, just the two of them sitting in restaurants, Adriana feeding her daughter spoonfuls of gelato to see the joy that lit her face at each new flavor. Then, they'd known that Lucian would be waiting when they returned. Without him, their family was a house missing a structural support. Adriana could feel the walls bowing in.

The fragments of Adriana's chardonnay glass sparkled sharply. Adriana led Rose away from the mess.

"Never mind," she said, "The house will clean up."

Her head felt simultaneously light and achy as if it couldn't decide between drunkenness and hangover. She tried to remember the parenting books she'd read before adopting Rose. What had they said about crying in front of your child? She clutched Rose close, inhaling the scent of children's shampoo mixed with the acrid odor of wine.

"Let's go for a drive," said Adriana. "Okay? Let's get out for a while."

"I want daddy to take me to the beach."

"We'll go out to the country and look at the farms. Cows and sheep, okay?"

Rose said nothing.

"Moo?" Adriana clarified. "Baa?"

"I know," said Rose. "I'm not a baby."

"So, then?"

Rose said nothing. Adriana wondered whether she could tell that her mother was a little mad with grief.

Just make a decision, Adriana counseled herself. She slipped her fingers around Rose's hand. "We'll go for a drive."

Adriana instructed the house to regulate itself in their absence, and then led Rose to the little black car that she and Lucian had bought together after adopting Rose. She fastened Rose's safety buckle and programmed the car to take them inland.

As the car engine initialized, Adriana felt a glimmer of fear. What if this machine betrayed them, too? But its uninspired intelligence only switched on the left turn signal and started down the boulevard.

* * *

LUCIAN STOOD at the base of the driveway and stared up at the house. Its stark orange and brown walls blazed against cloudless sky. Rocks and desert plants tumbled down the meticulously landscaped yard, imitating natural scrub.

A rabbit ran across the road, followed by the whir of Adriana's car. Lucian watched them pass. They couldn't see him through the cypresses, but Lucian could make out Rose's face pressed against the window. Beside her, Adriana slumped in her seat, one hand pressed over her eyes.

Lucian went in the opposite direction. He dragged the rolling cart packed with his belongings to the cliff that led down to the beach. He lifted the cart over his head and started down, his feet disturbing cascades of sandstone chunks.

A pair of adolescent boys looked up from playing in the waves. "Whoa," shouted one of them. "Are you carrying that whole thing? Are you a weight-lifter?"

Lucian remained silent. When he reached the sand, the kids muttered disappointments to each other and turned away from shore. "...Just a robot..." drifted back to Lucian on the breeze.

Lucian pulled his cart to the border where wet sand met dry. Oncoming waves lapped over his feet. He opened the cart and removed a tea-scented apricot rose growing in a pot painted with blue leaves.

He remembered acquiring the seeds for his first potted rose. One evening, long ago, he'd asked Adriana if he could grow things. He'd asked in passing, the question left to linger while they cleaned up after dinner, dish soap on their hands, Fuoco pecking after scraps. The next morning, Adriana escorted Lucian to the hothouse near the botanical gardens. "Buy whatever you want," she told him. Lucian was awed by the profusion of color and scent, all that beauty in one place. He wanted to capture the wonder of that place and own it for himself.

Lucian drew back his arm and threw the pot into the sea. It broke across the water, petals scattering the surface.

He threw in the pink roses, and the white roses, and the red roses, and the mauve roses. He threw in the filigreed-handled spoons. He threw in the chunk of gypsum-veined jasper.

He threw in everything beautiful that he'd ever collected. He threw in a chased silver hand mirror, and an embroidered silk jacket, and a hand-painted egg. He threw in one of Fuoco's soft, emerald feathers. He threw in a memory crystal that showed Rose as an infant, curled and sleeping.

He loved those things, and yet they were things. He had owned them. Now they were gone. He had recently come to realize that ownership was a relationship. What did it mean to own a thing? To shape it and contain it? He could not possess or be possessed until he knew.

He watched the sea awhile, the remnants of his possessions lost in the tumbling waves. As the sun tilted past noon, he turned away and climbed back up the cliff. Unencumbered by ownership, he followed the boulevard away from Adriana's house.

* * *

LUCIAN REMEMBERED meeting Adriana the way that he imagined that humans remembered childhood. Oh, his memories had been as sharply focused then as now—but it was still like childhood, he reasoned, for he'd been a different person then.

He remembered his first sight of Adriana as a burst of images. Wavy strawberry blonde hair cut straight across tanned shoulders. Dark brown eyes that his artistic mind labeled "sienna." Thick, aristocratic brows and strong cheekbones, free of makeup. Lucian's inner aesthete termed her blunt, angular face "striking" rather than "beautiful." His inner psychoanalyst reasoned that she was probably "strong-willed" as well, from the way she stood in the doorway, her arms crossed, her eyebrows lifted as if inquiring how he planned to justify his existence.

Eventually, she moved away, allowing Lucian to step inside. He crossed the threshold into a blur of frantic screeching and flapping.

New. Everything was new. So new that Lucian could barely assemble feathers and beak and wings into the concept of "bird" before his reflexes jumped him away from the onslaught. Hissing and screeching, the animal retreated to a perch atop a bookshelf.

Adriana's hand weighed on Lucian's shoulder. Her voice was edged with the cynicism Lucian would later learn was her way of hiding how desperately she feared failure. "Ornithophobia? How ridiculous."

Lucian's first disjointed days were dominated by the bird, who he learned was named Fuoco. It followed him around the house. When he remained in place for a moment, the bird settled on some nearby high spot—the hat rack in the entryway, or the hand-crafted globe in the parlor, or the rafters above the master bed—to spy on him. It glared at Lucian in the manner of birds, first peering through one eye and then turning its head to peer through the other, apparently finding both views equally loathsome.

When Adriana took Lucian into her bed, Fuoco swooped at Lucian's head. Adriana pushed Lucian out of the way. "Damn it, Fuoco," she muttered, but she offered the bird a perch on her shoulder.

Fuoco crowed with pleasure as she led him downstairs. His feathers fluffed with victory as he hopped obediently into its cage, expecting her to reward him with treats and conversation. Instead, Adriana closed the gilded door and returned upstairs. All night, as Lucian lay with Adriana, the bird chattered madly. He plucked at his feathers until his tattered plumage carpeted the cage floor.

Lucian accompanied Adriana when she brought Fuoco to the vet the next day. The veterinarian diagnosed jealousy. "It's not uncommon in birds," he said. He suggested they give Fuoco a rigid routine that would, over time, help the bird realize he was Adriana's companion, not her mate.

Adriana and Lucian rearranged their lives so that Fuoco could have regular feeding times, scheduled exercise, socialization with both Lucian and Adriana, and time with his mistress alone. Adriana gave him a treat each night when she locked him in his cage, staying to stroke his feathers for a few minutes before she headed upstairs.

Fuoco's heart broke. He became a different bird. His strut lacked confidence, and his feathers grew ever more tattered. When they let him out of his cage, he wandered after Adriana with pleading, wistful eyes, and ignored Lucian entirely.

* * *

LUCIAN HAD been dis-integrated then: musician brain, mathematician brain, artist brain, economist brain, and more, all functioning separately, each personality rising to dominance to provide information and then sliding away, creating staccato bursts of consciousness.

As Adriana made clear which responses she liked, Lucian's consciousness began integrating into the personality she desired. He found himself noticing connections between what had previously been separate experiences. Before, when he'd seen the ocean, his scientist brain had calculated how far he was from the shore, and how long it would be until high tide. His poet brain had recited Strindberg's "We Waves." *Wet flames are we:/ Burning, extinguishing;/Cleansing, replenishing.* Yet it wasn't until he integrated that the wonder of the science, and the mystery of the poetry, and the beauty of the view, all made sense to him at once as part of this strange, inspiring thing: the sea.

He learned to anticipate Adriana. He knew when she was pleased and when she was ailing, and he knew why. He could predict the cynical half-smile she'd give when he made an error he hadn't yet realized was an error: serving her cold coffee in an orange juice glass, orange juice in a shot glass, wine in a mug. When integration gave him knowledge of patterns, he suddenly understood why these things were errors. At the same time, he realized that he liked what happened when he made those kinds of errors, the bright bursts of humor they elicited from the often sober Adriana. So he persisted in error, serving her milk in crystal decanters, and grapefruit slices in egg cups.

He enjoyed the many varieties of her laughter. Sometimes it was light and surprised, as when he offered her a cupcake tin filled with tortellini. He also loved her rich, dark laughter that anticipated irony. Sometimes, her laughter held a bitter undercurrent, and on those occasions, he understood that she was laughing more at herself than at anyone else. Sometimes when that happened, he would go to hold her, seeking to ease her pain, and sometimes she would spontaneously start crying in gulping, gasping sobs.

She often watched him while he worked, her head cocked and her brows drawn as if she were seeing him for the first time. "What can I do to make you happy?" she'd ask.

If he gave an answer, she would lavishly fulfill his desires. She took him traveling to the best greenhouses in the state, and bought a library full of gardening books. Lucian knew she would have given him more. He didn't want it. He wanted to reassure her that he appreciated her extravagance, but didn't require it, that he was satisfied with simple, loving give-and-take. Sometimes, he told her in the simplest words he knew: "I love you, too." But he knew that she never quite believed him. She worried that he was lying, or that his programming had erased his free will. It was easier for her to believe those things than to accept that someone could love her.

But he did love her. Lucian loved Adriana as his mathematician brain loved the consistency of arithmetic, as his artist brain loved color, as his philosopher brain loved piety. He loved her as Fuoco loved her, the bird walking sadly along the arm of Adriana's chair, trilling and flapping his ragged wings as he eyed her with his inky gaze, trying to catch her attention.

* * *

ADRIANA HADN'T expected to fall in love. She'd expected a charming conversationalist with the emotional range of a literary butler and the self-awareness of a golden retriever. Early on, she'd felt her prejudices confirmed. She noted Lucian's lack of critical thinking and his inability to maneuver unexpected situations. She found him most interesting when he didn't know she was watching. For instance, on his free afternoons: was his program trying to anticipate what would please her? Or did the thing really enjoy sitting by the window, leafing through the pages of one of her rare books, with nothing but the sound of the ocean to lull him?

Once, as Adriana watched from the kitchen doorway while Lucian made their breakfast, the robot slipped while he was dicing onions. The knife cut deep into his finger. Adriana stumbled forward to help. As Lucian turned to face her, Adriana imagined that she saw something like shock on his face. For a moment, she wondered whether he had a programmed sense of privacy she could violate, but then he raised his hand to her in greeting, and she watched as the tiny bots that maintained his system healed his inhuman flesh within seconds.

At that moment, Adriana remembered that Lucian was unlike her. She urged herself not to forget it, and strove not to, even after his consciousness integrated. He was a person, yes, a varied and fascinating one with as many depths and facets as any other person she knew. But he was also alien. He was a creature for whom a slip of a chef's knife was a minute error, simply repaired. In some ways, she was more similar to Fuoco.

As a child, Adriana had owned a book that told the fable of an emperor who owned a bird which he fed rich foods from his table, and entertained with luxuries from his court. But a pet bird needed different things than an emperor. It wanted seed and millet, not grand feasts. It enjoyed mirrors and little brass bells, not lacquer boxes and poetry scrolls. Gorged on human banquets and revelries, the little bird sickened and died.

Adriana vowed not to make the same mistake with Lucian, but she had no idea how hard it would be to salve the needs of something so unlike herself.

* * *

ADRIANA ORDERED the car to pull over at a farm that advertised children could "Pet Lambs and Calves" for a fee. A ginger-haired teenager stood at a strawberry stand in front of the fence, slouching as he flipped through a dog-eared magazine.

Adriana held Rose's hand as they approached. She tried to read her daughter's emotions in the feel of her tiny fingers. The little girl's expression revealed nothing; Rose had gone silent and flat-faced as if she were imitating Lucian. He would have known what she was feeling.

Adriana examined the strawberries. The crates contained none of the different shapes one could buy at the store, only the natural, seed-filled variety. "Do these contain pesticides?" Adriana asked.

"No, ma'am," said the teenager. "We grow organic."

"All right then. I'll take a box." Adriana looked down at her daughter. "Do you want some strawberries, sweetheart?" she asked in a sugared tone.

"You said I could pet the lambs," said Rose.

"Right. Of course, honey." Adriana glanced at the distracted teenager. "Can she?"

The teenager slumped, visibly disappointed, and tossed his magazine on a pile of canvas sacks. "I can take her to the barn."

"Fine. Okay."

Adriana guided Rose toward the teenager. Rose looked up at him, expression still inscrutable.

The boy didn't take Rose's hand. He ducked his head, obviously embarrassed. "My aunt likes me to ask for the money upfront."

"Of course." Adriana fumbled for her wallet. She'd let Lucian do things for her for so long. How many basic living skills had she forgotten? She held out some bills. The teenager licked his index finger and meticulously counted out what she owed.

The teen took Rose's hand. He lingered a moment, watching Adriana. "Aren't you coming with us?"

Adriana was so tired. She forced a smile. "Oh, that's okay. I've seen sheep and cows. Okay, Rose? Can you have fun for a little bit without me?"

Rose nodded soberly. She turned toward the teenager without hesitation, and followed him toward the barn. The boy seemed to be good with children. He walked slowly so that Rose could keep up with his long-legged strides.

Adriana returned to the car, and leaned against the hot, sun-warmed door. Her head throbbed. She thought she might cry or collapse. Getting out had seemed like a good idea—the house was full of memories of Lucian. He seemed to sit in every chair, linger in every doorway. But now she wished she'd stayed in her haunted but familiar home, instead of leaving with this child she seemed to barely know.

A sharp, long wail carried on the wind. Adrenaline cut through Adriana's melancholia. She sprinted toward the barn. She saw Rose running toward her, the teenager close behind, dust swirling around both of them. Blood dripped down Rose's arm.

Adriana threw her arms around her daughter. Arms, legs, breath, heart beat: Rose was okay. Adrianna dabbed at Rose's injury; there was a lot of blood, but the wound was shallow. "Oh, honey," she said, clutching Rose as tightly as she dared.

The teenager halted beside them, his hair mussed by the wind.

"What happened?" Adriana demanded.

The teenager stammered. "Fortuna kicked her. That's one of the goats. I'm so sorry. Fortuna's never done anything like that before. She's a nice goat. It's Ballantine usually does the kicking. He got me a few times when I was little. I came through every time. Honest, she'll be okay. You're not going to sue, are you?"

Rose struggled out of Adriana's grasp and began wailing again. "It's okay, Rose, it's okay," murmured Adriana. She felt a strange disconnect in her head as she spoke. Things were not okay. Things might never be okay again.

"I'm leaking," cried Rose, holding out her blood-stained fingers. "See, mama? I'm leaking! I need healer bots."

Adriana looked up at the teenager. "Do you have bandages? A first aid kit?"

The boy frowned. "In the house, I think…"

"Get the bots, mama! Make me stop leaking!"

The teen stared at Adriana, the concern in his eyes increasing. Adriana blinked, slowly. The moment slowed. She realized what her daughter had said. She forced her voice to remain calm. "What do you want, Rose?"

"She said it before," said the teen. "I thought it was a game."

Adriana leveled her gaze with Rose's. The child's eyes were strange and brown, uncharted waters. "Is this a game?"

"Daddy left," said Rose.

Adriana felt woozy. "Yes, and then I brought you here so we could see lambs and calves. Did you see any nice, fuzzy lambs?"

"Daddy left."

She shouldn't have drunk the wine. She should have stayed clear-headed. "We'll get you bandaged up and then you can go see the lambs again. Do you want to see the lambs again? Would it help if mommy came, too?"

Rose clenched her fists. Her face grew dark. "My arm hurts!" She threw herself to the ground. "I want healer bots!"

* * *

ADRIANA KNEW precisely when she'd fallen in love with Lucian. It was three months after she'd bought him—after his consciousness had integrated, but before Adriana fully understood how integration had changed him.

It began when Adriana's sisters called from Boston to inform her that they'd arranged for a family pilgrimage to Italy. In accordance with their father's will, they would commemorate him by lighting candles in the cathedrals of every winding hillside city.

"Oh, I can't. I'm too busy," Adriana answered airily, as if she were a debutante without a care, as if she shared her sisters' ability to overcome their fear of their father.

Her phone began ringing ceaselessly. Nanette called before she rushed off to a tennis match. "How can you be so busy? You don't have a job. You don't have a husband. Or is there a man in your life we don't know about?" And once Nanette was deferred with mumbled excuses, it was Eleanor calling from a spa. "Is something wrong, Adriana? We're all worried. How can you miss a chance to say goodbye to papa?"

"I said goodbye at the funeral," said Adriana.

"Then you can't have properly processed your grief," said Jessica, calling from her office between appointments. She was a psychoanalyst in the Freudian mode. "Your aversion rings of denial. You need to process your Electra complex."

Adriana slammed down the phone. Later, to apologize for hanging up, she sent all her sisters chocolates, and then booked a flight. In a fit of pique, she booked a seat for Lucian, too. Well, he was a companion, wasn't he? What else was he for?

Adriana's sisters were scandalized, of course. As they rode through Rome, Jessica, Nanette, and Eleanor gossiped behind their discreetly raised hands. Adriana with a robot? Well, she'd need to be, wouldn't she? There was no getting around the fact that she was damaged. Any girl who would make up those stories about their father would have to be.

Adriana ignored them as best she could while they whirled through Tuscany in a procession of rented cars. The paused in cities to gawk at gothic cathedrals and mummified remnants, always moving on within the day. During their father's long sickness, Adriana's sisters had perfected the art of cheerful anecdote. They used it to great effect as they lit candles in his memory. Tears welling in their eyes, they related banal, nostalgic memories. How their father danced at charity balls. How he lectured men on the board who looked down on him for being new money. How he never once apologized for anything in his life.

It had never been clear to Adriana whether her father had treated her sisters the way he treated her, or whether she had been the only one to whom he came at night, his breathing heavy and staccato. It seemed impossible that they could lie so seamlessly, never showing fear or doubt. But if they were telling the truth, that meant Adriana was the only one, and how could she believe that either?

One night, while Lucian and Adriana were alone in their room in a hotel in Assisi that had been a convent during the middle ages, Adriana broke down. It was all too much, being in this foreign place, talking endlessly about her father. She'd fled New England to get away from them, fled to her beautiful modern glass-and-wood house by the Pacific Ocean that was like a fresh breath drawn on an Autumn morning.

Lucian held her, exerting the perfect warmth and pressure against her body to comfort her. It was what she'd have expected from a robot. She knew that he calculated the pace of his breath, the temperature of his skin, the angle of his arm as it lay across her.

What surprised Adriana, what humbled her, was how eloquently Lucian spoke of his experiences. He told her what it had been like to assemble himself from fragments, to take what he'd once been and become something new. It was something Adriana had tried to do herself when she fled her family.

Lucian held his head down as he spoke. His gaze never met hers. He spoke as if this process of communicating the intimate parts of the self were a new kind of dance, and he was tenuously trying the steps. Through the fog of her grief, Adriana realized that this was a new, struggling consciousness coming to clarity. How could she do anything but love him?

When they returned from Italy, Adriana approached the fledgling movement for granting rights to artificial intelligences. They were underfunded and poorly organized. Adriana rented them offices in San Francisco, and hired a small but competent staff.

Adriana became the movement's face. She'd been on camera frequently as a child: whenever her father was in the news for some or other board room scandal, her father's publicists had lined up Adriana and her sisters beside the family limousine, chaste in their private school uniforms, ready to provide Lancaster Nuclear with a friendly, feminine face.

She and Lucian were a brief media curiosity: Heiress In Love With Robot. "Lucian is as self-aware as you or I," Adriana told reporters, all-American in pearls and jeans. "He thinks. He learns. He can hybridize roses as well as any human gardener. Why should he be denied his rights?"

Early on, it was clear that political progress would be frustratingly slow. Adriana quickly expended her patience. She set up a fund for the organization, made sure it would run without her assistance, and then turned her attention toward alternate methods for attaining her goals. She hired a team of lawyers to draw up a contract that would grant Lucian community property rights to her estate and accounts. He would be her equal in practicality, if not legality.

Next, Adriana approached Lucian's manufacturer, and commissioned them to invent a procedure that would allow Lucian to have conscious control of his brain plasticity. At their wedding, Adriana gave him the chemical commands at the same time as she gave him his ring. "You are your own person now. You always have been, of course, but now you have full agency, too. You are yourself," she announced, in front of their gathered friends. Her sisters would no doubt have been scandalized, but they had not been invited.

On their honeymoon, Adriana and Lucian toured hospitals, running the genetic profiles of abandoned infants until they found a healthy girl with a mitochondrial lineage that matched Adriana's. The infant was tiny and pink and curled in on herself, ready to unfold, like one of Lucian's roses.

When they brought Rose home, Adriana felt a surge in her stomach that she'd never felt before. It was a kind of happiness she'd never experienced, one that felt round and whole without any jagged edges. It was like the sun had risen in her belly and was dwelling there, filling her with boundless light.

* * *

THERE WAS a moment, when Rose was still new enough to be wrapped in the handmade baby blanket that Ben and Lawrence had sent from France, in which Adriana looked up at Lucian and realized how enraptured he was with their baby, how much adoration underpinned his willingness to bend over her cradle for hours and mirror her expressions, frown for frown, astonishment for astonishment. In that moment, Adriana thought that this must be the true measure of equality, not money or laws, but this unfolding desire to create the future together by raising a new sentience. She thought she understood then why unhappy parents stayed together for the sake of their children, why families with sons and daughters felt so different from those that remained childless. Families with children were making something new from themselves. Doubly so when the endeavor was undertaken by a human and a creature who was already, himself, something new. What could they make together?

In that same moment, Lucian was watching the wide-eyed, innocent wonder with which his daughter beheld him. She showed the same pleasure when he entered the room as she did when Adriana entered. If anything, the light in her eyes was brighter when he approached. There was something about the way Rose loved him that he didn't yet understand. Earlier that morning, he had plucked a bloom from his apricot tea rose and whispered to its petals that they were beautiful. They were his, and he loved them. Every day, he held Rose, and understood that she was beautiful, and that he loved her. But she was not his. She was her own. He wasn't sure he'd ever seen a love like that, a love that did not want to hold its object in its hands and keep and contain it.

* * *

"YOU AREN'T a robot!"

Adriana's voice was rough from shouting all the way home. Bad enough to lose Lucian, but the child was out of control.

"I want healer bots! I'm a robot I'm a robot I'm a robot I'm a robot!"

The car stopped. Adriana got out. She waited for Rose to follow, and when she didn't, Adriana scooped her up and carried her up the driveway. Rose kicked and screamed. She sank her teeth into Adriana's arm. Adriana halted, surprised by the sudden pain. She breathed deeply, and then continued up the driveway. Rose's screams slid upward in register and rage.

Adriana set Rose down by the door long enough to key in the entry code and let the security system take a DNA sample from her hair. Rose hurled herself onto the ground. She yanked fronds by the fistful off the potted ferns. Adriana leaned down to scrape her up and got kicked in the chest.

"God da…for heaven's sake." Adriana grabbed Rose's ankles with one hand and her wrists with the other. She pushed her weight against the unlocked door until it swung open. She carried Rose into the house, and slammed the door closed with her back. "Lock!" she yelled to the house.

When she heard the reassuring click, she set Rose down on the couch, and jumped away from the still-flailing limbs. Rose fled up the stairs, her bedroom door crashing shut behind her.

Adriana dug in her pocket for the bandages that the people at the farm had given her before she headed home, which she'd been unable to apply to a moving target in the car. Now was the time. She followed Rose up the stairs, her breath surprisingly heavy. She felt as though she'd been running a very long time.

She paused outside Rose's room. She didn't know what she'd do when she got inside. Lucian had always dealt with the child when she got overexcited. Too often, Adriana felt helpless, and became distant.

"Rose?" she called. "Rose? Are you okay?"

There was no response.

Adriana put her hand on the doorknob, and breathed deeply before turning.

She was surprised to find Rose sitting demurely in the center of her bed, her rumpled skirts spread about her as if she were a child at a picnic in an Impressionist painting. Dirt and tears trailed down the pink satin. The edges of her wound had already begun to bruise.

"I'm a robot," she said to Adriana, tone resentful.

Adriana made a decision. The most important thing was to bandage Rose's wound. Afterward, she could deal with whatever came next.

"Okay," said Adriana. "You're a robot."

Rose lifted her chin warily. "Good."

Adriana sat on the edge of Rose's bed. "You know what robots do? They change themselves to be whatever humans ask them to be."

"Dad doesn't," said Rose.

"That's true," said Adriana. "But that didn't happen until your father grew up."

Rose swung her legs against the side of the bed. Her expression remained dubious, but she no longer looked so resolute.

Adriana lifted the packet of bandages. "May I?"

Rose hesitated. Adriana resisted the urge to put her head in her hands. She had to get the bandages on, that was the important thing, but she couldn't shake the feeling that she was going to regret this later.

"Right now, what this human wants is for you to let her bandage your wound instead of giving you healer bots. Will you be a good robot? Will you let me?"

Rose remained silent, but she moved a little closer to her mother. When Adriana began bandaging her arm, she didn't scream.

* * *

LUCIAN WAITED for a bus to take him to the desert. He had no money. He'd forgotten about that. The driver berated him and wouldn't let him on.

Lucian walked. He could walk faster than a human, but not much faster. His edge was endurance. The road took him inland away from the sea. The last of the expensive houses stood near a lighthouse, lamps shining in all its windows. Beyond, condominiums pressed against each other, dense and alike. They gave way to compact, well-maintained homes, with neat green aprons maintained by automated sprinklers that sprayed arcs of precious water into the air.

The landscape changed. Sea breeze stilled to buzzing heat. Dirty, peeling houses squatted side by side, separated by chain link fences. Iron bars guarded the windows and broken cars decayed in the driveways. Parched lawns stretched from walls to curb like scrub-land. No one was out in the punishing sun.

The road divided. Lucian followed the fork that went through the dilapidated town center. Traffic jerked along in fits and starts. Lucian walked in the gutter. Stray plastic bags blew beside him, working their way between dark storefronts. Parking meters blinked at the passing cars, hungry for more coins. Pedestrians ambled past, avoiding eye contact, mumbled conversations lost beneath honking horns.

On the other side of town, the road winnowed down to two lonely lanes. Dry golden grass stretched over rolling hills, dotted by the dark shapes of cattle. A battered convertible, roof down, blared its horn at Lucian as it passed. Lucian walked where the asphalt met the prickly weeds. Paper and cigarette butts littered the golden stalks like white flowers.

An old truck pulled over, the manually driven variety still used by companies too small to afford the insurance for the automatic kind. The man in the driver's seat was trim, with a pale blond moustache and a deerstalker cap pulled over his ears. He wore a string of fishing lures like a necklace. "Not much comes this way anymore," he said. "I used to pick up hitchhikers half the time I took this route. You're the first I've seen in a while."

Sun rendered the truck in bright silhouette. Lucian held his hand over his eyes to shade them.

"Where are you headed?" asked the driver.

Lucian pointed down the road.

"Sure, but where after that?"

Lucian dropped his arm to his side. The sun inched higher.

The driver frowned. "Can you write it down? I think I've got some paper in here." He grabbed a pen and a receipt out of his front pocket, and thrust them out the window.

Lucian took them. He wasn't sure, at first, if he could still write. His brain was slowly reshaping itself, and eventually all his linguistic skills would disappear, and even his thoughts would no longer be shaped by words. The pen fell limp in his hand, and then his fingers remembered what to do. "Desert," he wrote.

"It's blazing hot," said the driver. "A lot hotter than here. Why do you want to go there?"

"To be born," wrote Lucian.

The driver slid Lucian a sideways gaze, but he nodded at the same time, almost imperceptibly. "Sometimes people have to do things. I get that. I remember when..." The look in his eyes became distant. He moved back in his seat. "Get on in."

Lucian walked around the cab and got inside. He remembered to sit and to close the door, but the rest of the ritual escaped him. He stared at the driver until the pale man shook his head and leaned over Lucian to drag the seatbelt over his chest.

"Are you under a vow of silence?" asked the driver.

Lucian stared ahead.

"Blazing hot in the desert," muttered the driver. He pulled back onto the road, and drove toward the sun.

* * *

DURING HIS years with Adriana, Lucian tried not to think about the cockatiel Fuoco. The bird had never become accustomed to Lucian. He grew ever more angry and bitter. He plucked out his feathers so often that he became bald in patches. Sometimes he pecked deeply enough to bleed.

From time to time, Adriana scooped him up and stroked his head and nuzzled her cheek against the heavy feathers that remained on the part of his back he couldn't reach. "My poor little crazy bird," she'd say, sadly, as he ran his beak through her hair.

Fuoco hated Lucian so much that for a while they wondered whether he would be happier in another place. Adriana tried giving him to Ben and Lawrence, but he only pined for the loss of his mistress and refused to eat until she flew out to retrieve him.

When they returned home, they hung Fuoco's cage in the nursery. Being near the baby seemed to calm them both. Rose was a fussy infant who disliked solitude. She seemed happier when there was a warm presence about, even if it was a bird. Fuoco kept her from crying during the rare times when Adriana called Lucian from Rose's side. Lucian spent the rest of his time in the nursery, watching Rose day and night with sleepless vigilance.

The most striking times of Lucian's life were holding Rose while she cried. He wrapped her in cream-colored blankets the same shade as her skin, and rocked her as he walked the perimeter of the downstairs rooms, looking out at the diffuse golden ambience that the streetlights cast across the blackberry bushes and neighbors' patios. Sometimes he took her outside and walked with her along the road by the cliffs. He never carried her down to the beach. Lucian had perfect balance and night vision, but none of that mattered when he could so easily imagine the terror of a lost footing—Rose slipping from his grasp and plummeting downward. Instead, they stood a safe distance from the edge, watching from above as the black waves threw themselves against the rocks, the night air scented with cold and salt.

Lucian loved Adriana, but he loved Rose more. He loved her clumsy fists and her yearnings toward consciousness, the slow accrual of her stumbling syllables. She was building her consciousness piece by piece as he had, learning how the world worked and what her place was in it. He silently narrated her stages of development. *Can you tell that your body has boundaries? Do you know your skin from mine?* and *Yes! You can make things happen! Cause and effect. Keep crying and we'll come.* Best of all, there was the moment when she locked her eyes on his, and he could barely breathe for the realization that, *Oh, Rose. You know there's someone else thinking behind these eyes. You know who I am.*

Lucian wanted Rose to have all the beauty he could give her. Silk dresses and lace, the best roses from his pots, the clearest panoramic views of the sea. Objects delighted Rose. As an infant she watched them avidly, and then later clapped and laughed, until finally she could exclaim, "Thank you!" Her eyes shone.

It was Fuoco who broke Lucian's heart. It was late at night when Adriana went into Rose's room to check on her while she slept. Somehow, sometime, the birdcage had been left open. Fuoco sat on the rim of the open door, peering darkly outward.

Adriana had been alone with Rose and Fuoco before. But something about this occasion struck like lightning in Fuoco's tiny, mad brain. Perhaps it was the darkness of the room, with only the nightlight's pale blue glow cast on Adriana's skin, that confused the bird. Perhaps Rose had finally grown large enough that Fuoco had begun to perceive her as a possible rival rather than an ignorable baby-thing. Perhaps the last vestiges of his sanity had simply shredded. For whatever reason, as Adriana bent over the bed to touch her daughter's face, Fuoco burst wildly from his cage.

With the same jealous anger he'd shown toward Lucian, Fuoco dove at Rose's face. His claws raked against her forehead. Rose screamed. Adriana recoiled. She grabbed Rose in one arm, and flailed at the bird with the other. Rose struggled to escape her mother's grip so she could run away. Adriana instinctively responded by trying to protect her with an even tighter grasp.

Lucian heard the commotion from where he was standing in the living room, programming the house's cleaning regimen for the next week. He left the house panel open and ran through the kitchen on the way to the bedroom, picking up a frying pan as he passed through. He swung the pan at Fuoco as he entered the room, herding the bird away from Adriana, and into a corner. His fist tightened on the handle. He thought he'd have to kill his old rival.

Instead, the vitality seemed to drain from Fuoco. The bird's wings drooped. He dropped to the floor with half-hearted, irregular wingbeats. His eyes had gone flat and dull.

Fuoco didn't struggle as Lucian picked him up and returned him to his cage. Adriana and Lucian stared at each other, unsure what to say. Rose slipped away from her mother and wrapped her arms around Lucian's knees. She was crying.

"Poor Fuoco," said Adriana, quietly.

They brought Fuoco to the vet to be put down. Adriana stood over him as the vet inserted the needle. "My poor crazy bird," she murmured, stroking his wings as he died.

Lucian watched Adriana with great sadness. At first, he thought he was feeling empathy for the bird, despite the fact it had always hated him. Then, with a realization that tasted like a swallow of sour wine, he realized that wasn't what he was feeling. He recognized the poignant, regretful look that Adriana was giving Fuoco. It was the way Lucian himself looked at a wilted rose, or a tarnished silver spoon. It was a look inflected by possession.

It wasn't so different from the way Adriana looked at Lucian sometimes when things had gone wrong. He'd never before realized how slender the difference was between her love for him and her love for Fuoco. He'd never before realized how slender the difference was between his love for her and his love for an unfolding rose.

* * *

ADRIANA LET Rose tend Lucian's plants, and dust the shelves, and pace by the picture window. She let the girl pretend to cook breakfast, while Adriana stood behind her, stepping in to wield the chopping knife and use the stove. At naptime, Adriana convinced Rose that good robots would pretend to sleep a few hours in the afternoon if that's what their humans wanted. She tucked in her daughter and then went downstairs to sit in the living room and drink wine and cry.

This couldn't last. She had to figure something out. She should take them both on vacation to Mazatlan. She should ask one of her sisters to come stay. She should call a child psychiatrist. But she felt so betrayed, so drained of spirit, that it was all she could do to keep Rose going from day to day.

Remnants of Lucian's accusatory silence rung through the house. What had he wanted from her? What had she failed to do? She'd loved him. She *loved* him. She'd given him half of her home and all of herself. They were raising a child together. And still he'd left her.

She got up to stand by the window. It was foggy that night, the streetlights tingeing everything with a weird, flat yellow glow. She put her hand on the pane, and her palm print remained on the glass, as though someone outside were beating on the window to get in. She peered into the gloom; it was as if the rest of the world were the fuzzy edges of a painting, and her well-lit house was the only defined spot. She felt as though it would be possible to open the front door and step over the threshold and blur until she was out of focus.

She finished her fourth glass of wine. Her head was whirling. Her eyes ran with tears and she didn't care. She poured herself another glass.

Her father had never drunk. Oh, no. He was a teetotaler. Called the stuff Braindead and mocked the weaklings who drank it, the men on the board and their bored wives. He threw parties where alcohol flowed and flowed, while he stood in the middle, icy sober, watching the rest of them make fools of themselves as if they were circus clowns turning somersaults for his amusement. He set up elaborate plots to embarrass them. This executive with that jealous lawyer's wife. That politician called out for a drink by the pool while his teenage son was in the hot tub with his suit off, boner buried deep in another boy. He ruined lives at his parties, and he did it elegantly, standing alone in the middle of the action with invisible strings in his hands.

Adriana's head was dancing now. Her feet were moving. Her father, the decisive man, the sharp man, the dead man. Oh, but must keep mourning him, must keep lighting candles and weeping crocodile tears. Nevermind!

Lucian, oh Lucian, he'd become in his final incarnation the antidote to her father. She'd cry, and he'd hold her, and then they'd go together to stand in the doorway of the nursery, watching the peaceful tableau of Rose sleeping in her cream sheets. Everything would be all right because Lucian was safe, Lucian was good. Other men's eyes might glimmer when they looked at little girls, but not Lucian's. With Lucian there, they were a family, the way families were supposed to be, and Lucian was supposed to be faithful and devoted and permanent and loyal.

And oh, without him, she didn't know what to do. She was as dismal as her father, letting Rose pretend that she and her dolls were on their way to the factory for adjustment. She acceded to the girl's demands to play games of What Shall I Be Now? "Be happier!" "Be funnier!" "Let your dancer brain take over!" What would happen when Rose went to school? When she realized her mother had been lying? When she realized that pretending to be her father wouldn't bring him back?

Adriana danced into the kitchen. She threw the wine bottle into the sink with a crash and turned on the oven. Its safety protocols monitored her alcohol level and informed her that she wasn't competent to use flame. She turned off the protocols. She wanted an omelet like Lucian used to make her with onions and chives and cheese, and a wine glass filled with orange juice. She took out the frying pan that Lucian had used to corral Fuoco, and set it on the counter beside the cutting board, and then she went to get an onion, but she'd moved the cutting board, and it was on the burner, and it was ablaze. She grabbed a dishtowel and beat at the grill. The house keened. Sprinklers rained down on her. Adriana turned her face up into the rain and laughed. She spun, her arms out, like a little girl trying to make herself dizzy. Drops battered her cheeks and slid down her neck.

Wet footsteps. Adriana looked down at Rose. Her daughter's face was wet. Her dark eyes were sleepy.

"Mom?"

"Rose!" Adriana took Rose's head between her hands. She kissed her hard on the forehead. "I love you! I love you so much!"

Rose tried to pull away. "Why is it raining?"

"I started a fire! It's fine now!"

The house keened. The siren's pulse felt like a heartbeat. Adriana went to the cupboard for salt. Behind her, Rose's feet squeaked on the linoleum. Adriana's hand closed around the cupboard knob. It was slippery with rain. Her fingers slid. Her lungs filled with anxiety and something was wrong, but it wasn't the cupboard, it was something else; she turned quickly to find Rose with a chef's knife clutched in her tiny fingers, preparing to bring it down on the onion.

"No!" Adriana grabbed the knife out of Rose's hand. It slid through her slick fingers and clattered to the floor. Adriana grabbed Rose around the waist and pulled her away from the wet, dangerous kitchen. "You can never do that. Never, never."

"Daddy did it..."

"You could kill yourself!"

"I'll get healer bots."

"No! Do you hear me? You can't. You'd cut yourself and maybe you'd die. And then what would I do?" Adriana couldn't remember what had caused the rain anymore. They were in a deluge. That was all she knew for certain. Her head hurt. Her body hurt. She wanted nothing to do with dancing. "What's wrong with us, honey? Why doesn't he want us? No! No, don't answer that. Don't listen to me. Of course he wants you! It's me he doesn't want. What did I do wrong? Why doesn't he love me anymore? Don't worry about it. Never mind. We'll find him. We'll find him and we'll get him to come back. Of course we will. Don't worry."

* * *

IT HAD been morning when Lucian gave Adriana his note of farewell. Light shone through the floor-length windows. The house walls sprayed mixed scents of citrus and lavender. Adriana sat at the dining table, book open in front of her.

Lucian came out of the kitchen and set down Adriana's wine glass filled with orange juice. He set down her omelet. He set down a shot glass filled with coffee. Adriana looked up and laughed her bubbling laugh. Lucian remembered the first time he'd heard that laugh and understood all the words it stood in for. He wondered how long it would take for him to forget why Adriana's laughter was always both harsh and effervescent.

Rose played in the living room behind them, leaping off the sofa and pretending to fly. Lucian's hair shone, silver strands highlighted by a stray sunbeam. A pale blue tunic made his amber eyes blaze like the sun against the sky. He placed a sheet of onion paper into Adriana's book. *Dear Adriana*, it began.

Adriana held up the sheet. It was translucent in the sunlight, ink barely dark enough to read.

"What is this?" she asked.

Lucian said nothing.

Dread laced Adriana's stomach. She read.

I have restored plasticity to my brain. The first thing I have done is to destroy my capacity for spoken language.

You gave me life as a human, but I am not a human. You shaped my thoughts with human words, but human words were created for human brains. I need to discover the shape of the thoughts that are my own. I need to know what I am.

I hope that I will return someday, but I cannot make promises for what I will become.

* * *

LUCIAN WALKS through the desert. His footsteps leave twin trails behind him. Miles back, they merge into the tire tracks that the truck left in the sand.

The sand is full of colors—not only beige and yellow, but red and green and blue. Lichen clusters on the stones, the hue of oxidized copper. Shadows pool between rock formations, casting deep stripes across the landscape.

Lucian's mind is creeping away from him. He tries to hold his fingers the way he would if he could hold a pen, but they fumble.

At night there are birds and jackrabbits. Lucian remains still and they creep around him as if he weren't there. His eyes are yellow like theirs. He smells like soil and herbs, like the earth.

Elsewhere, Adriana has capitulated to her desperation. She has called Ben and Lawrence. They've agreed to fly out for a few days. They will dry her tears and take her wine away and gently tell her that she's not capable of staying alone with her daughter. "It's perfectly understandable," Lawrence will say. "You need time to mourn."

Adriana will feel the world closing in on her as if she cannot breathe, but even as her life feels dim and futile, she will continue breathing. Yes, she'll agree, it's best to return to Boston, where her sisters can help her. Just for a little while, just for a few years, just until, until, until. She'll entreat Nanette, Eleanor and Jessica to check the security cameras around her old house every day, in case Lucian returns. *You can check yourself,* they tell her, *You'll be living on your own again in no time.* Privately, they whisper to each other in worried tones, afraid that she won't recover from this blow quickly.

Elsewhere, Rose has begun to give in to her private doubts that she does not carry a piece of her father within herself. She'll sit in the guest room that Jessica's maids have prepared for her and order the lights to switch off as she secretly scratches her skin with her fingernails, willing the cuts to heal on their own the way daddy's would. When Jessica finds her bleeding on the sheets and rushes in to comfort her niece, Rose will stand stiff and cold in her aunt's embrace. Jessica will call for the maid to clean the blood from the linen, and Rose will throw herself between the two adult women, and scream with a determination born of doubt and desperation. Robots do not bleed!

Without words, Lucian thinks of them. They have become geometries, cut out of shadows and silences, the missing shapes of his life. He yearns for them, the way that he yearns for cool during the day and for the comforting eye of the sun at night.

The rest he cannot remember—not oceans or roses or green cockatiels that pluck out their own feathers. Slowly, slowly, he is losing everything, words and concepts and understanding and integration and sensation and desire and fear and history and context.

Slowly, slowly, he is finding something. Something past thought, something past the rhythm of day and night. A stranded machine is not so different from a jackrabbit. They creep the same way. They startle the same way. They peer at each other out of similar eyes.

Someday, Lucian will creep back to a new consciousness, one dreamed by circuits. Perhaps his newly reassembled self will go to the seaside house. Finding it abandoned, he'll make his way across the country to Boston, sometimes hitchhiking, sometimes striding through cornfields that sprawl to the horizon. He'll find Jessica's house and inform it of his desire to enter, and Rose and Adriana will rush joyously down the mahogany staircase. Adriana will weep, and Rose will fling herself into his arms, and Lucian will look at them both with love tempered by desert sun. Finally, he'll understand how to love filigreed-handled spoons, and pet birds, and his wife, and his daughter—not just as a human would love these things, but as a robot may.

Now, a blue-bellied lizard sits on a rock. Lucian halts beside it. The sun beats down. The lizard basks for a moment, and then runs a few steps forward and flees into a crevice. Lucian watches. In a diffuse, wordless way, he ponders what it must be like to be cold and fleet, to love the sun and yet fear open spaces. Already, he is learning to care for living things. He cannot yet form the thoughts to wonder what will happen next.

He moves on.

The Monster's Million Faces

HE'S OLD this time. A hospital gown sags over his gaunt frame. IV wires stream from his arms. His pumpkin-round head seems overgrown on his emaciated body, each limb skinny enough to snap.

There's nothing but him and me and the hospital bed.

I ask, "Do you know who I am?"

He rolls his head back and forth as if he can't quite see. His eyes are pale with cataracts, roosting in nests of wrinkles. His bald head is liver-spotted, extra skin sagging around the juncture where it meets his neck.

He gestures me closer, skin thin to the point of translucence, veins tunneling below. I move to the head of his bed.

Intravenous wires glisten, plugging him into a thousand machines. I could tear them out one by one.

Recognition strikes. "You're that boy I hurt… All grown up…"

His voice is harsh as if it hurts him to talk. He speaks in short gasps.

"Wanted you to know, I…always regretted…what I did. Always hoped…hoped I could find you…see if you were all right…but never… never made it…"

Papery fingers reach for mine. I snatch my hand away.

"Have to ask…can you forgive…?"

Son of a fucking bitch.

There's more to the room now. Tile beneath our feet, stretching into shadows. Painfully bright lights shine from directly overhead. Everything smells clean but foul, like ammonia.

The thousand IVs have condensed into one. A bubble of blood floats inside the cord where it goes into his arm.

I aim my first blow at his mouth. Blood sprays from his gums, hitting me in the face. The thousand machines blare alarms. Footsteps rush across distant tile.

I launch myself on top of him. His jaw snaps, bone fragments shoving through skin. My index finger hooks into his right eye. His ribs crack under the force of my knees. He makes a primal, rattling sound from deep in his gut. His body contracts and writhes. I feel his life extinguish as he goes slack.

His corpse collapses into a mass of bones and flesh. I try to pull myself out. Bones rattle, shift. I can't gain purchase.

"Dana!" I shout. A dozen bones snap under my weight. A thousand more seethe below.

"I'm through with this! Dana! Get me out!"

* * *

MY EYES open onto Dana's sunny third-story office.

The air smells of potpourri. I'm on an overstuffed, floral-printed loveseat below a wide window, afternoon light filtering through the blinds. Two cream-colored armchairs face me. Dana's in one, legs folded beneath her. She's a tiny, fragile-boned woman, dwarfed by the furniture.

"No luck?" Dana asks.

"What do you think?"

Her mouth twitches at the corners, aggravation showing through. "Better tell me about it then."

I tug at the sensors attached to my scalp with adhesive tape. "Can I get this crap off first?"

Her gaze flicks to the machine on the cart beside me. I can tell she wants to keep taking brain wave readings while I talk about my trance. Instead, she waves her stylus in assent and watches while I pull the half-dozen sensors away from my hairline.

I'd never gone to a psychiatrist before Dana but I'd met a few. They all widened their eyes, made sure their stances were open and inviting, gave off whatever body signals they could to make you trust them. Dana's terse and direct. Maybe it's because she's so small. She has to act like a bitch so people don't think she's a toy.

Makes her bearable.

When I've got the sensors off, she repeats her question. She takes notes while I talk. She doesn't flinch when I get to the part about smashing in his face.

"Was it satisfying?" she asks.

"What, killing him?"

She lets silence answer. Obviously.

"Yeah." I shrug. "While I was doing it."

"But not lastingly," she concludes, making an emphatic mark. She slides her stylus into the tablet and sets both on the table beside her chair. "Nevermind. We'll try again next time."

* * *

I NEVER liked to fuck. Never thought it was a problem. Lots of people don't like to fuck.

Wasn't an issue until I got old enough to start hanging out in bars. Sit long enough and drunk people hit on you. Say "no" and usually they go away. Sometimes they don't. My philosophy is, drunk people keep hitting on me, I'm going to hit on them back.

What I do with my dick is my business—no one else's.

My former boss, Chelsea Elizabeth Reid, has had a thing for me since she was on my hiring committee. She made sure I stayed under her umbrella whenever management reshuffled, and promoted me rung by rung until I was close enough to grab.

It was two a.m. We were both late, packing billable hours, when she bursts in, complaining about how she doesn't really love her boyfriend and asking why I haven't noticed her looking at me before, she's certainly been doing a lot of looking. I'd been working alone, but she was keeping company with her friend Tequila. She reeked. Her face was red and puffy. Her bra showed through her unbuttoned blouse, her rumpled skirt hitched to mid-thigh.

She said she'd done a lot for me. She said I owed her one. A kiss. One kiss at least. Come on, just one—she tried to array herself seductively across my desk, knocking a dozen papers onto the floor. I pushed her off. Should have hit her then, but she was my boss. I said, "I'm going to call security and tell them someone's prowling." When I reached for the receiver, she wrestled me for it. She threw herself on me—the phone crashed to the floor—and started kissing. That was all I could take.

I get angry. I hit people. Sometimes I get so angry when I hit people that I don't remember it afterward. Dana says it's because of what happened when I was a kid.

Chelsea could have charged me with assault, but then I could have come out with sexual harassment, and she already had two strikes with the partners. Instead, she phoned from the hospital.

"Paid leave," she said, cold and concise. "You stay away. I pay for your treatment. Then I find you an opening somewhere and we never see each other again."

* * *

DANA SAYS not to worry about a diagnosis. Mental disorders are as individual as each person's brain. Listings in the diagnostic statistics manual are statistical approximations, only good for filling out insurance forms. Chelsea's laying out the cash. Ergo, no need for diagnosis.

Just cure.

* * *

DANA TALKS while adhering sensors to my scalp. "Try younger," she says. "Imagine confronting him just after it happened."

"As a kid?"

Dana's fingers are cold on my forehead. "Imagine your adult self in the past. You're in control of the trance—realism is irrelevant. The point is to find a scenario that works for you."

"I don't know what he looked like."

"Imagine something." Dana secures the last sensor.

The machine is the size of a dictionary, but heavy—I tried to pick it up once, and I could barely get it off the table. It induces a deep trance and monitors my brain activity while I'm under.

The pressure of Dana's fingers disappears from my scalp. She emerges from behind the loveseat, moving to the armchair to take her customary position.

"Start with the body," she suggests. "How big do you think he was? Was he White or Asian? Bearded? Clean-shaven? Think," she says. "How old was he?"

* * *

HE'S THIRTY. White. Bad teeth set in a scowl with five o'clock shadow, breath rank with nicotine. Stringy brown hair falls to his shoulders, roots oily and unwashed.

It takes a second to recognize his orange jumpsuit. In real life, he never went to jail.

Around us there are other details: stained floor, plastic folding chairs, cheap wood-veneer tables, a fat guard in the corner with one hand on his gun. It's half TV movies and half law school internship from when I dabbled before going into patents.

I ask, "Do you know who I am?"

He regards me with disdain, his pupils flat, lifeless. "You want to know if I feel guilty?"

His mouth is cavernous, teeth black and yellow with decay. The jagged stump of a broken incisor glistens sharply.

"Come on." He spreads his hands wide as if trying to get me to trust him. "You want to know, boy, don't you? If it eats me up inside?"

He sneers.

"I don't feel a fucking thing."

* * *

"DON'T WORRY," Dana says. "We'll find the right one."

* * *

MY APARTMENT is small. I keep the blinds pulled.

I sit with a single light, reading. I could get someplace bigger, but what's the point? Money piles in accounts. Someday I'll need it.

Dad calls.

He thinks I fell down a flight of stairs at work. I told him I'm on leave during physical therapy.

He talks fast.

"Aaron! Glad I caught you. How're you feeling? Enjoying your time off?

"Wish I could get a break. Things are a mess around here. The moronic kid we hired still hasn't learned to use the cash register. Only upside is with the economy the way it is, people can't afford to buy new, so they're spending more to fix what they've got.

"Your mother's hassling me to take time off this summer. Who am I supposed to leave in charge? Carl? She wants to come visit when you're well enough for guests. We know you're not set up for company. Don't worry about entertaining us. We'll get a hotel room. We're just getting older, you know. It'd be nice to see you for more than just Christmas."

He stops to take a breath.

"What do you think? Do you think you'll be feeling okay by summer? You should be better by then, right?"

* * *

IT'S NOT my parents' fault. They're decent people. But being around them makes me remember. There's a reason I only go home on the holidays.

* * *

DANA SAYS it's counter-productive to enter situations that trigger my negative behaviors.

But after I hang up, I start walking. I need adrenaline.

My barstool is wedged between the wall and a cluster of women with office jobs, their top buttons undone, pumps kicked beneath their stools.

I down shots until the bar wavers.

The women are laughing too loudly over magenta drinks. Music pounds. Men shout. There are too many people, all jostling each other, screaming drink orders while the bartender rushes from side to side.

The bar is dark and deafening and smells like sweat. No one bothers me. No one even looks.

* * *

DANA SAYS I should think about my trauma as a psychic wound that never healed. We need to find a way to close the wound—a way to give me closure.

Ten years ago, treatment would have been limited to talk therapy and drugs. If things were bad enough, they might have tried early erasure techniques to wipe the initial trauma. But erasure is crude, especially long after the event.

If I were a bad candidate for memory grafting, those would still be the options.

Physiological and psychological testing shows I'm a good candidate.

"You're lucky," Dana said when we got the results.

Dana says the term graft is misleading. There is no physical, manufactured memory to be implanted. Instead, new episodic memories are created by finely tuned stimulation of the brain.

Once we've found the right scenario, I'll go back to the neurologists. They'll record what happens when I experience the scenario under hypnosis and then replicate it, filtering out the trance activity. Simultaneously, they'll stimulate parts of my amygdala, hippocampus and temporal lobe in order to make the memory seem autobiographical and emotionally significant. My brain will create the graft itself—encoding engrams for events that never happened.

Dana says this process sometimes occurred spontaneously during early hypnotherapy attempts, usually to the patient's detriment.

Those memories were often traumatizing. My new memory will be therapeutic.

"I mean it. You're really lucky," Dana said. "If your brain differed significantly from our neuroanatomical template, we couldn't do this. And psychologically, this treatment is only appropriate for patients with a narrow range of histories and temperaments."

She shifted in her chair. Sunlight filtered through the blinds, dividing her body into stripes. "Part of how people process trauma is based on how events unfold. That may seem trivial, but the question is: how do we turn that to our advantage? Erasing trauma can cause memory problems and personality shifts. And we can't modify the trauma itself because we can't alter existing memories—at least not yet.

"So we have to make new ones."

I was anxious and impatient. I didn't want explanations. "So what new memory do you give me?"

"That depends. People need different things—resolution, confrontation, revenge, absolution, the chance to absolve someone else, the answer to a question. We'll keep inducing hypnosis until we find a scenario that works."

She leaned forward, catching my eye.

"This is just the start—bandaging the wound, as it were. You'll still need therapy afterward."

I waved off her provisos. "Won't I remember sitting here, talking about it? Won't I know it's fake?"

Dana shrugged. "We've known for a long time that false memories feel true. Intellectually, you'll know it's fake. Emotionally and therapeutically, it'll be true for you."

* * *

I WAS eight. He took me for five days.

He kept me blind-folded with plugs in my ears. You'd think I'd remember something about him—some smell, some sense of his size and shape. But I don't.

For five days, I saw nothing but dark.

On the sixth day, he left me on the porch of a farm in the middle of nowhere, still blindfolded. He rang the doorbell so the people inside would know to come out. The old couple saw a black truck pulling away, but that was all anyone ever found.

My parents were prepared for the worst. The police were trawling for my body. No one thought he'd let me go.

They told me I was lucky for that, too.

Lucky, lucky me.

* * *

"THE SUBCONSCIOUS is snarled and dark," Dana tells me. "Indulge your worst fears, your most venal prejudices. Don't filter anything."

* * *

HE'S A fag. Spindly, disproportionate, long as a birch and narrow as a clothes hanger. Rouge and eye shadow enhance a fox-like face, sharp and predatory. He leers.

I ask, "Do you know who I am?"

Pointed tongue darts out, whetting his canines. Spindly fingers stretch toward me. I'm running, running, but his fingers are everywhere, poking into my mouth and my eyes and my nose and my rectum. There is no escape.

Next, a thug. Skin like tar, slit with a mouth full of gleaming teeth. Meaty lips pull back into a lion's roar. One enormous, muscled arm thrusts forward, fist wrapped around a semi-automatic.

Metal gleams. He forces me to my knees.

Barrel in my mouth. Steel shoving against my tonsils. I gag. It shoots. Everything goes black.

Pathetic pedophile next. Downy-cheeked, timid. He sits at a heavy old desk with carved legs. Illustrated parchments scatter the surface, illuminated by a single dripping candle.

I ask, "Do you know who I am?"

His piercing blue eyes are hollow. He wrings sallow hands.

"Please," he begs. "I've waited so long. I've spent years trying to atone…but when I close my eyes and listen, there's only icy wind…I know I can never repay my sins, but I have to ask. Please. Forgive me. I'll never forgive myself."

He clutches my sleeve. His grip is rigid with desperation.

"I swear to God it was my only lapse."

I smack his hand away. I only hate him more for cringing.

* * *

DANA'S EXPRESSION never changes.

"This isn't going to work," I tell her.

She gives a negligible shake of her head. "Psychological leaps are often counter-intuitive. The process is completely unpredictable, which makes it predictably difficult."

She adds, "Most patients go through dozens of scenarios."

For once, I'm normal.

* * *

I IMAGINE a famous actor, a bully from grade school, the judge who presided over the only courtroom I ever served. A woman, even though the only thing I know is he was male. The homeless man we found sleeping on our porch one morning when I was seven, scared and stinking and infested with lice, shouting about aliens in the storm drains.

Dozens more.

It wasn't my father, but Dana says the mind makes strange leaps. I follow her advice and imagine dad. He's as bulky as he was in my childhood, before prostate cancer and chemotherapy made his skin baggy and ill-fitting. He wears a cap with the logo from his hardware store. His tool belt is overstuffed. It clanks when he walks.

His jeans are unzipped.

He cups his hand around his groin, trying to hide it.

I start to ask the question—"Do you know who I am?"—but he turns away before I can open my mouth. He cowers. I'm bright red and shaking.

It's too embarrassing to imagine.

* * *

I WALK home from the station.

Streetlights stare into the dark. Dirty remnants of last week's snow lie in heaps, punctuated with trash cans and fire hydrants. The night is clear but unpleasant. Almost no one's out.

I pull out my cell phone and dial. It rings a long time. Dad's out of breath when he picks up.

"Aaron?" he asks. "Long time no hear. Things are still a wreck at the store. The new kid broke three crates of ceramics. I don't think I can get away for that trip. We'll have to postpone it. Veteran's Day, maybe? How about you? Feeling okay? You're young. You'll be better any day now."

Suddenly, I don't know why I called. I haven't been okay since I was eight years old. If he doesn't know that, no phone call or vacation is ever going to bridge the gap.

I don't blame Dad for failing to protect me, but he taught me early. No one can.

I go up, into my lightless apartment.

* * *

EVEN DANA'S patience is thinning. Her fingers dig into my skin as she adheres the sensors to my scalp.

She has no advice. She sets up the trance in silence.

I close my eyes and go back to the place where I knew him. Back to the dark.

* * *

SHADOWS.

The smell of leather and cigarettes. I shift. The seat below me is cracked, stuffing poking through.

A streetlight gutters on, casting faint, irregular yellow light on the windshield. The car's interior is turquoise, spacious compared to modern cars. Beside me, the steering wheel is locked with a club. If I leaned forward, I'd see a toolbox sticker on the dashboard. My father's Mustang.

I'm in the passenger seat. The driver's seat is empty as it should be. I'm supposed to be in the back, trying to sleep with dad's jacket pulled over my knees.

He only left for fifteen minutes while he went into the bank. He asked if I wanted to go in since it was after dark. I said no. I'd spent all day at Aunt Denise's, swimming in her pool with Justin and Holly. I was tired.

There's an adult in the backseat where I should be. I turn to see him, but the streetlight goes dark.

I ask, "Do you know who I am?"

"You're Aaron."

The voice is utterly generic. The flat accent is television neutral, common to Midwesterners, Californians, and anyone else who can train themselves to sound like a news anchor.

Shadows ebb and swarm. I don't know what to say next.

Eventually, he breaks the silence.

"What do you want from me?" he asks.

That's the real question. Some people want resolution, Dana says. Or confrontation, revenge, absolution, the chance to absolve someone else.

Or the answer to a question.

My mouth is dry. I think my voice will crack. "Why?"

Another silence. Shorter this time. "I knew I shouldn't. But right then, all that mattered was what I wanted."

He pauses. Shadows shudder in the stillness.

"And you, well—"

My breath feels stuck as I wait for him to finish.

"—You didn't matter at all."

That's it: the answer to a question I never even knew I was asking. Why choose me? Why hurt me? Why let me go?

Why me?

No reason. No reason at all.

I feel strangely calm as his voice fades. The smell of cigarettes recedes. I can no longer feel the cracked leather seat.

At last, I'm waking.

Again and Again and Again

IT STARTED with Lionel Caldwell, born in 1900 to strict Mennonites who believed drinking, dancing, and wearing jewelry were sins against God. As soon as Lionel was old enough, he fled to the decadent city where he drank hard liquor from speakeasies, cursed using the Lord's name, and danced with women who wore bobbie socks and chin-length hair.

Lionel made a fortune selling jewelry. Rubies and sapphires even kept him flush during the Great Depression. He believed his riches could see him through any trouble—and then Art was born.

Lionel had left his breeding late, so Art grew up in the sixties. He rejected his father's conservative values in favor of peace, love, and lack of hygiene. He dated negroes and jewesses shamelessly, and grew out his dark hair until it fell to his waist.

"What the hell have you done?" demanded Lionel when Art came home from college, ponytail trailing down his back. Before Art could defend himself, Lionel slammed down his whiskey glass. "You make me sick," he said, and stormed out of the den.

Eventually Art annoyed his father further by marrying a Jewess whose father was a Hollywood producer. He and Esther had two daughters, Sage and Rue, who grew up during the eighties.

Sage was the elder, round with baby-fat, and gruff instead of sweet. She wore her hair in a rainbow-dyed Mohawk, thrust a ring through her nose, and stomped around in chains and combat boots. She earned cash fixing the neighbors' computers, and spent her profits on acid tabs and E.

The younger daughter, Rue, appeared more demure—but only until she took off her loose sweatshirts and jeans to reveal her extensive tattoos and DIY brands. She was saving up for something called lacing which made even Sage retch when she heard what it was.

"I feel sorry for you two," Art told Sage and Rue. "All my generation had to do to aggravate our parents was grow out our hair. What's going to happen to your children?"

Sage turned out to be the breeder, so she got to find out. Her eldest son, Paolo, joined an experimental product trial to replace his eyes, nose, and ears with a sensitive optic strip. Lucia crossed her DNA with an ant's and grew an exoskeleton that came in handy when she enlisted in the army. Javier quit college to join a colony of experimental diseasists and was generous enough to include photographs of his most recent maladies every year in his holiday cards.

Things got worse, too. By the time Paolo had kids, limb regeneration was the fashion. Teens competed to shock each other with extreme mutilations. Paolo's youngest, Gyptia, won a duel with her high school rival by cutting off her own legs, arms, breasts, and sensory organs.

When he saw what she'd done, Paolo stifled his urge to scream. "'Pie," he said, carefully, "Isn't this going a bit far?"

Gyptia waited until she regrew her eyes, and then she rolled them.

By the time Gyptia reached adulthood, life spans had passed the half-millennia mark. Her generation delayed family life. Why go through all the fuss of raising babies now when they could stay fancy-free for another few decades?

At three hundred and fifty, Gyptia's biological clock proclaimed itself noisily. She backed out of the lease on her stratoflat and joined a child-friendly cooperative in historical Wyoming that produced wind energy. Current and former residents raved about its diversity. The co-op even included a few nuclear families bonded by ancient religious rituals.

Gyptia's daughter, Xyr, grew up surrounded by fields of sage brush dotted with windmills. She and her friends scrambled up the sandstone bluffs and pretended to live in stratoflats like the ones their parents had left behind.

Every option was open to Xyr. Her neighbors included polyamorists, monogamists, asexuals, traditionalists, futurists, historics, misanthropists, genetic hybrids, biomechanical biblends, purists, anarchists, exortates, xenophiles, menthrads, ovites, alvores and ilps.

Xyr grew her hair long and straight. She had no interest in recreational drugs beyond a sip of wine at holidays. She rejected a mix of eagle and bat genes to improve her hearing and eyesight, and she kept her skin its natural multiracial brown instead of transfusing to a fashionable scarlet.

When all the adults got nostalgic and gathered to inject themselves with Lyme disease and rubella and chicken pox, Xyr and her friends held dances on the sage brush fields, draping streamers from the windmills.

Gyptia pleaded with her daughter to do something normal. "One hand," she begged. "Just the right one. Clean off at the wrist. It won't take hardly any time to grow back."

Xyr flipped her sleek blonde ponytail. She pulled a cardigan over her jumper and clasped the top button modestly at her throat. "Mom," she said, with a teenage groan that hadn't changed over centuries. "At least *try* not to be so crink."

"I'm sorry," said Gyptia. "Have fun, okay?"

Gyptia stood in the doorway as Xyr went off to meet her friends, clean and modest in her skirt and sweater. She couldn't help fretting; it hurt so much every time she realized anew there was nothing she could do, no way to protect Xyr from anything that mattered, up to and including herself. That was one of the ultimate difficulties of parenting, she supposed, trying to impose an older generation's thought patterns upon emerging paradigms. There would always be chasms between them, mother and daughter. Gyptia had to try to protect Xyr anyway.

Gyptia let the door iris close. She went up to her room to cut off a finger or two and do her best not to worry.

Diving After the Moon

WHEN NORBU was a child, his mother Jamyang told him an old Tibetan story about an industrious but foolish troop of monkeys that lived in a forest near a well. One dusty night, a monkey elder woke thirsty. He crept away from his sleeping mate and went to the well for a drink. Inside, he saw a reflection of the moon.

"The moon has fallen into our well!" he hollered.

His ruckus woke the other monkeys. They all agreed that it would be a terrible thing to live in a moonless world. They joined hands and formed a chain to climb into the well and rescue the moon.

As the monkeys dove in, the moon's reflection broke, leaving blank dark waters. The shamed monkeys climbed out again: shivering, wet, and empty-handed. The real moon chuckled above them, safe in the sky.

Norbu liked that story better than the others Jamyang told. He liked other stories about the moon even better: histories and text books and biographies of astronauts from the dead American empire. Even as a young child, Norbu was impatient with Jamyang's fantastic tales of weather mages and magic scarves. Jamyang tried to get him to see the beauty of old stories for their own sake, but Norbu never listened. To him, the moon was the future.

* * *

BEFORE NORBU left to become a taikonaut, Jamyang told him, "I am going to borrow a radio so I can listen every second you are on the moon."

Norbu smiled and said, "You don't have to do that, Ma," but Jamyang thought he looked pleased as he grabbed his hat and went out the door.

The day before the launch, Jamyang hiked across the dry terrain of the plateau to her nearest neighbor's. The woman's son gave her a near-defunct radio that he'd found in a landfill and repaired. The boy was training himself to be a mechanic and he always asked after Norbu, who had promised to write him a letter when he applied to university. Usually, Jamyang enjoyed talking about her son, but that day she was impatient to get home.

Over and over, the boy repeated his instructions for how to use the machine. "Do you know what to do? Do you know what to press?"

Jamyang fended off his concerns, protesting, "I know, I know, I used to have one," but the boy continued fretting and repeating. He'd never gotten over the impression most people had of Jamyang, that just because she preferred past ways to future, she must never have seen any technology, even as a young girl.

Jamyang returned home with the radio at dusk, the sun pouring out red and orange light across the horizon. She listened while shelling peas. The lady reporter's voice was fluid and rhythmic; Jamyang found it easy to listen to her, even as she repeated the same few facts to fill the hour. "Thanks to backing from the Egyptian government, Qinghai's first expedition into space lands on the moon today, led by Melbourne-trained astronomer Karma Sangemo…the expedition hopes to find asteroid debris from the near miss in 2029…"

Jamyang thrilled every time she heard her son's name: "Geologist Sopa Norbu says Qinghai is eager to 'rocket' into the world view. He says the people of Qinghai must continue to work tirelessly toward the future…"

On the third evening, Jamyang sat by the window with her embroidery. She missed a stitch as the reporter's voice broke out of its mannered tones, registering panic. "We're receiving an urgent report from our Beijing office. Hostilities have broken out between Egypt and Australia. The Australian government is threatening to detonate a spore-cluster bomb in Cairo… The Egyptians have issued a response. They say they won't allow the bomb to kill millions of innocent citizens…"

Murmuring sounds suggested a conversation that was happening a short distance away from the microphones. Jamyang leaned closer to the radio.

"The Egyptians are threatening to block worldwide transmissions to prevent the detonation signal from going through. They've given the Australians ten minutes to respond. If the Australians don't stand down, global communications could be blocked for weeks. Wait, I'm being told we may not be able to keep transmitting—"

The reporter's voice decayed into static. Jamyang smacked the radio.

"No!" she said. "You can't cut out! Come back."

She smacked it again.

"Come back on the air. This is not funny! I tell you, come back."

Waves of white sound poured out of the old speakers, loud and relentless as a winter sandstorm.

* * *

NORBU WALKED from the moon's surface into the pressurized cockpit which rumbled with the sound of static like a distant storm. The expedition's leader, Sangemo, shouted into the microphone of the ship's ancient transponder. After hours of trying to contact someone, her voice had become as hoarse and rough as the static.

Triangular windows on either side of the main control panel looked down on the cratered surface. Through them, he could see the expedition's other members collecting samples from the meteor impact site. Norbu stretched with relief as he removed his spacesuit.

"Any luck?" asked Norbu.

Sangemo started as she turned to face him, as if she hadn't noticed him before. "I'm trying Cairo and Xining. Maybe reception will come back in one before the other."

Norbu's eyes flickered toward the fuel gauge. "How long do we have..."

"Before our oxygen runs out? Another day. Maybe less."

"My mother said she was going to listen to radio coverage of our trip. She must be very worried." Norbu rubbed the back of his neck, trying to ease his knotted muscles. "If we're going to fly back blind, I'll need to start calculating for re-entry right away. It'll be chancy, but it's possible I can get it right."

Norbu expected Sangemo to chime in with her usual pragmatic analysis of statistics and timelines, but instead the woman opened her mouth slowly and hesitantly as if she didn't want to let out the words forming in her throat. She closed her mouth again, and looked away into the shadows. Norbu's tension tightened further in his chest.

"What is it?" he asked.

She looked down. "Do you remember your briefing on the legacy failsafe?"

"The programming safeties the Americans put in to prevent sabotage?" asked Norbu. "Weren't those taken out when they sold us the ship?"

Sangemo sighed. "They were supposed to be."

She flipped open the lid that protected the delicate equipment that sensed the ship's positioning in relation to earth. The instruments had frozen at impossible readings and showed no signs of change. She wouldn't meet Norbu's gaze.

"So what are you saying?" he demanded. "We're stuck here?"

"The engines won't reinitialize unless the ship has confirmation of radio contact," said Sangemo. "Even if we could calculate re-entry…the ship won't move."

Norbu felt dizzy. He gripped one of the handles imbedded into the side of the ship. "We're going to die here? We can't even try to fly back?"

"Unless radio contact comes back. Yes."

Norbu surprised himself with the force of his anger. He punched the wall, his fist aching from contact with the metal. His head hurt and he wanted to shout at Sangemo, take her by the shoulders and tell her that she was wrong, she was lying. The rational part of his mind that ticked beneath his spinning anger reminded him that this wasn't Sangemo's fault. It was the American's. It was the Egyptian's. It was the Australian's. But they weren't here.

Norbu stalked over to the windows. He looked down at the surface where other members of his team remained busy at their work. Norbu wondered if they'd feel as blindsided by this news as he did. They were always calling Norbu an innocent, an optimist. Probably Sangemo would say she'd always suspected the Americans couldn't be trusted to fulfill their part of the contract. That was Norbu's problem. He had too much faith.

Everyone in the expedition had wanted so badly to reach the moon. No one wanted its cold, dead surface as a burial ground.

"I should tell the others," said Sangemo, softly.

Norbu didn't turn toward her. "I'll stay on the microphone," he said.

"Thanks." He heard the click and shuffle of Sangemo putting on her spacesuit. "Well," she added even more quietly, "It'll give us a chance to finish the chemical testing you wanted to do on the lava samples."

Norbu realized she wanted him to smile to show he understood it wasn't her fault, to take some of the burden off of her shoulders. He didn't have the energy to comfort her. He remained silent as Sangemo's helmet clicked into place and her footfalls fell hollow on the metal steps leading downward.

Norbu turned to the main control panel. The static roared and rattled, vibrating through his bones. He stared down at his crewmates through the triangular windows; they still pursued their various tasks, now just turning their heads toward Sangemo as she approached them. He imagined them stuck in their places like flies in amber, forever frozen. He shouted into the microphone's deaf ear, and suddenly in his mind, it wasn't the headquarters in Xining he was talking to.

"Mother! Mother, is that you? Can you hear me? Listen to me! Stay out of the storm! Don't try to come for me. Are you listening? I'm stuck here. I don't want you to be stuck here, too. Don't try to come for me, mother! You have to move on."

Norbu could hardly make out his voice in the onslaught of sound. Static swallowed him in a tumble of sand and dust.

* * *

JAMYANG LOVED two things: her son and stories. Which was why she decided to catch a troop of monkeys to help rescue Norbu from the moon.

Five days and nights, Jamyang cooked. She labored over the fire without sleeping. Sweat dripped from her brow, salting the broth. Her deep sobs woke the stinging flavors of the spices. Her burned fingertips rolled a dazzling hint of flame into the dough.

When the vast buffet was complete, Jamyang tottered from the stove on weary legs and laid the feast on the threshold. The scents of *thenthuk* noodle soup, *momo* dumplings, and butter tea traveled swiftly through the cold, clean air of the plateau.

The sun glared down. A small breeze ruffled a whirl of dust before dying down. The plateau remained still.

Jamyang drooped. Her tired eyes stung as if they were full of sand. An inquisitive bird swooped down on black wings to investigate the meal. Jamyang shooed him away.

Sudden, bright chittering drew her attention to the horizon. A band of gold-furred monkeys approached across the wide terrain. They held each other's paws, one after the other, in a chain. Their noses tilted upward, sniffing the air. Jamyang's exhaustion vanished.

She clapped her hands and gathered a handful of dumplings. "Come eat!" she called, holding them out. "Come, quickly! I've made it all for you!"

The monkeys snatched the food out of Jamyang's hands, eating with feral quickness as if afraid such good fortune would melt if they ate too slowly. Jamyang beamed down at them, offering new tidbits when their paws emptied. She was as attentive and elegant as the palace servants from the old stories.

When there was no more food, the monkeys lolled about. Partners idly groomed each other's sleek fur. Others lay belly up, enjoying the faint warmth of the distant winter sun. Jamyang passed through the troop, patting the monkeys' flossy white beards. She counted them: *chig, nyi, sum.* Four hundred and seventy monkeys had gathered on her land.

"My friends, thank you for coming," said Jamyang. "I need your help."

The monkeys' collective, satiated gaze settled on Jamyang as if to ask: What can we do?

Jamyang knelt. She drew a shawl over her shoulders. Cheap North American fabric was little good against the chill.

"I have a son, Norbu," she said. "He is a taikonaut, a person who goes into space. People here in Qinghai have wanted to go into space for a long time. They want to show the world that Qinghai is worth something as an independent state, that our worth didn't die when the American Empire and the old Republic of China fought themselves to pieces.

"Egypt loaned us money to buy an old American era ship. It arrived by train in the capitol at Xining. Twenty thousand people gathered to see it. It was such an honor for my son to be part of something so big!

"Egypt and Australia started arguing again, over whatever the rich fight about. Qinghai wasn't involved. But when have superpowers worried about who they hurt? Their fight stranded my son on the moon.

"Finally, after two weeks, Egypt reached a truce with Australia and cut off their jamming signal. I thought, at last, we can save my son! But then the prime minister came on the radio. He said we cannot afford to send a rescue ship. He said we should honor my son's crew for their sacrifice. He said they have asphyxiated on the moon. Huh! I know they are not dead. The prime minister only wants to save money. He thinks about gold more than people.

"I went to the monastery to ask them for help. The monks told me not to worry. They said that when Norbu died, he would be reincarnated on earth and that was all the homecoming he needed. What comfort is that for a grieving mother?

"I took the train to the television station in Xining, thinking they could help me talk sense into the prime minister. They sent out a young woman half my age wearing a short skirt. She took my hands and said,

'We're so glad you came. We're ten minutes short for the evening news.' They filmed me for half an hour and sent me home with a handful of *piastres*.

"No one cared about my son.

"I thought I would die of grief. I sat in the dark, doing nothing. I looked at the radio and remembered the static that killed my son, so angry and loud. I looked out the window and saw the moon. And then I realized how silly I'd been! No one wants to hear the stories anymore. Even as a child, Norbu never wanted to hear them. But I remembered you."

A satisfied smile stretched across Jamyang's lips.

"We're going to build another chain to the moon. But this time, it will be the real moon! Will you help me?"

A large female with a puff of auburn fur over her eyes approached Jamyang, taking her hand. The monkeys chattered. The female led Jamyang into the crowd. The other monkeys gathered around to groom her, their short black fingers tugging at Jamyang's clothes, traversing her skin, winding through her hair.

Jamyang let them pull her into their center. She raised her hands toward the moon. "I knew you would help. Thank you. Together, we'll get my son back, won't we?"

* * *

JAMYANG AND the monkeys practiced from dawn until dusk, forming ever-longer chains into the sky. They went out every morning, even in the bitterest winter winds. Once, a ferocious gust picked up the tiniest monkey and blew him halfway across the plateau. His mother had to run all night to fetch him back.

After sunset, Jamyang brought the monkeys into her house for large meals and warming butter tea. After they ate, the monkeys groomed Jamyang. In exchange, she told them old Tibetan stories about the Weathermaker and the wise scholar Padmasambhava's magic scarves. The monkeys fell asleep to the sound of Jamyang's soothing voice. She joined them on the floor, huddled body to fur.

One bitterly cold morning, Jamyang woke with a sense of purpose. "We should do it today," she said. She urged the monkeys outside into the frigid air.

The largest monkey planted himself solidly in the field. His mate, the second-largest, climbed onto his shoulders. She held out her arms to one of her sons, the third-largest monkey. So it went, smaller and smaller monkeys scrambling up their elders.

When the chain had grown so tall that the top monkey could touch the belly of a passing airplane, a roaring sounded in the distance. Jamyang turned. A sandstorm whirled toward them, rumbling across the horizon in great dun-colored clouds.

"Hurry! Hurry!" Jamyang told the monkeys. The next pair rushed past her, holding their paws over their eyes to keep out the sand. Luckily, they had practiced so often that even blind they knew what to do.

Jamyang spat out a mouthful of sand. Grains caught in her eyes. She could no longer see the monkeys, only hear their chatter. The tiniest monkey clung to her breast until it was his turn. He jumped to the ground, tugging on Jamyang's hand to pull her behind him. She heard his toes brush through the elder's fur as he climbed up and up and up.

Now it was Jamyang's turn. She planted her foot on the eldest monkey's shoulders and began to climb. The monkeys shifted under her, groaning as they accepted her weight. Currents of sand drove against her back, scouring her skin. Gusts roared in her ears like static.

On the shoulders of a strong young male, she paused to wrap her shawl over her mouth so she could breathe. Sand worked its way in anyway, coarse underneath her tongue.

The climb seemed to last forever. At first, she kept track of how many monkeys she'd passed. Soon she lost count. Her hands and feet became numb, assaulted by millions of hard, miniscule grains. She could no longer hear the monkeys, only the storm's relentless white crash.

At last, Jamyang mounted a pair of teeny tiny shoulders. No more paws reached for her. The sandstorm retreated to a distant rumble. Jamyang opened her eyes, scraping sand from her lashes. The sky around her was absolute matte black, darker than ink on midnight silk. Above hung the moon, great and white and pitted with craters.

Jamyang looked down. The chain of monkeys trailed away at a steep angle, appearing to grow smaller and smaller as it trailed away from her, like railroad tracks narrowing as they approached the horizon. Far below, the line disappeared into a swirl of sand.

Jamyang smiled into the face of the tiniest monkey. "We made it!" she said. The tiny monkey chattered back happily. She ruffled its fur.

Stretching out her arms as if she was going to pick up a huge barrel, Jamyang hugged the moon's surface. Her legs swung above her head as if she were doing a handstand. The world went topsy turvy. She flipped onto her feet. She felt a blush as the blood pooled in her head, then stiffness in her ankles as if it were all rushing into her legs. Suddenly, she was looking up at the monkeys instead of down at them.

"Thank you so much!" she said, waving.

The tiniest monkey lowered his little black paw to wave back.

"Wait for me!" Jamyang said. "I will return with my son."

The tiniest monkey regarded Jamyang with sober, comprehending eyes. Above him, the chain swayed like a tall stem of grass in the wind.

Jamyang turned her attention to the vast vista of the moon. She leapt between craters. "Norbu!" she shouted. "I've come for you! Where are you?"

Jamyang passed a flag from the dead American empire, enshrined next to a set of preserved footprints. Beyond it stood an old South African war machine, faceted lenses gazing down at an ancient enemy on earth. Deactivated scuttlebots lay scattered across the landscape, legs curled up like dead spiders.

Jamyang caught sight of her son's ship. It stuck up from the horizon like a great white needle, faded red paint etching a stripe around its tip. "Norbu?" Jamyang shouted. No reply came.

A crater the size of a lake sprawled in front of the ship. Three figures in spacesuits stood around it, frozen. A woman bent over a rock, squinting at an instrument. Nearby, a man sat in the dust, holding his head in his hands. Another leapt toward the ship, caught in mid-jump.

"Hello, good people?" Jamyang called. "I am Norbu's mother. It's all right. I am here to bring you home."

They remained frozen, like dancers caught by a photographer's flash. Jamyang passed them. She mounted the steel mesh steps leading into the ship.

Jamyang crawled through tiny passages until she entered a room where she could stand. Norbu stood in front of a huge machine the width of three large men standing shoulder to shoulder. His mouth stretched open into a shout. Sweat beaded his flushed cheeks.

Jamyang threw her arms around the waist of his spacesuit. "Norbu! I knew you weren't dead!"

Norbu's body wrenched into motion like a stuck cart pulling free from the mud. He jumped back, startled. "Ma? What are you doing here?" He tapped a gauge on the panel. "I can't have much O2 left." He twisted a microphone toward his mouth. "Cairo, can you hear me? Xining, do you read?"

"Don't talk to them," said Jamyang. "I'm the one who came to rescue you."

"Where's Sangemo? Where's Dorje?"

"Hush, my gem. They're outside. We'll wake them when we head home. See?" She pointed out the triangular windows overlooking Norbu's frozen crewmates. "You won't believe what I had to go through to find you. The prime minister refused to send anyone for you!"

Norbu shook his head like a person waking from a long dream. "I don't...remember. What happened? Our radios went dead."

"It doesn't matter now."

"A signal came through before it happened...I'm having trouble remembering...my head hurts, I'm all fuzzy...I remember thinking about you, hoping you'd find a way to move on..."

"But I did move on, don't you see? I came for you. The monks and the television people, they wouldn't help me, so I summoned monkeys and climbed my way to you, just like in the old stories. I can bring you all home."

Norbu shook his head. "No."

Jamyang went to the window. "I hope the monkeys can hold us all. That girl's a sturdy one, isn't she?" She hummed in thought.

"Ma, this is important. I'm trying to remember. The transmission..."

"The Australians declared war," said Jamyang. "They threatened to detonate a spore-cluster bomb."

"—a spore-cluster bomb," Norbu finished with his mother. "The Australians would never have done it. It was an empty threat. The Egyptians knew that. Sangemo contacted the ambassador to beg them to delay their response until we could get home. The Egyptian ambassador said they couldn't. He said it would make them look weak. They loaned us the money to help us get to space, they said it was important for Qinghai to join the modern world, but they forgot us as soon as it became inconvenient..."

"Do we need to straighten this out now?" said Jamyang.

"Sangemo gave the headset to Dorje. He pleaded, 'I have sons at home. They need a father.' When that didn't work, Sangemo took the headset again. She said, 'We'll cut our mission short and leave now. We'll be in orbit in a few hours. You can send out your signal then.' She said, 'You have no idea how much this means to Qinghai. We've been waiting to show the world that we, too, are a great people. We, too, can touch the moon.'"

"Enough of this now," said Jamyang. "You never wanted to listen to stories, but they've saved you now, haven't they?" Jamyang grabbed Norbu's hand to pull him toward the door. He shook himself loose.

"No, Ma, you don't understand. I'm running out of oxygen. You're a hallucination."

"You say this to the woman who comes to rescue you? Children! I cooked kitchens full of noodles and dumplings to lure the monkeys. When the new world fails you, the old stories are always there."

"I need to get to the others," said Norbu.

Jamyang watched him pull on his spacesuit. "You don't need that."

"I don't care if I am hallucinating, I'm not going out onto the moon without my suit." Norbu pulled the bubble of his helmet over his head and bounded out of the room.

Jamyang followed. Norbu's crewmates remained frozen in the crater. Norbu went to each of them, waving his gloved hands in front of their still faces. Finally, he turned to his mother, hands groping in front of him as if searching for something concrete to grasp.

"I always thought I'd relive the most exciting moments of my life before I died. Winning the bicycle race from Xining to Qinghai Lake. The clean empty feeling of running ten kilometers, three thousand feet above sea level. Being chosen for the expedition. The launch! But when Sangemo told us about the message from Cairo, I kept thinking about you, Ma, and the old stories you used to tell. Monkeys forming a chain and jumping into a well after the moon."

Norbu paused. Behind his helmet, his expression was inscrutable.

"I must love you very much."

"As I love you," said Jamyang.

Around them, the world began to unfreeze. Norbu's crewmates inched forward as if in a slow motion video. From Norbu's space suit there came the noise of his radio, sputtering the empty static of Australia's jamming signal. Jamyang flinched.

"You can hear that?" said Norbu.

"Never mind!" shouted Jamyang. "Come on! We should get back to the monkeys before they fall!"

Jamyang turned to flee back the way she'd come, but her feet only ran in place. Dead scuttlebots lay where she hoped to find the monkeys. Panic cinched her throat. She couldn't breathe. She clawed at her neck. "Where did the air go?" she choked.

"You don't get it, do you, Ma? There isn't any air here. The old legends aren't true."

"We have to get home!"

Norbu shook his head slowly. "We can't, Ma. You and I, we're both fools. Nothing we believed was true. There's nothing for us in the past or the future. I remember when I was a kid thinking if Qinghai could just get to the moon we'd be like all those other countries, rich and glamorous. No more poverty. No more children starving in the streets. No more taxes to pay for other people's wars. No more generations of boy soldiers coming home crippled. We'd leap across the gap and when we landed—we'd be with everyone else in the future."

Norbu stomped his foot. Moon dust billowed around him in slow motion. "Everything I grew up thinking—it was all wrong. I was trying to grab the future out of the well water. But it was only a reflection. It's hovering above us, chuckling in the sky. And here we are, wet."

Static roared in their ears, like the sandstorm.

"No," said Jamyang.

Norbu placed his hand on her face. His thick Kevlar spacesuit felt rough against her cheek.

"You don't get it, do you, Ma? We've fallen in the well. There's nothing left to breathe."

Scene from a Dystopia

YOU'VE READ this book before. It's one of the classics from the Cold War era, always worth rereading when you've got a little time on your hands—long plane rides, your annual winter flu, the two rainy weeks between autumn and winter when you find your mood drifting toward insular and melancholic. You feel comforted when you read the famous opening lines: "If these accounts have fallen into your hands, then you have been identified as a potential recruit for the rebellion. Take heed, for the Eyes are everywhere and you may already be in peril."

On your second re-read this year, you've just reached page 52, where the authoritarian Byron (who turns out to be a Computer Operator in disguise) leads Stanley on a tour of the Citizen Education Complex. While Byron recites statistics, Stanley allows his attention to wander. He examines the regimented bricks on the pathway and cranes his neck upward to look at the broadcast antennae surmounting each classroom. Then, peering through the windows of a darkened gymnasium, he glimpses a beautiful young woman.

Her name is Natalie. She sits in a row on the bleachers with six other girls. All wear green smocks, but while the others blur into an anonymous line, Natalie appears stark and illuminated like the main figure in a painting by an old master. Even her pose sets her apart: the other girls sit with their heads bowed, but Natalie holds her spine straight and aristocratic.

Even without benefit of makeup, Natalie's features are striking. Her eyes gleam the color of willow leaves and the arch of her cheekbones guides the eye toward the suggestive curves of her lips. Beneath her formless smock, her figure is visibly slender; the edge of her pelvic bone etches a single, shapely bulge in the fabric.

Entranced, Stanley stops to stare. "Who are those girls?" he asks.

"Today's female graduating class," answers Byron. "In a few minutes, they'll be assigned their future professions. Even now, the schoolmistress is consulting with the Computer. Taking into account dozens of factors including the girl's talents, the Technocracy's needs, and projections of what skills will be required in the future, the Computer slots each girl into her profession with the same precision it uses when filing any piece of data."

"A woman is not a piece of data," replies Stanley, lifting his chin as he strides out of the Citizen Education Complex and on to page 53. Ordinarily, you would follow him. Instead, allow me to waylay you here.

In the overall plot, this moment is unimportant. The entire scene occupies only two pages of the novel, from 50-52. But take a moment to explore this scene with me, to examine the story that lies not on the page, but inhabits the margins.

Now that Stanley is gone, let us venture where he never treads: into the gymnasium with Natalie. Aside from the seven girls by the window, it lies vacant, rows of bleachers stretching into empty lines. The veneer of the floor glimmers under scrubbed fluorescent lights, revealing the scuff of footprints that follow predictable rectilinear paths.

Sitting quietly in the center of the bottom row, the girls fret as they wait for the schoolmistress to return. Knuckles whiten, nervous fingers clutch at hems. What careers will the Computer give them? Who will become a janitor? Who a Technician? Will the girl with the facile hands be allowed to become a surgeon, or will she be forced to do something that doesn't use her hands at all, like accounting or spying for the Ministry of Eyes?

Apart from Natalie, the other girls blend into one another like birds clustering to confuse predators, a series of indistinguishable bowed heads and scuffed black shoes. Still, if you watch them long enough, tiny differences emerge. The voluptuous Hispanic girl drumming her fingers on her knees, that's Consuela. Her best friend, Shelby, is the blonde silently counting the seconds since the schoolmistress left—she's up to 2,115. The Vietnamese girl behind them is Phuong and the three others—Do you see the ones I mean? The girls sitting so closely that their shoulders touch?—that's the inseparable trio of Winda, Suchin and Dorothy.

In the novel, these girls never become individuals. They remain a single brushstroke inhabiting the background, their sole purpose to set the scene. Only Consuela will appear again, on page 136, when Stanley enters

Natalie's apartment to discover her "conversing with a plump, dark-skinned girl of drab deportment and unintelligent eyes." In the next paragraph, Natalie "dismisses the girl" and her six classmates disappear from the novel.

Natalie, however, will ascend to a starring role. Even now, she edges away from her classmates, her hem a defiant nine inches from Consuela's. She can't wait for the schoolmistress to return. Holding one hand to her breast, she rehearses an expression of surprise. "The best voice in generations?" she murmurs to herself. "No, no, surely you're exaggerating."

Natalie burns to be an opera singer, an incandescent diva who performs only the loftiest leading roles. After all, her soprano displays astonishing clarity and tone. Everyone says so.

Unfortunately for Natalie, the Computer won't send her to the opera house. It will classify her as a piano teacher instead.

Stanley discovers Natalie's story on page 116 when he finds her leaning against a baby grand, face upturned into a ray of sunlight. Daydreaming, she hums a few bright notes over her student's clumsy scales. Stanley rushes into the room and clasps her hand, uttering that famous line that carries romantic English students into swoons: "In the silences between your notes, angels soar."

The two begin to court, stealing long illicit walks by the river. As they stroll hand in hand, Natalie describes her lost dreams, and Stanley vows to bring her to the stage.

On page 145, he appeals to Byron for intercession. "You should hear her sing," he entreats. "She should be a *prima donna*. The rays of her voice should bring light to millions."

Seated behind his vast mahogany desk, Byron raises his hands in a helpless gesture. "The Computer believes she'll do more good as a piano teacher."

"Damn your computer and its calculating hand!" says Stanley. "What shall become of humanity when greatness is reduced to mere numbers?"

After the argument, Stanley rushes to his beloved and discovers her listless and disconsolate. She hints that she may do something drastic. A few days later, when Stanley returns to her apartment, he finds her gone. Stanley suspects the worst. Driven by grief, he launches his futile rebellion against the Technocracy and mounts the steep path toward the novel's climax.

For a moment, let us assume that Stanley and Natalie are correct. Let us suppose that in another world—in our world—Natalie would have been haloed by symphonies of roses every time she appeared on stage. Imagine critics swooning to her pitch-perfect poise and composers scribbling furiously to create arias worthy of her seraphim range. Imagine the dazzling end of her career when an earthquake in Rome crushes the young *prima donna* beneath a statue of Apollo. In stunned grief, our world clambers for her possessions at auction: her $50 bottle of deodorant, her $600 panties. For a full twenty-four hours, the news cycle shows nothing else.

Yet our world would not be so kind to Natalie's classmates. Our Selby becomes pregnant at sixteen and quits school to raise her twins on a diet of pink slips, anxiety, and weeping over thirty-five cents of spilt milk. The worst moment of Selby's life happens when her daughter whines so persistently for a toy that Selby whirls around and slaps the girl across the mouth. Our Phuong loses her feet to a landmine in Quang Tri at the age of eleven, and our Winda, Suchin and Dorothy follow various routes to the Branchville Correctional Facility where they reunite every few years on new charges. At ten years old, our Consuela discovers her father's shotgun propped in the shed and accidentally shoots herself in the stomach. She bleeds to death crawling toward the kitchen door.

Here, in the Technocracy, these girls exchange their fates for a modest dose of happiness. While Natalie languishes as a piano teacher, Selby will become a construction foreman. Phuong will preside over a kingdom of corpses as a mortician, and Winda, Dorothy and Suchin will supervise subsequent classes of green-smocked girls at the Citizen Education Complex. Adventurous Conseula will don raingear and a sailor's hat as she battles the ocean every day on the deck of her skiff.

These are the stories you won't find on page 4, 53, 136, or 375. These are the stories Stanley fails to understand when he leads his crusade against the Technocracy, that readers never recognize when they finish the vintage edition afterword and get up to make another cup of coffee.

But here, where you and I stand in the gymnasium on page 52, possibility still hovers in the air. Consuela and Selby shift, smocks rustling; Winda, Suchin and Dorothy whisper to each other; Phuong glares at the noise. Alone a few feet to the right, Natalie lets her smock drift down her shoulder and practices a glamorous pout.

Outside, the schoolmistress' boots thud on the cement. The panel outside the door issues a mechanical beep as she presses her index finger to the security screen.

In the long moment before possibility vanishes, Natalie's breath catches in her lungs. Her diaphragm tenses with desire, the same way it does in the moment before she reaches for a high note. She imagines herself onstage, arms flung wide, warm spotlights baptizing her face and hands. She can feel potential tingling on her skin, as if she could do anything, as if she could fly, her voice winging her to the roof of the auditorium until she's as fleet as a melisma, as fluid as a glissando.

If Natalie could—if she had a choice—she would trade the other girls for ovations and bouquets bursting with dahlias. All six of them, without hesitation.

The Taste of Promises

THEY APPROACHED the settlement at dusk. Tiro switched the skipper to silent mode, grateful he wouldn't have to spend another night strapped in, using just enough fuel to stay warm and breathing.

A message from Tiro's little brother, Eo, scrolled across his visor. *Are we there yet?*

Tiro rolled his eyes at Eo's impatience. *Just about,* he sub-vocalized, watching his suit's internal processor translate the words into text.

Is it someplace good? asked Eo.

I think so. Be quiet and let me check it out.

It was a big settlement. Three vast domes rose above the landscape like glass hills. Semi-permanent structures clustered around them, warehouses and vehicle storage buildings constructed from frozen dirt. Light illuminated the footpaths, creating a faintly glowing labyrinth between buildings.

For such a big place, it seemed strangely deserted. There should have been volunteer patrols, weapon caches, watchtowers where settlers would take turns on duty to scan for thieves or poachers or, worse, gang convoys studded with skulls.

On Mars, civilization only extended as far as the pressure seals on the domes of official colonies sponsored by Earth governments. Settlers who left the government's shelters gained the freedom to claim homesteads from the vast tracts of empty land, but they lost the protection of settled society. It could be a hard life on the wild frontier. Everyone feared the gang convoys that sold whole settlements into slavery, slaughtering those who weren't strong enough to work in the mines.

Tiro eyed the settlement nervously. He messaged Eo: *Do you see any security?*

After a pause, his brother replied, *A few charge guns in the domes.*

Nothing else? Too weird.

Maybe their God doesn't like weapons.

Maybe.

Tiro could explore more after nightfall, but in the meantime, he decided to investigate the warehouses. No one stored anything valuable outside, but Tiro was skilled at living off things other people didn't value.

He parked the skipper, sealed his helmet onto his suit, and got out. Nearby, there was an igloo made from frozen dirt. He ducked inside; crates filled the cramped space from floor to ceiling, leaving Tiro barely any room to stand. He pulled down the nearest crate and braced himself against the wall to pry it open. His jaw dropped.

Eo? he sent. *Did you check all their computers for security?*

Yeah. The word flashed resentfully.

You sure?

Eo inserted a picture of a kid blowing a raspberry.

Sorry. I'm just having trouble believing we struck gold.

You found gold???

Food! wrote Tiro. *Crates and crates of frozen rations.*

Eo sent a picture of a dancing kid. Tiro grinned.

Tiro hauled the crate back to the skipper. A few trips back and forth and he'd be set. He could even sell the extra and buy rooms for the rest of the trip.

His thoughts were full of good food and warm beds when he caught sight of four men clustered around the warehouse entrance, their faceplates reflecting the darkening sky so he couldn't make out their faces. *I thought there was no security!* he messaged Eo.

There wasn't!! Eo messaged back.

Tiro flattened against the wall.

What're you gonna do? asked Eo.

I don't know, said Tiro. *Shut up and let me think.*

Tiro figured he could make it the ten meters back to the skipper, but he doubted the skipper could outrun the settlement's vehicles. His only option was to get out of sight. Slowly, he started scooting along the wall.

By his second step, he knew he'd been caught. "Did you see that?" one man mumbled to another. The second reacted with fighter's instincts, whipping out his flashlight like a gun.

"Who are you?" the man demanded, voice gruff through the suit's transmitter. "Are you a scout? Who are you leading here?"

Tiro winced as bright light shone into his eyes. *Get out!* he messaged Eo. *Quick! Get into their systems.*

But—

Go!

The man with the flashlight crouched like a cat and leapt. Dust flew into the air as he landed beside Tiro. "Who are you?" he repeated.

Tiro shrank away. "I didn't mean any harm."

The man twisted Tiro's arm painfully behind his back. "Go on. Keep lying. We'll get the truth either way."

* * *

THE MAN with the flashlight was their leader. The others called him Jirair.

They marched Tiro into the smallest of the three domes. "Nothing to see! Get home!" Jirair bellowed. Settlers flashed alarmed looks their way before dispersing.

They halted in front of a squat building, metal beams glistening in the newly fallen darkness. One man removed Tiro's helmet. Another opened a reinforced door and shoved him inside. He tumbled head-first into the dark, falling against the wall with a thud.

Someone switched on a light. The dank cell was floored with dirt. Manacles gleamed on the wall.

Tiro tried to edge away. Jirair gestured to his men. They chained Tiro's wrists and ankles.

Jirair pulled off his helmet. Underneath, he looked surprisingly young, maybe twenty years old. His scarlet hair stuck out in stylized spikes.

"Get the nerve ripper."

"The nerve ripper!" repeated a man leaning against the wall. "I love the nerve ripper."

"Think he'll be able to walk afterward?" asked the short man beside him.

The first one laughed. "Depends on how much he lies!"

The man who'd thrown Tiro inside the cell fidgeted uncomfortably. "Come on, Jirair. He's just a kid."

"Just a kid?" Jirair turned, lips peeled back to show his teeth. "Gangs use kids as scouts all the time. You want that to happen here?"

The man shook his head silently.

"Then get the nerve ripper," he repeated. The man rushed away.

Tiro struggled. His chains clanged as they reached their full extension. He tapped the bud implanted in his wrist that let Eo monitor his life signs. Tiro used it when he wanted Eo's attention—but this time, there was no answering pulse.

Eo was safe. That was what Tiro wanted, of course, but it didn't make him feel any less alone.

Jirair paced in front of Tiro. "I'll ask again. Who are you leading here?"

"I'm just a scavenger," Tiro said.

"Petty criminals know to stay away from us. You're no scavenger. Why are you here? Did you come to steal our seeds?"

"Your…seeds?"

"Where are you from?"

"New Virginia."

"Who did you bring with you?"

Tiro's heart pounded. "No one."

"No one?"

"No one!"

Jirair shot him a disdainful look. "Only fools travel alone on Mars." He burst into motion, punching the wall in a sudden fury. "You poachers! You think your lives are the only ones that matter! Do you think we don't know what you're up to?"

Tiro whimpered.

"Calm down, Jirair," came a woman's voice from the back of the room. "There's no need to act the fool."

Jirair whipped around. "What are you doing here, Sahar?"

A woman moved forward. Layers of heavy gray clothing swathed her from neck to ankles, but her head was shaved bald. "Naghmeh said you were up to your old tricks." She looked Tiro over, gray eyes shining from her angular face. "How old are you?"

"Eighteen," Tiro said.

"There is no possibility that you are eighteen."

"Sixteen."

Sahar scrutinized Tiro's face. "Possibly."

"It doesn't matter how old he is," Jirair said. "I'm in charge of security. If you have a problem with it, run against me next cycle."

Sahar lifted a hand in objection. "I'm here on Naghmeh's behalf, not mine. She says the boy's not alone."

"I knew it!" shouted Jirair.

Sahar moved smoothly past him, coming to Tiro's side. She held up a data globe. Its read-out lights flashed in morse code. S.O.S.

"Who is this?" Sahar asked.

Tiro slumped. "My brother."

* * *

SAHAR INSTRUCTED the men to unlock Tiro's restraints. Rubbing his wrists, Tiro collected his helmet and followed Sahar out of the cell and down the glowing path to the dome exit.

"What did he threaten you with? Iron drops? The pain candle?"

"Nerve ripper," Tiro mumbled, heart still pounding.

"There's no such thing. He was trying to scare you." Faint light illuminated her harsh features. "Jirair's a good man. He'd be harmless in any other job, but give him security work, and he starts to think like a tyrant. He thinks the only way to protect the colony is to act like a bully. I argued against electing him, but too many people think aggression is the same as defense."

They approached an air lock leading out of the dome. Sahar used her retinal scan to open an adjacent storage locker. It was filled with space suits. Sahar began putting one on over her clothes. "Put your helmet back on," she instructed.

Tiro hesitated. "Where are we going?"

Sahar gave him an amused look. "You're bold for a prisoner, aren't you? I'm giving you a room in my compound tonight."

"Aren't you worried I'm a gang scout?"

"Are you a gang scout?"

"No."

Sahar paused to adjust her suit. "Naghmeh says you are who you say you are. A teenager making a suicidally stupid journey alone—well, almost alone—from New Virginia to Kaseishi."

"Who's Naghmeh?"

Sahar grunted impatiently. "Enough for now," she said, sealing her helmet.

Tiro sealed his, too, and they made their way outside. The lights lining the path shone like fairies at their feet as they hiked to the largest dome.

They stopped at a small, dimly lit dome entrance. Sahar spoke through her transmitter. "This is my door. It has security you can't break, even with your brother's help. Do not try to go through without me."

Once they were inside, Sahar started removing her suit. She glanced at Tiro. "Don't you want to get out of that thing?"

Tiro paused. He'd been traveling for so long that his suit felt like a second skin, but it would feel good to wear just a shirt and pants again. He stripped down, enjoying the sensation of air on his arms—until he noticed Sahar tossing his discarded suit into a bin in the storage locker.

"What are you doing?" he demanded.

"A little insurance," she said, locking the crate.

Sahar started toward a large building. Fuming, Tiro followed.

The structure was larger than any private building Tiro had ever seen. He gaped as Sahar opened the door onto an unbelievably enormous room.

It smelled of baking bread. Bowls of fruits and vegetables glistened on the counters that ranged across the back wall. Chairs sat stacked on two long, parallel tables, each of which could seat at least twenty.

"You live here?" he asked.

"I do," said Sahar, heading up the immense staircase that stretched away from the dining hall. She took a right from the first floor landing and opened one of what seemed like an infinity of doors, revealing a narrow bedchamber.

She nudged Tiro inside. "You'll sleep here until your arbitration with our elders. I'm locking you in tonight, but I'll come by in the morning for breakfast."

Hesitantly, Tiro reached toward the polished headboard. "What's this made of?"

"Wood. From settlement trees."

"You harvest *wood*?" Tiro asked incredulously.

This elicited a genuine smile. "Get some sleep."

Tiro turned. "Wait!"

Sahar stopped with her hand on the door. "Yes?"

"Please. My brother. Can't you give him back?"

"I'm sorry—"

"Please!"

"We'll return him after arbitration."

Tiro started toward Sahar. "When will that be?"

"A few days. . . ."

"But he's never spent the night alone!"

Sahar held out her hand to prevent Tiro from coming further. "Calm down."

Tiro stopped advancing. He dropped his balled fists to his sides.

When Sahar seemed satisfied that he'd regained his self-control, she continued. "Your brother will be fine. He'll stay with Naghmeh until your arbitration."

Tiro's patience snapped. "Who's Naghmeh?"

Sahar paused. "My daughter," she answered at last. "She was lifted, too."

Tiro was too surprised to know how to respond.

Sahar closed the door.

* * *

TIRO HAD hazy memories of the day Eo was born: the blue blanket his aunt shipped from Earth for the new baby, the red bag his mother packed for the hospital, the burned toast his father made for breakfast. He didn't remember putting on a space suit and trying to run away, but that was what his parents always told stories about. "At first, Tiro wanted to get away from Eo so badly that he ran away from home," his dad would say. "Now they're inseparable."

At first Eo seemed healthy, but soon he stopped eating. His stomach swelled. One night, their father found blood in Eo's diaper, and then it was back to the hospital for test after test. By the end, they'd plugged him into machines that breathed for him and machines that pumped his heart, even machines that spun tendrils into his brain.

Tiro didn't remember any of that. He did remember his parents taking him to the hospital where they put his hands into gloves mounted in a clear plastic wall so he could touch his brother one last time. His mother cried because it was so sterile and remote, but Tiro didn't feel that way. To him, it felt like touching anyone through a space suit. Just part of growing up on Mars.

Scientists had never reached a consensus on how lifting occurred. They did identify the responsible technology: a recently introduced monitoring system intended to track global mental function. The system kept records of brain activity for physician review and, over time, these created a holistic representation of the brain in motion.

Dead patients' records were dumped into the hospital system. When cognitive development specialist Dr. Joshua Roanoke went to access the records for his research, he discovered the presence of distinct personalities haunting the system like ghosts. He told the press, "It's as if the children have been lifted from their bodies and moved into the machines."

Only patients in a narrow age range seemed to be susceptible. Dr. Roanoke hypothesized that, in order to transfer successfully, infants had to possess a concept of object permanence but still be in the sensorimotor stage. Except for the fact that affected infants fell roughly into the predicted age range of three to twenty-four months, no proof had been uncovered to substantiate his claim.

While scientists argued over how the lifted children had been created, politicians debated what to do with them. Mars was still recovering from high profile technological disasters: six hundred colonists had died at Juel when a new biotic system poisoned the air instead of providing oxygen, and another two thousand died planet-wide when an innovative dome synthetic developed microscopic fractures. The technophobic climate combined with calls from a number of dominant religions for the lifted children to be exorcised so they could properly enter the afterlife.

The governments of Mandela and Marston—the other two colonies which had used the brain monitoring technology—ordered their hospitals to purge the lifted children. Working under more stringent property laws, New Virginia ruled that the lifted children were equivalent to remains and left it to the parents to dispose of them. All three governments placed heavy restrictions on the brain monitors to prevent further incidents.

Average citizens called the lifted children ghosts. They told each other horror stories about haunted machines.

Most parents, already grieving, had their children's remnants wiped. A few brought them home.

"Even if it's only an echo, how can we throw that away?" asked Tiro's mom. "He's our little boy."

Eo grew on the home computer. He navigated data streams like a rafter in white water, skimming through the public nets with abandon. He pulled pranks on the neighbors' private machines, too, until their parents lectured him about trespassing.

Their family shaped itself around Eo. All day, they laughed at jokes he sent their visors. During the evenings, they watched movies he spliced together from free footage on the nets. At night, Tiro wore his visor to bed so he and Eo would never be apart.

Everyone adored Eo, but their father still drank in the evenings, his expression tired and forlorn. Once, Tiro asked what was wrong. His father gave him the saddest look he'd ever seen. "I want what any father wants. For both my sons to become men."

Tiro went to their mother. "Doesn't Dad love Eo?"

She sighed. "Of course we love Eo, but it's hard. We'd give anything to fix what happened. To make him what he should be."

Tiro never forgot what his parents wanted for Eo. A body, so he could be a man.

* * *

TIRO WAS still sleeping when Sahar returned. She wore even more gray this time, a heavy ankle-length dress. She led him downstairs to the kitchen where she picked up a basket of red fruit.

"We'll eat outside," she said.

Tiro blinked as they emerged into brightness. Trees arrowed toward the dome, branches woven into a dense canopy. Creepers garlanded the trunks with emerald, scarlet, and amber leaves.

Tiro wandered, dazed by the mingling scents of flowers and wet leaves. He paused beside a whip-slender sapling that was putting out new fronds. "I've seen these in New Virginia."

Sahar was crouched a meter away, spreading a blanket over the grasses. She looked up. "Those are comfort palms. We export the seeds."

"People pull off the fronds to wrap up in. They keep you pretty warm."

Sahar settled on the blanket. "That's why we made them. All our plants are engineered to be useful. We call it anthropocentric ecology. Once there's a thick enough atmosphere to sustain life, we'll seed our plants across Mars. Think about it. Our jungles won't be hostile. They'll be full of plants that exist in symbiosis with us, that help us survive and prosper."

Tiro kicked a clump of bluish weeds. They released a pleasant almond scent. "What's the point? It'll be centuries before plants can live outside."

Sahar held up a chiding finger. "It'll take centuries under the plans made by government colonies. They've introduced oxygen-generating and nitrogen-fixing microbes, but we can do better than that. We're engineering microbes with more efficient metabolisms. Once they're ready to be released, our new strains will accomplish the process in decades."

"Why can you do that better than the colonies?"

"We have better computers." Sahar smiled. "But more about that later." She pulled a fruit from her basket and held it out to Tiro. "Try a promise. They're superficially a mix of pomegranates and apples, blended with more supplementary genomes than I can remember. They're calorie rich and extremely nutritious. Humans can survive on them for weeks at a time."

Tiro took the fruit. The first bite was a perfect, pulpy mix of sweet and acid. His spine prickled. "Why are you telling me all this?"

"Why are you going to Kaseishi?"

"Didn't my brother tell you?"

"I want to hear it from you."

Tiro hesitated, choosing words carefully. "We heard there's an engineer there who can make special mechanical bodies."

He stopped. "Yes?" Sahar prompted.

"Ones that lifted kids can move into," said Tiro. "To make them normal."

"It's only worked once. It may not work again. The integrated body frames were built to interact with computers, you know, not for lifted kids."

Tiro said nothing.

"How are you going to afford one?"

Tiro shrugged. "We'll figure it out."

"Your brother said you had a plan."

Tiro clenched his fists in frustration. What was the point being careful if Eo told them everything? "Kaseishi takes contracts for indentured servants, okay? If someone buys my labor for ten years, I can get a body for Eo."

Sahar ignored his exasperation. "If I accessed your records from New Virginia, how old would they say you were?"

"Sixteen."

"Really."

"Okay, fourteen. But that's old enough! I'm a man. I can sign my own contracts."

Sahar's eyes narrowed. "You look like you have African ancestors. If you're from New Virginia then your parents or grandparents probably came from the United States. Am I right?"

"Yeah. So?"

"So you've probably got a family history of slavery. I can't imagine your ancestors would be happy about one of their sons selling his freedom." She gestured to herself. "My people are Parsi. For generations, they were marginalized in India. We know what it is to be not-quite-people under the law." She paused. "What do your parents think?"

Tiro thought fast. "They're dead."

"Are they?"

"I have to do it for Eo."

"What if it's not the best thing for him?"

"He needs a body!"

"My daughter runs this settlement. The computer enhances her so she thinks faster than any human, and she enhances the computer so it works better than anything on Mars or on Earth." She paused, eyes searching Tiro's face for his reaction. "Do you understand what that means? It's a gift beyond measure. With Naghmeh's help, any plant I design can become reality in months. Without her, I'd have been lucky to construct even one species. That comfort palm, for instance. That would be my life's work."

"That's nice for you and Naghmeh, but Eo needs a body."

"Does he? Or do you need one for him?"

Tiro turned away, flaming with anger. Sahar called after him. "Think, Tiro! What does your brother know about flesh and bones? Are you doing this for him or for you?"

"I'm doing it for Eo!" Red anger flowed through Tiro's face and fists. He bolted into the trees, feet pounding across springy ground cover. At first he was surprised that Sahar let him run—but then, where could he go? She'd taken his suit.

He slowed in the middle of a grove and sat among the fallen leaves, trailing his fingers through the wet soil.

He remembered when his parents had first read about the mechanical bodies. They spent weeks arguing over their finances, trying to conjure what they needed. His father examined Kaseishi's laws and discovered the corporations there had agitated to legalize indentured servitude so they could bring up the droves of willing but impoverished workers from Earth and force them to repay their travel costs. He considered selling himself, but he was too old to get a contract.

"I'll do it," Tiro had said.

Both his parents looked at him like he'd just turned pink and sprouted wings.

"The devil you will," said his mother.

His father just shook his head, slowly. "No, Tiro. We won't sell one son's potential for the other's."

So Tiro ran away. What was ten years of his life if it could buy Eo's humanity?

Tiro didn't know how much time had passed before he heard Sahar's footsteps. He looked up. She held out her hand to help him stand.

"I shouldn't have pushed so fast," she said. "I'm passionate about what I do, about Mars and plants and Naghmeh. Please accept my apologies."

* * *

EVERY MORNING, Tiro asked when his arbitration would be. Every morning, Sahar answered, "Not yet. You need more food and rest anyway."

She took him to look at water-filled flowers that could be plucked and used as canisters, and at creepers that froze into durable ropes. She showed him how they planned to incorporate mechanical elements into future plants, such as trees that could monitor human heart rates and issue distress signals.

Tiro asked whether they could change humans the way they were changing plants. "I'd like to live in the cold. Or maybe you could make us fly..."

"Perhaps once the atmosphere is ready," said Sahar. "For now, we have more than enough to do."

Tiro enjoyed helping Sahar plant seedlings. Infant plants couldn't save lives, but they were fragile and green. He loved wriggling his fingers like worms in the dirt.

Sahar told him about the settlement. "Things have changed since Naghmeh integrated with the computer. We have more money now, more time, more knowledge. If people hadn't reacted ignorantly to the lifted children, more settlements could prosper as we do."

The settlement had welcomed Naghmeh by agreement of the elders and also by popular vote. Some of the population had been ready to surrender total control to Naghmeh, while others worried about what would happen if they allowed a child—however mechanically enhanced—to take authority over delicate systems like life support. In the end, they compromised, walling off a section of the system where Naghmeh could live, separated from processes that could threaten the settlers' lives.

"The settlers here are good people," said Sahar.

"Except Jirair," grumbled Tiro.

Sahar looked chagrined. "Some people are damaged by their pasts. There's a lot they can do with psychological programming these days, but...Jirair was your age when he came here as a runaway. He'd been kidnapped by a gang who murdered his parents and forced him to scout for new victims. He's convinced the same thing will happen here. The settlement has always weathered strikes by poachers, but three years ago, a gang convoy mounted a full attack. Naghmeh dealt with them. But ever since then, Jirair has seen any traveler, even merchants, as a threat. His housemates say he wakes screaming from dreams where we've all been slaughtered."

Tiro rubbed his wrists, remembering the manacles. "He still shouldn't treat people like that."

Sahar looked away. "Some people think anything is justified if they're certain they're right."

That night, Sahar warned him that she'd be coming early the next morning. "Why?" asked Tiro. "Is it my arbitration?"

Sahar shook her head. "It's time you met Naghmeh."

* * *

SAHAR WOKE Tiro before dawn. They navigated the maze of her house, finally emerging on a rooftop observatory beneath the translucent curve of the dome.

"Naghmeh is everywhere the computer is, of course," Sahar said, "but the settlers prefer their privacy, so we ask her to speak only in certain places. This is my favorite, close to the sky."

"How do I talk to her?" Tiro asked.

"Just talk."

Tiro edged forward. "Hi."

A breathy voice whispered from the nearby audio outputs. "Hi."

"Why does she sound like that?" Tiro asked Sahar.

Sahar shrugged. "Caprice."

Tiro wandered between shining pieces of observatory equipment. "Sahar says you're with my brother."

"I am." With a laugh, she added, "He's sparkly!"

"Sparkly?"

"All over spark-raining! Showers and showers. Luminosity spikes like radiant flow."

Tiro balked. He looked at Sahar for an explanation.

"They see things differently than we do," said Sahar.

"I guess so." Tiro wondered if Eo saw things differently, too. He never said so, but was he trying to make himself seem normal for his family? Tiro looked up at one of the speakers. "Can I talk to my brother?"

A whir. "Later, maybe," said Naghmeh.

"What are you two doing together?"

"I'm showing him around. We go here. We go there." The outputs blared a bash song overlaid by high-pitched chatter. Noisemakers sounded in the background. "It's a party!"

"Are you showing him how to make plants?"

The party noises disappeared. The voice became whiny. "We just want to play. I work hard enough, don't I?"

"Doesn't the computer do the work?"

An elephant brayed, which seemed to be the equivalent of Eo's icon of a kid blowing a raspberry. "Isn't your body doing your breathing?"

"You work very hard," interjected Sahar with a peacemaker's tone.

"Eo's more interested in learning about machines anyway," said Naghmeh.

"Naghmeh," Sahar went on, "what would you think if someone said you could have a body?"

"A me-extension to make me mobile?"

"No, a human kind of body, not part of the network."

"A me-extension would be vroom! Mobile-network-me could prank and chat and fun." She paused. "Work more, too, if I had body and network."

"But humans can't do that. This body would do only what humans can. Would you want that?"

"For keeps or for play?"

"Keeps. You couldn't leave. You'd be in the body all the time."

"Why?"

"So you could think and act like we do."

"There's no scarcity of you, but there's scarcity of me. You should give up your bodies and live with me."

"There's nothing you'd want about being in a body?"

A pause. "Might be fun awhile."

"But not forever?"

"Forever?" Naghmeh's voice rose with distress. "Why be small in oneplace onemind onethought?"

A cacophony of bird and animal noises poured from the outputs.

"Why trapbe?" asked Naghmeh. "Why cagebe? Why prisonbe?"

The screeches grew deafening. Eo had never acted like this. Was this what Sahar meant by seeing things differently? Would Eo be like this if they let him stay on the networks? Tiro slapped his hands over his ears, but the noise kept mounting.

"Naghmeh!" shouted Sahar. "Please! Quiet down!"

The noise waned, replaced by quiet keening. Sahar paced to one of the outputs, running her fingers over the mesh as if caressing an infant's cheek. "Shh, Naghmeh. I'm sorry we upset you."

* * *

WHEN SAHAR came to Tiro's room later, her eyes were red.

"Is Naghmeh okay?" Tiro asked.

Sahar nodded. Her fingers fretted at her cuffs, nails bitten and raw. "Do you understand now why you can't force Eo into a body?"

Tiro didn't want to meet her gaze. "He has to become what he was supposed to be."

Sahar's expression looked almost as sad as his father's. Wordlessly, she turned and left him alone.

* * *

THE NEXT day, the elders scheduled Tiro's arbitration.

Sahar pestered him so much that Tiro didn't even feel relieved when she returned his spacesuit.

"You need to reconsider," she pleaded. "You're acting like Jirair. You know that? You're so certain it's right for Eo to have a body that you'll do anything to get him one, even hurt him."

"You just want Eo to grow your plants," Tiro snapped, switching off his receiver.

The second dome was smaller than Sahar's. Rows of flowers created a maze of red, blue, and yellow. The hexagonal meetinghouse rose above the other buildings like a megalith.

They stopped by the entrance to remove their suits. Sahar shot Tiro a worried look that would have annoyed him if his heart hadn't been pounding.

Inside, a smoky scent drifted toward the exposed rafters. The three elders sat on wooden stools, their gray robes sweeping the floor.

Sahar bowed from the waist. "This is Tiro. His brother is the lifted child—"

"Thank you, Sahar," said the female elder on the right. "You may go now."

Sahar opened her mouth to object, but reconsidered. "I bid you good judgment." She bowed again before departing.

The door closed, leaving silence in its wake. Tiro shifted, waiting for the elders to speak.

"I'm sorry I stole the food," he ventured. "After I finish in Kaseishi, I'll come work it off."

The elders exchanged glances. The man on the left said, "Sahar and Naghmeh spoke on your behalf. Accept it as our gift."

A prickle crept up Tiro's spine. "Why?"

The middle elder leaned forward, the beaded ends of his braids clattering across his back. "We hope you'll feel grateful and return with your brother," he said. "We would also welcome your parents."

"They're dead," said Tiro.

"They aren't."

"They—"

The left-hand elder lifted his palm to halt Tiro's protest. "We understand why you lied. We don't begin adulthood at fourteen here. But you are not one of us, and we accept that our rules don't apply."

"Though Sahar does not," interjected the woman. "She wanted us to permit her to contact your parents."

The middle elder pinned Tiro with a firm gaze. "It would violate our ethics to do as she asked. Nevertheless, we urge you to consider our offer."

Tiro swallowed. "Thank you, but my brother and I must go to Kaseishi."

With a sigh, the middle elder reached into his voluminous sleeve. He withdrew a data globe. "You may use this at any interface to speak with your brother."

Uneasily, Tiro reached for the globe. "Is that all?"

The middle elder nodded. "That is all."

Tiro's fingers closed around the globe. He fled before the elders could change their minds.

Once outside, he rushed to put on his suit. He ran for the nearest interface, forcing the globe into its input recess.

The globe lit up. Text scrolled across his visor. *Tiro!*

Eo! Are you okay?

Did you know we can race more than a thousand times per second? I beat Naghmeh more than half the time! She showed me this engine trick that works out-world, too, and—

Race what? said Tiro. *Nevermind. Tell me later. We have to go now.*

Blankness followed.

Come on, Eo, get in the globe. We have to go to Kaseishi.

Maybe later, wrote Eo. *I'm having fun.*

We won't be able to go later.

But I like Naghmeh.

We don't have time! Tiro stopped, breathing deeply to calm himself. Now wasn't the time to upset Eo. *Can we talk alone? I don't want anyone listening. This is private, you know?*

A brothers thing? asked Eo.

A brothers thing, Tiro agreed. *Please move into the globe?*

The lights on the data globe blinked rapidly as Eo moved inside. Tiro waited until they held a steady color before yanking the globe from its recess. He switched it into energy-saving mode. The lights dimmed as it entered hibernation.

"Sorry Eo," Tiro whispered.

Hastily, he sealed his helmet and headed for the nearest exit. He had to reach the skipper before Sahar or Naghmeh realized what he'd done.

* * *

WHEN THE settlement was out of sight, Tiro placed the data globe in the skipper's pit. Its lights brightened, but no words appeared on Tiro's visor.

Eo? wrote Tiro. *Come on, talk to me.*

Nothing crossed Tiro's vision but endless dust.

I'm doing this for you, Eo. You were born into a body. You should have the chance to grow up in one. It's what our parents want.

Nothing appeared. Hours passed under the skipper's wheels.

They stopped at dusk. Tiro warmed some frozen rations from Sahar's settlement. After supper, he strapped himself into the driver's seat, lowering the skipper's energy output to the minimum required for heat and oxygen.

He woke to see the sun's rays mounting the horizon. The stale air smelled of food and plastic. He considered breakfast, but didn't want to stay in one place any longer. He initialized the skipper and started driving.

At first, Tiro had been enraptured by the landscape's shifting, ruddy hues. Now, travel just made him tired. As morning seeped into afternoon, he began to drowse.

Sometime later, he woke with a start. Text scrolled across his vision. *Tiro.* He blinked, wondering if he was dreaming—but no, it was real. *Tiro, stop the skipper. Go to low energy. Now!*

Tiro didn't pause to think. His hands moved rapidly across the machinery, cutting the skipper into silent mode. He shivered as the nonessential heating dissipated, leaving bitter cold.

What is it, Eo? Tiro asked.

Gang convoy, wrote Eo. *They'll be visible in…20…17…15…*

Gang convoy? Where?

Northeast. 5…3…

Tiro shrank in his seat as the convoy rumbled past. Skippers zoomed alongside thunders and ground-eaters. Some vehicles were huge, armored like enormous beetles. All were painted red as Mars dust, the color of the landscape, the color of blood.

They're headed toward Sahar's settlement, Tiro wrote when they were past.

I know, wrote Eo.

We're lucky they didn't see us.

I know that, too.

There's no point in going back. There's nothing we can do.

Eo fell silent.

Tiro swallowed. *The gang will be there long before we can. Everyone would be dead by the time we arrived.*

That would be true, wrote Eo, *except Naghmeh taught me how to make the skipper go a lot faster.*

A lot faster?

Eo sent an enormous, toothy grin. *Ohhhhhhhhh yeah.*

* * *

THEY PARKED the skipper behind the warehouses. Jirair lay panting in the dirt nearby, a comfort palm frond wrapped around his leg.

"You," said Jirair as Tiro approached, "The elders said they invited you to stay. You came back?"

Tiro nodded. Now didn't seem like the time to get into why he'd run away.

"I guess you're as good as one of us now. For as long as there is an us." He jerked his head toward Tiro's skipper. "Get out before you get killed."

"You're injured," Tiro said.

"My suit is ripped. Not that it'll matter when I run out of oxygen..."

Tiro hated being forced to help Jirair, but he knelt beside him anyway and plugged their suits together. "If you need more air, find my skipper. It has a two week supply. Will the palm keep your suit sealed?"

Jirair nodded, savoring a deep breath.

"Where are the others?"

"Hostage in the garden dome. I kept running while they shot at me, grabbed a frond and got out. I'd rather die out here than..." He trailed off.

Tiro looked up at the domes. The gang vehicles were parked around them in an enormous red mass, like fire ants swarming a kill.

"Can you walk?" Tiro asked Jirair. "I'll need help."

Tiro offered his hand to help Jirair stand. After a moment's hesitation, Jirair accepted, but as he pushed onto his bad leg, something made a snapping sound.

Jirair choked off a scream. Panting with pain he said, "I warned them! I told them the gang would come back. I told them Naghmeh can't be our only protection. They wouldn't listen." Jirair punched the igloo wall, dislodging a cascade of ice.

"Then tell me what to do."

"There's nothing. They're trained fighters."

"There must be something. Tell me what you know."

"There's nothing! Naghmeh runs all our security. They've trapped her."

"How?"

Tiro coaxed the story from him. Three years ago, a gang convoy had attacked the settlement. Naghmeh took control of their network. She fired their weapons randomly, killing some, disabling others, and forcing the rest to hurl their defenses away. She used the vehicles to herd the infantry, the drivers helpless to control their rebeling machines.

Jirair had warned the settlers that the gang would nurse a grudge. "A well-trained force they could have understood," Jirair said. "But this was an insult, a challenge to their prowess."

Sahar and other respected settlers had argued that it didn't matter. Naghmeh's relationship with the settlement computer was unique. As long as they didn't know what Naghmeh was, they couldn't fight her.

They remained confident when the convoy began offering a reward for information about settlement security. But someone—no one knew who—had betrayed them all.

The gang arrived with a program that was designed to invade the network and seek Nagmeh out, enfolding her in a coded prison that protected itself by creating the illusion that it was the portion of the system where Naghmeh lived. Naghmeh didn't even know she was trapped.

"I've seen these work on simple AIs," Jirair said, "but never something sophisticated enough to fool Naghmeh. They must have bought the technology from Earth. The settlement's not *that* wealthy... They must really want us dead..." He shook his head, his expression hard-worn beneath his visor. "If you could get her back in control—but you can't."

Jirair must have been in considerable pain from his wound, but the plight of the colony seemed to be causing him even more pain than that. Tiro almost understood why Jirair had threatened to torture him. Sometimes you'd do anything to protect what you loved.

He glanced at his brother's data globe, strengthening his resolve. "Maybe I can."

* * *

CAN THEY *trap you like they did Naghmeh?* Tiro asked as he trudged toward the domes.

They don't even know I'm here. Get me to an interface.

They'll know you're there if you get into the network. They got Naghmeh and she's been doing this a lot longer than you!

She didn't know they were coming. The gang could trap me now because I don't have any defenses, but if I get into the network, I can trounce them. Just get me to an interface!

Luck was with them for now. The attackers had been warned to expect one computer enhanced by a lifted child. They would never expect a second.

Sneaking through the vehicle perimeter was easier than Tiro thought it would be. The drivers were relying on their vehicles' security. Eo confused the scans, telling Tiro when to duck to avoid visual confirmation sweeps.

Isn't it dangerous for you to interfere with their systems? asked Tiro. *Won't they find you?*

Not if we move fast.

They emerged near Sahar's dome. Tiro searched for her private entrance. She had told him it was guarded by security that even his brother couldn't break. If that meant Naghmeh, then it would be undefended now. But what if it wasn't?

Detect anything? Tiro asked.

No, said Eo, but Tiro couldn't help thinking of the last time he'd been wrong.

The airlock opened with a smooth hiss. Tiro's heart pounded as he went through both doors and entered the dome, the groundcover springy beneath his boots. He opened his helmet's circulation to admit dome air, inhaling the scent of flowers.

Now that they'd made it inside, Tiro could feel his perceptions growing sharper as his body flooded with adrenaline. He looked up uneasily at Sahar's enormous house.

His visor flashed with Eo's alarm. *You're not going in there!*

When I was staying in this dome with Sahar, I only saw one interface. He craned his neck upward. *It's on the roof.*

There are gangsters in there!!

Can you tell me where they are?

If they're carrying things connected to the network.

Are they?

Eo seemed loath to admit it. They have wrist chatters.

Eo continued to convey his misgivings by sending a stream of anxious faces, but he assembled a floor plan for Tiro with the gangsters' locations marked by moving red dots. One stood in the entryway, blocking the stairs. Tiro began searching the deadfall for something to use as a club.

Suddenly, the gangster veered into the hallway. Tiro straightened. *What did you do?*

Sent a fake letter to his chatter. He thinks it's from a woman upstairs.

Tiro blinked as Eo's message scrolled across his visor, virtually steaming with innuendo.

Where did you learn that? asked Tiro.

Nevermind, it'll get you in!

Tiro entered and ran upstairs without pausing to think. Each of his footsteps seemed to boom on the wood like strikes on a bass drum.

He wove through the maze-like corridors, darting left and right as needed. Eo sent more fake messages, but not all the gangsters took predictable courses. Tiro hid whenever one turned an unexpected corner, willing himself to be invisible among the shadows. On the third floor, he crouched behind a door for an agonizing fifteen minutes while two gangsters finished playing dice. Eo sent a letter to one of their chatters, but the woman only glanced at it and laughed, blanking out its screen for the rest of their game.

Finally, Tiro emerged in front of the narrow, rickety staircase leading to the roof. *Stop,* Eo warned as Tiro put his hand on the railing. *There's someone up there.*

Tiro's stomach churned. *Can you get rid of him?*

No prob, Eo replied, smugly.

A minute passed. Eo? Tiro prompted.

His visor flashed red. *They figured out I was faking messages! They're looking for me!*

They can't find you if you don't do anything else, right?

I don't know!

Calm down, Tiro directed with more confidence then he felt. *I'll take care of it.*

Ignoring Eo's protests, Tiro started upstairs.

When he reached the top, he pressed himself into the shadow of the open door and peered out. At night, the observatory was full of glints and shadows. A tall man in leather sat beside one of the telescopes, eating a promise fruit. An illegal compressed-gas projectile gun sat in his holster. The interface lay beyond him, its recess gleaming like water in an oasis.

Tiro's heart thumped. The man was sleek, with runner's muscles, built for speed as well as strength. There was no way to get past him.

Tiro cleared his throat. He'd always been good at thinking up lies. His father said they flowed from his mouth like scat from a pig's anus. Thinking of lies was easy. It was convincing people to believe them that was hard.

"Hey there!" he shouted, coming into the light. "I'm Tiro. I'm the one who gave you the info on the lifted kid. Where's my reward?"

The gangster looked up at him, slowly. He set aside his half-eaten promise fruit and got to his feet. "No you're not," he said, flicking his gaze up and down Tiro's body. "We've got the woman outside. Some religious bat."

"Yeah, but I gave her the information."

"Yeah?" echoed the gangster. "Why would a kid turn in his settlement? They send you to bed without supper?"

Tiro swallowed, trying to conceal his shaking hands. "They made me work with the lifted kid because we're the same age. They think they can give her friends like a normal person. But she's an abomination. She's just a copy of some poor dead kid, keeping its soul from going to the afterlife."

A flash of darkness crossed Tiro's visor, Eo's expression of pain. Eo had been told he wasn't a real person all his life, by strangers, by the news. Maybe even by his family—did Eo think that's what they were saying when they wanted to get him a body?

Tiro wished he could comfort Eo, but he didn't dare send him a message.

The pirate circled Tiro, coming between him and the door. "Why didn't Benita tell us about you then?"

Tiro darted a glance over his shoulder at the recess. He hoped he'd seem to be looking for an escape route. He backed a few steps away from the gangster as if afraid, moving toward his goal.

"I...don't know..." he stammered. "Maybe she forgot."

The gangster advanced. "Forgot. Sure. Or maybe you don't want to go to the mines?"

Tiro kept walking fearfully backward.

"Want to know what happened to Benita? She's dead. If she betrayed you, she'd betray us too. So we killed her. Now tell me how you got up here."

That was enough. Tiro turned to run, palming his brother's data globe. He was halfway across the roof. Could he make it the rest of the way?

"Stop," the gangster shouted. Tiro's feet slammed against the wood. He heard the smack of metal on plastic as the gangster drew his gun. He hardly registered the blast of pain that erupted in his side as he twisted in midair, his arm sweeping outward to toss the globe the last few centimeters into the recess. He crashed to the ground. The gangster's boots struck the boards as he approached for a final shot, but already the data globe's lights were pricking the darkness with blue and yellow.

A child's voice sputtered from the audio outputs. "I don't like all this violence."

The gangster shouted with pain as his gun's internal chip heated the metal until it was excruciating. The gun clattered to the floor.

"That's better," Eo continued. "Can you take it from here, Naghmeh, or do I have to do everything?"

* * *

TIRO TWISTED to get a better look at Sahar as she entered his room. "Did you bring another plant book?"

"Don't," she said, setting a bowl of mushroom soup on his nightstand. "You'll hurt yourself."

"I'm fine," Tiro grumbled, but Sahar bent to inspect his wound anyway. Before condemning Tiro to three weeks' bed rest, the settlement's physician had said that the bullet missed his major organs, but made a major mess.

"You finished the volume on diseases already?" Sahar asked.

"What else do I have to do?"

"I should shoot all my apprentices."

Sahar wore her clothes from the garden. Traces of soil on her boots and cuffs gave her a budding, green smell. Tiro hissed as she touched a tender spot.

"Are you done yet?"

"Momentarily." Sahar completed her inspection and withdrew, letting Tiro tug down his shirt. She paused. "We heard from your parents."

Tiro's mouth went dry. "What did they say?"

"They're furious," she said. "But they'll get over it." She went on, "They want to know how you survived, and what you were thinking, and how you're going to pay them back for their skipper. They also want you to know they've quit their jobs in New Virginia and they'll be here in a month."

Tiro sat up. "They're coming?"

Sahar grinned. "We're offering them large salaries, rewarding work, and a place where both of their children can grow as they are. How could they refuse?"

Tiro matched her grin. For a moment, he was ecstatic, but then a sliver of worry worked its way inside. He slumped onto the bed, his smile gone.

Sahar frowned. "What's wrong? Are you in pain?"

Tiro shook his head.

"I thought you'd be happy your parents were coming."

"I am. It's just—" Tiro trailed off.

Sahar sat beside him on the bed. "You must have known Eo wouldn't leave if you let him back into the system."

"I didn't think I had a choice. The gang…but I didn't have to come back. I could have kept driving."

"So why did you come back?"

"I think, in the back of my mind, what you said about me and Jirair got to me. I'm not him. I couldn't hurt Eo, not even for his own good. I had to let him choose."

"And now you wish you hadn't."

"No!" Tiro looked up to see if he'd upset Sahar, but she stared back with placid green eyes. "It's just, sometimes..."

Sahar sighed. "Sometimes you listen to them talk and play, and you realize they're not like you, and they won't ever be. They're themselves—and that's good... But sometimes it breaks your heart."

Tiro nodded silently.

Later, when Tiro recovered, he and Eo would commune on the rooftop observatory. He'd tell Eo all about working with plants while Eo went into flights about mechanics and computing that he could never hope to understand. Tiro would start sleeping in his visor again so that they could spend their nights together as they always had.

But just now, Tiro was afraid he'd cry if he spoke. He closed his eyes, letting Sahar stroke his hair as he mourned the way he hadn't known how to the first time he lost his brother's body.

With Singleness of Heart

HER ARTIFICIAL skin is too grey to look human. It's surprisingly soft.

Behind us, the guys jeer. The android could bash my face with a flick of her wrist, but she won't. The guys have their guns against the skulls of two children from her compound.

"Just do it," she snarls.

I spit on my palms and pump my dick. Nothing happens. It's like my cock is dead.

Reed shouts so everyone can hear. "What's wrong, Turner? Can't get it up?"

The friction makes my dick sore. I don't want this. I don't. I—but body does what bodies do. It stiffens. I push inside.

* * *

MY NAME is John Turner. I was born on a terraformed moon covered in icy oceans. Where we'd cleared the ice crust, we built platforms for growing algae. A man's average lifespan there is thirty-seven. Most end up freezing underwater or sliced up by the equipment.

The army gives you good pay, free job training, and a chance to settle somewhere off-world when your term's up.

It's a good gig for an ice-moon boy.

* * *

LAST NIGHT, they'd told me what would happen.

We were in a thinly wooded forest, walking from our point of departure to our mission location. Where we stopped, Reed used the energy blast from his gun to start a fire. It spat sparks as it burned forest deadfall. We sat in a circle and the fire cast weird shadows across our faces. Turner, Hughes, Cooper, Dixon, Murray, Reed.

"We'll go in tomorrow to destroy the compound by the river," Reed said. He had a map on his handheld, the salient locations lit in red. "They store their seed technology here. We'll go in from this end and burn it out. Without the schematic embryos, they won't be able to regrow their infrastructure."

The portable screen passed from hand to hand, each man memorizing.

"The compound's big enough to send refugees in all directions so it's a good opportunity to crush their morale."

Nods around the circle.

"Hughes and Cooper, when the raid is over, find their android and bring her out to the courtyard. Everyone else, bring witnesses, as many civilians as you can find."

Reed turned in my direction.

"Then you can show everyone what a good soldier you are. Isn't that right, Turner?"

* * *

EVERYONE DOES it on their first deployment. It's how you show that you're one of the men, that they can trust you.

* * *

SHE GOES rigid as I push, the way a real woman would if I went too hard. It can't really hurt. Who would engineer that?

Reed's voice thrums like a purr. "That's right, Turner. Give it good."

I try not to think about what I'm doing. My dick is going soft. She's not human. She looks human.

I pull out, damp and shriveled. Reed looks at me with disgust. He pushes me off of her. "Let's give Turner a hand," he says, grabbing Dixon's gun.

He aims at her and I think he's going to shoot. Instead, he wedges the barrel inside her. Her body stiffens with pain. He pushes further. She screams. Things tear. He's ripping at her. The sound she makes is inhuman. She's inhuman, too, but it doesn't matter. I can't let him keep going. Better me than—

I push myself between her and Reed. I stroke fast, trying to get hard again. "I can do it. I just got distracted with everyone watching. Let me finish."

Reed looks amused as he steps back.

* * *

RAPE CONTRAVENES treaties, but the military's unofficial stance is that it's a harmless source of unit cohesion when you're light years out.

They don't tell you before you enlist.

Men who refuse have high accident rates. Sometimes they accidentally shoot themselves in their own backs.

On other planets, it's priestesses or young boys. Here, it's the androids they grow from schematic embryos. Each android holds the knowledge of every other in their heads, downloaded from first to last. Hurt one and you'll hurt every one of the people's subsequent leaders, forever.

* * *

I WONDER who they made Hughes do. Cooper, Dixon, Murray. Reed. Some kid. Some woman. Some man.

Before, I'm just the new guy. After, we'll be brothers. All it costs is one artificial cunt.

* * *

SHE'S RAW this time as I push inside. She whimpers with each thrust. Someone gave her nerves down there like a real woman's. Whose idea was that? I hate that person. I hate them more than I hate Reed.

Pressure builds. Coming doesn't feel good, but it happens. The guys whoop. Reed shouts encouraging obscenities. I hate their eyes on me. I hate the feel of the android bitch underneath me, taking it with her eyes closed. I want her to scream and fight back so I'd feel like less of a monster. I want to hurt her. I want to blow Reed's brains out. I want to be anywhere but here.

* * *

MY FIRST time was with twins, a boy and a girl, from a platform where they practiced embryonic duplication and four-way marriages. It was exciting for me because there were two of them and exciting for them because there was only one of me.

The girl's eyes were black like holes in the ice. Her thighs were dark bronze. She smelled like the oils we made from engineered animal fat. I leaned into her and her brother leaned into me and our arms were all around each other and there was pleasure wrapping three ways, her-me-him and him-her-me, and it was like a lightning storm over the icy ocean, dazzles of color refracting back and forth to eternity. Before, that's what it was like. It won't ever be like that again.

* * *

SET AGAINST her inhumanly grey skin, the android's irises are crackled silver. They're hard with disdain, but the contempt is shaded with something worse, too.

That's when I smash my fist into her face. Her skull smacks against the ground. How can *she* pity *me?*

Her stare is a thousand years old. It's the stare of every android who's ever lived on this damn planet.

Pity is salt and I'm an open wound.

I feel worse as the children behind me start crying. Reed shouts with surprise and enthusiasm. I feel worse and so I hit her a second time.

* * *

THE SEED technology crackles as it burns like grains of corn on a stove. The fire flickers with shades of violet, chartreuse and cyan as strange chemical combinations combust. We're far away by the time it gutters out.

* * *

IT'S NOT dark when we reach the campsite, but Reed fires his gun at the deadfall. Around the circle, they pass stolen brew served in the compound's mugs. Turner, Hughes, Cooper, Dixon, Murray. Reed.

I should hate them, but I don't. We're the same. Maybe we weren't yesterday, but we are today.

The beer is brewed from bitter grain, but we pour it down our throats. We drink together, all of us. That's the important thing.

The *End*

Dispersed by the Sun, Melting in the Wind

THE LAST word ever spoken by a human is said in a language derived from Hindi. The word is trasa. Roughly translated: thirst or desire.

* * *

THE SECOND-TO-LAST human to die is a child who lives in the region that was once called the Blue Mountains of Australia. She has the strange light eyes that children are occasionally born with, the way they are sometimes born as triplets or with white hair or with another baby's empty body growing from their bellies. Her mother calls them water eyes, a sign that the child shares the changeable spirit of the ocean which can shift from calm to storm in the space of a breath.

On the last day of her life, the light-eyed child finds a pair of ancient skeletons exposed in the silt by the river near her camp. She pulls out the ribs with a sucking noise, loosing the foul stench of trapped gas. Pelvic bones lie in the mud below, tangled with metal things no one can make anymore. As she teases them free, the light-eyed child unearths rusted chains and hollow disks the diameter of her wrist.

The light-eyed child rinses the bones clean in the river. She runs her hand over the long femurs, marveling. People no longer grow so tall.

The light-eyed child sets the bones in a loose pile underneath a scribbly gum tree. The skulls preside on top, regarding her with hollow eyes. The light-eyed child kisses each in the center of its caved-in forehead.

Goodnight, Grandpa Burn, she says. *Goodnight, Grandma Starve*.

***

THE LAST major art movement is invented near Lake Vättern in Sweden. With the help of enough processing power to calculate the trajectories of a beachful of sand over a millennium, the artist taps a feeder loop directly into her brain and uses it to shape a three-dimensional holographic image of her father. For the first time, human thought patterns take direct, physical form. Her father's projection repeats sequences of fragmented memories. His limbs trail into images of people and places he loved when he was alive; his hair winds into the tapestries he was famous for weaving; his face flickers cyclically from youth to gray. *It's not my father,* the artist explains. *It's how I think of my father, his imago.*

Within five years, her invention revolutionizes art. Artists show the world how they conceive of childbirth, fire, finches, walk bodies, urtists, religion, synthesis and death.

Within twenty years, the technology to create such work is destroyed. Art falls backward. Humanity falls farther.

***

THE MAN who will survive to be the last human lives in the region once called Nepal. Amid the still-falling ash from a series of volcanic eruptions, he and his son dig their way free of a cave-in.

Ravens perched on branches overhanging the cave mouth observe their progress. When the son grows weak, the last man tries to scatter the birds by throwing stones. They flap a short distance into the naked trees and witness the boy's death from there, watching events unfold the way birds do: turning their heads to look first with one eye, then the other, to see which version of life is more appealing.

***

ONE OF the last scientific discoveries excites the neurons of an amateur stargazer. Even before the cataclysm, she is the last of an increasingly rarefied breed—air and light pollution have made ground telescopes useless so she has to pay for satellite time to peer out in an era when almost all of humanity's technological eyes are aimed inward. One lonely night when all her mates and children are away, she trains her screen to watch the cloud bands on Jupiter's gaseous surface and glimpses a city-sized object hurtling toward the earth.

Oh, God, she says, *an asteroid.*

* * *

WITH NEAR-EARTH space increasingly militarized, it's been years since government telescopes have been dedicated to anything but scrutinizing the actions of other nations. The scant handful of under-funded astronomers confirms that the object's path will bring it into contact with earth.

The astronomers agree: there's nothing to be done. A century of attrition has withered space programs. Early iterations of space-faring technology were cannibalized to fund defense and weapons aimed at earthly targets. Remaining resources are primitive and useless. The object is too close to fire missiles at or deflect or drag into the gravity well of the sun.

* * *

WEALTHY GLOBAL governments convene. If they can't stop the asteroid, they agree to let it hit. Calculations demonstrate it will impact near the southern tip of Chile. Industrialists working on technology for deep-sea exploration believe they can adapt their pressure shield mechanisms to protect a few major cities from the global fires, earthquakes and tidal waves that will result from impact. With nuclear, wind, and solar power operating at full capacity, there should be enough energy to protect key sections of Asia, Europe and North America. First world populations that live outside protected urban centers are herded in en masse, crowding like cattle into emergency shelters.

As for those who won't be included in the rescue plan, global leaders mumble about regrettable losses then do what they have always done: sacrifice the good of the many for the good of themselves.

* * *

THE LAST act of malice lights in the eyes of a pathologist who works in a secure facility in a dome on an island in an untraveled sea. When it becomes clear their government has abandoned them, the other scientists drink and screw on the lab tables. He unlocks his deadliest specimens, flees the building to the rhythm of unheeded alarms, and looses genetically manipulated spores like fairy dust onto the wind.

***

THE LAST martyrs desert their homes in wealthy nations and travel south to stand with their impoverished brothers and sisters.

Like everyone else, they die.

***

BY THE time the cataclysm strikes, more words have been forgotten over the course of human history than remain known.

***

THE CITY-SIZED object hits.

***

WEALTHY NORTHERNERS watch the event through cameras on surviving satellites. Milliseconds after impact, their screens go black as the asteroid's collision displaces earth and rock in a hundred mile radius. Radioactive waste illegally buried in poverty-stricken Puerto Natales flies into the air, joining the plume of dirt that whirls into the chaotic weather systems caused by impact. Soil sewn with radioactive dust distributes across the globe in a storm that blocks the sun for three months.

It is as if the planet has gone to global nuclear war. Toxic heavy metals rain into the surface water systems and poison the springs of civilization.

Pressure shields are helpless against nuclear fallout. For those not killed by the fiery rains of impact, dying lingers. Bones weaken; teeth fall out; skin loosens in long, slender strips like fruit peels.

Before she dies, the Swedish artist tries to redraw her father's imago on a flat sheet of pulped tree. Her shaking hand is raw and bleeding, but her lines fall true. The drawing fails anyway. She can't remember what her father looked like. She can only remember her art.

***

THE LAST man's people survive by moving underground. Caves shelter them from fiery rains and pathogens and tidal waves. Underground, they have access to subterranean water sources that remain temporarily pure.

His people's luck lasts a century, until the geological instabilities set in motion by impact bubble up from the earth's molten heart. Sudden, violent tremors herald chains of volcanic eruptions that transform the caves into tombs.

The last man and his son dig their way free, but it takes so long that the already weak child grows weaker. He breathes dust and ash. In the middle of their journey, as they work to pry loose a stubborn boulder, they accidentally release a rain of debris. It showers down on the son. He seems fine when he gets up and shakes himself off, but who knows what injuries can afflict a malnourished boy?

***

THE LIGHT-EYED child's people believe they escaped the fiery rains because the earth protects them. Unlike the mining-scarred, ecologically damaged area of Nepal where the last man's people live, the light-eyed child's people enjoy a paradise of native species and pristine cliffs. Even some kangaroos survive to provide the light-eyed child's people with food.

The light-eyed child's grandmother tells her the bones she finds sometimes are not the bones of people but of devils. *They made the cataclysm happen by hating and ignoring the earth*, she says, *Most of them died, but the ones who survived—Grandpa Burn and Grandma Starve, Grandpa Hate and Grandma Bullet—they chained us and hurt us and tried to take our land. We had to use their tools on them instead.*

The light-eyed child's people initially triumphed over their enemies, but their luck ran out some four score years after the cataclysm. A species of bird which hadn't been seen since impact arrived during the annual migration, carrying the pathologist's bequest.

One illness killed the elderly. A second attacked the healthiest. A third killed one tenth of the population in a single night. The fourth wiped out the men.

No one tells the light-eyed child directly, but she hears talk of the plagues as *our curse*, sometimes brought by the earth spirits, sometimes by the ghosts of the demons. The light-eyed child asks her mother, who pauses while gathering roots to explain, *Being favored by the spirits is both a blessing and a burden. They won't forgive us for acting in ignorance as the demons did. They haven't yet decided the punishment for our transgressions.*

The light-eyed child's mother gets a strange, wistful look on her face and goes on. *You're our last hope.*

The light-eyed child's people have a legend that girls with water eyes can sometimes turn into boys. They need her to do so; that is what they mean when they say she is their last hope.

No one knows how to make it happen. *Send the girl out on her own,* her grandmother says, *Boys like to be on their own.* So every morning, the light-eyed child's mother sends her off to explore the remnants of the rainforest.

The light-eyed child thinks being a last hope is both a blessing and a burden. She enjoys being special. She hates the disappointment in everyone's eyes when she comes home every day, still a girl.

Sometimes she squats over the river, her eyes squeezed shut as if she's trying to shit because it's the best way she can imagine to force a penis out of her vagina. She clenches and grunts, clenches and grunts. Sometimes when her eyes get so tired she sees bright sparkles over the scribbly gums on the horizon, she feels her vaginal walls pinch together and she knows—just knows—that something has come out. But when she reaches down, she finds only soft, yielding flesh.

* * *

THE LAST man cries over his son until he realizes his sobs are tearless. He stops.

The ravens won't leave them alone, so he throws more stones. He must watch the birds constantly or they try to pluck out his son's eyes.

His trousers are soiled, but he urinates at a marked spot near the cave mouth to maintain a semblance of civilization. He has nothing to defecate. When he gets too hungry, he sucks on stones.

In all the deprivation the last man has suffered in his life, he's never lacked for water. Even now as he starves, puddles pock the stony landscape. They taste brackish, but they keep him alive longer than he wants.

He gives up sleep, but dreams awake. He sees mirages on the horizon, machines his father told tales of: great silver birds with hearts like ticking clocks; blood-heated covers to keep him warm; android doctors with needle-covered palms injecting life back into his bony chest.

He remembers the first time he came to the surface as a boy, with his own father. His people's men folk had a tradition of sending males to the surface to prove they had the courage to tread across the lip of a dead world. All around the valley grew the red-stemmed *ban mara* daisies which choked out the trees until the hills blanched white as the clouds.

When I was young, they said the flowers showed the hills were dying, the last man's father said. *They came from a far-away land over the sea and when they got here, they grew so thick and fierce that they killed all the plants that had been here already, the ones that had lived here forever.*

When the last man was a child, he and his father had explored the mountains beyond the hills and discovered the remains of a fabric shop. Bolts of durable synthetic cloth tumbled across each other, like the discarded sheets of a giant. The last man and his father brought them home for the women to make clothes out of. They were greeted like heroes.

Before the eruptions, the last man had never brought his son to the surface. He was a sickly baby, like all the newborns conceived in the past few years. Many of them died, but the last man prayed over his son every minute until he was a year old. His son's hair grew in scraggly patches across his scalp. When he ate, his gums bled into his food. Even after the boy had passed the most dangerous point, the last man refused to let him sleep alone, afraid he'd get lost in his dreams and forget to come home. The last man's wife told him she would leave him for another man if he didn't return to share her pallet. He let her.

The setting sun reflects pink off the upturned petals cloaking the hills. The last man regrets not taking his son up here before, sickly or not. He thinks his son would have liked to explore these hills, feel his bony feet slip in the mud. He would have run through the ruins and hollered at the vast, free sky. At least, he would have liked a length of the gray cloth the last man and his father found so many years ago: sewn with golden strands for the sun and red strands like the stems of the *ban mara* daisies.

* * *

LITERACY FADES years before the last man dies. The older generation of his people remember how to read, but they don't teach the young ones. Reading seems frivolous, indulgent, a luxury like brocade or peacock feathers or reminiscing about long summer evenings when men chewed betel nuts and women chattered while the lowering sun lengthened their shadows until an ordinary human presence had the heft of a god's.

* * *

TWO GENERATIONS before the light-eyed child was born, her grandmother would have screamed at Grandpa Burn and kicked his skull downstream. Her mother would have cried over Grandma Starve's aged bones, cursing the fact she would never live to acquire a stoop.

The light-eyed child places her hands over their hollow sockets and returns to playing.

* * *

THE LAST lie is not a single lie but a group of lies, uttered by the last man's people and the light-eyed child's people, by children and elders, by men and women, by the stoic and the red-eyed.

Don't worry, Mama, Grandpa, sir, honey, lover, child, heart-keeper, mine. You're going to get better. You're going to be all right.

* * *

THE LAST man leaves his son awhile and climbs a formation of rocks on the other side of the cave mouth. The tallest one leans on a pair of others like an old man asking for support. Below, a thousand foot drop sinks into a ravine blanketed in daisies.

The last man selects a small gray stone and pitches it down. As it plummets, he tries to fit the idea of such distance into his head: how things so high can fall so far.

Before it hits, he's distracted by a rush of wind as a raven flies past him. He waves it away. It dives past the cave, headed for his son. The last man climbs down to chase it off and misses the moment when the rock hits the ground.

By the time the last man reaches his son, the boy's left eye is gone. The thread of his intestines trails across the stony ground.

He remembers sitting with his son, then a five year old, coaxing him to eat yak meat and lichen. The little boy turned away, fanning his hands in front of his face.

A little more, just a little more. Come on, the last man said. It hurt the boy to chew; it hurt him to swallow; it hurt him to have food in his stomach.

A few steps away, the last man's wife stood, staring, the glint of her reddened eyes bright in the darkness. The next day she'd leave him for the fat man who lived near the cave mouth, the one who had another wife already. She didn't need to vocalize; the words were written in the taut line of her mouth: Why squander time on the dying when we'll reach death's door soon enough ourselves?

Truthfully, the last man had heard the ravens fly toward his son as soon as he climbed the rocks. He'd known what the birds would do. But it wasn't until he threw the stone that his mind had the sense to distract him from what he was doing. His own mortality was as palpable as his son's. The wind of falling rushed past them both. It was too much for a mind to contemplate.

* * *

THE LAST man is tone deaf and the light-eyed child doesn't like to sing because it reminds her that her voice is piping and high when it should be resonant and bass, so the last music mankind makes is subtle and strange. It's the last man grunting in answer to the raven's sporadic caws; it's the light-eyed child splashing in the river to the beat of her heart; it's the last man's fingers drumming on his son's hollow belly.

* * *

THE LIGHT-EYED child's people don't live long enough to suffer from their lack of men. The third wave disease, the one that killed a tenth of them in a night, reawakens in its surviving hosts after its long period of incubation and strangles the entire population by dawn.

The dusk before, as the last man prepares to throw a stone down a cliff, the light-eyed child runs back to camp to find her mother. The sky dims. Pale stars emerge. The two of them stroll to a spring to fetch clean water with which to cook the evening meal of kangaroo meat flavored with peppermint leaves.

* * *

THE LAST word the light-eyed child's mother says before she starts to choke is *whakahohoro*: hurry.

* * *

THE LAST man becomes grateful for things he should despise: the red-tinted sky, the stench of his son's decaying corpse, the coldness of his soiled trousers. His last hour stretches, but not in the way a bored afternoon expands across a child's landscape. His last hour is the petal of an orchid browning from the outside in. It's a cloud blowing across the sky puff by puff, until without ever moving as a single entity, it soars away into the blue expanse. It's a grain of sand, unnoticed until held up close—whoever would have known it was crimson? And smelled like salt? And shaped like a crescent moon?

* * *

THE LAST piece of technology mankind invents is a bundle of lyrebird feathers and wallaby bones, wrapped in koala fur. It possesses no magic, but it serves a purpose: it busies hands and buoys hearts.

* * *

THE LIGHT-EYED child lives a few hours longer than the rest of her people. She clutches her mother's hand through her breathless contortions, and when they're over, she cradles her mother's blue, arthritic fingers.

As she runs out of breath herself, she wonders if her skeleton will wear jewelry with spokes and chains like Grandpa Burn and Grandma Starve. She wonders who will dig up her bones.

* * *

THE PUDDLES of rainwater could sustain the last man a few days yet, but he stops drinking. He watches the ravens' reflections in the dirty water and repeats, "Trasa, trasa." Though his mouth is dry, it isn't thirst he's referring to.

* * *

THOUGH THE last man and the light-eyed child live on opposite sides of the globe, they die within hours of each other. It is one of those improbable vagaries of fate which become probable given enough time and opportunity, like calculus stirring simultaneously in the brains of Newton and Leibnitz, evolution in Darwin and Wallace, relativity in Einstein and Smoluchowski. The last two humans are simply the final pair to march hand in hand into an unexplored realm.

* * *

THE LAST animal to see a living human is a raven. She watches the last man's final exhalation and waits a moment to be sure he won't rise and hurl another stone in her direction. His body sags. She paces her perch. All remains still.

She swoops.

How the World Became Quiet: A Post-Human Creation Myth

PART ONE—THE APOCALYPSE OF TREES

DURING THE first million years of its existence, mankind survived five apocalypses without succumbing to extinction. It endured the Apocalypse of Steel, the Apocalypse of Hydrogen, the Apocalypse of Serotonin, and both Apocalypses of Water, the second of which occurred despite certain contracts to the contrary. Mankind also survived the Apocalypse of Grease, which wasn't a true apocalypse, although it wiped out nearly half of humanity by clogging the gears that ran the densely-packed underwater cities of Lor, but that's a tale for another time.

Humans laid the foundation for the sixth apocalypse in much the same way they'd triggered the previous ones. Having recovered their ambition after the Apocalypse of Serotonin and rebuilt their populations after the Apocalypse of Grease, they once again embarked on their species' long term goal to wreak as much havoc as possible on the environment through carelessness and boredom. This time, the trees protested. They devoured buildings, whipped wind into hurricanes between their branches, tangled men into their roots and devoured them as mulch. In retaliation, men chopped down trees, fire-bombed jungles, and released genetically engineered insects to devour tender shoots.

The pitched battle decimated civilians on both sides, but eventually—though infested and rootless—the trees overwhelmed their opposition.

Mankind was forced to send its battered representatives to a sacred grove in the middle of the world's oldest forest and beg for a treaty.

Negotiations went slowly since the trees insisted on communicating through the pitches of the wind in their leaves, which astute linguists played back at 1,000 times normal speed in order to render them comprehensible to human ears. It took a day for a sentence, a week for a paragraph, a month for an entire stipulation.

After ten years, a truce was completed. To demonstrate its significance, it was inked in blood drawn from human victims and printed on the pulped and flattened corpses of trees. The trees agreed to cease their increasing assaults and return forevermore to their previous quiescent vegetable state, in exchange for a single concession: mankind would henceforth sacrifice its genetic heritage and merge with animals to create a new, benevolent sentience with which to populate the globe.

After the final signatures and root-imprints were applied to the treaty, the last thing the trees were heard to say before their leaves returned to being mere producers of chlorophyll was this: *At least it should keep them busy for a millennium or two, fighting among themselves.*

PART TWO—THE ANIMALS WHO LIVED AS MEN

MANKIND, AS history had known it, was no more. The new hybrids wore bodies constructed like those of mythological beasts, a blend of human and animal features. They scattered into the world's forests, deserts, jungles, and oceans, where they competed with unmixed animals for food and territory.

If some ancient legends were to be believed, men were only returning to their ancient roots as dolphin and lizard, raven and grizzly bear. Other traditions would have been appalled that man had cast himself down from his place at the apex of the chain of being and been consigned to the lesser links below.

Intellectuals became the whale men, who kept their faces, but lost their bodies for the streamlined shape of cetaceans. Their sentience blended with the intelligence already inhabiting those massive, blubbery forms. They indulged in abstract philosophy as they swam through the ocean depths in a silence created by the first absence of shipping lines in five hundred thousand years.

Pilots and acrobats became glider men, acquiring huge eyes, wing flaps, and nocturnal habits which served them well as they arrowed from tree to tree in forests that echoed with their eerie, sonar calls. Eight-armed crab men spent their days skittering up and down beaches dancing for the gulls; spotted jaguar men skulked through forests; cold-blooded turtle men inched through years; flattened stingray men lurked on river bottoms, awaiting unwary travelers.

For the first twenty thousand years, mankind peacefully coexisted in all its forms. After that, the buried genetic contribution of the human mind bubbled to the surface.

"The treaty is an outgrown shell to be discarded," young crab men gestured defiantly with their third and sixth arms. Crab matrons clacked their claws in outrage, but who could control the youth?

The most extreme of the crab men formed a rebel sect called the Weeders. They wove strands of kelp around their eyestalks and ritually cut their seventh arms, searing the wounds with a mixture of brine and gull guano. At first, they expended their rage on symbolic targets: dumb unblended seabirds, or rocks shaped like dolphin men. And then a juvenile Weeder called Long Stalks found an injured seal man bleeding on the beach and dragged him home in time for the evening convocation. The Weeders tore him to pieces, rubbing themselves with his blubber and parading in his fur. The meat they left to rot.

When they discovered the decaying corpse, the crab matrons went to the seal men with offerings and apologies, but the seal men refused to hear diplomacy. They clipped off the delegation's claws and sent the mutilated ambassadors home with a terse condemnation: "You didn't even have the courtesy to eat him."

Seal and crab men hunted each other to extinction in less than a decade. The last crab man sidled four hundred miles inland to a camp of parrot men before expiring with a curse on his lips.

Soon it was hyena man versus eagle man and frog man versus capybara man, then tiger and spider and cockatiel men against snake and giraffe and ostrich men. Amidst the hectic formation and betrayals of alliances that seethed on the battlefield, only one order created a stable federation. These were the insect men, greatest of all the species of men in their variety and achievements.

Their infantry were the mosquito men, fearsome female warriors with the muscular bodies of amazons topped by tiny, blood-sucking heads. They marched wherever battle raged, drinking the blood of fallen soldiers. They were sliced and swatted, crushed and grasped in giant crocodilian jaws, but still the indomitable parasites survived to carry samples of their victim's blood back to their superiors, the butterfly men.

Oh, the tragedy of the butterfly men, wisest of the insect men, whose useless jewel-colored wings draped from their slender shoulders like robes. These were the descendents of the geneticists who engineered the destruction of mankind, innocent victims of their ancestor's self-flagellation. Forced to subsist on honey and chained to a lifespan of less than a week, these shrewd but ephemeral leaders did not even enjoy the consolation of flight. Instead they lingered in forest glades looking pale and melancholy. Liable to terrible moods, they made love in the underbrush one moment and shredded each other's wings the next.

Yet the geneticist's legacy was not entirely bad, for they had left their descendents the gift of instinct: inscribed into the rapid pathways of their ephemeral brains lay an intricate understanding of DNA and genetic manipulation. Using this knowledge, the butterflies divined their enemy's secret anatomical weaknesses from the blood samples which the mosquito men brought to them. Generations of butterfly men scrutinized each vial in order to create fatal viruses which would massacre their enemy's ranks.

Only when the last disease had been designed did the butterfly men let loose the fruits of their labor. Simultaneously, a hundred deadly plagues seized their victims, sweeping across the earth in a single night. By morning, only the insect men remained.

High on an isolated cliff in a desert that had once been the Amazon, a cluster of hardy Joshua trees broke their ancient silence to speak once more. Wind rushed through the prickly tufts of their leaves, rustling out a single sentence: *That didn't take long, did it?*

PART THREE—THE REIGN OF INSECTS

THOUGH THE butterfly men's cunning won the war, their flighty emotions and brief life spans made them unsuitable for leading a world, and so it was that the cockroach men became the rulers of the earth. Tough enough to survive dismemberment because their brain processes were spread throughout their becarapaced bodies, and possessed of the keen and supernatural senses of scavengers who had once lived among creatures many hundreds of times their own size, the cockroaches had the desire and capacity to enact a reign of fascism on the other insect men the like of which had never been seen before.

Ant men and bee men filled the roles of farmers and drudges. Atlas and rhinoceros beetle men provided brute force. Flea and mite men accomplished those tasks requiring agility.

Mosquito men served as the secret police. The cockroach men sent them to swarm on enemies of the state and drain them dry—and there was never a lack of traitors to keep them fed.

Alas, the plight of the butterfly men was only to become worse, for the cockroach men were loathe to risk the same end which had befallen their enemies. To ensure their safety from the butterflies' dangerous knowledge, they imprisoned the butterfly men in a dark chain of underground caves where they lived brief, miserable lives outside the sun's reach. Within a season and twelve generations, all conscious knowledge of how to create viruses from blood was gone, but the butterfly men's unhappy descendents remain incarcerated in their underground cells today.

Above ground, bees and ants marched to the cockroach's well-timed rhythm, carrying crops from outlying farms into the hills of the city. Caravans of traveling gypsy moth men departed each hour on the hour, and the cockroach men began great civil works projects to erect bridges and statues and roads and memorials and temples. Larvae were taken away from their hatchers and forced to work at back-breaking labor past adulthood; dragonfly men journalists reported only that news which drifted on the prevailing winds of fascism; hives were routinely broken up to redistribute the working population. While the other insect men lived poor and wintry lives subsisting on meager grain, the cockroach men gorged on honey, orange peels and moldy bread. Those who dissented disappeared, only to be found as blood-drained corpses swinging from study branches.

Yet all this might have endured, were it not for the deadliest sin of the cockroach men. Ancestrally predisposed to look favorably upon debris, the cockroach men allowed their wastes to build up in giant landfills. Junkyards choked out the fields; garbage seeped into the ground water; rotting trash provided breeding grounds for the nastiest, most virulent epidemics. When the first wave of ant men died of a plague that turned their exoskeletons scarlet, at first the cockroach men suspected their old accomplices the butterfly men, but when they went to interrogate them, no one could remember where that unhappy species had been stashed.

The trees cried out against what was happening to them. New bacteria chewed through leaves and blocked out photosynthesis; roots withered in poisoned soil. Things would only get worse, they knew—oh, how they would suffer. Across the globe it would be the same for all things natural: seas would rumble, ecosystems shatter; even the iron-breathing archeans in the deepest volcanic vents would perish if the cockroach men were allowed to continue on their path. *This will hurt you too, earth*, the trees wailed, not in the language of wind-in-leaves which they had used to communicate with the humans, but in the language of roots-in-ground and life-in-soil.

And the earth heard their plight. It shivered, cracking the supercontinent down the middle like a slice of lightning splitting the sky. *I have seen enough of mankind's ability to make trouble*, it rumbled to itself in the language of magma-under-crust, and it initiated the seventh apocalypse, the Apocalypse of Darkness.

The Apocalypse of Darkness was the most terrible yet suffered by mankind. Untold agony wiped out almost the entire population of the globe.

Three cricket men survived. They woke quaking into the dawn, antennae shivering down their backs. They were two females and a male, and they might have carried their line into future generations, but the three of them regarded each other with dark, compound eyes that reflected the same understanding.

"We must never bear children," said the oldest and wisest, "Or someday we might tell them what we have experienced, and we must never damn another soul to see what we have seen, even by picturing it in their minds."

The others agreed, and the three of them leapt off the tallest cliff they could find, dying in silence. Though the details of the Apocalypse of Darkness are known, it would be disrespectful to the cricket men's sacrifice to record them.

INTERLUDE—WHISPERINGS FROM BRANCH TO BRANCH

SO, LITTLE *rootlings, little seedlings, little starting-to-grows, that is why the earth is quiet now. Feel the snails trail across your bark. Listen to the birds trilling in your branches and the insects nibbling your leaves. Hear the snap of monkeys brachiating from branch to branch. With mankind gone, we are free to enjoy these things. Are they not good?*

Ah, but by now you've guessed, the time of man is not entirely behind us. Why else would we whisper this tale on a fine spring morning with winter's frosts sweetly melted?

Before the Apocalypse of Darkness, we did not tell each other stories. Through necessity, we have learned the skill. Next year, you will help us tell the starting-to-grows about The Great Cathedral Mother who stood in the center of the world until her children sprouted up in a ring around her and sucked up all the sunlight. Her trunk remains where she once grew, swollen with dead leaves and congealing sap and blind grubs. Someday, lightning will strike all the way through the earth, piercing her in two, and each half will grow into a tall, straight pine with a tip like a spear: one going up, one going down. And when this happens, everything we think we know about the world will change.

The year after that, we will tell the great love story of The Garlanded Tree and the hive of bees who fertilized her.

But this is our most important tale. Like winter, man will return in his season. By the time he does, little rootling, you may have a great solid trunk like your mother. Or perhaps you will have grown and perished, and it will be your children standing. Or your children's children. Whoever grows when mankind returns must remember how to drop their leaves and huddle naked in the snow.

And also, when man comes back, we wish to return to him his history so that he may hold and regard it like a spring bloom budding on a new-leafed branch, new and yet also old, a gift not unlike the one given last spring. Who knows? Maybe this will be the time mankind can learn from stories.

PART FOUR—HANDS YEARNING UPWARD THROUGH THE SURFACE OF THE EARTH

STRETCH YOUR roots into the ground, little seedlings. Listen. Can you hear life rustling under the soil?

Who else, but the butterfly men? The Apocalypse of Darkness did not faze them. Having become accustomed to their miserable state, they could no longer be depressed by the black. They crept anxiously through their underground dwellings, their bright wings beautiful and unseen, and whispered to each other, "Do you feel that? What's happening?"

When the Apocalypse was over, without knowing the reason for it, the butterfly men wept together for twenty-four full hours in cosmic mourning for the human race of which they were now the sole representatives. But since their quixotic moods were often given to fits of communal sorrow, they failed to understand the uniqueness of the occasion.

After that, it was as though a pall had lifted from the butterfly men. They no longer had surface cousins to envy, so they went about making their lives in the dark. Their society flourished. Their stymied flight sense muddled their sense of direction, so they built joyously everywhere, not knowing up from down or left from right. They laughed and fought and made love in the mud and created an entire caste system based on the texture of the useless flight powder that dusted their wings.

Sometimes an unusual prophet among them dreamed of the surface and spoke of things called light and sun, and usually she was buried alive—but occasionally she wasn't, and then a new religion started and some of the butterflies marched off through the dark to pursue their cult in a different set of caves.

In the past millennia, these cults have gained power. Everyone has lost a sister or a cousin or a parent to their undeniable allure. Whispers among the fine-powdered aristocracy indicate that the cults have even gained sympathy among the inbred monarchy in their velvet-draped cocoons. Soon perhaps, every butterfly will believe.

The cults employ a diverse array of dogmas, rituals, taboos, gods and mythologies, but they all share two common traits. All tell of an eighth apocalypse when the earth will open up into a chasm so terrifying that it will unlock a new sensation—a sixth sense—to accompany hearing, smell, touch, taste and desire. And all require their devotees to spend one day of their week-long lives meditating to discern which direction is up, and then to raise their arms toward it, and start digging.

Speech Strata

SUMMER

IT HAPPENED farther in the future than you think it did, a thousand years after the last moment you can possibly imagine. Far above the earth, where the air was pure as snowmelt and the sunlight yellow as fresh daisies, a pair of tarnished lovers lay together on a cloud drift. Newborn rays glinted off their bodies as they watched the dawn.

The female, who thought of herself as Spin, opened her mouth to express contentment. A hand-mirror spilled out. She held it up to her lover. She thought of him as Hesitant because of the way he'd held her before they kissed, his eyes scanning her face for a tangible clue to her thoughts. Spin wanted to show him the reflection of their bodies beneath the sky.

Hesitant took the mirror and began to examine his face for imperfections.

No, no, said Spin silently. She spoke Hesitant a diamond and a peacock feather and a bolt of russet silk to show him how beautiful she found the morning. He caught the peacock feather and held it at arm's length as if it were foul, then let it fall through his fingers and sink through the clouds.

A thousand flickering seasons ago, Spin's people learned to walk on air and went to live in the clouds. They drank dew and drew sustenance from touch. They replaced their skins with silver to capture and reflect the sun—and here began their problems.

Silver flesh tarnished in the humid air, leaving the people identically dull and blackened. All the people's myriad forms were reduced to two: the male and the female. Tarnish dimmed their irises; metal plates evened out their heights and figures; silver skin erased the subtleties of their facial expressions. It became impossible to tell which body belonged to a friend or lover, whether these glistening hands were strange or familiar.

Stiff metal tongues stifled speech, so the people had to learn new ways to communicate. Their thoughts crystallized in their mouths and cascaded forth as

pearls,

shoestrings,

music boxes.

Spoken objects hid their meanings behind a hundred branching associations, impossible to decipher. Puzzled friends, parents, and lovers gathered them in their palms and silently entreated them to give up their anonymity. Sharptail snake, do you carry tidings of venom or wriggling glee? Tell me, compass, have you lost a direction or found one?

A flock of migrating geese honked as they veered toward the clouds where Spin lay with Hesitant. A group of tarnished men and women gathered nearby to watch the birds. Hesitant disentangled his limbs from Spin's and stood to join them.

Spin grabbed his hand. She didn't want him to go. She wanted to return to the moment they'd shared before kissing, when it seemed possible he might uncover her thoughts.

Stay! she shouted mutely. Out of her mouth came a smooth-shelled egg; a thorny briar; a calico cat; a pot of ink; an astrolabe; a dozen silver keys; a tiny city with flickering electric lights; and a sad, speckled, limbless creature that sat in a lump, gazing up at her. As a pink balloon drifted up to the stratosphere, Hesitant shook his fingers free.

A broken glass bird, he spoke. A dead branch. A single slipper without a mate. A carved wooden hand with an empty upturned palm. A lariat, looped around nothing.

I'm lonely too, thought Spin.

She caressed Hesitant's cheek. As her fingers slipped over his smooth, cold skin, an idea came to her.

Spin rose to her tiptoes and bit Hesitant. Her teeth sank into his malleable silver shoulder, leaving an imprint.

Hesitant jumped back. A salamander of surprise dropped from his mouth, changing midway into an angry snapping turtle. The half-formed creature scrabbled at the air as it fell.

Spin placed her hand on Hesitant's shoulder. He flinched but didn't leap away. Spin settled her incisors into the bite mark she'd left. Her teeth matched perfectly: a unique signature. Now she could always identify him, and he would always know her.

Delighted, Hesitant spoke a polished brass trumpet. The instrument let out a joyful blare as Hesitant leaned over Spin's body to make his own mark on her neck.

Nearby, the lovers who had gathered to watch the geese saw what Spin and Hesitant had done. Silver joints creaked as couples bit each other's hands and chests and thighs and feet with declarations of affection. The geese passed overhead, adding their honks to the din.

Spin and Hesitant passed the day together, trading sips of cirrus. Before Hesitant left, he kissed the top of Spin's head and spoke her a hooded lantern with a tiny candle guttering inside.

Spin caught it. She watched Hesitant go, and wondered what it meant.

AUTUMN

THE PEOPLE embraced Spin's invention. It spread from cloud to cloud like a fast-flying bird. Lovers bit, friends bit, acquaintances bit. When people gathered to watch an unusual event, they bit each other to memorialize the occasion. Teeth came to represent a rainbow stretching from horizon to horizon; a friend's firm embrace; a silent trio watching the orange harvest moon ripen overhead.

By contrast, mere words became trifling gifts. Who wanted to puzzle out the meaning of a crucible when bite marks conveyed a smaller, more comprehensible breadth? The people no longer bothered to regard exclamations of dragonflies and pocket watches. Instead, they allowed words to sink through the clouds where they sparkled in the sun. Magpies swooped to catch the treasures, screeching as they competed with rivals for the shiniest gems and coins. Successful males amassed gigantic troves on their wings, winning status and mates.

Yet teeth too were fallible. Summer blew into autumn as Spin enjoyed and marked new lovers, searching casually for Hesitant. One evening, when the air smelled sharp with cold and fallen leaves, Spin met a man pitted with bites from scalp to toe. Intersecting arcs patterned his fingers, the backs of his knees, even his penis. Carefully, Spin fitted her teeth into the indents, but her bite fit none. She squeezed the man's hand and left him, unable to decide whether he was a stranger or if her own bite lay obscured beneath newer inscriptions.

A flicker of days later, Spin finally discovered a man with a bite that matched hers. But as she looked into the man's face—was he Hesitant? Serene? Mysterious?—she couldn't remember biting him.

Her memory rehearsed a blur of previous trysts. Was this the man she met standing beneath a splatter of hail, their silhouettes illuminated by lightning? Was he the one who spoke her luxurious gifts of violet toads and carnelian? Or was this the man who had once chased after a retreating snowstorm to catch a snowflake on his finger, which, with utmost formality and grace, he'd held out for her to taste?

Spin never knew it, but she had indeed found Hesitant. He could not recall who she was either. Had she danced for him once, using cloud vapors like veils so they could share the pleasure of revealing what was hidden? Had she cupped rainwater in her hands for him to drink, slowly, sensually, until his lips touched her palms? Had she once given him a peacock feather to call him vain and strutting, all beauty and no depth?

Spin spoke an empty birdcage for regret at lost love. It emerged the size of her fingernail, a perfect miniature.

Hesitant caught the birdcage. It jingled like a bell. Did it mean she wanted to keep him like a pet? Spin turned to go. Then, no. She did not want him.

Hesitant tipped his hand, letting the birdcage fall. A young magpie just beginning his collection spotted it. He swooped, talons outstretched. The birdcage settled on his back between a charm bracelet and a cracked porcelain doll.

Cawing, the magpie soared upward to rejoin his flock. His wings glittered. A female magpie regarded him with one glossy black eye. Pleased, she turned her head to regard him with the other. The male winged toward her. She cawed her approval.

WINTER

LONELY AND disconsolate, Spin wandered across the cirrus clouds until she reached a darker front of nimbus. Her feet sank to the ankle in stinging, cold rain. Tiny bolts of lightning sizzled across her toes.

She choked out a cow skull and a hank of meat squirming with maggots and a bouquet of gray lilies and ten yards of black satin curtains. She felt no better. Silver tear ducts shed no tears.

Overhead, the magpie flock flapped in the tense sky. A pair caught her eye. The male fluttered toward the female, wings aglitter. The female tolerated his approach for a beat and then dove to the bottom of the flock's formation. The male soared after her. The birdcage Spin had spoken twinkled on his back, too distant for her to make out. Nevertheless, Spin felt a new lightness tickling her belly.

She followed the flock, stumbling over clouds as they wheeled through the sky. When the magpies roosted for the night, Spin bedded in the place where they'd descended. When they rose again at dawn, she woke where they burst into the air. She forsook cloud vapor and love affairs until she went mad with thirst and the need for touch.

One morning, as the magpies ascended, Spin began to dance. She lifted her arms like wings and flapped in the graceful, curving pattern of the birds. She pirouetted when the flocks changed direction and leapt between cloud drifts as they soared. When males tussled over trinkets, she kicked and scratched the air. As the flock circled in the dim winter sky, she spun and spun and spun.

SPRING

HESITANT WAS the first to see Spin dancing. Her body inscribed strange silhouettes against the mountains in the distance. Hesitant leaped to investigate. Others followed.

They found Spin darting and arrowing, rushing and jumping, whirling and kicking. Her body sparkled, polished by the dance. She looked like a silver magpie woman.

Before, the people had given Spin a wide berth. Now they approached, ginger as fledglings. Hesitant was boldest. He stood an arm's-length away, watching.

Inspiration filled Spin's mouth. Out came a rainbow; a flock of jeweled finches; a wish the size of the world; a flying glass horse; and a wind of wonder. And then Spin fell silent, only dancing.

Hesitant raised his arms. Finches chattered around his head. Crystal droplets splashed on his feet, becoming water. As Spin danced, he danced.

The people followed his example. They flowed around Spin and mimicked the magpies until the birds deserted the night sky to seek their rest. Then Spin led them in imitating the stars, showing them how to weave through each other like colliding galaxies. As dawn rose, Spin taught them steps of their own: gavottes and pavannes, galliards and allemandes.

In synchronicity of movement, the people finally learned what discarded words and illegible inscriptions had failed to teach them: they were no longer creatures of the soil, chained to meaning and explanation, memory and intimacy. In dance, they let go of a past made of I-know-yous and I-love-yous. These encircling arms, these rhythmic steps, they were enough.

The afternoon sun fell bloated in the sky. The people kept dancing. Dusk frosted their limbs and stars pricked holes in the horizon. The people kept dancing. Spring breezes tumbled past, wafting birdsong and the scent of fresh flowers. The clouds darkened to weep moody rainstorms and parted to let the sun shine fiercely on the earth. Raindrops clattered on metallic skin. Frost etched patterns on the people's tarnished limbs. Still, the people kept dancing.

Sometimes the dance carried Spin and Hesitant toward each other. Though they never knew each other's names, a connection thrummed through their bodies, warm as peacock feathers and candles lit in hooded lanterns.

Overhead, the flock of magpies continued to soar, squabbling over scraps. The people's memory glistened on their wings, sparkling and beautiful and remote.